· THE CAIRO DIARY ·

After stints as an actor, night watchman and bookseller, Maxim Chattam studied criminology in Paris. He is also the author of several plays, a well-received trilogy, *The Soul of Evil, In Darkness* and *Evil Spells,* as well as the recently released thriller *The Mysteries of Chaos.*

THE CAIRO DIARY

Maxim Chattam

PAN BOOKS

First published 2007 by Minotaur
an imprint of St Martin's Press, New York

First published in Great Britain 2008 by Pan Books
an imprint of Pan Macmillan Ltd
Pan Macmillan, 20 New Wharf Road, London N1 9RR
Basingstoke and Oxford
Associated companies throughout the world
www.panmacmillan.com

ISBN 978-0-330-45191-8

Originally published in 2005 as *La Sang du Temps* by Michel Lafon, France

1 3 5 7 9 8 6 4 2

A CIP catalogue record for this book is available from
the British Library.

Printed and bound in the UK by CPI Mackays, Chatham ME5 8TD

.❧.

· AUTHOR'S NOTE ·

.❧.

Reading is an entirely personal experience: a crazy feeling of exaltation, resulting from a meeting between black marks on fragments of wood treated with spirit and a brain that captures the words and interprets them, according to its particular sensibilities. The engine that drives every story is the reader's mind; his or her imagination is its fuel. All the author does is describe a more or less malleable landscape, and then works hard to ensure that the reader follows the guardrail.

But it's all about the senses.

And I would like to share with you my experience as a reader, before I leave you alone with these pages.

For a long time I liked silence when I was reading.

The peace and quiet of a kind of impersonal nothingness, which enabled me to savor fully the sonorous cataclysm of the words.

Then I made an effort: I began using music for reading. Symphonic music.

At the start, the idea didn't really tempt me. Then it won me over. The perceptive process of reading involves the senses. And music adds enormously to their power.

Read a novel at home with music floating all around, or in a train car, with a personal stereo glued to your ears, or even slip a CD into the computer during your lunch break at work and plug the headphones into the CPU, and the magic of the imagination is set in motion.

Believe me, if you're not already an enthusiast, it's an experiment well worth trying. The use of intoxicating music increases the already incredible power of reading tenfold.

But not just any music.

Making the right choice of background music is as difficult as choosing which book to open next.

Usually, when I write, I deny myself any kind of distraction, anything that might make me lose my concentration (however tenuous it may be). For this novel, I tried a different approach . . . out of curiosity, to find out what kind of effect it might have on me.

I was lucky. At my very first attempt, I discovered *the* music for the novel.

Or perhaps it was the book that was inspired by the soundscapes.

I work with music from films. It's perfect, created to add sound to an image without supplanting it. Original film soundtracks are composed with the aim of being shared; they never make a name for themselves all on their own, so they are the ideal reading companions.

Here are my recommendations, in the form of a few recordings, should you decide to follow my advice for the book you are about to read. True, it does demand a small amount of preparation, but I am sure that you will be rewarded emotionally.

If you are tempted before even reading the first chapter, try to obtain the music from the film *The Village* by James Newton Howard. Careful now, don't confuse the issues. We're not talking about the film here, so it doesn't matter whether you liked it or loathed it. The music itself is intoxicating.

This recording should serve as your ideal companion for this novel. I listened to it on a continuous loop, day after day, throughout the time I was writing the part about Mont-Saint-Michel. And I never tired of it.

If you wish to take curiosity and enjoyment still further, then you will have to find a second recording for the whole of the part about Egypt. For this, there are two possibilities, as far as I am concerned: either Peter Gabriel's *Passion* or *The Passion of the Christ*, composed by John Debney, whose mysterious, Middle Eastern–influenced soundscapes should carry you far, far away into that strange land we call the imagination.

I have told you everything. My reading secrets are now yours.

In regards to myself, music changed the way I perceived things as a reader. The stories acquired more emotional density—which I would have considered unthinkable before. I felt like an amateur baker who discovers the existence of yeast.

Of course, this is only a piece of advice, but it is like those good, small restaurants whose details friends like to pass quietly to one another, like an affectionate secret, and then hope to be there when the other finally arrives, to witness the smile on his face. In any case, I shall be around while you are reading; I simply hope to see those smiles appear on your faces.

Finally, in this time of doubt, I shall allow myself to remind you that the time machine does exist. It is magic.

And magic really exists. In words.

That is the key to this story.

Happy reading . . .

—MAXIM CHATTAM
Edgecombe, October 12, 2004

Only he who carries the load knows how much it weighs.
—ARAB PROVERB

Man will occasionally stumble over the truth,
but most of the time he will pick himself up
and continue on.
—SIR WINSTON CHURCHILL

THE
CAIRO
DIARY

.

·⚬⚬·

· PROLOGUE ·

·⚬⚬·

Tombs of the Caliphs, East of Cairo,
March 1928

The setting sun filtered through an ancient tomb, shining right across its immense structure from one window to the other like a red eye, tingeing the stone with a fleeting touch of blood. The necropolis had all the elements of a ghost town: its deserted streets, its structures inhabited only by sand and wind, and its increasingly dark shadows.

The damaged monuments were dotted among more modest tombs. They were disproportionate in size, buildings of several stories surmounted by dizzy cupolas and flanked by silent minarets; they had courtyards, fountains that had forever run dry, spacious loggias, and everywhere those darkened openings, accolated windows or holes designed to play with the light.

All at once the sand in the streets whirled up and was borne away by the dusk wind.

Stone remains emerged from the ground, rough stelae toppled by the centuries.

Several acres of large, majestic tombs, as fine as palaces, waited at the gates of Cairo, like the last hope before the desert. A tardy, forgotten hope.

Not far to the east, hills danced under the city's ramparts, like a strangely fossilized sea-swell. Hills not of earth or sand, but of detritus: eight centuries' worth of debris, abandoned here by organized city-dwellers. Heaps of rubble, shards of pottery, fragments of carved stone in a sea of picturesque remains.

The silhouettes of the last people who had been crouching there, working, moved off in the direction of Bab Darb el-Mahrug, a gate leading into el-Azhar district. A group of three kids were squabbling, as was so often the case here, over a piece of enamel that could easily be sold. The question was which of the three had seen it first, lying among the rubble. The eldest was twelve years old.

The children came here every day to dig through the debris, in search of the most insignificant, vaguely historic crumb that might bring a little money if offered to the wealthy tourists who swarmed all over Cairo.

For once the dispute did not result in blows and the eldest child let the other two leave with their trophy, in exchange for a few threats about their future fate if he saw them hunting around there again.

Seleem, who had been watching the scene from the steps of a tomb, finally stood up. He had been there for more than an hour, waiting for them all to leave. He did not want to take the risk of being seen.

His presence in the necropolis was too important for that.

And secret.

Now that the sun was setting, Cairo was gradually lighting up, the ocher city progressively gaining color from the modern brilliance of the European-style buildings. A forest of minarets rose up above the old city wall.

Seleem saw his city through the eyes of a ten-year-old boy who had never even crossed the Nile: with the feeling that the center of the world lay at the heart of those narrow alleyways.

Nothing was more beautiful or more important than Cairo.

Except perhaps this evening, this meeting.

He adored legends. And he was on the point of experiencing one. He had been promised.

It must be time.

Seleem walked down the steps and along an interminable wall. He walked past the funerary mosque of Bars Bey until he found the place he had been told about.

A cramped passageway disappeared between two tall mausoleums.

Splintered wood was strewn across the sand.

Seleem watched where he was stepping and entered.

It was dark; the first stars were not enough to light up the narrow passage.

Seleem walked to the end of what turned out to be a blind alley, and he waited.

Night had fallen, and now the stars were glittering powerfully above the tombs of the caliphs.

Seleem let out his first scream.

The echo of his cry rose up into the empty structures that surrounded him. Instinctively, without rational thought, he had just invented a language, and this cry was the most original definition of it.

It had just given substance to terror.

Before the ends of his hair had finished turning white, he was able to let out a second scream.

This time, he spoke the language of pain.

* * *

A stray dog abandoned the old rag it had found and turned its head toward the blind alley. The screams had just stopped.

The dog opened its mouth and the tip of its moist tongue lolled out. It headed toward the passageway.

It stopped at the entrance, where the thick shadows began.

Then it moved toward the source of those screams.

Its canine curiosity vanished after a few feet, when it scented what haunted the air at the end of this blind alley.

Its eyes saw through the darkness, making out the stocky figure that was moving above the body of a child.

The shape unfolded, became tall.

The smell spread out until it reached the dog's maw.

And the animal began to back away.

When the shape advanced toward it, the dog urinated.

It urinated on itself.

The wind raised up its offering of sand and bore it away, far away, into the mysteries of the desert.

· 1 ·

Paris, November 2005

Paris was muttering angrily.

A storm of indignation was shaking the entire city. The thunder of public rallies battered the fronts of Haussmann's buildings, echoing through the alleyways on the great boulevards, until it reached the ministers.

A leaden sky had lain across the roofs since the scandal began, strangling the capital like a too-tight scarf.

Never had France known a November like it: so icy and yet so electric.

The press had been dining out on it for the last three weeks; certain journalists went as far as stating that November 2005 would relegate May 1968 to the ranks of an anecdotal skirmish if things continued in the same way.

The newspaper stands flashed past like milestones in one of the rear windows of the powerful sedan, issuing their information in regular doses, vital for survival in a civilized environment. All the front pages gave details of the Affair as they saw it; there was scarcely any room for the rest of the news.

The sedan was running alongside a large truck.

Suddenly, the reflection of a face appeared in its rear window.

Marion flinched imperceptibly as she suddenly came face-to-face with herself.

Her face was a ghost's. Her pleasant features were not sufficient today to make her easy on the eye; she had grown too pale, her split lip divided her face like the comma in an eternally unfinished sentence, her sandy hair showed a few streaks of white, and, in particular, her eyes had lost all their brightness. The inquisitive, jade-green flame had given way to two dying embers.

She was approaching forty, and life had just presented her with a really great gift.

The leather squeaked as the man at her side leaned toward the driver and asked him to take a right. Marion blinked in an attempt to forget her face.

Three males, as virile as they were cryptic, were surrounding her in this silent car. Men from the DST.

Direction de la Surveillance du Territoire—the French equivalent of the CIA.

The acronym struck a heavy, slightly terrifying chord.

Especially for Marion, who had never had any problems with the law, who had only been stopped by the police once in her life for a routine identity check, and whose job as a secretary at the Médico-légal Institute and morgue in Paris was the only original thing about her—if indeed it was original.

She had always felt herself to be identical to the millions of other people she lived with in this country, caught up in the system of work, lifting her head a little higher after each year, so she could stay afloat and go on breathing.

Nothing in her life had prepared her to find herself one day in this car, heading for the unknown.

Until she'd returned from her holidays, at the start of October.

Until that morning, very early, when she had entered the cold autopsy room. Each detail was engraved on her mind. Even the stuttering of the neon lights when she pressed the switch. Once again she saw the flashes of white light reflecting off the tiles, the immaculate stainless steel of the dissection table. Her heels echoed at each step. The antiseptic smell hadn't completely masked the other, more acrid smell of cold meat. The only reason she was there so early that morning was to find Dr. Mendès, who was neither there nor in the adjoining storeroom.

Marion had turned around to walk back across the room.

Her eyes fell on it by chance, as though drawn to it.

It wasn't very eye-catching, hardly a cartoon strip.

But it had changed her life.

Until the DST came to see her and told her she was going to die. Probably.

Unless she agreed to disappear. For a time at least, long enough for things to calm down, for a place to be found for her, for them to rely on her, for a system to be set in motion.

Everything had been so quick.

Paranoia is a virus. Transmit it in the right circumstances and it will develop all on its own. From that moment on, Marion had spotted shadows in her wake, individuals spending the night in darkened cars in front of the building where she lived, and her telephone sounded strange, as if it had been bugged.

Then the attack.

She swallowed, ran her tongue across her lips. The cut was still there.

A warning.

Marion had agreed to disappear.

Before the media discovered the identity of this woman, the initiator of the greatest scandal the Fifth Republic had known; before other people, dangerous in different ways this time, returned to attack.

The man from the DST who took charge of her case had told her just to bring warm clothes, and her most personal possessions, as she wouldn't be returning home for a long time; it could be a month, maybe a year. She knew nothing about her destination.

The vehicle with the darkened windows passed through La

Défense tunnel, heading toward the A13 Autoroute, and in a few minutes disappeared toward the west, evaporating into the anger and the gray-white horizon that encircled Paris.

The smell of the sea gave Marion her first clue, but darkness fell too quickly for her to spot any landmarks as they passed by. She rested her head back against the seat, rolled up her window, and confined herself just to following the few lights with her eyes. For now, her future was nothing but a roar in the darkness, a doubt moving at eighty miles per hour, speeding toward the unknown.

She reopened her eyes to find that the car was climbing a forgotten road, with nothing on either side but emptiness. Marion sensed that they were almost there, and pressed her face to the glass like an impatient child in need of reassurance. The vehicle slowed down and turned left before coming to a halt beside a stone wall.

The front passenger immediately got out and opened the door so she could get out. Stiff after the journey, Marion had difficulty straightening her long legs. She stood up gently, numb with sleep. They were standing at the bottom of a steep hill.

Ancient structures rose up from the slope, forming a collection of fortifications and dwellings worthy of a medieval film.

Then the moon pierced through the low clouds, and trained its silver searchlight on the summit.

Out of the shadows loomed a colossal tower, dominating the entire bay, its foundations crushing all architectural pretensions for miles around.

Marion closed her eyes with a sigh.

Behind her, one of the men had just placed her two suitcases on the ground.

She had arrived at the bottom of what was going to be her retreat for the weeks, or maybe months, to come.

Mont-Saint-Michel.

As fleetingly as it had appeared, the summit sank back into the darkness, as the moon withdrew behind its nocturnal sieve, like an insect slipping away, sheltering from predators.

· 2 ·

The wind suddenly rose, capturing Marion in its vise; her clothes flapped about in the darkness. One of the men accompanying her turned his head toward her. His eyes were cold. *Cold like this journey, cold like in bad films,* thought Marion. He stared at her and blinked. For a moment she detected the man behind the professional, some mercy beneath the austerity. Guessing that she was the intended recipient of this pity hurt her, and her heart felt hollow.

Beneath a tower close to the main entrance, metallic hinges began to grate. A narrow postern gate opened, creating a hole in the wall.

A frail silhouette detached itself from the wall and came toward the group. It was holding up a lantern, which glimmered faintly in the darkness as if it were guiding the person and drawing it into the blackness. The person was draped in a robe that changed shape as the wind gusted around it with increasing ferocity. Suddenly, he or she lifted a hand to hold down the linen headdress that concealed the face. The driver of the sedan approached and they exchanged a few words, which were rendered almost inaudible by the distance and the wind.

Then he came back to Marion.

His was the only voice she had heard. He bent forward as he addressed her, so as not to have to talk too loud despite the gusting wind. His eyes only rarely settled on Marion; they swam above her, toward the far distance, already preoccupied with a world elsewhere.

"Anne will show you to your new home. Trust her, she has performed this kind of service for us before. She knows what must be done, so listen to her. Sorry I can't be gallant enough to carry up your cases, but the less time we spend here, the better."

Marion opened her mouth to protest, but no sound emerged.

"You will receive news via Anne as soon as things start moving."

"But . . . aren't you going to . . . I don't know, search my room or something?"

A half-smile appeared on his lips. In it she saw a degree of affection for her own naïveté.

"That won't be necessary," he replied firmly. "You have nothing to fear here. Trust me, at least about that."

She sensed that he was about to turn away and placed her hand on his arm. "How . . . what do I do to contact you if . . . "

"The mobile number I gave you the first time, call me on that if you need to. Now I must go."

He watched for her reaction for a moment, then pursed his lips and gave a slight nod. "Good luck," he added, with more kindness in his voice.

Then he walked away and signaled to his two companions to get back into the car.

A few seconds later the vehicle had disappeared onto the jetty, leaving behind it two tiny red marks upon the bosom of the night.

"Come on, let's not stay here," a voice said behind her.

The voice was calming, gentle. Marion turned around to face it. Under the onslaught of the elements, Anne appeared more vulnerable and fragile than a tender young sapling in the storm. The wind had carved myriad deep lines that furrowed her face.

"Let's go in," she said. "I'll take you home, where you can rest."

Home.

Marion swallowed with great difficulty.

Everything was moving too fast, she no longer had any control over anything; and she was submitting to it all with disconcerting neutrality.

Already Anne was walking toward the postern gate, carrying one of the two suitcases.

What happened next owed more to the world of hallucinations than to free will. Later, Marion remembered walking up a narrow street, with ancient housefronts made of stone and wood. Then several steps and a passageway winding beneath tiny buildings, on the fringes of a sinister cemetery.

The gate closed again and Anne raised her eyes to look at her. Blue eyes that were smooth and determined, in opposition to the rest of the face.

"Here is your new house," she said.

That and other words, distant words. Words devoid of meaning, logic, life.

Words that traveled for an instant between the two women before being lost in tiredness. The entrance light was on; it was swaying as though on a ship. It was shining increasingly brightly. Blindingly.

Marion closed her eyes.

Her legs were trembling from the effort of the climb. Her breath was all spent.

She remembered nothing more of what happened next.

Except for the draft of air when the door opened.

And the low rumbling sound of a man's voice.

· 3 ·

A leftover piece of Babel.

That's what Mont-Saint-Michel was. A proud finger pointing toward the heavens. Marion saw in it not the marvel of religious devotion, but rather a conceited attempt to get closer to God. A gull sniggered as it skimmed the dizzying wall that dropped more than seventy yards. Marion stood bending forward, her hands placed on the low stone wall, overlooking the whole of the mist-drowned bay. A milky tide was gradually receding, releasing smoky trails as it licked at the ramparts. The white cloth coated absolutely everything. Nothing escaped: not a single lost mast or distant cliff, not even the causeway that provided the link to the mainland.

The Mount rose up out of this sea, colossal, like the cutting edge of a patiently shaped flint laid upon an immense expanse of mother-of-pearl.

Marion turned her back to the sight and faced the forecourt of the abbey church, which stretched out at her feet.

"We are on the western terrace," explained Sister Anne. "Apart from the lace staircase on the church roof, one cannot enjoy a more agreeable view."

Marion confined herself to a brief nod, as she did with all the sister's comments. Together, they had walked up the main street, then climbed the two "great stairs"—two long series of steps leading to the roof of the world—Sister Anne taking on the role of guide for the occasion.

"I am going to introduce you to our community. They are as impatient to make your acquaintance as they are aware of the need to be discreet regarding your presence among us."

Marion cast a last glance at the view. The mist was flowing over the ground as if the Mount and its inhabitants were all drifting away, out to sea.

She closed her eyes for a brief moment. Drifting. That was the word that best characterized her these past few days.

Waking up in that strange bed had immediately made her feel sick, gripped by the muted anguish that tightens the chest when a situation seems to be overflowing in all directions, completely out of control.

Anne approached her. She gave a faint, but reassuring smile. The icy wind emphasized the whiteness of her face. Lines lay deep between sections that were completely smooth. It put Marion in mind of a folded mask, like the skin of cream on hot milk.

"I know how you are feeling," said the nun quietly. She was right beside her now.

She laid a hand on Marion's back.

"Confusion thunders inside here, doesn't it?" she added, placing an index finger on her brow. "With a little time that will pass. Trust me."

Marion gazed at the little woman. "Is this something you're used to?"

Hardly had she spoken the phrase when it disappeared, swept away by the tone, the weakness of her voice. She had always hated showing her weak points, her difficulties, or her worries.

"Not in the way you imagine," replied Sister Anne. "I have indeed performed this service before. But it isn't . . . usual."

Marion was still staring at her.

"I'm going to say this to you now, so it is done: I know nothing about the reasons that have brought you here, and that doesn't interest me. I just want to help you so that the time you spend among us is as pleasant as possible."

She bore Marion's gaze without defiance or hardness.

"For everyone," she went on. "Pleasant but discreet. Nobody undesirable will come and find you on the Mount, have no fear. It is the ideal place to spend these few weeks, or months. Famous all over the planet for its remoteness. You will melt into the background."

She rubbed Marion's back. "I will be with you for as long as it takes you to get your bearings. All will be well. You'll see."

Marion opened her mouth to speak, but could not expel the air. She must look frightful, she thought. With her hair blown all over the place by the gusts of wind, her damaged lip, and her sunken eyes. *An old harpy, that's what you are. . . . A harpy rendered decrepit by events.* Overtaken *by events. Drowned, even.*

"Let's not linger, everyone here is in turmoil. They won't have much time to spare for us, with the storm that's coming."

"The storm?" Marion repeated quietly.

"Yes, you didn't hear the news. . . . A few days ago, they announced that there's going to be an enormous storm on the coast, the like of which hasn't been seen for several centuries. Even the army has been mobilized in rural areas to help people prepare their homes and to assist in the event of emergency. Everyone here is busy making the Mount as waterproof as possible, and protecting what needs to be protected."

Sister Anne scanned the western horizon. "You might think it was going to be fine, that this carpet of mist would lift to reveal a sunny day. But tonight, it'll be war."

Her eyes were shining with excitement. "Anyhow, come, you have work to do. A whole list of names to learn, and the faces that go with them, of course."

Marion slid her hands back into the pockets of her woollen coat.

She fell into step behind Sister Anne and entered the abbey church.

The eastern sun dissolved in a gigantic and blinding gray puddle, which bathed the high windows of the choir. A long procession of massive columns ran along the central aisle as far as the transept. Starting at the entrance, all of the architecture converged on the flamboyant choir in a sort of optical illusion, as if the nave was no more than a prolongation of the earth's entrails, toward the supreme elevation right at the end, below the high windows, before the altar.

The abandoned feeling lasted only a few seconds, but it was enough for Marion to rid herself of the weight on her chest, like an excess of breath that had stayed in her lungs too long, expelled all at once in a spontaneous exhalation. Since it had happened—*no! for the last few weeks*—Marion had been unable to create a state of emptiness in her mind, unable to avoid feeling crushed by the situation. Each of her words, and each of her actions were motivated by—or a consequence of—this escape. And for the first time, she had opened her eyes and really looked, without any thought related to her exile.

For an instant, the majesty of the place had washed away her troubles.

The semblance of a smile appeared on her lips.

Marion raised her head toward the ceiling. High up, the arches of an ambulatory formed patches of opaque shadow.

These were not completely still; they turned around and around and stretched out as if long, black silk sheets were moving around each arch.

Marion watched intently, her nose in the air.

The door had been left open, and the wind gusted against her back.

The flames of a few candles danced, faltering dangerously in this ever-stronger breeze.

Marion heard Anne's footsteps as she walked away down the nave, paying her no attention.

She felt as if she was being observed.

The little hairs on the back of her neck stiffened.

The more she became aware of it, the more the feeling spread with increasing confidence.

Her tongue was coated. She knew this searing feeling of paranoia. The past weeks had brought both emotions closer together, turning them into veritable rivals in a fierce competition, in which serenity was at stake. An almost daily match. And all that was required to unleash the paranoia was an ounce of anxiety; once it had that, it spread like burning oil on a lake.

Marion swallowed, forcing herself to curtail all speculation, all imagination, to rid herself of this anguish by refusing it any fuel.

The sensation grew less acute.

Sister Anne had disappeared, turning into the northern arm of the transept.

Marion started walking again, along the rows of cold benches. All the same, she glanced briefly at the dark arches before turning.

The ambulatory that stretched out behind these mysterious mouths was still just as invisible. And the shadows were still moving.

Sister Anne was waiting for her at the top of a staircase leading down into the depths of the building. Her eyes scrutinized Marion to assure herself that all was well and the little woman set off first down the stairs. They came out at the lower level, in an enclosed chapel, with fewer than ten tiny benches, a handful of lit candles, and a very low, rounded ceiling that reinforced the impression of warmth and intimacy. An amber half-light trembled on the walls of the crypt of Notre-Dame-des-Trente-Cierges.

There, in the dusk of the last bench, seven motionless silhouettes were waiting, their heads bowed beneath masks of fabric. Seven pious statues, as immovable as stone.

All seven were dressed in religious habits.

They all wore coarse, inhuman faces, with irregular, clumsy features, distorted mouths, and monstrous eyes, like a group of gargoyles staring at the crypt's altar.

Then the Mount's spell was broken.

And the stone changed.

The fabric of a cowl gently folded back.

And suddenly a hand appeared. It rose to make the sign of the cross, and the fabric mask crumpled as the priest pushed back his hood.

· 4 ·

There were four men and three women.

The most striking thing was how similar they all were in shape.

Apart from one brother who was much taller than the others, the six followers were of the same height, and of a relatively slender build, as though forged from the same mold.

I can't help it, it's my job, Marion thought. *Too many autopsy reports to draw up properly and file, and you find yourself focusing on people's external aspects: their physical data.*

It was true, she couldn't deny it. Her job overflowed into her judgment. When she encountered new faces, she often saw first of all a piece of funereal statistical data relating to their appearance. A portly fifty-year-old man with flabby skin who'd clearly enjoyed the high life made her think of heart attacks, while a white neck whose tendons were forever protruding beneath the chin because of stress raised the specter of a ruptured aneurysm.

Whereas others tended to catalog people according to their socio-professional category or in relation to their general cultural background, she did so according to the probable circumstances of their death.

Sister Anne rubbed her hands together as she turned toward Marion.

"Here is a part of our community," she said. "Marion, let me introduce you to Brother Damien."

The man in question emerged from the group to come and greet the newcomer. He was around forty. His hood was drawn back, revealing cropped gray hair and a full face that contrasted with his rather svelte body. There was a certain joie de vivre in his eyes. He greeted Marion with a bow of the head, his eyes constantly on the move.

Hyperactive, always cheerful, you might say; the type who eats too quickly and swallows without chewing. He'll probably choke to death when something goes down the wrong way.

She adored that expression. Dying because something "goes down the wrong way." So as not to say: "death by suffocation, due to the presence of a foreign body in the airways." The classic story of a Sunday afternoon that turns into a nightmare. Lunch with friends, plenty of wine, everybody eating hungrily and then . . . one mouthful too many, swallowed too quickly, without really thinking about it. The food gets stuck in the diner's throat, and panic grips the impatient eater. You found them each Sunday evening, lined up in the basement at the Médico-légal Institute, one behind the other on their aluminium gurneys, while their relatives were howling somewhere that it was impossible, that people couldn't just die, not on such a peaceful Sunday, not like that.

Marion had seen an awful lot of "impossible corpses" like that, in her ten-year career.

It was settled. Brother Damien was to be "Brother Wrong Way."

Giving free rein to her idiotic little game did her a world of good. She relaxed, became herself again.

Next was Brother Gaël, a young man of around twenty, with the look of a babe in arms, and by all accounts the son of a good family—*the second son of the noble ancien régime family, the one who's destined for the Church*—too young to inspire Marion in her guessing game.

Sisters Gabriela and Agathe had no greater effect on Marion. They were young—around thirty—and at first glance as smooth as a block of polished marble.

The tallest of the seven was a man approaching fifty, slow in word and deed, pale, and visibly on the verge of breathlessness after welcoming her. Marion opted for "Brother Anemia" in place of his real name: Brother Christophe.

The two last members were Brother Gilles and Sister Luce, two individuals of a highly respectable age, whose eyes were as piercing as they were taciturn; two eagle faces, prominent noses, and thin lips, so alike that one might think they shared the same blood.

Marion had no desire to play with them. It wasn't funny anymore.

Brother Gilles stared at her for a long time without saying a word. He merely folded his long, wrinkled fingers upon his belly.

"I think you know everybody now," commented Sister Anne.

Brother Gilles coughed exaggeratedly to indicate his disagreement.

"Ah, yes! Almost everybody! There is still Brother Serge, the hierarchic leader of our community. He could not get away, but you will meet him a little later."

There was an uncomfortable silence. Brother Damien leaned toward Marion. "If you need anything, don't hesitate to ask."

There was nothing forced or overly charitable about his affability, thought Marion. His sincerity was actually rather touching.

"Thank you," she whispered, rather too softly for her liking.

Sister Gabriela, who had the face of a porcelain doll, laid a hand on her arm. She had not pushed back the fabric headdress that hid her hair, and this gave her an even more angelic appearance.

"You will get used to this place very quickly, you will see," she confided in a musical voice.

"On that subject," interrupted Sister Anne, "we thought it would be best to organize some way for you to pass the time during the days to come. For today, that will take the form of a tour of the Mount, which will acquaint you with your new environment. After that, Friday and the weekend will be a little strange, with the storm. . . . And next week, Brother Damien suggested he might take you with him to the library in Avranches, to classify some books in the reserve collections, if that appeals to you. . . . "

Marion nodded without great enthusiasm. She noted that every eye was on her.

"Don't worry," Sister Anne said finally. "Here, within these walls, you will spend a winter . . . like no other."

Marion froze. No, she wasn't going to spend the winter here. It would only be a matter of weeks, perhaps months, one or two, in the worst case, but not a whole season. She swore to herself that she would be home for Christmas.

"Soon our faces will be familiar to you," continued the nun. "These halls will be like a series of drawing rooms for your soul; you will enjoy strolling through them. Give yourself a little time. That is all the Mount demands of you: a little time. It will do the rest."

"Very well said," Brother Gilles said abruptly, in a rough voice.

Marion observed him. Thick gray and black hairs peeped through his withered skin. His face was marbled with numerous fine red veins and white creases, like a crumpled garment. He looked back at her without blinking, the keen brilliance in his eyes bearing witness to a fierce stubbornness.

"We shall leave you with your protégée, Sister Anne," he continued. "We shall all have time to get to know her better; right now, the storm demands all our attention."

Marion could not take her eyes off him.

He didn't like her. Her or her presence among them, that was obvious. In other circumstances, she would have allowed herself a cutting remark on the pointlessness of welcoming someone if that welcome was a chore in his eyes, but she was hardly in the mood. And she had only just arrived; one could begin the introductions better than that.

Bit by bit, she was regaining consciousness. And her sodden character was awakening, she noticed.

Everyone left by the little door at the far end, taking their leave of her with a swift wave of the hand. The majority seemed nice, even pleased that she had come.

When they were alone, Sister Anne turned to her. "I am sorry if Brother Gilles seemed a little less than—"

"That's not important," interrupted Marion. "In any event, I think we shall have to get along together during the weeks to come."

She managed to crack a friendly smile. "We'll get used to each other, don't you think?"

Sister Anne nodded with pleasure. "I am happy to see you smile at last."

Me too, Marion almost said. She caught herself as she drifted with the tide for a moment, as she took in what was happening to her with a benevolent sense of fatality.

"A long guided tour awaits us, are you ready?"

"Lead on."

Sister Anne took the same door as her comrades and they slipped into the Mount's limbo.

They passed through the Devil's Dungeon, a modest room at the end of a staircase leading from the church level, which provided access to the Merveille.

A long corridor dotted with pillars stretched eastward: the promenade. At its far end, in the half-light, Brother Gilles was conversing in a low voice with another monk, whose identity could not be discerned because he had his back to Marion.

Brother Gilles noticed her from a distance and his gnarled hand rose suddenly from beneath his robe to grab hold of the other monk and lead him into the darkness, where they disappeared.

Marion sighed softly.

She had only been there twenty-four hours, and already internecine strife was becoming apparent.

The time spent on this granite mountain was going to be long.

Behind her, Sister Anne turned a heavy iron key in an age-old lock, which grated as its catch sprang back.

Then the door opened with a creak.

· 5 ·

They spent all morning there.

Sister Anne moved about between these corridors with bewildering ease. In Marion's eyes, it was as if she had grown up here.

The two women carried out their tour to the sound of hammer blows, nailing plywood planks to the most fragile windows. Several times they encountered a brother or a sister in the midst of sealing a narrow window with the aid of large pieces of damp cardboard. The preparations were moving on apace. The storm that was rolling in their direction must be a monster to arouse so many fears.

Beyond a general impression that there were staircases everywhere, chambers in every nook and cranny, and convoluted corridors, Marion managed to retain a few essential facts.

First of all, the structure of the abbey could be divided into three levels, even if a multitude of intermediate rooms and slopes did swiftly truncate this point of reference. The upper level was that of the immense abbey church. The middle level contained the crypt of the Thirty Candles and a large number of small side chapels. Then the lower level, the one with the dungeons, had held Marion's amused attention, especially the one that provided easy access to the exterior of the north side, through the abbey's gardens. And then there was the Merveille. A fabulous construction on the northern slopes and adhering to the rest, which could also be divided into three levels: the vast storeroom with the chaplaincy at the bottom, in the middle the formidable Salle des Chevaliers with its powerful columns, next to the Salle des Hôtes, and finally the refectory and the cloister, which left Marion speechless.

The hanging garden and its calming greenery were surrounded by covered galleries, whose magical, staggered rows of columns, arcades, and carved crockets offered an endless approach to contemplation and meditation. The western slopes opened onto a triple picture window, which emphasized the fact that three elements mingled here: the earth for a foundation, the sea for life, and the air for the spirit.

Sister Anne explained that when there was high, thick mist, the cloister garden was reflected in it, creating the illusion of an accessible Eden, brought to the eyes of men by the breath of the angels.

Marion noted that the majority of the rooms they encountered had heavy, locked doors, whose passkeys Sister Anne kept with an almost ridiculous bunch of twenty keys, which were huge and clinked loudly. When the sister took her imposing key ring from a fold in her robe, Marion had the impression that it was far too heavy for those apparently delicate wrists. But Sister Anne seemed hewn from rustic leather, resilient and capable of being stretched at will.

And her limpid blue eyes pierced through everything they looked at.

The Mount in its entirety was divided into two parts: the village on the one hand, climbing up the southwest flank from the causeway to the south, and the abbey itself, on the summit, with the Merveille stowed away to the north. After walking up the rue Grande and a whole succession of steps known as the Grand Degré Extérieur, the great outer staircase, you eventually reached the barbican, the dividing point between the village and the abbey. The latter, which was gigantic, was guarded in its southern part by a very tall building: the abbot's residence; while the Grand Degré Intérieur, the great inner staircase, ran along the foundations of the abbey church and climbed as far as the forecourt: the western terrace.

Lunch was served in a shared room at the abbot's residence. Marion was struck by the simplicity of this room designed for living. Here there were no historic furnishings, nothing but exposed stone walls and Formica tables. She even stifled a grin as she picked up her stainless-steel knife, worthy of a school cafeteria; this was a long way from the mystical image she had retained from her morning visit.

With the exception of Sister Agathe and Brothers Gilles and Gaël, all the members of the community who had been introduced to her that morning were present at the table.

"It is my turn to serve," declared Brother Christophe.

He spoke with a disconcerting slowness. She hadn't been mistaken in nicknaming him "Brother Anemia," thought Marion.

Ravioli and cheese were served in a large pan.

"As you will notice, there are days when we have less time to prepare the meals and others when we are more . . . indulgent."

Marion, whose face was buried in her plate, easily recognized the sweet, singsong voice of Sister Gabriela. The young woman was looking at her with a degree of anxiety at the thought that the newcomer might be put off by their lunch.

"This suits me very well," she reassured the nun. "I'm no great cook myself, and I don't often have the time, either."

Brother Wrong Way jumped at the opportunity. "And what do you do, if that's not indiscreet?"

Marion had no time to open her mouth. Sister Anne reprimanded her colleague's jovial curiosity in a scathing tone, "Brother Damien! Your question is inappropriate—"

"No, it's okay," cut in Marion. "It's not a problem."

She turned toward the forty-year-old man, who had just lost his jovial air. "I am . . . or I was"—she sighed—"a secretary at the Médico-légal Institute, in Paris."

With amusement, she scanned the faces as the idea of what her daily duties might entail sank into each of their minds.

"The Médico-légal Inst—" began Sister Gabriela.

"Yes, that's right. The place where corpses are stored before autopsies."

Eagle-faced Sister Luce raised her eyebrows. The old woman gazed fixedly at the food she was calmly ingesting.

"Don't be alarmed, the secretary isn't based in the dissection rooms, although that may have happened to me. My work is clearly less . . . incisive, if I can say that."

"But you have relatively direct contact with death?" emphasized Sister Gabriela.

"In a way, yes."

"Isn't that too heavy a burden to bear?"

"It's . . . at the start, I admit it's hard. Then as time progresses you get used to it. I think over the months and years, the sheer volume of deaths reduces the dramatic element."

"The notion of the mortal individual becomes lost in a generic, less personal, more distant death?" suggested Sister Gabriela.

"Yes, that makes me think of that saying," interjected Brother

Damien, laying down his fork and raising an index finger. "If you kill a man you are a murderer, but if you kill several you are a conqueror."

Marion blinked. She knew an additional part to this maxim: And if you kill them all, you are a god. The place and company weren't perhaps ideal for this extension.

"In a way," she eventually conceded.

"It's a little crazy all the same," the brother went on. "In the end, one becomes more moved by the death of a single individual than by genocide! If you look, one murder close to where we live makes the front page of the newspapers, but they're completely silent about what's going on in Africa, for example—"

Sister Luce put down her glass too quickly, and it almost shattered. "I do not think ruling on a dramatic scale of death is a very pious attitude, Brother Damien," she reprimanded him, in a voice as sharp as a billhook.

"No, of course not. I am simply saying that death does not merit different degrees of feeling. It is always tragic without discrimination, it—"

"That is enough."

The monk remained openmouthed for a brief moment, disappointed not to be able to correct this mistake. His gaze slid toward Marion.

Soon there was nothing left but the clinking of plates to lighten the atmosphere. Marion finished her food and addressed Sister Luce, "What does your daily life consist of?"

"That depends on the day. At the moment it involves preparing the Mount to withstand the coming storm. In fact, if you will kindly excuse me, there is still a great deal to do."

Sister Luce collected up her cutlery and her plate, stood up to put everything on a tray, and left the room.

Marion nervously tapped her glass with her index finger. "That's a good start," she muttered.

Sister Anne's look told her that she had sensed her uneasiness.

"Marion," began the sister, "will you permit me to call you Marion? This afternoon, I shall show you round the village and—"

"I think there are more urgent matters," she cut in. "If this storm is so fierce and there are so many things to do all over the place to protect the Mount from it, perhaps we could help?"

Marion then hastily added, with a hint of malice, "I think Sister Luce would appreciate it. And I must admit that a little activity would do me good."

Sister Anne remained openmouthed for a moment, then agreed. Farther off, Sister Agathe burst out laughing and swiftly put a hand over her mouth.

Marion observed the sky through the window.

It was gray, a uniform gray, without relief.

If the storm was approaching, it was doing it very gently, crawling along like a predator preparing to pounce suddenly on its prey.

For three hours they dug in the northern garden to remove plants or shrubs, which they transplanted into terra-cotta pots before storing them in the Merveille's vast storeroom for a few days. Marion had tied back her hair with an old elastic band and spared no effort to get as much work done as possible. When the light began to fail, she could no longer feel her fingers.

From time to time she raised her head to scan the abbey's ramparts, looking for signs of life, but never distinguished more than a furtive shape. Mont-Saint-Michel had all the appearance of a wrecked ship. With no one left on board.

An arrogant yet divinely beautiful *wreck*.

The sole sign of the approaching storm was the wind, which was now blowing harder. A stubborn wind, which eventually numbed the skin and bit into the flesh.

Marion entered and placed the last pot in the row of previous ones, then allowed herself to sink onto a bench, facing the door of the storeroom.

Outside the light was ashen, tarnishing the garden's last colors. Sister Anne joined her, tools in hand, and sat down beside her.

"Well, another bit saved," she said finally.

"As you say."

Sister Anne nodded toward the outside. "I hesitated to tell you when we were there, but now. . . . Did you know that we were digging the soil of the 'jardin de pleine mer,' the garden of the open sea, and that before it was given that name, it was known as the 'monks' cemetery'?"

"That's nice . . . "

"Nonjuring priests were buried here during the Revolution. They are still there," added the nun, with a restrained laugh. "And the administrator of the Mount wants to organize cocktail parties and wedding breakfasts here, can you imagine?"

"All in the best possible taste."

"Indeed."

Marion almost remarked upon the apparent vitality of the plants that grew there, accompanied by a sordid joke about their roots, but decided against it; bad taste was decidedly in the air.

She contemplated the rows of pots, which ran for several feet. "Sister Luce will be pleased," she commented. "We have spared her an additional job."

New laughter lines appeared at the corners of Sister Anne's mouth. "Don't hold her slightly distant manner against her, she wasn't trying to hurt you. We are a small community here, we have our customs, and your arrival necessitates a few alterations to everyone's perceptions, like an old bachelor who finds he suddenly has to live as one half of a couple. It's very positive for everyone. And if she seems a little . . . sour-tempered at first sight, Sister Luce is a remarkable woman at heart, you will see."

"If it requires you to make an effort, why did you agree to take me in?"

Sister Anne's smile grew less broad but did not disappear. "It's a little peculiar. . . . We are tenants here. The Mount belongs to the state, and is managed by an administrator. We pay rent, and provide certain services. As we did today, running about all over the place preparing for the storm—"

"Or as you do when you agree to hide people whom the state entrusts to you. It's imposed on you—"

Sister Anne shook her head gently. "Nobody is imposing on us. The question was asked four years ago, and after discussing it among ourselves, we agreed to provide this service. The Mount is our retreat, not our shrine."

Marion lowered her eyes to her hands. They were covered in soil and scratched all over.

"Come along, I'll take you back to your house, where you can warm up and have a wash. I'll call for you this evening, so we can go to dinner—"

"I would prefer to remain alone this evening, if you don't see any problems with that. It's . . . getting my bearings. I've only just arrived."

Sister Anne nodded. "Of course, I understand. We have filled your refrigerator, so you'll find something to eat. And if you need us, our telephone number is on the entrance table."

They walked back via the north and the east, but Marion couldn't quite work out where she was. They walked back down rue Grande as far as the little parish church, behind which lay a staircase, which one must climb in order to walk around the edge of the cemetery. Opposite the headstones stood a row of tiny, one-story houses. Sister Anne patted Marion warmly on the back, by way of goodbye, and walked off, leaving her protégée to enter her new lair.

Marion pushed the door shut and leaned back against it.

She let out a long breath before opening her eyes again.

The entrance hall was narrow, flanked by a staircase that led up to the bedroom. This was her home.

She must get used to that idea. For a few weeks, minimum.

She hadn't yet taken the time to really explore, to get the measure of the place, and that was going to be her program that evening.

She placed the key on the hall table, walked past the wall of the kitchen, and entered the living room, *her* living room.

A long, tall window ran almost the entire width of the room, right at the back, divided vertically by slender beams that gave it a medieval feel. A sofa stood at a right angle underneath, opposite a cabinet hiding the television and hi-fi system. The place had clearly been fitted out as a not always successful compromise between an ancient house and modern comfort. But the view was pleasant. The pointed slate roofs and the redbrick chimneys led down in a gentle slope to sea level, toward the south and the entrance to the Mount, toward the causeway that led off into the distance, cleaving the gray expanse until it finally rejoined the land.

The attics and the pointed windows of the lofts were all dark. One lone ribbon of white smoke rose from a chimney lower down in the village, and was immediately dispersed by the wind.

Marion laid her coat on the sofa and sat down beside it, her hands folded behind her head. Noticing that she was covered in soil, she got up again rather quickly, clicking her tongue against the roof of her mouth in annoyance.

It must be around six. She wasn't hungry, just in need of warming up. There was a bath upstairs, a chance to relax, and why not take the time to take a little care of herself? How long was it since she had done that? Taken two hours in one evening for herself, for her body, to smooth cream over her blemishes, exfoliate with the aid of gel, wax away excess, slather, rub, sound out, and improve its appearance so she felt good? Make herself a new skin.

Yes, that was what she needed, in order to find herself again.

Marion leaped to her feet and climbed the steps, which creaked under the carpet that covered them. The staircase led directly into the bedroom, which had no door; a double bed, a sofa with a low table, a wardrobe, a few shelves, and a dressing table were sufficient to fill it. Three mansard windows opened up, two to the south onto the same view as the picture window downstairs, and the other to the north, onto the little cemetery.

The two suitcases were lying on the ground, underneath the shelves, waiting to be emptied. Marion crouched down to take out a pair of clean underwear and her dressing gown, then headed for the bathroom.

She turned her head as she got up, her eyes sweeping the room very swiftly. From right to left, linking the pieces of information with a blurring sensation.

Sofa . . . low table . . . lamp . . . pile of magazines, placed there through Sister Anne's good offices . . . beige carpet . . . bedside table . . . night-light . . . bed . . . sheet of paper . . . other bedside table . . . other wardrobe . . . carpet . . . and the door leading to the bathroom.

Marion had already taken two steps when she stopped.

Sheet of paper?

This time her attention was drawn back to the bedspread.

It wasn't a sheet but a vellum envelope bearing a single word: *Mademoiselle.*

Her heart started thudding in her chest, and she opened her mouth to breathe. What message lay inside?

She closed her eyes, immediately reassuring herself. Those who wished her ill in Paris were the type to strike, not leave her an envelope.

Marion's fingertips felt her split lip.

If they had found her, she would no longer be standing.

It was Sister Anne or one of her companions who had left this. Nothing more.

Marion nervously pushed a lock of hair behind her ear. She didn't like the attention. The envelope hadn't been there when she woke up; she had made the bed before leaving and could swear to it. If she must spend the coming weeks here things must be made clear: That they gave her shelter, so be it, but she would demand a certain privacy, beginning with the place she lived. She didn't want people to be able to come in here behind her back.

She picked up the envelope and opened it.

Inside she found a piece of cardboard on which was written in beautiful black handwriting:

Do you like playing games?

 45 35 51 43 22 11 12 43 24 15 32/41 24 15
43 43 15 25 11 51 34 15

 I shall say only one thing to help you: There are twenty-five of them, although one may add another, which would be the double of its predecessor, aligned in a square, 12345 across and 12345 down.

Yours.

Marion blinked and reread the note.

"What is this bullshit?" she murmured.

Her first reflex was to lift her head and look through the curtains to see if anyone was spying on her from the cemetery opposite. It was built on a terrace, which brought it up to the same height as the upper floor. The house was separated from it only by an enclosed alleyway between the buildings and the cemetery wall.

Nobody.

It was particularly dark outside.

Marion lit the lamp beside the bedroom sofa and sat down on the cushions.

What did this mean? All these figures . . .

"Fine, okay . . . you want to play. . . . What is this? A kind of welcoming ritual? Hazing?"

Marion had spoken out loud.

Her heart started to calm down.

She placed the card on the low table.

What now?

Her eyes scrutinized the succession of numbers.

It's a bloody riddle. A coded message . . .

And she had always loved this kind of mystery, ever since she was very small. Even crosswords fascinated her. In a certain way they were, in her eyes, semantic riddles, divided up.

So these few figures here . . .

Yes, she had to admit it: This intrigued her.

And so?

"And so, shit! If it occupies me," she declared, getting up to fetch a notepad and pencil from her bag.

Whether this was the idea of Sister Anne or one of the brothers, that had no importance in itself.

"Let's see . . . "

They didn't look like coordinates, more like a coded message.

The figures were all grouped in pairs. One pair could designate one letter rather than one word; that seemed like the most logical explanation.

Marion closed her eyes to try and remember that word she had learned as a teenager. . . . It had haunted her mind for years. . . . A word with an *o* in it. . . . God, it was something everybody knew. . . .

"*Esarintulo!*" she exclaimed.

The order of the letters most used in the French language. First the *e*, then the *s*, the *a*, and so on. She could try to link the most commonly recurring figures with the most used letter.

"That gives us . . . "

Marion counted. The forty-three and the fifteen appeared the most, four times each. *E* and *s* probably. The fifteen was in the middle and ended the message, whereas two forty-threes succeeded each other in the center. Two letter *e*s in the middle of a word? Unlikely. On the other hand, two instances of *s* were feasible. Marion opted for *s* as forty-three and *e* as fifteen.

Next, eleven and twenty-four appeared twice.

An *a* and an *r*?

Marion wrote down her first deductions in her notebook, leaving a cross for the unknown letters:

xxxSxAxSRЕx/xRESSЕxAxxE

Nothing obvious. Eleven letters in both words, she noticed. It was very short. Perhaps too short for Esarintulo to work properly.

On the spur of the moment, the sentence supposed to be a clue had seemed incomprehensible to her and she hadn't included it in her reasoning; now it was time to reintegrate it into the equation.

> *There are twenty-five of them, although one may add another, which would be the double of its predecessor, aligned in a square, 12345 across and 12345 down.*

Twenty-five what?

Marion ran her tongue over her lips.

She drew a rectangle in her notebook. Starting at the top left-hand corner, she wrote 1, 2, 3, 4, and 5 at equal distances apart, following the horizontal axis, as for a graph. She repeated the operation with the vertical, the y-axis.

	1	2	3	4	5
1					
2					
3					
4					
5					

"And now?"

There were indeed twenty-five boxes to fill, but with what?

> *There are twenty-five of them, although one may add another, which would be the double of its predecessor.*

Her hand fell, hitting the sheet of paper.

"What bullshit!"

She tried to replace figures with letters.

"The alphabet!"

Double its predecessor was the letter *w* . . . a double *v*. And from twenty-six you then went to twenty-five.

She filled the square in ascending order, the most logical.

	1	2	3	4	5
1	A	B	C	D	E
2	F	G	H	I	J
3	K	L	M	N	O
4	P	Q	R	S	T
5	U	V	X	Y	Z

Then she went back to the series of figures.

45   35   51   43   22   11   12   43   24   15   32/41   24   15
43   43   15   25   11   51   34   15

All she had to do was intersect the columns. One vertical and one horizontal coordinate gave a letter.

Following this method, the first, forty-five, that is four and five, could give either *t* or *y*. Since few words began with *y*, the first figure in each number must indicate the horizontal, the second the vertical. She started replacing each pair with its designated letter.

Her nails were black and the soil emphasized each crease in her fingers. Dark particles sometimes came away and soiled the paper.

TOURGABRIEL/PIERREJAUNE

· 6 ·

A bluish light was falling on the bedroom now that the sun had vanished. All that remained was an amber-colored circle around the sofa and the little lamp.

"Gabriel tower, yellow stone," Marion read.

She rested the notepad on her knees.

What exactly did they want from her? To drag her outside on a treasure hunt?

She lifted her eyes to the window. The cemetery had aged three centuries with the advent of darkness, its crosses becoming menacing, its lichen taking on the unpleasant appearance of sticky flesh, flowing from stone to stone. Far above, the abbey's mass sat atop its rock and watched over the little house.

Marion went and fetched the map Sister Anne had given her that morning, and unfolded it on the low table.

The Gabriel Tower was a structure that stood a little apart, on the western flank of the Mount.

A round tower, beside the water, which could be reached by two paths. One was impractical at high tide. It necessitated a circuitous route, leaving the village by the main gate to reach the fortification. The other was a little more complicated for a neophyte. It meant climbing to the top of the village, to the path that circled the abbey, then going down again by the one called "la montée aux Fanils" in order to reach the Gabriel Tower.

Nevertheless, with the aid of a map it shouldn't pose any problems.

Marion refolded the map and went down to get her coat.

Of course she was going to go, now that her curiosity had been aroused. What would she do otherwise? Take a bath and ponder for an hour on the reasons behind this little game? Pointless.

Pointless and irritating.

She adjusted her warm coat, swallowed a glass of water in a single gulp, and went out, taking care to lock the door firmly behind her.

The narrow street was as dark as a sewer. It resembled a sordid medieval alley: the wall of the cemetery's foundations on one side and the row of little houses on the other, old stone everywhere, and in lieu of a lamppost an unlit lantern made of wrought iron, which creaked softly in the wind. Marion realized that she didn't have a flashlight to light her way or even allow her to keep an eye on the map. Fortunately, she had a reasonably clear idea of which way to go. It was pointless to consider taking the lower route; she had seen the sea rising during the afternoon, and by now it must be licking the ramparts.

She took the path to the left.

The ground was paved and invisible. Marion was walking on a sieve of shadows, through which only sound could filter.

A staircase appeared to the right, following the boundary of the cemetery, and climbing to higher levels of the Mount.

She turned up her collar to protect her neck from the cold, slid her hands into her pockets, and kept her elbows tightly to her sides as she climbed the steps.

The way was narrow and turned several times. It wound between low, decrepit walls and age-old houses. Marion was soon looking down on the village, from which very little light was emanating.

The streets were deserted.

She found herself in front of the abbey. A formidable fortress of faith, powerful and dominant, facing the bay. Marion walked for a moment under its protection, until she found a large staircase, which led to a road that wound between trees and led down to the fortifications.

The wind had strengthened.

The Gabriel Tower appeared down below, partly hidden by the

vegetation that covered the western and northern part of the hill. Quite tall but particularly wide, it was isolated from the rest of the buildings on the Mount, like a pariah.

The sound of the surf now joined with the wind's lament.

Marion eventually reached an open postern gate, which led to the side of the tower.

A fierce wave thundered against the other side, breaking violently against the stone.

After looking down on the landscape for several minutes, Marion was disturbed to find herself on the same level as the sea. She had lost that impression of assurance and control, and had become vulnerable, snatchable.

Yes, that was the word. *Snatchable*.

Seen from above, the dark immensity that surrounded her seemed beautiful and as inoffensive as a picture, but now the sea could snatch her with just one tentacle a little wilder than the others. All it took was a sudden burst of anger to carry her off, out to sea.

The absence of real light gave each sound a disconcerting amplitude. Marion drew her neck down even further into the collar of her coat. She was not terrified. Not at ease, because of her proximity to the sea in the darkness, but she was not afraid.

By this time, she had reached the Gabriel Tower. She had still to find a yellow stone.

The road had disappeared behind her; the earthen pathway sloped gently down toward the shoreline.

Suddenly, the gleaming arc of a circle appeared at the end of the path. It howled as it shattered against itself, spitting its spume onto the rocks. The sea remained motionless for a second then drew back, like the tip of an immense tongue that had tasted the flavors of the earth in that place. The sky's timid twilight was reflected in it, creating a chaotic interplay of mirror effects.

Marion stood almost twenty-two yards from the edge of the world, her hair driven to madness by the lashing wind.

She didn't regret coming down. The atmosphere was worth the trouble.

A yellow stone. You still have to find a yellow stone, and see where this little game is supposed to lead us.

She advanced step by step, scanning the ground and trying to make out the rare lighter patches scattered across it. She quickly walked beyond the tower, coming closer to the sea, which was now scarcely more than three feet below her.

It undulated constantly, noisily crushing its edges against the banks. Marion stood as far away as possible, receiving the ocean's salty dross in return for her temerity.

There was no trace of a yellow stone.

Unless it was small and hidden in the bushes, and without a flashlight it would be impossible to make out.

Marion reached the end of the path. Beyond it stretched out the sea's kingdom.

Yellow stone . . . yellow stone . . . I still have to bring it to light!

She turned around and walked back toward the tower.

A multitude of whitish dots were scattered across the ground like constellations.

A larger, duller patch lay against the wall of the Gabriel Tower, a small rock. Probably yellow.

Marion pulled it backward. It was heavy.

The block rolled onto its side, the sound swallowed by the roaring of the waves.

Marion pounced on the envelope that had just been liberated before it had a chance to fly away.

Nothing written on it.

She put it in her pocket.

There was a whistling sound above her.

At first it was faint, then it began to swell. Something began to breathe the air forcefully, like an enormous asthmatic creature.

Marion carefully scanned the tower and its top, from which the breathing sound seemed to come. The noise was drowned out.

Its last notes were swallowed up by a liquid sound, like a valve suddenly closing on the water.

Suddenly the air gave a violent crack, sharper and deeper than thunder. Marion started.

The echo resounded inside the tower. And Marion understood as she saw the sea drawing back. There were long openings, practically at the bottom of the tower, like horizontal arrow slits, through which a powerful wave could sometimes enter and strike the internal structure of the building. As it withdrew, the water caused an indraft that produced a long, whistling sound.

Marion had seen enough. The cold was starting to overwhelm her and if up to now she had been merely uneasy, this time she had to admit that she felt less sure of herself.

It was as she was climbing back up the circular path around the abbey that she saw the shadow for the first time.

A shape down below, in an adjacent narrow street, a few yards below her. An individual whom she had just noticed and who had without a doubt noticed her too, as was evident from the frequent halts he or she made to look up in her direction. Unfortunately it was too far away for the person to be recognizable.

Marion walked faster. It wasn't late, but the wind really was blowing very hard, hard enough to dissuade people from going out. They were in the antechamber of the storm, there was no longer any doubt about that. And the presence of this individual did not reassure her.

Carried along by the speed of the wind's gusts, the silhouetted figure was making swift progress, continuing to keep watch on Marion.

Marion had no desire to encounter whomever it was, still less a stranger. Not now.

She walked down the first flight of steps, then jumped down the next. The narrow corridor turned to the right, between two empty houses, then to the left, swerved again, and then there were more stairs. Marion literally hurtled down them.

Her ears were hurting from the attacks of the coming storm.

Finally she came out in the street, *her* street, panting for breath.

She covered the last few strides down the dark alley.

Before stopping suddenly in front of an unexpected obstacle, a mass battered by the elements that bounced off it.

He was there.

In front of her.

The light came up suddenly, pointed directly at Marion's face. She took a step back, protecting her eyes with one arm.

"Hey!" she protested.

There was no reaction from the figure in front of her.

Marion had only had sufficient time to spot that the stranger was much taller than she was, and very powerfully built.

"Will you please lower your flashlight!" she snapped. "You're blinding me."

She could no longer see him, but heard him moving. His shoes squeaked on the paving stones.

"Hey, I'm talking to you!"

The torch went out.

"I don't know you. Who are you?" demanded a man with a strong Northern accent.

"Excuse me? Are you joking? You're the one who's attacking me, with your light!"

"That's my job, little lady. I'm the Mount guard. So who are you?"

Marion relaxed a little. She detected the release of a more intense tension than she'd been aware of. "I . . . I was invited here by the brothers and sisters to—"

"That's what I was telling myself. You're with the brotherhood. That's what I thought when I realized that I didn't know your face. Gaël, Brother Gaël, informed me that they were playing host to a woman on retreat for the winter. Excuse me if I frightened you."

Marion was annoyed that someone had said she was going to stay all winter. "That's okay, let's not talk about it again," she said. "My name's Marion."

"And I'm Ludwig."

He raised his torch and lit his face from beneath, to show himself. "Now you'll recognize me," he chuckled.

He was indeed very tall, a good six foot two, a little overweight, with plump cheeks and a circle of beard enclosing his mouth. His eyes were as dark as his close-cropped hair. Around thirty, Marion estimated.

"You shouldn't stay outside, the storm's coming," he warned her. "Pretty soon it's going to be blowing a gale around here."

"I was just going back home, I've been out for a little walk."

"Yeah, well, don't hang about. I'll finish off my round and then I'm getting under cover. After then, there'll be nobody left on the streets."

Marion pointed to the narrow street that ran behind him. "I live down there . . . "

"Oh, 'scuse me."

He stepped aside to let her pass. "Right, anyhow, we'll have a chance to get to know each other if you're spending the whole winter with us. Good night, madam."

She nodded and felt a surge of relief as she reached her front door.

The man's "madam" hadn't pleased her. Too overdone. How old was he himself? Five or six years younger than she was? He had spoken the word as if a whole world existed between them. As if she were . . . old.

Thin-skinned.

Yes, so what?

She locked the door and switched on the ceiling lamp in the entrance.

What had come over her, going out like that?

She slid a hand into her pocket and removed the envelope.
She shook her head gently, bemused by her own attitude.
And she placed the envelope on the hall table.

· 7 ·

The dawn was gray.
And noisy.
The storm had launched its first attack during the night, waking
Marion many times. For the time being, all that was left of it was its
tail end, a continuous wind that whistled against the walls and
transformed the whole bay into a vast, sooty sky in which nobody
could tell the difference between sea and air.

Marion opened her eyes gradually.

On the bedside table a cream-colored sheet of good-quality paper lay, unfolded. An elegant fountain pen had written the following words upon it:

> *Bravo.*
> *Bravo, and welcome.*

The sheet of paper was newly crumpled, a gesture of irritation
the previous night, when Marion had opened the envelope before
going to bed.

She got up before eight o'clock. She went down wearing a
dressing gown "borrowed" from a fine London hotel during an
international symposium on legal medicine, to which she had
accompanied the female director of the Médico-légal Institute.
Somebody had dropped a note through the letter slot and it had
slid onto the tiles in the entrance hall. Marion sighed as she
picked it up.

Neither a riddle leading to nothing, nor anonymous, thankfully.

This time there were no obscure phrases. Sister Anne explained that she was at the abbot's residence for the whole day and that Marion could join her there. As Friday was the day of the Passion, no member of the brotherhood would be taking any meals, so she would have to eat alone, and she ended by hoping that the storm hadn't disturbed her sleep too much.

Marion arched her eyebrows and let the note fall to the ground.

Still dazed with sleep, she opened the refrigerator and found some orange juice. She ate some crackers, sitting on the big sofa, staring distractedly the tops of the roofs through the window.

She had no desire to be among the brothers and sisters today, and especially not to listen to any talk of Christ, God, the Church, or religion as a whole. She aspired to a real, entirely personal peace.

She took a shower, dressed in jeans and a thick woollen sweater, then rang the abbot's residence, whose number was on a list beside the telephone. She explained to Sister Anne that she would like to be alone, and hung up. She had made no mention of the previous evening's riddle, and still less the fact that she'd gone out. Either thing would become clearer on its own, or not at all.

In any event, the day passed more quickly than she had imagined.

In the morning, she braved the wind, which was still just as strong, to wander along the main street of the village. Apart from Mère Poulard's restaurant, there was only one shop open. The handful of resolute winter tourists had melted away at the announcement of the storm. Marion was alone in the street.

When she entered the souvenir shop, the saleswoman offered her most beautiful smile and begged her to buy a postcard, so that she wouldn't have opened up for nothing. They laughed and quickly hit it off. They drank a few coffees as they got to know each other. The saleswoman's name was Béatrice, she was forty-four, and she lived on the Mount with her eighteen-year-old son, Grégoire. Several times, Marion remarked that she was a beautiful woman, with bobbed red hair and high cheekbones that led to a slender nose, and that it was a shame for her to live alone in this exile, at the end of the world. There couldn't be hordes of attractive men around here, apart from the usual ones, you'd get through them all pretty quickly, and if she hadn't found one who suited her—

Béatrice swiftly replied that she was divorced, and had been single for a long time. "How about you?"

Marion answered with a nervous laugh. "Never married, no children, never divorced, in other words I've never taken any risks," she said in a single breath.

"So was it your career, or haven't you ever met the right guy?"

"I think one influenced the other, and vice versa."

"Shit, you say that as if everything was already over and done with. You're delightful, Marion, and that's not just flattery, it's what I really think. How old are you?"

"Thirty-nine."

Béatrice spat out the smoke from her cigarette as she gave her a sidelong look. "And you've come to Mont-Saint-Michel to look for your Grail? My dear, you can't go questing for an escort, sorry, for your Prince Charming in a place where there isn't anybody. . . . "

"I'm on retreat. With the brotherhood."

Marion followed to the letter the story Sister Anne had given her. She was on retreat for the winter or at least for a few weeks, fleeing the stress of the city to find herself again, regain serenity. Sister Anne had asked her not to mention anything about her real life, to make up a false surname for herself if she had to give one. Nobody outside the religious community must know her real identity, as a safety precaution.

The worst thing, she realized, was that she found it disconcertingly easy to lie. Her apartment in Paris, near the Gare de l'Est, was transformed into a house in Choisy-le-Roi, her job at the institute became artistic director for a small advertising agency, and so on and so forth for all the "formalities" of her existence. The most difficult thing was lying about the spiritual aspect of her presence on the Mount. She was not a believer, and not into Zen or Feng Shui and the rest, either; she found her own personal spirituality in the records of Aretha Franklin, Janis Joplin, and Rickie Lee Jones.

Béatrice invited her to lunch at her home, above the shop. Grégoire wasn't there. He had left school a year earlier and was looking for work in one of the region's small or medium-sized businesses. He borrowed his mother's car and spent most of his time away from the Mount.

The two women joked a lot and found out more about each other. Marion offered to look after the shop for a day or two, if that would be of help to Béatrice, and in exchange Béatrice promised to take her for a trip to terra firma if she should feel too hemmed in behind the fortifications.

Marion got back home late in the afternoon and made herself some dinner with the fresh vegetables she found in her refrigerator. Sister Anne had explained about shopping. All she had to do was provide a list, and at least once a week, one or two of the brothers would go to Avranches to buy everything.

At least she had gained a home-delivery service.

The storm began again early that evening. The rain poured down on the roofs with impressive enthusiasm. The chimneys soon disappeared in a grayish haze, spangled with the occasional distant flash of lightning.

Marion was beginning to get used to her new living room. The long window was its soul, she realized. A direct view into the life of this place, the village, then the bay, and the mainland in the distance.

She fell asleep in front of the television, and when she opened her eyes it was pitch-black. The rain was still falling, but with a more muffled sound, and the thunder had deserted the shore. Only solitary flashes of lightning remained on the horizon.

Marion gazed at the sight for several minutes.

This must resemble what it had been like during the landings in

1944. Spectral lights that tore through the darkness, and the vague echo of the guns. And not one human voice in all the chaos.

Marion switched off the TV and went up to bed.

The weekend was cast in the same mold. The brothers and sisters held a Mass in the abbey, before an audience of the staunch faithful who had defied the bad weather to come to Mont-Saint-Michel. Marion chose to remain on her own. She went to visit Béatrice and spent the two days arranging her few possessions in the house.

On Monday morning, the storm had ceased.

As had been planned, Brother Damien came to fetch Marion that morning to drive her to Avranches, where they were going to do some classification of the age-old collection. The old Simca carried them a good distance from the Mount, to the town hall square, where they parked between the brown puddles that filled the potholes.

Brother Damien showed his credentials, greeting all the members of staff by their first names, while Marion followed in silence. They climbed a staircase adorned with paintings to the glory of the great individuals who had created the town's history, and entered the library.

Marion thought she had entered a wooden cathedral.

The shelves reached very high, transforming the books into a single body of knowledge, accessible only by sloping ladders. A narrow and fragile-looking U-shaped gangway ran around almost the whole room, serving the top shelves, some five and a half yards above the ground.

Brother Damien roused her from her contemplation. "Do you know that among the manuscripts stored here are fragments of an eighth-century Bible? Phenomenal, isn't it?"

"I'm completely overwhelmed," murmured Marion.

The floor creaked like the deck of an ancient three-master as they walked along.

"It is kept in an adjoining room, in an enormous safe, like the ones they have in banks. You have to put on white gloves to touch it, you know!"

"I can imagine . . . "

Brother Damien chatted with the chief librarian, a small and jolly man who wore half-moon spectacles perched on the end of his nose; then they set off up the spiral staircase that led to the upper gangway.

The books stretched away in rows until perspective made them appear as slender and small as a fingernail. Marion leaned on the guardrail, laying her hands upon it. Since her adolescence she had developed a theory, which held that all the keys to the cosmos were assembled at various earthly points: libraries. An individual who knew all the books in a few libraries could understand the universe, right down to its most intimate, most savage elements. You'd have to read everything, in order to be equal to the task of cross-checking, to know what had—sometimes stupidly—escaped the scientists. The main part was already within our reach, but dispersed, so one mind must assimilate it all; there were experts in each discipline, but nobody covered them all. All you had to do was choose your libraries well, perhaps ten or so, and the kinds of material oriented toward the absolute, and the mind would become the possessor of knowledge. Its reasoning would carry out the analyses, exchanges, and conclusions leading to knowledge. The impossibility of the task for a single brain and a single life reflected all the truth of this ultimate knowledge: It was not within the grasp of mankind. Marion had often thought about it. Why not accept that we were simply not capable of really understanding the whole cosmos? How could we imagine a cat working on the implications of the theory of relativity? And yet that doesn't mean it is incapable of thinking, at its own level, according to its means. This reasoning did not imply that we should stop wanting to understand, of course, but that Man should become humbler, less greedy, and that his conception of knowledge should be less a violation than a reflection. For sooner or later the Earth, on its own scale, will remind us of the cost.

Marion's hands gripped the guardrail.

She hadn't had these types of thoughts for a long time. Imitation eco-freak, hippie fever. None of the things she respected or wanted to be. And yet . . . the routine of work, the need to integrate into society, having a bank account, bills, a social life: From year to year, all of this pushed further back what she had been when she was younger, with her hard-line, anticonformist ideas. What others regarded as maturity suddenly appeared to her like a sort of brainwashing. And finding herself abruptly isolated, no longer seeing her few friends, being shut away in her home, doing nothing but thinking . . . little by little, all of this awakened that part of herself that she had forgotten, or at least believed had moved on.

"Get back!" the librarian shouted up from below. "Don't lean on the rail like that; it's not very stable!"

Marion straightened up and gave him a nod.

Brother Damien had disappeared.

She followed the one and only path to the corner, from where four steps led up to a minuscule door, which stood ajar.

"Come in, don't be afraid." Brother Damien invited her in with his usual bonhomie.

Marion entered the attic. It took the form of a rectangular, low-ceilinged room, lined with shelves that groaned under the weight of books, old magazines, local periodicals, cards, and ornithological sketches. A fanlight at each end allowed in a little light, just enough to move without tripping over the piles of encyclopedias or old magazines that grew here and there on the floor.

"This is our office for the days to come," joked the brother.

"Is all of this part of the heritage of Mont-Saint-Michel?"

"Not at all, it belongs to the town of Avranches. We come here to draw up an inventory; the town hall employs us for that. Each brother and sister in our brotherhood earns a salary, not for personal gain but simply to earn his or her living. Generally we work part time. Right, well, we've got plenty on our plate!"

Brother Damien handed her a notebook and a pen and allocated her the left-hand section. Her task was to list all the works in minute detail, by hand and with no classification system save the one in which they were already more or less arranged.

Marion faced the hundreds of well-worn spines lined up before her. And she set to work.

Seeing that they were going to be there for several days, she suggested to Brother Damien that they should equip themselves with a radio the next day, so they could at least listen to a little music. He grimaced at the idea, and reminded Marion of the virtues of working in silence, for thought and prayer.

Behind his permanent good humor, Brother Damien was still a member of the brotherhood like all the rest, Marion reminded herself.

For more than three hours, she sorted and listed periodicals, newspapers, and newsmagazines covering all of the second half of the nineteenth century and up through the 1940s. The covers gave off the forgotten smell of the colonies, the Roaring Twenties, the fox-trot, and of journeys by steamer or airship. And the smell of war.

The industry of death.

By the end of the morning, from superannuated images of bygone cultures and their delicious fascination, Marion had declined into a misanthropic melancholy.

At noon, Brother Damien took her to a café in the square, along with the librarian and a few members of staff from the town hall. Marion remained silent, introduced by Brother Damien as being on retreat in their community. She left them while they were having dessert and went to buy *Ouest-France* at the café opposite, where she settled herself at the counter to read.

The scandal that had forced her to leave Paris was still on the front page.

Nobody was talking about anything else.

She skimmed through the newspaper. Then her eyes lit on the telephone next to the toilets. She longed desperately to phone her mother. To hear the sound of her voice, tell her over again that everything was okay, that she mustn't worry.

The man from the DST had explicitly forbidden her to do it. For her safety, and for that of the people she loved. Marion had had only a few hours to say goodbye to those close to her, to explain to them that she had to go into hiding for a while until things calmed down, perhaps until a court case was opened. If that was possible.

She had a telephone card in her purse, next to the debit card the DST had given her, forbidding her to use her own until they gave her permission. There was next to nothing on the account, just enough for basic needs.

Just one quick phone call . . . to hear the sound of her voice . . .

And screw everything up!

She paid for her coffee and went out. The others were still sitting at their table.

Marion crossed the square and entered the town hall. She climbed back up to the attic, where she set to work again, although she was unable to find the switch to work the fluorescent lighting. It was dark between the shelves. The most badly damaged books were difficult to identify, and she had to take them out and open the flyleaf to read the title inside. She did this for a quarter of an hour, before reaching the lowest shelf.

Marion took the weight off her knees and sat directly on the floor, sucking the end of her pen. Here the books were smaller, but heaped up any which way, one on top of another and covered in dust. An index card was stuck in at the end of the shelving: "Bequest of the library of the abbey of Mont-Saint-Michel—1945 or 1946—to be listed and classified."

The card was yellowed, and had probably been there for fifteen or twenty years.

Everything in this room constituted the unwanted castoffs from the library. The most beautiful items were stored downstairs, while the ones that had little value had been slumbering here for a long time.

Marion returned her attention to the abbey bequest.

Around fifty works. At first sight, they all seemed to be in foreign languages.

Briefly scanning them, Marion noticed especially the books in English, a few in Dutch, and a handful in German.

She had always had a slight weakness for old books, especially those for children, which smelled of dust, mildew, and time. She read English perfectly, so she was interested in the titles of the first volumes.

Authors whose names were unknown to her.

Henry James appeared suddenly. Marion seized it by the edge and pulled it out to smell it. She closed her eyes.

Then she replaced it and moved on. Virginia Woolf was lost between manuals on good etiquette in society.

One folio volume was distinguished by its black color. It was injured; the base of its spine lay open, and twisted threads hung down from it. The letters of its author's name had half-disappeared between two cords, eaten away by the decades.

Marion deciphered the English title, which remained legible because it was gilded.

As she drew out the book, white particles fell to the ground and rolled away into the gaps between the floorboards.

It was a story she loved.

The Narrative of A. Gordon Pym by Edgar Allan Poe.

A novel that finished on a sentence in suspense, the only one Marion knew that had no end, ending in the middle of a chapter, with an open ending. She stuck her nose in it. It had the characteristic smell of antiquity. When she was little, she often went to her grandfather's house, where he had a splendid library, with a large number of very old books. Marion adored their smell; she thought it was the scent of the fingers of thousands of readers that formed this magnificent bouquet.

Poe had the same powers of memory as Proust, thought Marion.

The flat side of the book was a little swollen, the leather cracked.

Marion opened the first page.

Then she turned the pages that followed.

Her eyebrows shot up.

Lines appeared beneath her lower eyelids.

The pages were indeed in English.

But there wasn't a single printed letter.

Nothing but pages of manuscript writing, upright and joined.

"March 16. I asked Azim to fetch . . . "

Marion flipped through the pages. It was the same throughout the book. She found the start of what appeared to be a private diary.

"March 1928, Cairo."

It wasn't light enough. Marion had to get her nose right in among the pages in order to examine the stitching.

Somebody had meticulously removed the original printed pages, in order to replace them with this notebook, which had been sewn in with great care.

In her hands she was holding a private diary dating from March 1928, written in Cairo, which someone had tried to hide. Marion closed it and placed it on her thigh.

Thick droplets began to fall onto the fanlight.

Harder and harder, until they made the attic drum to the rhythm of their sad song.

· 8 ·

The door of the attic banged as it slammed shut.

Marion rushed to pick up the phony novel and replaced it on the pile. She felt as if she'd been caught red-handed, like a child, although she hadn't done anything. The feeling was curious, both disconcerting and exciting at the same time.

"You're here already!" exclaimed Brother Damien in astonishment, as he left his umbrella at the door. "What an appetite for work, I congratulate you!"

Marion was about to reply that she hadn't been sixteen for more than twenty years, but she refrained, particularly since a moment ago that's exactly how she had felt.

They recommenced their work for the afternoon, while the rain fell continuously.

Around five o'clock, when Brother Damien informed her that they would be leaving soon, Marion returned soundlessly to the foreign-language shelf.

The black volume was on the top.

She checked that the brother couldn't see her, and grabbed the book.

It disappeared under her sweater.

"Why did you take it?" asked Béatrice as she spat out cigarette smoke.

"I don't know. Out of curiosity, I think."

"What is it? A personal diary?"

"That's what you'd call it. From 1928, written in English by someone who was living in Cairo."

"An English expat. I wonder how your diary ended up in Avranches?"

Marion swallowed a mouthful of coffee. "I have my own idea about that."

"You haven't even read it!"

"It was part of a bequest from the abbey of the Mount dated 1945 or 1946. Say the brothers at the time housed an English soldier during the war, and he died, or left them his diary. They would have stored it with the rest of the books in English in their library, before giving everything to Avranches at the Liberation, perhaps to make some room."

"I'm not convinced; 1928 is a long time before the war. I can't see your British soldier trundling around with his private diary in his pocket for more than ten years!"

"All the same, it's an idea . . . "

A few feet away, Grégoire was stretched out on the sofa with a magazine in his hand. He stood up. "I'm bored, Mom, I'm going to take a trip into town, to Pontorson."

He stretched and his jaw cracked as he yawned unrestrainedly.

Good-looking boy, Marion had told herself when she saw him for the first time. Although he was eighteen, he still had baby skin on his cheeks, pink and soft. His spiky hair was messy, and the tufts fought for possession of his head. A diamond sparkled in his ear.

"Don't be late."

"I promise."

He put on his leather jacket and went out, the keys to the car in his hand.

After a silence, Marion nodded to the door he had just left by. "It must be hard for him to live here, isolated from the mainland and his friends."

"Greg is a loner, but it's true that it's not paradise for him. Sooner or later he'll go and live on dry land."

"Why, isn't that what's here? You talk about the Mount as if it's an island!"

"It is one, in the minds of the people who live here anyway.

You'll come to realize that; they have a real island mentality! They stick together, take the blows, and if they have to, they can keep a secret, a secret that shouldn't leave the Mount."

Marion looked deep into her eyes. "Why do you say that?"

Béatrice shrugged. "Because it's true. People say that islanders live on the margins of the continent; that it's a special kind of life, and it is. And also, this place is very small. There are just a handful of us and it's a real tourist trap, but imagine the people who live in Jersey, for example!"

"You talk as if you've experienced it yourself. Am I wrong?"

Béatrice grimaced. "I grew up on Belle-Ile. Believe me, it's a state of mind."

Béatrice got up from the kitchen table and switched on the ceiling light. "Weren't you supposed to be having dinner with the brotherhood this evening?" she wanted to know.

"No, Brother Damien explained to me that Monday was a day of religious abstinence. He is exceptionally driven to work, but none of the others leave their cells."

"What a life!"

"And besides, since I've been here they've been making an effort, in particular at mealtimes. Usually they eat in silence, or somebody reads from the Bible. . . . "

Marion slammed her hand down on the cover of the black book. "Right, I'm off home."

"Aren't you staying to eat?"

"No, I've already outstayed my welcome and I've got reading to do," replied Marion, brandishing the private diary. "I intend to fully satisfy my curiosity before I put it back."

A few minutes later, Marion was walking back up the main street toward the little parish church, with the book under her arm and her hands in her pockets, savoring the veil of dampness settling on her face.

"Out for another stroll?" inquired a masculine voice behind her.

She turned around and saw Ludwig, the night watchman, who

was addressing her from his great height. "No, this time I'm on my way home."

"Sorry again if I frightened you the other evening."

Marion nodded. His Northern accent was very pronounced, and it amused her. There was an appeal to friendship in this linguistic peculiarity.

You're just thinking that because he doesn't have the same way of expressing himself, that's all. . . .

"Anyhow," he went on, "if you're looking for me one night, my place is right down at the bottom, in the square at the entrance to the village. The door is always open, and if I'm out on my rounds, you can call me on my mobile. Here's the number."

He handed her a card he had prepared.

"Thank you, Ludwig. Good night then, and good luck."

Marion nodded a farewell and set off again. She didn't feel in the mood for a chat. She went back home, put a pan to heat on the stove, and was about to throw in a chicken breast and a spoonful of crème fraîche when somebody knocked at the door.

"What now," she muttered.

Brother Damien was standing on the doorstep. "Good evening, I'm sorry to disturb you, I won't keep you long. It was simply to remind you that I'll be calling for you at nine tomorrow morning. And take this, it's for you."

He handed her a box of Xanax. A tranquilizer. "Sister Anne thought you might need it, what with the circumstances. . . . And with the wind blowing so hard at night. . . . Anyway, it might help you to sleep."

Marion took the packet and thanked him.

She noticed that the brother's attention was drawn to something behind her back. Marion remembered that she had placed the purloined book on the hall table, just behind her.

"I'll leave you now, I shouldn't really be here anyway, seeing as it's Monday. Have a pleasant evening, and I'll see you tomorrow morning."

If he had recognized the book, which was unlikely, he had not shown any sign of having done so.

"Good night, Brother Damien."

She closed the door and threw the package onto the hall table, beside the black book.

She ate a hearty dinner, sitting in the living room with a little music on the stereo, to give the house some semblance of life. Then Marion went and settled herself on the corner sofa, propped herself up comfortably, and opened the private diary. On the first page, she read in English: "Logbook, by Jeremy Matheson, March 1928."

She turned the page.

"March 11. I have decided to . . ."

Marion blinked. She had a very good command of English; she just needed to recall the vocabulary.

"March 11. I have decided to take up my pen, not to confide secrets and relieve a guilty conscience, or to write down the details of my day-to-day existence, but in an exceptional way, to relate this immense story in which I have recently become embroiled.

"This exercise, if it may be considered such, is purely experimental. I am beginning it only to satisfy my desire to resolve these strange hours by means of writing, and I am not in a position to define what its end will be, if it is to have an end. I shall try to be as comprehensive as possible, to relate the facts without allowing myself to be corrupted by empiricism, empathy, or my simple subjectivity of interpretation.

"This diary is my account of this insidious story, which now haunts me."

Marion looked up. The living room was lit by a single lamp placed beside her, leaving part of the room in darkness.

She liked this restful ambience. She returned to her reading.

* * *

"First of all, I would like to . . .

". . . introduce myself. My name is Jeremy Matheson. I am a detective 'on behalf of the Empire of His Majesty King George V' as one must say, stationed in one of the British colonies: Egypt; in Cairo to be precise. I am thirty-three years old and . . . "

And so began the story of Jeremy Matheson. Within the space of a few dozen words, Marion had entered the tale.

Feeding her imagination with what was written in the diary, she plunged into this vanished world . . .

· 9 ·

Jeremy Matheson wiped the ink from his index finger, then resumed his tale.

An oil lamp was burning above the desk, suspended from one of the rail car's beams.

Close to the entrance, the carpet was striped with amber ridges, where the grains of sand had collected into sparkling veins. His habit of shaking his shoes in the same spot before removing them had produced these ramifications, which were building up into a welcoming delta.

A thermometer a yard tall was hanging by the door. Although night had already fallen, it was still indicating excessive heat.

The further into the rail car you looked, the more timid the light became, loath to unveil Jeremy Matheson's privacy. The good-quality materials reflected or drank in the flame's brightness. The varnished wood was worn but robust, and the velvet wall-hangings were still soft.

Beyond the door, farther on than the wide desk where the detective was working, two cracked leather settees stood opposite each other, roasted by so many days in the middle of this steam-room, separated by a low marquetry table. Crumpled sheets of typewritten paper with the Cairo police letterhead lay in heaps on the settees. A few photos stuck out from the paper, warmed by the scorching heat.

Black-and-white photos.

The first had a long line of red ink across it, as if to condemn it.

It showed a white wall, and a man in a suit, impossible to iden-tify as he was bending forward, clinging with one hand to a hole in the mortar. Strings of saliva ran from his mouth to the ground, like a spider's web under construction.

On the left side of the photo, the wall opened onto a nebu-lous side path. The thick shadows made it impossible to make out the human shapes forming a circle around a mass on the ground.

The second photo showed a close-up of a doll of woven straw, coarsely made. It was already pretty threadbare, ready to fall apart if handled carelessly.

Someone had clumsily painted the semblance of a dress on it.

A painting or a stain.

Dark and damp.

The third photo revealed city shoes, Western shoes, freshly waxed although dressed in a filmy veil of dust. They were all sur-rounding something in the middle, placed on the ground. Several men were standing at the edges of the image, yet the frame of the photo went no higher than their calves.

The snapshot centered on a little, chubby arm lying on the beaten earth of what must be an alleyway.

And a half-open hand.

The skin was too smooth to be old.

The same sticky, dark substance as on the doll stained the wrist.

Ten other photos lay on top of one another, all turned facedown on the leather settees.

The light from the lamp's flame hardly reached any farther now, into the place where the space narrowed to form the entrance to a bathroom. On the right, a gangway led away to the back. To the bedroom.

A large cheval glass gave this final room an illusion of depth, by reflecting the most distant corners. Opposite the dressing table, covered with issues of *Picture Show Magazine,* next to the Voltaire armchair hidden beneath a heap of clothes, stretched a double bed with crumpled sheets. At its foot lay a carved wooden bowl, overturned on the carpet, with masses of cigarette butts drowned in a sea of ash overflowing from it.

The photo of a woman decorated the bedside table. Not enough of the night's brightness filtered through the two windows to identify her face.

At the other end of the rail car, the kettle on the cast-iron stove started to whistle.

Jeremy stood up, and grabbed a dirty rag to lift it and make himself some tea. The dried mint leaves swiftly filled the vast room with their fragrance.

Jeremy savored his burning-hot drink, leaning back in his chair. Unusually, he had not removed his boots. His feet were dissolving inside them.

He always wore his shirt with its many pockets, even if he had to keep it open, baring his chest. He was unshaven. He hadn't had time that morning. It suited him, slightly veiling his excessively hollow cheeks, reducing the impression that his mouth was too fleshy.

Jeremy ran a hand across his face.

His nose was slender, hooked.

His eyebrows ebony-black.

And a coppery halo emanated from his bare forehead, which was surrounded by black hair, smoothed back.

To hear the women who chatted on the terraces, sipping their *sahleeb* outside the clubs he frequented from time to time, Jeremy Matheson was "ardently desirable."

The brutishness of Africa and British elegance had come together in the same man.

Everyone knew that he was a detective, and a brilliant hunter, who had already been on a reckless safari in the wilds of the Great South.

Everyone also knew that no woman in Cairo could boast of having shared her bed with Jeremy Matheson.

People whispered that he was highly selective.

And secretive.

There were rumors . . .

The glass tinkled as Jeremy placed it on the table. He cracked the joints of his fingers, which were very long and vigorous, like his hands, which attracted many glances from the women of Cairo's colonial society. He rose and opened the door of the rail car.

A flight of three steps led to the canopy that was attached to the side wall. A carpet covered the sand, with chaise longues, a wooden pole, and several cases of equipment and food, labeled ARMY PROPERTY.

Jeremy nonchalantly pulled out a chair and sat down in front of the tent.

The night calmed the sun's ardor. It was much nicer now, but it would take another hour or two before the interior of the rail car cooled down.

Opposite him, rails wove across a landscape he loved, a procession of endless worms, undulating in the moonlight, heading toward infinity, just like the skein of existence.

And lower down, behind the building that housed the rail museum, beneath the massive mouth of orange stone, the central rail station cocooned its steel snakes and its anonymous travelers in the shelter of its vaulted roof.

About a hundred yards from the carriage where Jeremy Matheson lived, a streetcar jolted past, wearing its sparking crown of electricity like a headdress. The line served the beautiful districts of Heliopolis, away from the city. Inside, women and men traveled separately.

The faces were smiling; one young woman was even laughing out loud. There were lots of young Westerners.

Jeremy watched them until the streetcar was no more than a blur with shining red lights.

His lips pursed and began to whiten.

He swallowed noisily.

His hand searched the pocket of his beige linen trousers.

From it, he took a small piece of torn paper. Several lines of elegant handwriting filled the first half of it. Jeremy's hand masked its content.

All except what was written at the bottom.

"Samir. 5 years old."

Jeremy's hand clenched into a fist.

Despite all the resilience he was summoning up to stifle this pain in his throat, the lower rims of his eyes began to swell with moisture.

His jaw jutted beneath the fine skin of his cheeks.

Like veritable Cyclops of the heavens, the millions of stars trained their lone eyes upon him, trembling and immaculate.

A droplet fell beside Samir's name.

The paper absorbed it instantly.

It grew within the fibers, broadening more and more until it touched the edges of the name.

· 10 ·

When Brother Damien came to fetch Marion that Tuesday morning, she was looking cheerful and trim.

She was wearing a white woollen coat over her sweater and jeans, a hat of the same material, and a bag was slung across her chest. Her abundant hair was hidden under the hat, and Brother Damien paid real attention to her features, in a way he had not yet done. He noticed the green of her irises, which looked less lifeless in the cold. Her rounded cheekbones gave her a Slavic appearance.

He wondered for a brief moment about that injury to her lower lip, before driving the curiosity from his mind.

They reached Avranches before half-past nine, and went directly up to the attic.

They inventoried the works in silence until midday, when the brother suggested going out for lunch. Marion had hoped she could get away on her own to read the journal, which she had brought in her bag, but the circumstances hardly lent themselves to it. The library's curator insisted on inviting them to eat with him, in order to paint them a detailed history of the Mont-Saint-Michel manuscripts.

She didn't know if it was because of the concentration needed to read titles in the semidarkness, or the dust, but she was starting to get a migraine when she got back, late that afternoon.

She found some painkillers in a cupboard in the bathroom, and lay down on the bed until the pain began to fade.

The twilight cradled her until her sight clouded.

She slipped into unconsciousness.

All she could see now was the open wardrobe.

The different-colored stripes of her clothes piled on top of one another.

The colors were mingling . . .

A sharp focus returned. Suddenly Marion could make out perfectly the details of her clothes.

The sleeves of her shirts weren't properly folded; they were sticking out at the sides. That wasn't like her at all.

She knew she was a fanatic about that sort of thing. Everything had to be impeccably arranged so that she didn't have to iron it again in the morning. And as it happened, she remembered quite clearly having cursed at the lack of coat hangers; she had taken very special care to fold her shirts in piles, the sleeves skillfully folded underneath.

And now they were sticking out. Not all of them, but some.

Sufficient for her to know that somebody had moved the clothes. Or at least lifted them up.

Marion leaped out of bed. Too quickly. Her head spun.

She stood at the end of the bed until her dizziness disappeared.

Then she inspected the bedroom. The sofa, the bed, the bathroom. She did the same downstairs.

She had difficulty breathing, searching every nook and cranny, ready to shout out and strike the slightest suspect shape.

She came back regularly to the front door, watching the telephone, checking that it was still there.

She didn't know the place well enough. She hadn't yet had enough time to get to know it properly, so it was difficult to know if anything else had moved. And yet a persistent intuition whispered to her that this was indeed the case.

Should she ring the DST straightaway?

The house was empty; there was nobody there, no direct danger.

Someone had got into her house during her absence.

She forced herself to breathe more normally.

Nobody had traced her here, nobody. She was safe. The DST had taken care of that. That was their job, they were professionals; she had nothing to fear.

Her heart gradually started to beat in a more regular rhythm.

The lock hadn't been forced.

Someone from the brotherhood. Whoever had the key to the house.

This time it was too much. She seized the phone and dialed one of the numbers Sister Anne had written down.

She heard the singsong voice of Sister Gabriela.

"Sister Gabriela, it's Marion. Could you put Sister Anne on, please?"

She didn't have to wait long. Sister Anne picked up the handset almost immediately. "What can I do for you? Are you joining us for din—"

"Who has the keys to my house?" asked Marion.

"What? Hasn't something ha—"

"Who has the keys?"

"Well . . . we do. I mean, the brotherhood. There is a copy of all of our keys here, at the abbot's residence. The majority of the brothers and sisters use them every day to get about, and there are keys to all the doors, including the ones to our different buildings, such as the one you're living in. What's wrong, Marion? I can sense you are nervous. Is there a problem?"

Marion mentally analyzed her reply; she hadn't expected this.

"Marion?"

"Yes . . . no, no problem. I . . . I had an attack of paranoia, I'm sorry . . . "

"Then come up and join us for supper, we—"

"No, thank you, but I shall stay here. I have things to occupy me. Thank you, good night."

She hung up.

The entire brotherhood had keys to her quarters.

So what now? What was happening to her? It wasn't a case of identifying a suspect, and she wasn't at the heart of a conspiracy either.

But somebody had entered her home to search through her things.

Sister Anne or one of the others, she assumed, *to reassure herself that I didn't have anything that might be dangerous for me. . . . No weapons. . . . She's in charge of my safety, or of keeping an eye on me, and she's making sure that if I get depressed I'm not going to do anything silly. . . . That's what I'd do in her place.*

And what about the letter. The riddle?

A game.

Who from? And what is the point?

To divert me, make me think about something else. . . .

Marion wasn't convinced.

All of this wasn't clear; the ideas were all mixed up in her head. Her only certainty was, for the time being, not to give too much of herself away. Whether it was a game by the brotherhood to keep watch on her and help her to pass the time here, or the fruit of one mind, working toward a personal goal, Marion must remain in the background and observe, so as to take action when the time was right.

That didn't prevent her taking certain measures.

She couldn't call a locksmith without everyone knowing. But she could at least declare her privacy.

She took the few items off the hall table and pushed it up against the door. As she straightened up she gave a long, slow breath. This would guarantee that nobody got through as long as she was here.

The precaution was rather excessive, it seemed to her.

If she really was at some kind of risk a hall table wouldn't protect her. It would be better to call the DST immediately and tell them about the problem. On the other hand, if she really believed that all of this was the result of measures designed to protect her, she had nothing to fear and her improvised "blockade" had no purpose.

But it does. For me. For my head. So that I can sleep, reassured.

And it didn't do any harm to anyone.

That evening, Marion didn't eat much. She spent most of her time watching the door from the sofa, while half-watching the television.

Her mind came back regularly to Jeremy Matheson's diary. He had a way of talking about his life that was very much his own, a way of describing the place where he stayed, that once-luxurious, untidy railroad car. He presented himself as a handsome man with a total absence of modesty, and put across the melancholy that dwelled within him with an absolute lack of shame that astonished Marion. The choice of words was crucial; it filtered through in the reading. Matheson had taken time composing his journal. And, as he himself confessed, one soon realized that there was no egotistical purpose in it, but just the will to leave a record of a drama that was already making its presence felt in the early pages.

Marion's eagerness to read had been checked by her discovery early that evening. After that, she hadn't felt in the right frame of mind.

But it was returning now.

Curiosity.

Who was Jeremy Matheson, above and beyond this introduction?

What kind of man could he be?

And why this somber story of children, in which he admitted he had wept over the list of victims?

Marion went to fetch the book with the black cover.

She started on a bottle of gin, pouring herself a glass with some orange juice, and she sank back onto the sofa.

The village was going to sleep before her eyes, behind the glazed window.

She opened the book and began again at the exact place she had reached.

· 11 ·

Detective Jeremy Matheson had connections in Cairo.

Not only through his professional capacity, but because a good part of Cairo's Western society knew of his existence, either by reputation or because they had requested his good offices.

Matheson had no equal when it came to sorting out misunderstandings.

A wayward mistress, a *baksheesh* that turned into a backhander and that had to be forgotten, or quite simply a request for a few judiciously gleaned nuggets of information.

His notoriety had passed into the salons, private clubs, and parties; people whispered his name in one another's ears like a miracle cure. For nothing about him would lead a person to think he could be this man of society. There was nothing worldly about him.

Neither his almost savage appearance, nor his excessively withdrawn behavior. People came to him on the tips of their toes, wary and feverish at the thought of requesting a service from this unfathomable individual. He always regarded the petitioner with the same sidelong glance, lips pursed, then finished with "I'll see what I can do."

And he untied knots with skill.

His greatest qualities in this respect were his discretion, of course, and on the other hand his address book. His name was familiar to many benches in the *qawha,* and beside old Cairo's public fountains, as well as to the concierges of large hotels or the secretaries at the ministries.

Matheson had been in Cairo for nine years. He had come at his own request, as soon as he entered the police force, once he had obtained his law diploma. Cairo made sense with its exoticism, adventures, sunshine, and above all its less rigid hierarchy, more inclined to promote him swiftly and enable him to become an investigator. The reality had proved him right.

Moreover, he enjoyed a freedom to maneuver here that it would have been impossible for him to find in London or anywhere else in England. And after nine years spent tanning his skin beneath the heat of the pyramids, he had never asked to return home. On the contrary, he did everything to ensure that his file remained forgotten in the archives. He had seen three British High Commissioners arrive, one after the other; he had been present at the anticolonial demonstrations, and at their episodes of violence; he had witnessed the birth of Egyptian independence, and the discovery of the tomb of Tutankhamen—almost a decade filled with glory and dramatic incidents that had fascinated him. And Cairo had him in its grasp.

His points of reference were in the line of minarets on the rooftops, in the song of the muezzins that punctuated the day in a less martial manner than Big Ben, in the splendor of an Englishman's life among the Arabs. And also in the daily spice that wafted in from the desert onto all their heads: the threat of a danger that might rise up at any moment, in any possible form. This is how his life played out in the city of *One Thousand and One Nights*. Although Matheson was quintessentially British, the London fog and the predictability of life beside the Thames had lost their charm.

Here, all Westerners had the right to carry a weapon; here, the nights might flare up in a moment under pressure from the nationalists; each meal had a flavor of antiquity. In Cairo, history was no longer made, but punctuated; people lived with it for company; the mysteries had a material quality that was found nowhere else; the legends became reality; the sand and the sun edged the city and life with a bitter taste that incited people to live ever more intensely.

Cairo was a cobra, lurking between the Mokattam Hills and the Nile. Rather than proving lethal, its bite caused a total dependence, which could never be broken.

The Egyptian police, under the command of Russel Pasha, carried out the main body of the investigation work, although still overseen here and there by Englishmen in strategic posts. Jeremy Matheson's main responsibility was for matters involving Western people or goods, but his role was above all political. Two-faced Egypt owed it to itself to function with this cumbersome, two-headed power—to satisfy sometimes the colonial whims of one set of people, sometimes the fervor for identity of the others.

Just as he didn't give a damn about promotion now that he was a detective, Jeremy Matheson cared nothing for this demagogic will. He served the interests of his office, beyond that of the nation, he told himself over and over again. He carried out his investigations, playing on both cultural stages like a true juggler.

He handled the murder of a vagrant and a theft from a rich Englishman's home in exactly the same way.

He knew only too well how his Cairo colleagues could classify an investigation and its importance in accordance with the interests at stake, the social classes concerned, or quite simply according to their own preferences. And Matheson made it his duty to stir up ill-feeling in this world where a total absence of probity reigned. Not because he was himself a man of integrity—far from it—but simply to give the occasional hefty kick to this nest of snakes and watch them writhe about convulsively.

Matheson had built up his own boundary, extremely narrow, yet permeable, between his official work and the work he did privately to render services. He very rarely obtained money for these services, but he nourished his address book, created biographical dossiers on this person and that person, when necessary giving himself permission to ask for a service in return. This was how his extended network of knowledge operated.

When, at the end of February, he had heard talk in the corridors of his department about the body of a child found in an abandoned house in the northwest of the Abbasiya district, Jeremy Matheson had stopped to listen.

The news in itself, although macabre, was not inconceivable. That part of Cairo was an assembly of hovels where death struck very often; what worried him more was the condition of the child when discovered.

Matheson had left his office to join the two police officers. The one who had just come back from the scene still looked as pale as the sail of a felucca. He didn't allow himself to give precise details, however he confided that the child had been broken in two around the pelvis, as if it were made of light wood, snapped at an atrocious angle, the torso bent backward, the flesh pierced by the hip bones.

There had been no rape, but there were traces of a sexual nature.

The investigation was entrusted to an inspector named Azim Abd el-Dayim, a native of Cairo who knew el-Abbasiya district well: the very least that was needed in order to work there without running the risk of being cut into pieces in such a place. He found no witnesses, no convincing clues.

On March 2, a six-year-old girl was found in a sordid alleyway in el-Huseiniya. She was not broken in two, but her state was horrible in other ways. Five men had seen her, and not one had managed to retain his dignity; all had dissolved into tears, some had vomited, and others had nightmares for several nights.

Samir was the third innocent to be wiped out.

His head lying flat on the stone of a tomb in the cemetery of Bab el-Nasr.

The link between these crimes was in no doubt. The violence was different each time, but exercised with such ferocity that one might doubt the human nature of the culprit.

The three children came from poor areas, from families without resources.

The three children were around the same age.

The three children had been tortured to death, clawed, bitten until pieces of flesh were torn away.

The three children had been sullied.

In less than two weeks.

Jeremy Matheson had picked up his phone, and then got moving. He abandoned his investigation into the murder of an archaeologist carrying out excavations in the basements of Cairo; the case wasn't coming to anything anyway.

And he obtained the investigation into the dead children.

Azim Abd el-Dayim became his colleague, because he spoke Arabic and because he didn't have the same color skin.

Three days later, on March 14, 1928, the telephone rang.

And Jeremy Matheson's life was turned upside-down forever.

· 12 ·

Marion rested the black book on her knees and drank the last mouthful of gin and orange juice, before pouring herself a second glass.

The alcohol was still burning her throat, producing a bitter aftertaste. A taste that echoed many others, among the pages of the notebook she was reading.

Her fingers began stroking the cover.

For a private diary, it was pleasant to read—the start, anyway.

The author had started writing a little after the beginning of the facts he related. This introduction to the subject was a kind of long flashback.

In the first sentences the melancholy came through. Jeremy Matheson was a wounded man, stanching his suffering with words on paper bandages. Contrary to what he stated in the prologue, his writing felt much more than just an account written for the purposes of information. He was emptying his overflowing soul.

The other element that disturbed Marion was that he very seldom said *I*. Instead, he preferred to include himself among other people so as to say *we*, using the police, the English, men, and other groups as often as possible.

On the other hand, the events heralded in the latest pages she had read were highly disagreeable to Marion. The murders of those children.

She wasn't sure she wanted to know.

And yet there was this feeling of curiosity.

She bent over her alarm clock to check the time.

11:12.

She didn't feel particularly tired. The intrusion into her home had shaken her up too much. The fear and the anger had evaporated with the tale.

She glanced briefly at the sloping roofs of the village.

Then the book fell open in her hands again.

As soon as he had hung up, Jeremy Matheson informed Azim, his colleague, and they headed for the *sharia** Muhammad Ali, which they drove along before forking off eastward, beneath the ramparts of the Citadel. They left the city, crossing an ancient cemetery to reach the Tombs of the Caliphs.

In the vehicle, they went over Azim's investigations to date. Managing everything on his own, he had delegated as much as possible, in order to gain time. Police officers had gone to take statements from each family, while others went from door to door, to ask the inhabitants of the districts concerned if they had seen or heard anything unusual on the nights of the murders. Azim centralized the reports, went over them with a fine-tooth comb, and attempted to identify a lead, without success. He had made hardly any progress since the first day; all he had was a clear conscience, knowing he had done his work to the best of his ability.

Three victims, perhaps four today.

Children just a few years old, living in the same area, northeastern Cairo, all from very poor families. That was all they had.

*Street

A tarred road ran parallel to the necropolis, and they were able to park alongside the vehicles that were already there; Jeremy and Azim covered the rest of the distance on foot, along the fringes of the desert.

It was late morning, and the temperature was around eighty-five degrees. The heat seemed to emerge from the ground itself, weaving blurred wreaths in the air, which climbed toward the heavens, obscuring the horizon. The tall minarets of the tombs cast their shadows on the sand, outlining a calm path, inviting others to walk in their footsteps, like a religious message filtered beyond the stone.

Roofless walls followed one another in successive waves, their multicolored bricks forming pink, red, and white battlements around the cells. The domes and towers rose up all around, in buzzing hives beneath the one eye of Ra.

Richard Pallister, the police photographer, was at the entrance to a blind alley, seated on a small boulder, his hat on one knee and his camera bag at his feet. He was mopping his brow with a handkerchief, less from the heat than from the shock.

And yet the heat was unusually powerful for the season.

Pallister lifted his head to look at the new arrivals; his eyelids were swollen and red, his gaze vacant.

Pallister looked for a landmark. The one that distinguished men from beasts, the landmark that shines permanently like a red boundary stone on the verge of consciousness, and that looms up in front of it when thoughts go too far.

His face was colored with a transparent film that slid little by little from his hair to his chin, in salty droplets, leaving pallid skin in its wake. His lips were trembling.

When Jeremy reached him, the photographer murmured something, but it was the emotion in his eyes that made Jeremy understand. He was begging him not to go there.

Nevertheless, Jeremy entered the narrow alleyway. He heard Pallister begin to sob.

The right-hand wall belonged to a tomb that looked above all like a house with a flat roof, white and blind. Opposite, the wall was much older; it had been crumbling for a long time. Its skeleton of bricks was as black as charred bone, a loose mesh with the purple hues of the desert grew between each stone, similar to dried blood; the construction was now no more than a geological corpse, conferring upon the alleyway a suffocating appearance and a smell of dust.

It ran on in this way for twenty yards.

Two natives of Cairo, wearing cheap suits and *tarbooshes** were standing right at the end, their hands on their hips. The two men stood in silence, avoiding looking at the ground.

As soon as they spotted Jeremy Matheson they came to meet him, only too happy to be able to distance themselves for a moment from this cursed place.

"A *dragoman*† found it this morning, while preparing his itinerary," reported the first man with a pronounced accent that made him roll his *rs.* "They thought about telling you straightaway; it's too much like the previous ones. . . ."

Without a word, Matheson laid a hand on the man's shoulder to move him out of the way. He approached what was spattering the beaten earth and the walls of the alley.

A child aged around ten.

Bled-out and distorted, as if by an all-powerful giant who had discovered this strange toy, and manipulated it until it was worn-out and broken, kneading it, shattering it, bursting it; and now the child was lying like a shapeless parcel, its only remaining human aspect its arms and legs, and a swollen head whose hair had turned white with terror.

Matheson swallowed his saliva, and it went down his throat with a moist echo.

* A red hat similar to the fez mostly worn by Muslim men
† A local tourist guide and translator whose knowledge is often more linked to his address book than to his historical learning

There were pins and needles in his legs. He closed his eyes to concentrate on his breathing. Swiftly he noticed how fast his heart was beating.

Calm down. Breathe.

Azim took hold of his arm gently.

"Are you going to be all right?" he asked in a reassuring, almost maternal voice.

Almost white, Jeremy turned to look at him.

Azim was wearing the traditional turban, and a Western shirt and trousers. His finely shaped, ebony-black mustache danced on his upper lip. He carried his excess weight with grace, ever serene, his movements always catlike.

"Mr. Matheson?" he said. "Are you sure you want to stay here?"

Jeremy breathed out slowly and nodded. "Yes," he murmured. "Yes. I want to stay."

The two men with tarbooshes contemplated him without judging, too deeply affected themselves.

In turn, Jeremy stared at them. "Right," he said, regaining a little substance and trying to steady his voice. "Have you obtained any particular clues?"

"No," replied the first man, "there was too much movement in the sand. It's impossible to say what is old and what is recent, not to mention the dragoman's footsteps and our own. On the other hand we have not really examined the area around," he said, indicating a circle around the lifeless body.

"And what about the dragoman? Where is he now?"

"We took down his details and . . ."

"And?"

The man twitched nervously, foreseeing trouble. He raised an eyebrow and a shoulder at the same time, ill at ease. "And he left . . ."

Jeremy opened his mouth when Azim—who was still holding

his arm—loosened his grip. "Don't dwell on it," he whispered, "it's pointless, what's done is done."

Jeremy breathed out for a long moment, without taking his eyes off the two men in front of him. "Very well," he said finally. "Stay at the entrance to the alley, and watch for the arrival of the stretcher-bearers."

He spun around to confront the extent of the carnage once more. "Nobody touches the body," he commanded after a moment's silence. "The doctor will take care of it. We shall search the sand and everything else, in search of clues."

He and Azim divided the area around the body between them, and started to walk around it gradually, examining each inch of the ground and the walls.

The shadow cast by the tombs had protected the site from the sun, and the bodily fluids had not had time to be absorbed or totally assimilated by the earth. There were still long, brown trickles, between which they had to step with care.

Jeremy opened the top buttons of his shirt to allow a little air to his chest. He was not breathing well.

One long track had not been erased by his predecessors' footsteps: two times five parallel lines, running for two yards from one corner to the little body.

The child had dug his nails and his entire fingers into the sand to hold on while he was being dragged backward.

Toward a greedy mouth.

Jeremy drove this image from his mind.

He would have none of it. It was a parasite to considered thought. What mattered was to concentrate here, now. Nothing else. No mad images.

He went back to inspecting the scene, taking all the time necessary not to omit any detail. There were too many humps and hollows in the sand to deduce anything from them; it was complete chaos.

"I may have something here," said Azim in his singsong voice.

Jeremy joined him, facing the decrepit old wall. Azim was hanging a yard from the top, his feet balanced in holes he had managed to find.

He pointed to a fresh gash in a brick just under his nose, at the top, which was less than nine feet up. The gash was shallow and was a little more than one inch long and less than one wide.

"How did you find that, Azim?" exclaimed the English detective.

"It's my job," replied his companion joylessly. "It looks like a claw mark."

Azim exclaimed something in Arabic. "There's another one here," he pointed out immediately.

The second, which was similar, was about eight inches away. Both were close to the top of the wall.

The sun was beginning to illuminate this part, covering the textures with its rough brilliance; its rays were so pure and hot that they brought out the shadows, while dulling the brightness of the colors.

A glint of quartz or gypsum caught Jeremy's eye. It was coming from the end of the gash.

"What's that?" he asked.

"I just saw it, too. Wait . . ."

Azim steadied himself with one hand and freed the other to extract the shining object delicately.

His expression darkened.

"What is it?" demanded Matheson, suddenly impatient.

"I don't know. . . . It looks like a bit of ivory . . . a pointed bit."

"Let me see."

Azim jumped down beside him and held out the white fragment.

It was triangular and sharp. Its material was reminiscent of slightly damaged horn. Jeremy raised his face to the claw marks in the brick.

Something made of horn had grazed the top of the wall, in much the same way as it had eight inches away.

Suddenly, Jeremy placed his hand on his colleague's abdomen to prevent him from moving anymore. He scanned the ground attentively.

Among the multitude of minuscule dunes that had formed, he swiftly detected one hole that was much deeper than the others.

At first, he showed Azim two other depressions just in front of him. "Look."

"I made those, sir," replied Azim. "When I jumped down from the wall. My feet sank in and left those hollows."

"Yes, I know, precisely! Now look at this other hole, here."

He pointed to the one he had spotted. "And this sort of jumbled mass of sand beside it, about eight inches away, must have been its twin before it was wiped away."

Azim nodded his understanding. Someone had jumped from the top, an adult to judge from the depth.

"He was balancing at this height when he jumped," explained Jeremy, pointing to the holes. "He leaned on the brick to propel himself, and scratched it because he was holding a weapon made from horn, apparently in both hands; that's what caused these marks."

"In both hands? Not practical for jumping."

"That is true. That being said, I can scarcely believe that his nails could make such gashes!"

Jeremy immediately started scaling the masonry. "The child was caught unawares, terrified even, to judge by the color of his hair. He must have seen his attacker at the last moment, standing or crouching in this very spot," he said, reconstructing the scene as he hoisted himself up.

He took the time to find his balance and stood up slowly to look down on the alleyway from a height of almost nine feet. Then he turned to look from the other side, which hid the multicolored wall.

"Do you see anything?" Azim wanted to know. "Wait, I'm coming up—"

"Pointless! You might break your neck, the bricks aren't well joined together, it's very old. There's a level a few feet lower down."

Before Azim advised caution, Jeremy had already jumped to the other side. His shoulders rose above the top of the wall, and he bent forward to signal to him; all was well. And he started to search.

Down below, on the other side, Azim could see only the upper part of the Englishman moving about, sometimes disappearing completely when he kneeled down. Detective Matheson gritted his teeth and shook his head somberly as he combed the roof of what must be a mausoleum.

Suddenly, after a few minutes, he stopped. He bent forward and briskly stood up, a hand in front of his mouth. He stroked his chin.

"Something?" inquired Azim.

The Englishman nodded.

"Do you want me to come up?" Azim continued.

"No." The word was brusque, yet spoken with a disconcerting softness. "No, I don't think there's any need for you to," added Jeremy in the same almost inaudible tone, as though confiding a secret.

"So what is up there?"

Jeremy bent forward to look down on the whole area. He gazed at the towers, the fortifications, and the cupolas that gave this place such an original aspect. Because of the sun he was obliged to screw up his face in order to see without closing his eyelids completely.

His words were spoken so faintly, as if to himself, that Azim had great difficulty in catching them all. "We are dealing with a hunter, Azim. A hunter without pity, a hunter whose trophies are children . . ."

What came next, if anything did, was lost for all eternity among the tombs.

· 13 ·

It was midnight.

Marion laid down the diary on the edge of the sofa.

The gin and orange juice was starting to make her head spin.

She gazed about the dimly lit room, asking herself what she was doing there. The décor resumed its place in her memory quite quickly.

The afternoon's break-in was no more than a bad memory, clouded by the alcohol.

She felt disoriented, thrown totally off-balance by what she had just read.

Thinking about it, she hadn't really read it; that was the problem. She had *lived* the discovery of the dead child. The power of the words.

They are a door.

They are the magical incantation.

The source of spells.

A gateway to the imaginary world.

They had carried her off into the film of the past, and she had got lost there.

Marion groaned as she stretched.

She was tired.

"And you're a little bit drunk, my dear," she commented out loud.

She went up to the bedroom and just as she was about to get undressed, she remembered that she had left the black book downstairs. She hesitated; she had no desire to go back down, and yet she wanted to keep it with her, very close. She sighed and went to fetch it.

Darkness was cradling the village beyond the picture window.

Marion stood still in the darkened living room, gazing out at the roofs and lifeless windows. Then she went back to her bedroom and took off her clothes. While she was placing her clothes in the little bathroom that adjoined it, she noticed the reflection of her figure in the mirror.

She still had magnificent legs. She turned around.

Her backside wasn't bad either, she told herself.

A modest greed was bringing roundness to her belly, which had still been flat not so long ago. Her breasts weren't as firm as they used to be, but all the same they were fine, she reckoned. It was her arms that displeased her most in the end. That elasticity under the triceps, that ribbon of flabby skin under the biceps.

She knew this inventory by heart.

The mirror was of no more use to her than the prompter in a theater.

The most difficult thing to accept was not this body, which was ripening in the face of everything, despite the absence of regular sexual activity, despite her peculiar way of life, or the fact that it had never served to carry or build life; no, the hardest thing was her face.

The furrows of existence that grew more insistent with the years, the complexion that was fading without the unrestricted use of the institute's ultraviolet facilities, the sandy blond of her hair, which was losing ground in favor of the white of resignation.

And yet the overall sight wasn't an unpleasant one. Marion had nothing to complain about; she was still a beautiful woman. Her features were soft, and the lines merely emphasized a degree of wisdom . . .

Marion burst out laughing. Her thoughts were wandering; it was time to sleep, to forget about her body and about questioning herself. Women agonized over the idea of withering and consequently losing the love of their husbands or the admiring looks of men in the street and she, Marion, feared she might never overcome her solitude. Before you could hope to keep something, you had to win it.

"You're talking nonsense," she murmured, noticing that her breath smelled of alcohol. "You're drunk."

She slipped between the cold sheets on the bed, without bothering to put on pajamas or a nightshirt, and she closed her eyes.

Her hands slid down her hips. One slipped beneath her hip, and brushed against her pubis.

Her fingers lightly caressed the hollow of her sex.

And she rolled onto her side, holding onto the covers so as to pull them right up to her neck. Not tonight. She was too tired.

The sun of Egypt was still shining, somewhere in a corner of her thoughts.

The heat cradled her.

Jeremy Matheson was holding her by the shoulders, and tenderly smoothing her hair.

He smelled so good. . . . Virile, almost bestial. Attractive, as if he exercised an irresistible charm. Magnetic.

Marion saw his mouth approach hers.

Her hand tightened again about the covers.

She slept.

Marion sorted the books in the attic of the library in Avranches along with Brother Damien all day Wednesday; these were their last hours of toil in the stacks.

She almost asked him questions about what each member of the brotherhood had done the previous afternoon, to try and ferret out the prowler who had broken into her house, but she decided to say nothing so as not to arouse the monk's curiosity.

She returned home around five o'clock, and the telephone rang almost immediately. She was expected at the abbot's residence in order to meet Brother Serge, who was the head of the brotherhood.

Marion climbed the external great stair and crossed the Châtelet to arrive at the long and imposing façade of the residence.

Sister Agathe was waiting for her at the entrance. The sister was younger than she was, relatively insignificant in terms of physique, and almost spectral in her discretion. She led Marion through the corridors and staircases and knocked at an arched wooden door.

Brother Serge opened it and invited Marion to enter. Sister Anne was there too.

The man was in his fifties. A large, twisted nose and several dark moles marked his face. Beneath his thick, brown eyebrows, his eyes formed two placid, elongated lakes that reflected no emotion. Looking at him for the first time, Marion found herself comparing him to Robert De Niro, only less charismatic and more drained.

"I am pleased to be able to make your acquaintance at last," he said by way of introduction. "You have been here a whole week, and I have scarcely had a moment to myself. Do please take a seat."

Marion did so, not far from Sister Anne, who kept a benevolent watch on her. The monk's voice was familiar to her, but she couldn't quite identify it.

"Are you becoming accustomed to your quarters?" Brother Serge wanted to know.

"Yes, in my own time. I'm starting to feel 'at home,' as they say."

"Perfect. I was worried about you settling in, it's a little awkward. But I was given to understand that Sister Anne had taken you under her wing, so I know you are in good hands."

So he was pretending to inform her that everything had had to be orchestrated well in advance of her arrival, presumed Marion. She wondered how many people had passed between these walls before her, entrusted to the brotherhood by the DST. Was it a well-oiled mechanism? That was unlikely; frequency and quantity would have placed the system in danger. A too-predictable procedure was of no interest for this kind of mission, which consisted of making an individual disappear for a given length of time. Nobody must be able to follow the trail back.

Marion decided not to play any longer. "Are you in permanent contact with the DST?" she asked.

Brother Serge hid his broad smile behind his even broader hand.

He turned his head toward Sister Anne to share his amusement before answering Marion. "No, on the contrary. Silence prevails. All I have is a telephone number to call if it is absolutely necessary. We are merely a spiritual community, Marion. Will you allow me to call you Marion?"

She gave a casual nod to invite him to continue.

"Not secret agents," he concluded.

"I was just curious. Wondering."

"We render a service. We were asked to do so one day, we agreed, and it happened again, and it is exceptional. That's all."

"That's all," repeated Marion, gazing fixedly at him.

"How do you pass your days? You are helping Brother Damien, I understand."

"Yes. It isn't very exciting, but it keeps me busy. Alas, the cataloging is over and tomorrow I'm back to my idleness."

"I'm going to give you this bunch of keys. Please take the greatest care of it. With it, you will be able to go wherever you wish."

He picked up a metal ring, from which a dozen large keys hung. "Be as discreet as you can; the Mount's administration thinks you are on retreat with us. They would not look favorably on us allowing you such a privilege."

Sister Anne leaned toward Marion. "I will explain the purpose of each of these keys to you," she said.

"It will be as good a means as any other of amusing yourself. I must confess that your worst enemy here will be boredom. We shall keep you company as often as possible; having said that, I shall not hide from you the fact that our brotherhood has to keep to its normal routine. We cannot find you an official job on the Mount; that would not be sensible."

"Were you told how long I was going to stay?"

Brother Serge scratched the nape of his neck. "No, not at all. I have no idea. We were asked to watch over you during the winter, for as long as it takes for 'things to settle down or move forward.' I don't even know what those things are"—he brandished his index finger in front of her face—"and I don't want to be told. It might last three weeks or three months."

He paused, then added, "Since we do not know, prepare yourself to spend the coming months here."

Marion took the bunch of keys.

"In the meantime, if I can be of any assistance to you . . . ," he said, trying to be reassuring.

Marion thanked him briefly.

She knew where she had heard that voice.

The night of her arrival. While she was falling asleep, a deep masculine voice with extremely clear enunciation. He had come to her bedside on that first evening with Sister Anne.

Marion declined when she was offered dinner with the other members of the brotherhood; Brother Gilles—and his aquiline profile—was going to read from the holy writings during the meal. She went back to her house, more curious than anxious to find out if she had received another mysterious visit. Marion walked through all the rooms, but there was nothing to make her think so.

Perhaps it was over. . . . She had been titillated by the enigmatic letter, and checked out to see that she wasn't hiding any dangerous objects, and now she was going to be left in peace.

Marion prepared herself some instant soup, too lazy that evening to cook.

She placed the bowl on the living-room table, with a bottle of water and a yogurt, and took the black book from her woollen bag.

Marion settled down to eat and opened the diary where she had left off.

· 14 ·

Jeremy Matheson and his colleague Azim elbowed their way through a pedestrian street in the el-Musky district. Here, everyone moved around on foot, or on the back of a donkey if absolutely necessary; the density of passersby and stalls was such that nobody could do otherwise.

Beneath the high, dilapidated façades with their jutting balconies, the deep shops overflowed at their leisure as far as the middle of the street, thus arranging the rainbow-colored bouquets and veils of exotic fragrance into a long procession.

Jeremy passed beneath a large carpet made from camel skin, displayed on high like a tent, and from which an acidic, sickening smell was emanating. A seller of silk fabrics hailed him, only to withdraw instantly when he saw Azim dismissing him in his own language.

The silken stoles in red, green, blue, yellow, and their variations disappeared behind one another, leaving the way clear to a labyrinth of baskets filled with dates and fat, sugary-scented figs.

Everyone was talking, shouting in Arabic, exchanging money for goods. The men were laughing and guffawing, revealing toothless mouths. People were watching each other and looking covetously from underneath the low rims of fez, tarboosh, or turban, protected from the sun by the awnings of tanned hide, fabric canopies, and other representatives of an ancient architecture.

"Why a 'hunter'?" asked Azim. "Just now, you talked about the murderer as if he was a hunter. He's certainly a beast, a madman ripe for execution, but why did you say a 'hunter'?"

"Because that's what he did. When I go on safari, I roam the savannah for hours, keeping watch on my prey from a distance, approaching it very gently, if possible from above. If it spots me I try to bring it where I want it, to enclose it in a natural circle or some kind of cul-de-sac, so that it is imprisoned. And if I have an elevated viewpoint, all I have to do is swoop down on it, and swiftly put it to death."

"He is above all a sick man, sir. He must be sick in the head to kill a child. And he did not just kill it, he slaughtered it. He is demented!" thundered the little Egyptian.

"Not only that, Azim, it goes much further. He didn't just kill that child, he tracked it. He hunted it down. And when you're hunting, the pleasure isn't in the last second, once you've pressed the trigger, even if that is part of it. It is in the ritual that precedes it, the slow and meticulous quest to detect your prey, track it, manipulate it from a distance, imprison it. That is where the pleasure lies. And that's what he did, this killer; he hunted the child. He takes pleasure in tracking."

Azim's hand swept through the air in protest.

"And yet," Jeremy went on, "the murderer was hidden behind the wall, on the roof of a mausoleum, watching for his victim to arrive. He waited, so that he could swoop down on him suddenly, leaving him not the slightest chance of escape. And then he toyed with him. . . . He has the mind of a hunter, and a perverted one at that. He loves what he does."

"Why do you say that? Were you inside his head?"

"The clues enable us to state it as fact."

"Are you finally going to tell me what you found up there?" Azim raged.

They walked between sacks of spices hanging along an endless tunnel, their nasal passages suddenly assailed by successive waves of aromas.

"The reason why I speak of him as a perverted hunter, Azim. Semen."

"What?"

"You understand me perfectly well. His own, I am certain. He could not hold it in, his excitement was so great. There are whispers that it happens to the greatest hunters, you know, that they have an ... *erection* at the high points of their hunt. He couldn't control it. And that is good for us."

"Good for us? What kind of Englishman are you to say such a thing? You talk to me of hunters, of sexual acts, and ... good for us?"

"Yes, highly informative if you prefer," Jeremy Matheson corrected himself, paying no heed to his colleague's astonishment. "First of all, we can work out his personality more easily. Next, we know that he is definitely a man and not a woman who has escaped from an asylum. We know that he probably wears a bubu or a djellaba, otherwise the semen would not have fallen on the ground; I have difficulty believing that a hunter on the point of swooping down upon his victim would have his trousers undone; and finally, the most important thing assuredly: We know that there is a lead to be followed relating to the way the child spent his time."

Azim stopped in the middle of the ever-teeming street; a few people bumped into one another, but did not protest.

"I don't follow you," he admitted.

"Think, my friend. . . . If the man was there, ready for the hunt, it is because he knew the child would come. Such excitement builds up; I can't imagine it just surges up out of nowhere, all at once—no, he had already been thinking about it for a while when the child appeared. He kept watch on him, before attacking him. And you will surely agree that the caliphs' necropolis is not a place where one meets many children! He knew that his victim was going to come, because he lured him there, or because he knew how the child spent his time. And that's where we must look."

Jeremy wiped the sweat from his brow with the back of his sleeve.

"There's still the child's terror," he added lugubriously.

"The white hair, you mean?"

"Even caught unawares, I don't see how the boy could have been so afraid."

Azim searched his English vocabulary before saying, "The killer's physiognomy. Perhaps he is as ugly on the outside as he is on the inside."

"That's possible, that's possible . . ."

Azim nodded, producing folds of flesh beneath his chin. "In any case I am impressed by this lesson in deduction. A little mad, admittedly, but completely logical. And this does indeed lead us to a trail, bravo. What is more, using the hunter-killer hypothesis one can then add in an element that has worried me ever since I began conducting the inquiry: He has a feeling for the area. Notice how he has always chosen his victims within a very localized area: the northeast of Cairo. From the walls of the Citadel to el-Abbasiya district. He has defined the limits of his hunting ground."

"Yes, exactly. We may have to go into this further, but to begin with we must deal with the most urgent matter: identifying the child."

Jeremy took a date he had filched on his way past a few seconds earlier, and popped it into his mouth.

"You have a brilliant analytical mind," commented Azim. "When you allow the detective within you to express himself, it is a treasure to accompany him in his reasoning."

Jeremy stared at him for a moment before correcting him. "It wasn't the detective who spoke, Azim; he would not have sensed all that. No. It was the hunter."

They found themselves in the basement of an age-old building, which extended back far enough for the interior to remain cool despite the high temperatures outside.

The room was vaulted, with a rather low ceiling, lit both by gas lanterns hanging on the wall and by oil lamps that gave off a persistent, fatty odor, mixed with the more terrible stench of meat. It was a pungent aroma, mingling the smell of rotting ham and the mustiness of different foodstuffs that had been allowed to spoil over several days inside a bag before it suddenly opened.

Four wooden tables covered with greaseproof paper stood in a row under two large blackboards.

Trolleys stood alongside the tables. On them, slender, sharp instruments had been set out, each more terrifying than the last; fine blades, notched or with teeth, wire cutters, saws, and even hammers. In one corner lay a half-yard-long ruler, whose yellow paint was now spattered with ring-shaped red dots.

And in the lone, but imposing sink lay a substantial accumulation of sticky instruments immersed in stagnant water the color of Bordeaux wine, in which more solid, stringy substances swam.

Notepads with sheets wrinkled by repeated wetting were piled on a small table at the entrance to the room.

Jeremy Matheson was standing, facing a man of around fifty with a white beard and hair. His black apron gleamed strangely moist in the light from the lamps.

"This is the last time I work in such a rush," he warned.

"You know it is important, Doctor," said Jeremy. Then he demanded, "So?"

The old man turned toward the sheet-draped shape on the nearest table. "The poor kid had a very bad time of it, believe you me. He was beaten to a pulp; he has bruises all over his body. His left arm was broken, shattered in three places, the elbow too, plus several ribs. . . ."

He spun around to face one of the large blackboards, on which different observations were written. "Four, to be exact. In short, I'll spare you the rest. It will all be in detail in the report you'll receive shortly from the office. This is what interests you: He was killed by manual strangulation, I am almost certain of that. Though, in view of all his injuries, the little chap wouldn't have survived very long. The disturbing thing is the appearance of the marks on his neck."

He half sat on the edge of the table. "You know, Detective, when you strangle someone, it requires so much force to cut off the circulation of air and/or blood that you must press very hard indeed. . . . And in general, you push your fingers into the skin, leaving traces of the nails, grazes or dermabrasions. In this case, there are actual holes, savage cuts, sometimes quite deep."

"What does that mean? That the murderer had a knife?"

"No, not really. The mark of the fingers is there; the hematomas are shaped almost like the hands. No, it means that the killer of this child had very hard, very long nails, almost like blades."

The doctor picked up a porcelain bowl containing the triangular piece of horn found a few hours earlier by the two investigators. "If you want my opinion, this thing here could very well be one."

Jeremy bent toward him, inclining his neck. He didn't understand. "How do you mean?"

"I am simply saying that this fragment here could be nail."

"What? You surely don't think so! That's a bit much! The killer would have to be a monstrous giant!"

"Listen, I am not the one who makes the comparisons; each to his own work, and mine inclines me to think that this could be the tip of a nail. Pointed, thick, hard, certainly, but why not? In any case it corresponds to the type of wound the child has on him. Ah, yes, because he does not just have these marks on his throat but all over his body, or almost. Everywhere where he was held, we find these cuts, like a hand with overlong nails."

"With claws, you mean. . . ."

"Given the size and the sharpness, yes, one may talk about claws."

"Was he attacked . . . sexually?"

The doctor seemed to hesitate. "Not in the strict meaning of the term. Rather like the others, there is sperm on his body, but no penetration."

"Anything else?"

The doctor ran a hand through his beard. A line of blood had dried around the rim of his nails. "Details of a biological kind, but nothing concerning the criminal aspect. When I opened the child I noted that he was situs inversus, that his organs were the wrong way around; that is to say that his heart and liver were on the right side, not on the left. Normally, in an adult one notices this even before the autopsy, because in theory the right testicle is lower than the left; it is the opposite for men whose hearts are on the left."

"And does this change anything?"

"Absolutely nothing, it is merely a peculiarity. Another thing: He was a hemophiliac. I could not swear to it, but it seems fairly obvious to me. The digestive tract and the joints bore marks of trauma linked to hemophilia. And with regard to the wounds, the blood flowed far too strongly for injuries of that nature; there is almost no trace of coagulation."

Jeremy cast a glance toward a notebook that lay in the middle of some used scalpels. A constellation of little red droplets spattered the pages with their spidery notes. "Thank you, Doctor."

"This is the last time I work in such a rush," repeated the doctor. "Next time, you will wait."

"I know—"

"No, you know nothing," he snapped with an anger that surprised Jeremy. "Working in a rush means taking the risk of rummaging around inside and cutting oneself. Do you know all the illnesses that are transmitted in that way? Two doctors died recently in this manner, one in Alexandria this winter and the other here, last year. Erysipelas—have you ever heard of it? No? It's an infection that has been decimating doctors for a few years. One small cut and it's too late. . . . A fold of swollen flesh, fevers, and you're gone. I didn't survive the war in France to die so stupidly! That was the last time."

The man grabbed a clean rag and wiped his hands mechanically. He moistened his lips and rubbed his beard, bringing the circulation back to his jaw. Then he turned toward Jeremy Matheson, who gazed at the too-small mass that lay on a table, covered with a sheet.

"Sad, isn't it?" said the doctor.

He approached the detective, the rag in his hand. "You know, sometimes when I'm toiling away in our entrails, I stop for a minute and contemplate the body of work that we are. The extent to which we are all unequal. Some have resilient, wide arteries, which are harder to block. Others on the contrary have frail, narrow ones. Why? There are no rules to it. Probably not hereditary; it's the chance fault of nature—either you are born with a strong propensity to die early, or not. For this poor lad, it happened more quickly than he'd imagined. His heart beat what, a million times before it stopped? More or less. A million calls to life, for nothing. Nobody heard. He returns to dust."

"You're depressing me, Doctor." Jeremy patted him amicably on the shoulder and made to head for the exit, a sordid staircase.

"Are you going to find whoever did this?" demanded the doctor behind him.

Jeremy halted on the first step. He had absolutely not expected this sign of involvement from this man who had seemed to maintain a casual distance from the situation from the start. Then, in the moving light from the lanterns, the doctor added, "If you find him, Detective, do me the pleasure of putting a bullet into him from me."

Jeremy rejoined Azim a little later, toward the end of the afternoon. The little Egyptian had done the rounds of the police stations to check any reports of missing children. He was looking for a boy aged around ten, whose description might correspond—insofar as they were able to determine—with the child found that morning in the blind alley.

But in vain.

It was more than probable that the boy came from a poor district, and very often, in such areas, the inhabitants first tried to sort out problems among themselves, before turning to the authorities. It might take several days for a disappearance to be reported.

Jeremy gave a detailed report to Azim of everything the doctor had told him, omitting nothing. Azim took no notes; he memorized the information without showing any trace of emotion.

"Azim, I am going to call at the asylum to reassure myself that nobody has escaped or any former child molesters been freed lately. We should also tour the hospitals to check that no children have been admitted recently following a savage attack of this type. You never know, perhaps there have been previous failed attempts."

"Indeed. If I may say so, do not forget to call at Ibn Touloun, the old mosque. There are plans to restore it this year, but for the time being it still houses senile old men. They say that its patients are sometimes dangerous; it's a lead like any other."

Matheson nodded and thanked him, and the two men split up. The English detective went back to sharia Abbas, where he spent three hours obtaining the information he wanted. More than five thousand patients were housed there, in conditions that were far from salubrious.

When dusk fell over Cairo, Jeremy Matheson took refuge in his usual *qawha*—a small dive, devoid of decoration—situated near the central railroad station. The owner—the *qawhagi*—immediately served him an *arriha* coffee, flavored with cardamom; the Englishman's preferences were well-known.

A little distance away, old men were playing *mankaleh* and chatting, while a storyteller told one of his numerous legends in Arabic to anyone who would listen.

The wreaths of smoke from the hookahs thickened the air, flavoring it with an oily apple taste, or tainting it with clouds of *ma'assil*.

Jeremy let himself be soothed by the storyteller's voice, imagining all sorts of spectacular sights, straight out of the desert and ancient times.

He soon moved on to alcohol. This *qawha* had no hesitation in serving it, something that was becoming increasingly rare since the more orthodox Muslim sects had strengthened their authority. He drank his glasses of house brandy with a speed that did not bode well, systematically throwing under the table the ice that the owner insisted on putting in his glass.

He staggered back to his railcar, his vision blurred, and collapsed onto his unmade bed.

He had scarcely laid down when he stretched out a hand to the bedside table. He knocked over various objects placed on it before grabbing hold of a frame containing a black-and-white photograph of a woman.

"Jezebel . . . ," he groaned. "Jeze . . . bel . . . who transcends time through nights of pleasure. . . . Jezeb—"

The frame slipped from his fingers and fell onto the carpet, beyond his reach in his nauseated state.

He buried his head in the feather pillow to hold back the rising tears.

A blinding flash shattered his dream of pleasures now gone.

The image lasted only a second. The image of a body.

The body of a child.

The fragile collarbones were jutting out through the thin skin of his chest.

And through all the horror of today.

He had wanted this investigation and its burden of atrocity. Now he was going to have to wear its uniform, in order to be able to enter the firmly closed circle of truth. In order to approach it, dance with it. Was he capable of that? Without putting a foot wrong, without stumbling from the slippery path and falling into shadow.

Jeremy pulled his pillow over his mouth to muffle the sound and howled with all his strength.

· 15 ·

The entire village was shrouded in mist when Marion awoke on Thursday morning.

She took her shower and saw the cotton-wool clouds thinning out beneath her window as she emerged from the bathroom. The carpet of innocence was flowing back toward the sea.

She dressed in jeans and a roll-neck sweater, then put on her trench coat to go out and take the air.

Outside, the walls and paving stones were still damp. Three-quarters of the shops were not open. Behind her she heard someone panting as they ran; the sound growing gradually louder. She stepped aside to make room and was surprised to see Brother Damien in jogging gear, running down the main street at quite a pace. None of his customary bonhomie was now visible on his features; nothing but a fierce determination. He waved at her as he ran past and disappeared into the downward-sloping curve of the street.

Marion stopped outside Béatrice's shop; she was one of the few hopeless cases who almost never closed.

"Sporty kind of guy, Brother Damien," commented Marion as she entered.

"What, him?" chuckled Béatrice. "He could run the whole pilgrimage to Compostela! A proper marathon runner, he is. He goes running almost every day on the causeway. So, how's our beautiful Parisian lady?"

Marion leaned her elbows on the counter. "I'm taking advantage of the great outdoors . . ."

"Here when you say that it means you're bored stiff."

Marion answered with an amused smile.

"So, what's the latest from that book of yours?" asked Béatrice.

"It's intriguing."

"Intriguing? Isn't it supposed to be a private diary? In what way is it *intriguing*?"

"The way in which it's written, for a start. It's the account of a police investigation."

Béatrice giggled. "What, really?"

"Or rather, it's the point of view of the man who led the investigation."

"And?"

"And that's all for the moment. I'm making Jeremy's acquaintance."

"Ah! So it's Jeremy, is it? . . . You're on a first-name basis now, are you?"

Marion winked at her and straightened up. "Anyhow, I think I'm going to spend today reading. Can you recommend a good place on the Mount? You know, as a setting; somewhere pleasant."

Béatrice sought inspiration from her ceiling before suggesting, "You could sit up on the ramparts. But the ideal place is the abbey, right at the top. At least in one of the big rooms you'll be shielded from the wind. If you ask at the entrance desk, they might let you through."

Marion almost answered that as a matter of fact she had free access with her keys, but something held her back. She wasn't from around here, and feared people might see her in a bad light if she flaunted the favors she was enjoying.

They chatted for an hour before Marion went back up to her house to fetch the diary. She picked up the magic bundle and scaled the interminable steps to reach the summit. Before she'd even reached the Châtelet, she found a black door that formed part of the edifice. Out of curiosity, she approached and tried several keys in the lock before hearing the mechanism click open.

Now that she could get through any door she liked, she was really in business.

Stimulated by her success, Marion slipped inside with the joy of a child doing something forbidden. She took care to lock the door properly behind her. She walked across a room partially occupied by maps designed for tourist visits and carried on until she reached the northern slope. Outside, she discovered an entire steep flank covered in foolhardy vegetation, constantly battered by the winds.

Marion followed the wall of the Merveille back to the western gardens; heading back up the winding slope, she found herself back at the door that led into the Merveille via its lowest level, where she had dug up the plants with Sister Anne.

She arrived in the storeroom, a gigantic chamber crisscrossed by columns. All the plants and shrubs she had dug up with Sister Anne were still there, freshly watered. Marion considered the place too dark and too cold for sitting and headed up the spiral staircase to the floor above and the Salle des Chevaliers. She remembered passing through it during her tour with the nun. Suddenly she missed the old woman.

You can't treat her like an old *woman! How old is she? Fifteen years older than you? It's ridiculous. . . . It's her skin. . . . The moment she displays any emotion, it crumples into myriad lines. . . .*

Sister Anne's blue eyes came back into her mind, suddenly inspiring her to great good sense.

What was happening to her? Was it the setting? Marion crossed the fabulous stone forest and wandered along a gnarled corridor, climbed up and down steps, opened doors that protected crypts or led outside, and in a very short time she realized that she no longer knew where she was.

Then she entered Belle-Chaise, the abbey's old courthouse. An army of benches with backs stood in serried ranks, facing a long table that looked like an altar. With its slender windows and its high wooden ceiling shaped like an upside-down ship's hull, the room made Marion feel that she could spend a few tranquil moments here, particularly when she spotted a chair with a cushion in one corner. She picked it up and wedged it behind the enormous fireplace, not far from a window that filtered in the gray light appropriate to this sullen day.

Now that she was at her post, Marion reminded herself of one of those attendants you meet in the Louvre museum, sitting at the entrance to the galleries. She wriggled about on her chair to get comfortable, then stood up to drag over a bench, which sent a horrible grating noise echoing right through the hall. Marion listened for a moment and, detecting nothing but the wind whistling through the corridors, she dragged it a bit further and sat down, stretching out her legs on it.

This time, she was all set.

When she opened the diary, it was with the desire to discover the exact link between this Jezebel woman and Jeremy.

Marion shivered as gooseflesh climbed up her arms. It was cool and damp.

She read the first few lines of the passage where she had halted previously, while the sentences that followed dissolved to form an image, sounds, smells . . . and the characters sprang to life, before her wondering senses.

· 16 ·

The two investigators, Azim and Jeremy, met up for breakfast on the terrace of a café, opposite the Ezbekiya gardens. An arid heat had already taken hold of the city, bedecking every forehead with a salty veil. The two colleagues ate nothing, confining themselves to steaming cups of tea. Behind them, a group of hotel employees, dragomans hired for the occasion, and a variety of individuals in the pay of Westerners were lining up to procure tickets for the forthcoming Oum Kalsoum concert.

The two men ran over the previous day's research, which had borne no fruit for either of them.

"I can't stop thinking about what the doctor said about that piece of horn," confided Azim. "He really thinks it is a fragment of nail? How is that possible? How could anyone have nails like that?"

"I agree with you, the old doctor is mistaken. That being said, it could form part of a costume. . . . "

Azim drew back in his seat. The early-morning sun lit up his round face and his mustache and hair shone with the brand-new South American pomade, *gomina argentina*.

"I can see what you're getting at; I too have told myself that the murderer must be an Arab," he announced. "Those children did not speak English, and even one of yours who spoke a little Arabic could not have made them trust him enough to come alone to such sordid places each time."

"Except with the lure of profit," Jeremy corrected him. "But I must confess I rather agree; an Englishman would have drawn attention more easily. On the other hand, a black from Sudan could have done it."

"Why?"

"Because there are many of them in Cairo, they speak Arabic, are sufficiently integrated not to be noticed, and because certain ethnic groups have probably retained traditional dress. Again, it is the hunter slumbering within the killer who provides me with this lead. In many southern tribes, men don tribal dress to go hunting, together with charms, made from ivory or horn, for example. . . . "

Azim wore a sad smile. "Still this idea of the hunter? But it's coherent, I give you that. It is entirely coherent. Where I am less in agreement with you is regarding the integrated status of the blacks. In your eyes perhaps, but"—he leaned toward the Englishman—"in the eyes of a native of Cairo, a Sudanese is still a Sudanese. I shall go and ask a few questions in the districts where the victims lived. You never know."

They set off around ten o'clock, when they felt it was no longer too early to go and question the families of the previous victims. Azim was to play the principal role, as Jeremy did not speak Arabic. However, he wished to be present, to show that British authority was openly involved and especially so that he could evaluate the atmosphere and people's attitudes himself.

They began with the el-Huseiniya district, above the cemetery of Bab el-Nasr. They had to abandon the car at the entrance to sharia Negm el-Din, and continued on foot through the labyrinth of alleyways, darkened by tall, crumbling façades. The streets were of beaten earth and some of the buildings had been around for several centuries, without ever benefiting from any maintenance whatsoever.

It took them three-quarters of an hour to find the tiny house where the eight members of Samir's family lived, crowded together. Samir had been discovered in the nearby cemetery.

They were invited to sit down on patched and mended cushions, and offered burning-hot, sugary-sweet tea.

Several children in rags shouted and played in the adjoining room.

Azim conversed with the patriarch, a man worn-down to the tendons, with skin like parchment and the physique of a seventy-year-old even though he was probably twenty or thirty years younger. Pain twisted his features as Azim spoke his son's name.

The low table on which his wife placed a round tray was a chicken cage, turned upside-down. As he noticed this, Jeremy had even more difficulty drinking his sweetened tea, knowing what a treasure it must represent with regard to their finances.

Words were exchanged between the two Arabs, Azim interrupting the other man from time to time, probably to obtain clarification.

Several times, Jeremy caught the expression of fear that the mistress of the house was having difficulty concealing. Azim seemed to be focusing solely on the father.

From time to time, a brown face made an appearance in the opening that led to the kitchen; never the same one, never the same age. From the sound of the voices and the stridence or low pitch of the children's shouting, Jeremy deduced that there must be at least one adolescent aged around fifteen, and several little ones between five and ten. As quickly as it had appeared, the child vanished back into the noisy horde that did not seem to have been subdued at all by the death of one of their number.

Jeremy sat in frustrated silence, the language and cultural barriers making it impossible for him to do anything. He could see that it was necessary to ask the wife some questions too. To have her opinion. Sound out her feelings as a bereaved mother. And understand her anxiety.

As he was finishing burning his lips on his tea, the unexpected happened: Azim turned suddenly to the wife and addressed her. The husband tried to reply but Azim silenced him with an imperious gesture.

The poor woman, caught between the devil and the deep blue sea, scarcely dared open her mouth. Azim added something.

She began to stammer.

And as if the floodgates of the Aswan Dam had suddenly opened, the words came pouring out. She held back her tears until she had said everything.

Jeremy thought he caught the last word, as she spoke it after a moment's silence, almost whispering it, fear adhering her tongue to the roof of her mouth: "*Ghul.*"

"*Ghul?*" Azim repeated, in surprise.

In haste, they were shown outside, politely but firmly. Just as he was leaving, Jeremy said to Azim, "Tell them this is to thank them for their cooperation."

"Excuse me?"

Jeremy handed a few Egyptian pounds to the mistress of the house. The Englishman detected a certain reticence in the woman's tear-filled eyes, but the mother in her took the upper hand and clasped the notes eagerly.

A little later, the two investigators were walking back up an evil-smelling alley toward their car.

"What did you find out?" Jeremy wanted to know.

"I asked the usual questions, which had already been asked at the start of the investigation, and the answers are the same: no particular details in the days preceding their son's disappearance, no strange individuals in the vicinity of their home, nothing like that. I asked them specifically about a black man, but nothing. Their son was a good boy and had no reason to follow a stranger. The night he was killed, he should have been in his bedroom with his brothers. He went out while everyone was asleep. It wasn't difficult: It's a very old house and it is possible to enter or leave without making a sound."

"I saw you questioning the mother; what did she say to you?"

"Well . . . not very much, actually. She talks a lot with the neighboring women, who have all been comforting her since the death. And they gossip. Is that the right word? Gossip?"

"Yes, Azim," said Jeremy, somewhat exasperated by this detour in their conversation.

"One of them is the friend of a friend of the mother of the little girl who was murdered at the beginning of the month. Do you follow me?"

"Yes, I think so."

"That creates links, associations. And the women in these places are the consciousness of the district, and its eyes and ears too. Some have seen things. Here, others at Abbasiya, in the very poor district. And they think they know what is killing their children."

Jeremy halted midstep. He stared at Azim, eyes wide. "And?"

"Oh, it won't please the little Englishman in you."

"Tell me anyway."

"You haven't been here long enough to believe in our fairy tales, have you?"

"I don't even speak Arabic, Azim."

"The women think that what is killing their children is a *ghul*."

Without asking him to repeat it, Jeremy shook his head, indicating that he was listening to the hypothesis, but was unable to believe it.

"A ghoul, is that it? Where did I read about those? In Bram Stoker, I would imagine. . . . So what is it, a sort of vampire?"

"The *ghul* is a female demon, an evil creature, like the jinn for example. *One Thousand and One Nights* mention them frequently. It is a monster that eats the dead, and which can assume an appearance that is sometimes hideous, sometimes attractive."

"Azim, these women make up stories, they frighten themselves, and they dig up the old superstitions. This one fits the bill because it is a metaphor for what the killer really is. A man in appearance, capable of luring children, and a monster inside, capable of torturing them."

Azim smoothed his mustache. "It is not a metaphor if you believe what they say," he objected. "Because there are witnesses to its presence. A strange being was seen prowling at night, sniffing the children's clothing that was drying on the roofs, attempting to climb through the windows into the children's bedrooms, fortunately without success. A thing dressed in a black robe, and a deep hood to conceal its horrible appearance. Its hands are hooklike and it moves silently; few have seen it. It is even whispered that animals are so terrified that they run away from it."

"Let's see, you know we won't find any witnesses, any who will give their names, I mean to say; it's a myth, and there are heaps of spiteful people willing to make others believe they have seen this creature, but when you investigate, you never find anybody."

"Because that is how Cairo is, built from darkness and light, knowledge and ignorance, on myths and promises. And look at the result! The largest city in the Arab world! Proud and coveted! And you whites come all the way from the Americas just to see its pyramids."

"Spare me the militant speech, Azim. Right, so is there nothing other than this ghoul story?"

Azim seemed disappointed by his colleague's brusqueness. All at once his flow tailed off, along with the beginnings of a smile.

"No. This evening I shall write up all the small details I have noted down about the child and what his parents told me."

They reached their car in silence and went off to visit the other families, which took all day.

Each time, it was a large and very poor family. Nothing unusual had been noticed before their child's disappearance. Jeremy insisted on giving a few banknotes to each family, and in so doing divested himself of a large sum, as Azim looked on with as much surprise as admiration.

The two investigators separated at the end of the day, Azim heading off to the police station to write up his notes, and Jeremy to his usual *qawha* to shake off the weariness of an additional day.

He had been there only an hour when Azim entered, sweat dripping from his brow. He looked round the café, a sheet of paper in his hand. When he spotted Jeremy, he rushed to his table and laid down the document.

"The same school!"

Jeremy sank back into his chair.

"I am a fool!" thundered Azim. "I did not make the connection when the parents gave me the information, and my men did not think to ask for the information when they were conducting the investigation. The dead children all went to the same foundation. Keoraz. It's not really a school, but they went there to receive training, and that is a point common to all of them!"

In the haze of tobacco smoke, Jeremy's eyes suddenly held the same vacant gaze as a blind man's.

"Are you all right?" Azim asked anxiously, furtively checking that the glasses placed in front of the Englishman did indeed contain the vestiges of coffee and not alcohol.

Eventually Jeremy nodded.

"I know somebody at that foundation." He laid a hand on the sheet of paper. "Let me deal with this, if you don't mind." And the report vanished into his pocket.

· 17 ·

M arion slammed the diary shut.

She was seething with impatience at the thought of reading what came next, but first she must relieve herself. Out of curiosity, she nevertheless turned a few pages and caught surprising words, a scene beneath the pyramids . . . an animated conversation . . .

Marion was about to place the book on her chair and head off in search of toilets, but changed her mind. She chose instead to take it with her, along with her bunch of keys.

A door creaked at the entrance to the Belle Chaise.

Marion turned her head, ready to explain herself, but there was nobody there. The door was shut.

The wind intermittently whistled between the gaps, creating a hissing, breathing sound throughout the abbey. Was that him, the culprit?

Don't start imagining things . . .

Marion went out and soon crossed a little overhanging kitchen garden, from where she could look down on part of the village and the bay.

A small sandy recess was shielded from eyes and from the elements.

She was in such dire need that the thought of urinating there passed through her mind. She dismissed it hastily, put off less by the indecency of the act than by the fear of being caught.

Marion went down some steps and got lost again in the building's endless corridors. A spectral light forced its way as best it could through the rose windows, loopholes, and pointed windows.

Walking by a pillar, she stopped in her tracks and suddenly turned around, realizing she had just been past there.

As she turned, she became aware of a movement in the distance. In the time it took her to focus on this distant shadow, it had gone.

She thought she had made out a habit similar to those worn by the men of the fraternity. She had seen nothing more, neither a corpulent stomach nor a distinctive walk, and still less a face.

Had someone spotted her?

If so, the brother would certainly have stopped, at least greeted her, she assumed.

"He wouldn't reprimand you for being here and he could tell you where the toilets are," whispered a little voice inside her head.

Marion rushed forward. She reached the steps, climbed onto the granite bridge where the individual had disappeared, and dashed through an arch.

At top speed, she crossed the next room in the direction of the one and only staircase the figure she was pursuing could have taken.

Running down the spiral staircase, she paused for breath by a window and saw a long courtyard down below.

The figure was trotting quickly across it. It was impossible to identify, for it was entirely covered by a black robe with a hood pulled down over the head; from a distance, it looked like a monk's habit.

Marion sped up and was soon outside again, breathing hard.

There was now no trace of her fugitive.

Because the more she thought about it, the more it seemed to her that the other person wasn't just walking, but in a hurry to escape.

That's nonsense. . . . It's that police story, going to your head. . . .

Marion sighed noisily as she got her breath back.

What an adventure! Yes, but . . . let's face it, adventure is a very big word. . . .

She thought of Brother Serge again. Of him, and of his concern for Marion to be occupied, not unduly bored.

Right, let's look on the bright side. Taking a pee isn't urgent anymore, any minute now it's going to become a catastrophe. . . .

The courtyard led into the guardroom, which Marion crossed, rejoicing as she saw the empty entrance booth. The cashier was warming herself with a coffee, along with one or more of the guides who were forced to wait all day in case some visitors turned up. She passed under the barbican and hurried home.

After relieving herself, she made herself some tea and took it to the corner sofa, to continue her reading.

The sight of that person fleeing in his mysterious robes titillated her.

Did the brothers usually walk along with their hoods up? She didn't have that impression. . . . But anything was possible.

All the same, what with the riddle she had received on her arrival, the "secret" visit to her quarters, and this strange presence, that was enough to make her ask herself a few questions! Undoubtedly the riddle was just a game, the intrusion well-meaning and designed to promote her safety, but nevertheless Marion felt the combined effect oppressive.

It's the place. It's making you paranoid. I mean even more paranoid than you already were.

Sooner or later, she was going to discover that the brother she had pursued had nothing to do with her; he just happened to be there and was in a hurry.

The creaking door . . . in the big room where I was reading. The door creaked when I stood up, as if someone was watching me and then withdrew so as not to be caught.

This hypothesis implied that she had been followed through the Mount's corridors, and spied upon. . . . With what aim? The fraternity had agreed to hide her, not to keep her under permanent surveillance; that wasn't part of their arrangement. She mustn't go crazy. Marion shook her head; she was going a bit too far.

It was time to move on to something else, to plunge back into Egypt during the 1920s.

From her place on the sofa, she swiftly ran through the list of items in her fridge and remembered that she had a pan of fried vegetables for lunch. Everything was settled; she had the whole day to herself.

To read.

She hadn't read three words when she got up and pushed the hall table up against the front door.

"There," she said. "That way, my paranoia will be happy too."

Marion stretched out under the bay window, the cup of tea in one hand and the diary in the other.

· 18 ·

While Azim was attempting to identify the fourth victim, Jeremy Matheson was being jolted about at the mercy of the streetcar taking him to Giza.

After the indefinable contours of the city, the desert had an exceptionally linear appearance.

Jeremy had spent some quite long periods in this sea of sand, where the interminable horizon of saffron dunes tore at the retina, overtaxed by the contrast with an incredibly deep, indigo sky. The desert was infinity, placed within the reach of mankind. There, silence became opressive; after a few days, the absence of all sound created a continuous buzzing, before the ear and the brain became acclimatized to this scorching torpor.

Jeremy placed his palm against the glass as they approached the Giza plateau.

The triangle of pyramids imposed itself on him forcefully, like a warning of his own ephemeral nature. They did not rise up out of the desert; on the contrary, it was the desert in its entirety that unfurled before them in an endless carpet, offering as many tributes as there were grains of sand.

From the high ground in Cairo, they excited curiosity; once you were at the foot of them you trembled, both with wonder and with a fearful respect.

Line fourteen of the streetcar system terminated, five miles from the center of Cairo, in front of the Mena House Hotel, a caravansary prized by all of Western high society.

The tourist season was nearing its end, but the pyramids were attracting as many visitors as ever. The sun hadn't been up for more than two hours and already thirty or so white heads sporting extravagant hats were moving over the ridges of the Great Pyramid, standing out against the blue sky as little marks bent under the weight of effort.

Egypt was the foremost destination for all European aristocrats, all the planet's crowned heads, and their interminable hangers-on.

The Mena House Hotel was an oasis of luxury in the middle of the emerging desert, offering incomparable terraces where guests could take their rest under the watchful eyes of these outsized tombs.

Jeremy knew he was going to find her here, taking her breakfast facing the marvels. He had called the villa in Heliopolis that very morning, very early, but had been told that "Madam is not here." At this time of day, the only place she could have spent the night was here.

She adored their rooms.

Jeremy recalled her face in the shade of a fan, and her eyes, shining with greedy lust. She and he, eating lunch at the Gezira Sporting Club. And her mouth, whispering above the fan about how she adored making love with him beneath the benevolent pyramids.

Her irreverence, her verbal effrontery in such a place, still left a hollow feeling in his belly. She had no equal when it came to asserting herself, or playing on her self-assurance with men; she did it with such charming, sexual grace that nobody ever dared say anything to her. All you could do was laugh, lower your eyes or swell out your chest when she decided to provoke, to play, and she did so with sufficient delicacy that nobody else noticed.

The heat was emerging from the ground in a thick layer as fiercely as it was descending from the sky.

Jeremy swallowed with difficulty. He was desperately thirsty.

Thirsty for what? For whom?

He closed his eyes to forget these idiotic words, these futile thoughts, and entered the hotel.

She still had the same room, the one that was set apart a little, "so we don't have to keep quiet," as she used to say in her daring moments.

Jeremy took off his sunglasses and knocked at the door.

In the silence that followed, lucidity returned to him and he knew he had no business here. It was dangerous. For him.

A part of him began to hope that nobody would answer.

The door opened a little way, revealing a man in white-and-gold livery and a red fez.

"Sir?"

"I should like to speak to Miss Leenhart, please."

The servant frowned. "You must be mistaken, sir. There is no Miss—"

"Show him in," said a woman's voice behind him.

The man did so and Jeremy entered the suite with its broad bay windows, which let all the light of the plateau into the vast living room.

A wooden balcony ran along the entire length of the room. Through the open windows, the heady scent of jasmine wafted up from the hotel gardens.

Jeremy walked out to the table that had been laid out under a fabric parasol. The finest porcelain cups and plates were set out on the embroidered tablecloth, between pots of jam.

And in her rattan armchair, a woman dabbed her lips with a napkin and sat up.

Although he knew her beauty well, it took Jeremy's breath away all over again.

Her long black hair against her snow-white skin.

Her large, green eyes beneath a fringe of incredibly long lashes.

Her cheeks, whose roundness was emphasized on the left by a beauty spot right in the middle. Her arms, so long and slender.

She was wearing a green dress that fell open at both sides below her hips, and that Jeremy had never seen before; there was a large knot on the low neckline. A dress he had never touched, never unfastened. This thought clutched at his heart.

Her lips, which were a timid pink, opened in a polite smile. "Have you forgotten? I am Mrs. Keoraz now."

"As you wish . . . "

She inclined her head, and an ebony-colored lock of hair fell over her forehead. She could be as elegant and beautiful as she could be cold and distant. In a moment she had switched to the second of these aspects.

"If you have come to take up my time, then respect what I am," she cut him short, all traces of a smile gone.

She picked up a slice of bread and spread it with rose preserve.

"You know I will never call you that," he said, dragging over a chair in order to sit facing her. "I need you."

"That need is not reciprocated. What do you want?"

Still the same repartee, capable of trading her velvet tongue for the serpent's fangs, mused Jeremy. This allusion brought to life a whole host of memories, which tortured him inwardly.

"Well?" she demanded.

He took a long breath before beginning. "I need your help. It is about your foundation."

"Francis's, you mean."

Jeremy clenched his jaw, hollowing his already emaciated cheeks still further. "And which you are involved with," he said between clenched teeth. "Don't play this game with me, Jezebel."

"What game?"

"You know very well! This business of blowing hot and cold. Not with me, I know you too well."

She put down her slice of bread and stared coldly at him. "So? Doesn't it work? Dare to tell me it has no effect on you. I know how to make men suffer, don't underestimate me in that art; you are all transparent to me. I was curious, I loved you all, I collected you all, I observed you from every angle, and then, I became tired. You are transparent to me. I see through you as I see through all the others. So don't come here to ask for my help and tell me that I produce no effect on you, otherwise why would you be wearing an expression like that?"

Jeremy sat up straight, aware that he had hung his head too much. She classed him among all the others, accorded him no importance whatsoever; she counted him as just one more name, one more pleasure, without taking account of what he was.

Yes, she was right, she knew what to do to make him suffer. That was exactly right. Grant him no importance and act as if their affair had been just one more domino in her own personal game.

"Jez . . . " he said, very quietly, after a time.

He could not continue; she started eating as she observed him, without helping him, waiting to see what words would extricate themselves from the turbulent mess inside him.

Jeremy made what he knew was a terrible mistake in her presence. He lowered his eyes. He escaped the vise of her emerald irises to sweep his gaze across the windows that led to her apartments. Behind her, the glazed door opened onto the bedroom. Onto an immense, soft bed whose sheets spilled onto the floor. Jeremy swallowed his saliva as the ditch within him became an abyss.

"He . . . is he there?" he managed to ask.

"Who? The man who is giving me pleasure?"

Jeremy wanted to hate her. Detest her to the point of banishing her from his existence.

She had not said "Mr. Keoraz" or "my husband," which would have been painful enough; no, she had used him as an instrument for her pleasure. Which was even worse. And she knew it. She knew that Jeremy had loved her beyond the emotions of the mind or the heart, to the point of considering their lovemaking as the sole materialization of this powerful love. Carnal love had been everything. Because she was not playing during those moments, it was the only time of rest, the sole moment when she was herself, naked, stripped bare. And he who possessed her in the moment of orgasm could gaze upon her true soul.

This jealousy went beyond all those petty emotions of daily life that Jeremy had lost. She knew it. She was sneering at him.

"He is showing some friends from London around," she confided. "Why? Do you wish to speak with him, perhaps?"

"Stop. I need you to help me. It's not about me. It's about children."

A subtle movement in the alchemy of the constituent parts of her face indicated to Jeremy that he had hit home.

"Children from your foundation who are dying."

She put down the piece of bread she had started eating directly on the tablecloth, and her eyes narrowed to two long, dark slits.

· 19 ·

In the meantime, Azim was wearing out the paving stones and beaten earth of Cairo's eastern districts. An artist often used by the police had agreed to produce as accurate a portrait as possible of the last victim, taking care not to reproduce the wounds that had deformed the face. Detective Matheson had asked him to leave him with the investigation into the foundation that had educated the dead children, but he had not asked him to keep his distance.

By going to the head office, the little Egyptian had identified the fourth victim. He had succeeded in meeting a certain number of people involved, until one of them immediately recognized the child's portrait.

Seleem Yehya, aged ten.

Azim transferred the information to the police secretary. As luck would have it, in order to be accepted by the foundation, the children had to supply as much information as possible upon registration. Beginning with the address where they could be found. The old districts of Cairo had the peculiar characteristic that the streets did not all have names, still less numbers. When you asked the way, in general you had to be guided by landmarks like a fountain, a house with blue shutters, or a crossroads with five branches. . . . Seleem's address had been transcribed according to this code.

Before noon, Azim had found the child's parents, and become the bearer of the terrible tidings.

He had questioned them briefly, between the sobs and the shouts of rage, before vanishing into the sordid street where they lived.

Seleem had the same profile as the preceding victims. A calm, lively, and curious child—hence his presence at the foundation— and one who did not go looking for trouble.

And, above all, he was described as obedient.

How could the murderer succeed in getting good children out of their homes, in the middle of the night, and of their own free will?

The desire to find out a little more about this foundation made him seethe with impatience. But he had promised Detective Matheson that he would do nothing, that he would wait for him.

The key to the problem was in the murderer's method of making the children come to him. Azim could sense it.

How do you lure a little boy or a little girl to you? How do you persuade them to leave their homes soundlessly, without a word, right in the middle of the night?

A Westerner with money or simply original objects bought from his country could incite this curiosity. But this hypothesis implied an Englishman who could speak Arabic, capable of making these children trust him, and who moreover ran the risk of being noticed more easily in these districts than an Arab. Unless he moved around in a djellaba. Or if he knew the district very well, so as to avoid the busy streets. Everything was possible in the final reckoning.

Azim repeated these questions to himself, over and over.

He did have one small idea, but it was unacceptable.

A magic spell.

An evil enchantment, in the manner of the *ghuls*, who lured their prey through demoniacal manipulations, lies, and enchantments.

Of course, that didn't stand up.

No more than that rumor that was haunting the eastern districts. That the killer was a *ghul*.

And yet . . . that could explain a lot of things. *The extreme violence*—no man could be so brutal with a child, except a madman who had become an animal. *The traces of enormous claws*—they had no plausible explanation for the time being; nobody apart from that cynical old doctor could believe that it was really nails that had produced such deep wounds, and moreover he had not come to this opinion through his medical knowledge, but through a lack of other ideas. *The spells*—that would explain why the children came deliberately to the killer. And above all—*the witness reports*—the hypothesis came from them after all, from witnesses who had seen the beast.

Witness reports.

"If that's where the foundations of this monster's existence lie, that's where we must search if we are to have a clear conscience!" said Azim out loud as he walked along a street in Darb el-Ahmar, an old district of the city.

He stopped to drink from a fountain and splashed his face and neck before setting off again for el-Abbasiya, to find the family he had visited the previous day with Jeremy Matheson.

On the way, he was astonished that his English colleague had not refuted the *ghul* hypothesis. He was so closed to anything irrational that he hadn't even wanted to listen.

Azim had told him that *ghuls* were female demons. But sperm had been found on each victim. The Englishman had not paid sufficient attention.

Azim had already been turning this question over and over in his mind for a while. Evidently this *ghul* story was just a legend to frighten people . . . but what or who was hiding behind this thing that wandered through the alleyways at night? For Azim had no doubt that there was indeed something. He knew people like himself, prompt to liven up events, but there was never smoke without fire. Behind the story of the *ghul,* a reality was hiding.

Azim reached the house of mourning. The children were not there, only the father and his wife. The detective questioned the wife for several minutes, asking for the names of the women who could give him information, and where to find them. Then he left in search of them.

He found two of the three. The first mentioned her uncle as the direct witness of the creature; Azim asked to meet him. He lived in the Gamaliya district.

The second spoke to him of another woman whose husband said he had watched the *ghul.* Azim's heart leaped when he learned that this couple lived under the cemetery of Bab el-Nasr, also in Gamaliya. They were not the same people. Azim obtained the necessary information and thanked her.

An hour later, he was in the company of an old man, with a gray mustache and skin tanned by decades of burning sun, walking along in a blue djellaba, the color worn by the Tuaregs, the "Blue Men of the Desert." Azim told the man why he had come, and explained that his niece had sent him about this "beast" he said he had seen.

They walked side by side down a street so narrow that the superannuated buildings that rose up on either side made it look like a deep gulf.

"Tell me in what circumstances it occurred," said the detective.

"It was late, and I had spent the evening with a friend who still keeps a *ghoraz*.* You know, it's just more of the same with these Englishmen now. They say we are independent, and yet they want to close all the places where we smoke. Who are they to impose that on us, eh?"

"Of course. But let's get back to that evening. You say you were in a *ghoraz*. Had you smoked a great deal?"

"Not more than usual."

"And you were on your way back home when it happened?"

"Yes, it was a little lower down, we're almost there. I was walking slowly; the smoking had made me a little light-headed. And then suddenly, I sensed that there was something. First of all, the nape of my neck shivered. I thought my hair was standing on end all by itself! Anyhow, I didn't think about it, I flattened myself against the wall. I have to say that it was quite dark—there's none of your fancy gaslight here!" The old man had begun to talk loudly, almost shouting.

"I understand." Azim calmed him, placing a hand on his elbow as if to guide him.

"I flattened myself against the wall, really you know! It was my body that guided me and saved my life! And do you know why? Because the hashish had opened my mind to a better understanding of the world. My mind was open to the things of the world beyond! And it sensed what was approaching, and it gave the warning to my body, and it passed it on to me, so that I—the man on the surface—could understand that something inhuman was approaching."

This testimony must be taken with a large pinch of salt, thought Azim, almost disappointed. The old man had probably been too

* A place for smoking hashish

much under the influence of the drug that evening to think clearly. One must separate what might be true but embroidered from what was just the fruit of a delirious mind.

"And the *ghul* emerged from the darkness, wrapped up in its black robe, a big hood on its head to hide it. It was walking slowly and it was very tall, almost seven feet, and it entered the blind alley down below."

Indeed, they arrived at a crossing of ways, itself as narrow as the streets that led off from it. The old uncle indicated the place he had stood that evening and pointed his finger toward the blind alley the beast had entered.

"Even if my body was in control of me, I would not have known what it really was if it hadn't raised its head before leaving. It wanted to look up high and there, in the moonlight, I saw its demon's face. It has no face, nothing but flesh and teeth! I have been having nightmares about it every night since."

Azim bent to examine the interior of the blind alley. It was not very deep or tall in relation to the rest of the district. Several single-story houses stood in a line, some of them so dilapidated that living there was unthinkable.

"Did you stay long after that?" demanded the detective.

"At least five minutes. I was paralyzed, I was really afraid, you know. And then I kept close to the houses and walked home as fast as my legs would carry me."

"So you walked past the blind alley?"

"Yes. I couldn't see clearly, but I think it was empty. In any event the monster hadn't come out again when I passed."

Azim nodded as his eyes swept across the house-fronts. He counted thirteen doors. But it was possible to flee by climbing the wall at the far end, which was not very high.

"Do you know the district well?" Azim asked the old man, who nodded. "Then you perhaps know where one would come out on the other side of the wall, at the far end?"

"In a backyard, full of rubble."

So it was possible to leave in any direction. Azim had difficulty hiding his disappointment. "Have you seen it again since?"

"Oh, no! And I don't want to!"

Azim thanked the man and left in search of the second witness, a seller of clothing. He found him at his shop, in the midst of prayer. The muezzin had called the faithful for Asr, the afternoon prayer. Azim waited outside the door until it ended. He recited his prayers from the Koran in silence. In agreeing to take up such an important office in the police, he had also agreed to put his religious practices to one side during working hours.

The trader had seen the same creature: tall, covered by a black robe and a hood.

"How tall?"

"I don't know, a head taller than me."

The man measured around five foot five. All the same, less than the immense size claimed by the old hashish smoker, who had seen a *ghul* seven feet tall. Maybe six one or two, Azim supposed.

"I was on my terrace," the witness continued, "and I saw it pass by just below, on the neighbor's roof. There, it took an interest in some children's clothes that were drying, and it jumped onto the next house, where it spent a little time by a skylight, trying to get inside. It's a way of getting into the bedroom where my neighbor's children sleep. It wanted to go in, but as it couldn't open it, it left. I am certain it is what killed the children. That's what it is searching for at night."

"It moved from roof to roof?"

"Yes, and with a great deal of agility; it makes no sound."

"Could you make out the face?"

There was a silence between the two men.

"Yes."

The trader caught his breath and took the plunge. "It often looked behind itself. And when it passed beneath my eyes, it walked forward and then, just before jumping onto the neighbor's roof, it turned its head."

He sat down on a stool, his eyes staring into nothingness. "Allah be thanked, I did not see its eyes. I think it would have robbed me of my reason. It had no . . . "

He slid a hand over his own cheeks, his nose, then his chin and his lips. "There was nothing human about it. No skin, no contours, nothing but tendons, blood, and teeth. Teeth that gleamed right to the edges of the jawbones, almost as far as the ears. I shall never be able to forget it."

Azim was captivated by the account. He forgot where he was and what he was doing amid all these fabrics, hanging from the ceiling.

"And its hands . . . I saw its hands too, and even in the darkness I could see that they weren't human. Its fingers were too long, and . . . and it had enormous claws, even more menacing than an eagle's talons."

Azim blinked and his mind cleared. He asked the trader for a little information and discovered that he lived less than five hundred and fifty yards as the crow flies from the place where the *ghul* had been spotted by the old smoker.

"Do you have children?" asked Azim.

"Four."

"Then do not let them sleep on the roof, even if it is hot."

The man approached Azim. "Are you mad? I *saw* that monster. I would never do anything of the kind! And my children never go out alone."

"A wise precaution. Even if I do think that it is unlikely that this . . . *thing* will come back through your district—"

"Didn't anyone tell you?" asked the trader in astonishment. "It didn't come just once. I have seen it three times."

· 20 ·

Fantasy.

Marion got up to stretch her numb muscles.

This tale of a creature prowling the darkness, this ghoul, was pure fantasy.

She considered the diary's black cover.

What kind of text was it? What had she happened upon? For the first time since she had begun reading, she felt uncomfortable. She had felt uneasy during the descriptions of the children's murders, and yet that was part of the story, part of the investigation. But this tale of a monster betrayed a certain naïveté that Marion didn't know if she should impute to the man or to the era.

The author, Jeremy Matheson, wrote down in the first person what he had experienced or felt, and wrote a long parenthesis on what his colleague, this man Azim, had done during this time, giving glimpses of the fact that they had spoken about it subsequently. It was curious to note how precise he could be in his descriptions, almost romantic in places. He even attributed precise emotions to Azim, so intimate that it was unlikely they had really discussed them. No, Jeremy had made calculated guesses, deduced, or imagined.

Nevertheless, the theory of the ghoul remained hard to swallow.

Marion stifled a yawn.

It was midafternoon, she had only paused briefly for lunch, and her hours of reading had made her feel groggy.

The weather was sad, the sky displaying an entire spectrum of grays, from broken white at the zenith to an ashen horizon.

She pulled on a warm sweater and opted for the trench coat in order to go for a walk; the cold had intensified over the last two days. The feeling of the diary in her pocket was almost reassuring.

If the notion of the ghoul beggared belief, she had to admit that she was gripped by this tale, and excited by what the yellowed pages still held in store for her. Since she had found it, she had almost never separated herself from her precious treasure. It exerted a perverse fascination over her. It provoked a voyeurism that she could never hold back.

She walked along the edge of the little cemetery, and skirted around the entrance to the parish church of Saint-Pierre to get back to the rue Grande. From there, she headed into a passageway between two ancient buildings and reached the curtain wall. From one tower to the next she walked along, buffeted by the wind's powerful breath. Down below, the sea had left stretches of water in its nocturnal wake, puddles with absinthe-colored reflections, some of which reflected misshapen images back to the skies.

The Tombelaine rock loomed up in the distance, standing alone with its cloud of barnacle geese. It inspired a certain melancholy in Marion, this lost fragment of France in exile, damned forever amid the mists and tides of the bay.

Damned or privileged, she corrected herself.

Its stark, ascetic shape made her feel even sadder.

A dark shape was moving diagonally between the Mount and Tombelaine. Marion strained her eyes and confirmed what she had sensed: A man was calmly walking back toward her.

He made a large detour and Marion was just thinking that there was no reason for it, when she recalled what people said about the bay. The moving sands had claimed their share of victims. They bit ankles and drew down calves, sucking on their food at leisure, until the rising tide came along and drowned whatever jutted out above the sands.

The stroller clearly knew the way, and was getting closer to the curtain wall.

When he was a short distance away, Marion took in the details of his appearance. He was a mature man, tall and slender, not brown-haired as she had at first thought, but wearing a sailor's cap over his white hair. He moved elegantly, hands thrust into the pockets of a navy blue pea jacket.

He hailed her with a little wave of his arm.

She was at first astonished, then realized that she was the only person on the entire length of the ramparts and that she had been watching him for a while already, which he was sure to have noticed.

Marion responded with an answering wave.

To her own surprise, she started walking along the curtain wall, parallel to the walker, descending toward the entrance to the village.

They met under the arch of the Porte du Roy.

The stranger took off his hat, leaving his lily-white hair ruffled, and bowed slightly, hands behind his back. "Madam."

He was much older than she had at first thought. At least eighty, thought Marion. His face was half-invisible beneath a week's growth of beard, as dazzlingly white as his hair, and two deep furrows ran vertically down his cheeks. His eyes were barely discernible under the protection of his half-closed eyelids, yet they radiated an astonishing vivacity, seemingly piercing right through her. The man held himself perfectly upright, his bearing in no way forced, and accompanied by a certain natural charisma. As a young man, he must surely have been stunning for, despite his age, Marion found him very attractive.

"I don't believe I've had the honor of meeting you before, however I think I know who you are. The village is small, and information circulates quickly, even more so than on that Internet everyone is talking about. You are on retreat with the brotherhood, are you not?"

"That is correct."

"Allow me to introduce myself: I am Joe."

"Joe?" she repeated.

"Yes, that's my name. I bid you welcome, madam . . . ?"

"Oh, I'm sorry, Marion."

She held out her hand and he shook it affectionately. His skin was like parchment; *perhaps because of the cold,* she thought.

"Delighted to make your acquaintance. The thing is, we don't have many visitors during the winter, and even fewer long-term residents."

He had a hint of an accent that Marion couldn't quite place. *Alsace,* she thought uncertainly.

The Mount really was a veritable Tower of Babel. The majority of the inhabitants she came across were not natives of the area but had been imported from the four corners of the country.

"I spotted you on the ramparts just now. It's a magnificent walk, and if I may offer one small piece of advice: Go up there at dusk, it is beautiful enough to burn your eyes. From a distance, the grasses take on orange and violet tints; it's incredible."

Marion replaced a stray lock of hair behind her ear. "I shall make a note of that, thank you. Have you been to Tombelaine?"

"Indeed."

"It must be a beautiful place."

"That it is. I can take you there sometime if you would like; it's around four miles, there and back. On the other hand, don't try your luck alone; the edges of the bay are treacherous. You have to know your way to get there."

"That's what I've heard. I'd be delighted to accompany you next time. You . . . you live here, if I understand rightly. . . . "

"Yes, a little higher up, but come along and have some tea, if you're not busy?"

Marion nodded and followed the old man as he started walking up the rue Grande.

"Is the brotherhood's welcome to your taste?" he asked.

"Yes, everybody is very nice," replied Marion. "And I have all the tranquillity I was dreaming of."

"Tranquillity! You were certainly inspired when you chose Mont-Saint-Michel if it's tranquillity you're after. And there is no better place than the abbey in which to meditate."

"From what you say, it sounds as if you've been here a long time."

"Oh, yes. But no time at all in comparison with that . . . stone," he said, looking up at the soaring mass of the summit.

As they walked up the street, Marion was surprised to note that he was really much taller than she was; he must be almost six two.

"Where are you staying?" he inquired. "Opposite the cemetery, I assume?"

"Yes, does news travel that fast here?"

"Faster than you can imagine," he said, laughing. "In fact, the brotherhood usually houses people on retreat in attic apartments lower down in the village if there are several of them, and in that little house if there is only one."

He leaned toward her with a knowing smile, and added, "I told you: I've been here a long time. . . . Everyone knows everybody else's business on the Mount."

"I can see that. . . . On that subject, how many of you are there living there at the moment?"

"Well . . . there's Béatrice the shop owner, and her son. The postal clerk only comes here to work at this time of year, like the hotel staff and the people who work at the Mère Poulard restaurant. . . . Ah, Ludwig the night watchman lives among us. The members of the brotherhood, and myself. So that makes . . . thirteen! My God, I'd never realized. So you are now doubly welcome! The fourteenth resident of the Mount, to dispel bad luck!"

"Oh, don't give me such an important part to play; people might not want me to leave," said Marion with amusement.

"Here we are."

They entered a medieval house, with lofty ceilings, broad windows, and a wooden floor that creaked underfoot. Dampness and the smell of wax shared the place between them. Joe showed Marion into an outsized living room, in which the fireplace took up more space than a Norman wardrobe.

"Do sit down, I'll be right back."

He returned a few minutes later, carrying a tray, and poured out piping hot tea accompanied by buttered biscuits.

"So, how did you end up here, if I may ask?" he wanted to know.

"By chance."

Joe gave a brief nod. "How do you mean, by chance?"

"Almost. I wanted . . . needed some rest. To recharge my batteries. I found out what was possible for me to do, the different places where I could go on retreat. The temporary vow of silence isn't my thing, so I ruled out a convent in Savoy, and the next one on my list was Mont-Saint-Michel. I didn't ask myself any more questions, and I decided to try my luck," she lied with aplomb.

Joe gazed at her, his eyes lingering on the cut in her lip, which was beginning to scar over. Then he looked her straight in the eyes. Marion observed him in return. He seemed ready to receive her confidences, imagining that here he had a battered wife fleeing from her husband, or the victim of an attack who had come here to regain inner peace. Whatever he might think, Marion saw that he was not fooled and that he could guess at a few more dramatic reasons for this retreat.

"What would you say to a good fire?" he asked with sudden enthusiasm. At which he stood up and laid a log and some twigs in the hearth. "For my part, I've been here since the war, you know!"

Marion lifted her cup of hot tea and blew gently on it. "So you know everyone, and every nook and cranny of this place, I presume."

Joe grabbed an old newspaper, which he tore into strips, crumpling them up before sliding them underneath the heap of wood. "I certainly hope so!"

Marion held back from asking him the question that kept running through her head.

She swallowed a mouthful of tea.

The living-room windows looked out onto a tiny neglected

garden, over which the ramparts loomed. The grayish sky diluted the daylight in a vast cupola.

Joe struck a match and lit the balls of paper in the fireplace.

Marion allowed her curiosity to overcome her reserve and asked, "If you've been here since the forties, perhaps you've heard of an Englishman who apparently stayed on the Mount . . . "

Joe lost interest in his burgeoning fire. "An Englishman?" he repeated. "Why an Englishman?"

She made up her reply on the spur of the moment. "It's . . . oh, just a chance thing, stuff people have told me; I just wanted to know if it was true or if someone had been playing tricks on me."

"Who told you that? Brother Gilles?"

Marion made an effort to place Brother Gilles in the whole brotherhood. He was the eldest, not very nice, with his aquiline profile. *An old grouch,* she recalled instantly. He was too close. She'd have to find somebody else, or her lie might be discovered.

"No, not at all," she replied. "It was in Avranches. A group of men trying to be funny, I would imagine. They told me that an Englishman came to the Mount for a stay . . . "

Joe shook his head. "Ah, the town. . . . They're not trustworthy. In any case there weren't any Englishmen here, not as far as I know. Was it important to you?"

Marion caught herself lying with an intoxicating ease. The words and the confidence came to her spontaneously, without hesitation, without fear; her hands were not moist and her legs were not shaking. She had revealed herself as a thoroughgoing liar in the pay of the DST, in a way.

This idea pleased her. In her own way, she embraced this new career, that of spy.

"Why are you interested in a visit by an Englishman?" asked Joe. "There are hundreds of more entertaining and mysterious things in the history of the abbey, so why that?"

"It's just that I was told that an Englishman had stayed here a while before going away again and leaving a private journal behind him. But apparently nobody has ever found this journal. I was so bored that the story was enough to appeal to me."

Joe opened his hands in a sign of powerlessness. "Sorry, but I've never heard such a story, and yet I'm the kind of old fellow people come and question about that sort of thing; I'm in a way the eyes and ears of this lonely rock. If I may permit myself, don't listen too closely to what you're told in town; the Mount gives rise to many rumors, but they are rarely true."

Behind his back, the flames rose little by little, making the branches crackle as they licked at them.

Marion drank some tea and enjoyed a biscuit as she warmed her hands before the hearth. "Just now, you asked me if it was Brother Gilles who told me that story about the Englishman. . . . Do you know him well?"

Joe bit into one of the biscuits and wiped his chin with a paper napkin. "Yes, we're both a bit like this old stone. Almost immovable in the middle of the bay."

"I don't think he likes me much," confided Marion.

"Don't fret about it. He doesn't like anybody, not you, not me, not the tourists who pass through. In any event, nobody who is not directly attached to the Mount. If you weren't born here or as good as, in his eyes you're a parasite on 'his' abbey, a cockroach liable to damage this legacy of ancient times."

"Then why doesn't he like you? You were here long before, weren't you?"

"Brother Gilles? No, he arrived a year before me, with Sister Luce, whom you must surely have noticed."

Marion remembered a very old woman, with a profile strangely similar to that of Brother Gilles, and every bit as taciturn and sour-tempered. "Indeed . . . "

"And since then they have been the repositories of the spirit of Mont-Saint-Michel, or at least they think so!"

Joe started to laugh, his mirth restrained but sincere.

"Brother Gilles and Sister Luce, are they . . . from the same family?" asked Marion with interest.

"That is a vast debate! I don't know. To see the pair of them, one as acerbic and disdainful as the other, you might think so. But in the end, I still don't know if they already resembled each other back then, or if it's this bitterness that has brought them closer together in terms of physical appearance. I just can't remember what they were like, when they were younger. That's what old age is like, my dear, it means forgetting, or getting confused. Or no longer having the strength to go far in efforts of memory. So we harp on about what we have left."

"You seem in very good form to me, for someone who's saying such things."

"Don't trust appearances, Marion, still less here than elsewhere."

He took the plate of biscuits and offered it to her so that she could take one, then took one himself. "Have you met everyone?" he asked.

"Yes, everyone you have mentioned."

"All fine folk."

"That's what they seem to me. Actually, it's quite funny because I'm discovering each inhabitant of this . . . this island in one way or another, and I find myself liking them all for the little I know of them, even though I am generally suspicious by nature, not to say misanthropic. You know, I have often thought, stupidly I agree, that only people with sinister secrets to keep could want to set up home on a pebble like this one, set apart from the world."

Joe joined his palms in front of his nose and leaned his chin on his thumbs as he gazed at the fire. "Secrets, all the families in the world have them," he confided. "All. More or less well-kept. It isn't the secrets that lead people here. It's the answers. The men and women who live here do so because their souls are like this Mount, made up of truth sometimes concealed by mists, sometimes unveiled by the sun. We are here because we are all made up of fluctuating memories, like the tide. No other place could suit us better."

"Are you talking about yourself?" Marion dared ask.

"No, I don't think so. More in the name of all the Mount's inhabitants."

Joe pointed a gnarled index finger at her. "I can see you turning pale," he said, laughing. "Don't be afraid, I'm talking in metaphors. Mont-Saint-Michel isn't the lair of melancholic people; I just . . . decode souls. That being said, I'm often wrong."

At that, he laughed even more. "I haven't frightened you, anyway?"

"No, it would take more than that. And since I've been here, I'm beginning to stop jumping at the slightest thing."

"Really? That is preferable; this village is full of indefinable sounds, especially at night. So if you are becoming accustomed—"

"I'm not afraid of sounds, but jokers."

Joe frowned. Marion swallowed. Now that she had started, she couldn't go back. And besides, the old man inspired confidence in her.

"The day after I arrived, I found an envelope in my house, well, the one I'm living in. Someone who wanted a bit of amusement, in the form of a riddle. It was no more than a game to wish me welcome . . . and to test me, I think."

"Test you? What makes you say that?"

"A simple practical joker would have wished me welcome directly in the envelope, and merely placed it inside the house. But in this case, I had to decipher a code and go out onto the Mount to find out the real meaning of the message."

Joe nodded. "It's original. And you had the determination to follow it through to the end. Congratulations."

"I had nothing else to do." Her reply fell like a guillotine, cleaving the air. They remained silent for a moment. Eventually, Marion put down her cup and stood up.

"Thank you for everything."

"If I may permit myself to paraphrase your joker: welcome here, to my home. Now that you know where I live, do drop in and pay me a visit."

Marion said goodbye and stepped out into the cool wind, which was whistling along rue Grande. She walked down the paved road to the little staircase that skirted around the parish church, then along the edge of the cemetery to her door.

On the way, she thought of Joe. About his agreeable presence, his smiling, trusting face, and about his age. She didn't understand why she liked him so much. He was at least eighty, even if his bearing was such that he looked thirty years younger.

She left her coat in the hall and switched on the lights in the living room.

It took her less than five seconds to notice it.

It was flaunting itself there, like an insult to her privacy.

A large envelope, lying on the sofa.

· 21 ·

The same paper as in the first message.

This time, there was no riddle.

No game, either.

Nothing but a request. Almost a warning.

Because you were the first person to visit us in a long time, I wanted to play with you. I note with surprise that you have happened upon something that belongs to me. That was in no way planned in our little game, a game whose only goal was to amuse us both on this immense, over-tranquil rock. But hardly had the game begun when it ended. For by appropriating what is mine, you have offended me. I know that this was not your wish, so I am inclined to put things behind us straight-away. On the sole condition that you give me back my possession. Place

it this evening in the place where you found the welcome message, at
the Gabriel Tower. And we shall call it quits. Hoping to be your friend,
once this misunderstanding has been rectified.

There was no doubt as far as Marion was concerned that the possession in question was the diary. She hadn't come into possession of anything else since her arrival.

She returned to her trench coat and took the notebook from one of the pockets.

Its cracked leather cover was cold to the touch. *The Narrative of A. Gordon Pym* stated the title in old gilded lettering. In the long run, it was becoming even stranger than a work by Poe.

And the bizarre nature of its contents was echoed in reality, noted Marion. Like the book found by the hero of Michael Ende's novel *The Neverending Story*. Who hadn't dreamed of possessing a book that *really* opened onto another world?

Marion opened the cover and flicked through the worn pages.

The magic of this text had been in operation since 1928, and was stretching out its inky arms so far that it had even altered time this winter, more than seventy years later.

Who knew that she had found the diary?

Brother Damien.

On the evening of the discovery he had dropped in to see her. The diary was on the hall table, and his eyes had lit on it. Although he had said nothing, perhaps he had recognized it. In that case, the entire brotherhood might know about it.

There was Ludwig the night watchman, too.

She had bumped into him on her way back from Béatrice's place. The book was under her arm; he could have seen it.

In fact, anybody could have written those letters.

Marion went into the kitchen for a glass of water.

If she must follow a process of elimination, she could strike Joe from the list of suspects. He had been at Tombelaine that afternoon, and then with her. And the letter had been placed in her house while they were together. The Mount was sufficiently small for people to watch her comings and goings; if she was seen leaving, it was easy to get into the house.

That was perhaps the solution to the problem.

The author of these letters had a key. And the brotherhood had copies of them, according to Sister Anne.

If she must continue her process of elimination, Marion chose to retain only the men of the religious community. In the last letter, the French text contained no feminine word endings—it spoke of being *votre ami* rather than *amie*. This could be a decoy. For the moment, Marion continued with her original logical method.

Five people remained.

Brother "Wrong Way" Damien, permanently excited and apparently sporty.

Brother Gaël, the youngster of the group. Timorous.

Brother Christophe, "Brother Anemia." Perpetually slow and out of breath.

The old and unpleasant Brother Gilles and finally, the great manitou of the whole bunch: Brother Serge, with his almost disturbing physique.

All the same, she was suspecting men of the Church.

Were they exempt from all failings or vices, for all that?

Marion shook her head emphatically. The writer of this letter was hiding among those five.

And now? What was she going to do?

"If you want your book back, you're going to need more than a letter you've sneaked in behind my back, old chap," she announced out loud.

She was annoyed by this cowardice, disguised as a mystery.

Not only was she not going to abandon the diary in the middle of the great outdoors, but she wasn't going to give it up at all.

And that evening, when the coward would be waiting outside, in the cold, for her to go out and give back the book, she would be comfortably sitting here, reading it.

And if he wanted to get his hands on it, he would have to show his face to her, and ask her for it.

Then she would see what ought to be done.

She had had enough of secrecy and jokes.

At the start, that riddle and the intrusion into her lodgings to check her things—all of that was almost amusing in context. But with this, he had gone a little too far.

She might be a stranger on this mount, but they would have to accept her.

Nobody had a choice; least of all her.

· 22 ·

Jeremy Matheson and Azim had dinner together in an Italian restaurant on Boulevard Sulliman Pasha.

Azim ate hungrily, proud of the significant advance he had made in the investigation. "It's not a legend anymore; we now know that it is real!" he exclaimed, with his mouth full.

"All the same, Azim, we are not going to believe the wild imaginings of two . . . cranks, as a basis for conducting our investigation! You have said as much yourself, the first man was under the effect of drugs when he thought he saw that . . . ghoul!"

"I agree that we must review what he said with a grain of salt, but he definitely saw something that evening; I gazed upon the fear in his eyes, and both men's descriptions tally."

"Common popular imagery. They have the same references, the same myths; so when one of them mistakes a cripple escaping with his plunder for a monster, the others do the same."

"Listen, we may have a chance to trap this thing, or whatever it is, if we station some of our men in that district. The shopkeeper told me he spotted it three times in three weeks, each time when he had gone out onto his roof at night to smoke. He's an insomniac."

Jeremy drank the rest of his wine in a single gulp. Then he shook his head. "I am not going to mobilize thirty men at night for one or two weeks, on the pretext that a crazed insomniac thinks he's seen the monster that haunted his childhood. We have more important things to do."

"Such as?"

"Tomorrow morning, we have a meeting at the Keoraz Foundation, with its director."

Azim remained silent, seething with frustration. "How do you know this foundation?" he asked eventually.

Jeremy gave a composed smile as he wiped a piece of bread around his plate. Azim had the impression that his English colleague had been expecting to arrive at this question since the start of the meal. He finished chewing, taking his time, before pushing away his plate, and saying softly, "Because of a woman, my friend."

Azim was about to raise a glass of water to his mouth, but he halted, one hand on the crystal stem.

"Some time ago, I fell in love with a woman who is today the wife of the patron who created that foundation."

"Mr. Keoraz?"

Jeremy played with his napkin as he spoke. At the mention of Keoraz's name, Azim saw his grip on it tighten so much that his knuckles whitened.

"The very same. He is the paymaster; it is he who fills the foundation's coffers, but there is also a director, Mr. Humphreys."

"And you are still in contact with this woman?"

"If you can call it contact. But I am as knowledgeable about this foundation as Jezebel is benevolent toward it, and I confess that for her, I too played a part."

"You?"

The image of the solitary, taciturn Detective Matheson everyone knew did not sit well with that of a Jeremy in love and doing good works with underprivileged Cairo children.

"Yes. . . . It lasted a few months in the autumn and winter of 1926, and then we parted." He opened his heart in a lower voice, with less assurance in his body, and fell forward, one elbow on the table.

"How long ago did you separate from this woman?" asked Azim.

"January last year, a little more than a year ago. She met her husband at a New Year's Eve celebration, a dinner organized by the foundation's patron for all his volunteers."

"Were you among them?"

Jeremy nodded, his eyelids blinking.

Azim's lips vanished inside his mouth as he replied. "Whatever the case, it is a coincidence that is going to help us," the little man remarked.

"In the final analysis, the English community in Cairo isn't as extensive as all that; it's clear that at some point one will have to carry out an investigation into one's close acquaintances. I don't call that a coincidence, no more than a 'foreseeable inevitability.' By the way, congratulations on identifying the boy; I found out just now, when I called in at the office."

"I called to see the family, to inform them of the death. The foundation is in all cases the common point among the victims, there is no doubt about that."

Jeremy wiped a hand across his face. His features were drawn. When the waiter came within reach, he hailed him and ordered more wine.

"May I ask a service of you, Azim? Until tomorrow morning, we shall not speak further about all this, if you would be so kind."

Azim took the request like a lash from a whip. It was their work, and Jeremy had expressly demanded to work on this investigation.

The presence of this Jezebel woman in the investigation had something to do with this sudden discomfort, Azim could have sworn to it.

"As you wish," he replied.

Jeremy poured himself another large glass of wine and drank half of it in a single swallow.

For a second, Azim had the firm conviction that the Englishman was hiding something from him. But as quickly and strongly as it had come, that certainty mutated into doubt, then faded away.

The headquarters of the Keoraz Foundation stood on the long and broad sharia Abbas, where its neighbors were a Catholic church and the building housing the telegraph and telephone company.

It was early morning and there were many vehicles about, zigzagging between the streetcars and filling the still-cool air with the raucous cries of their beautiful machinery.

Once again, Jeremy found the contrast striking.

Between one city to the west, rich and Western, and its eastern—and far more chaotic—counterpart. One was made up of a well-spaced-out network of perpendicular streets, with European architecture, sidewalks planted with decorative shrubs, buildings as tall as they were modern, and shops worthy of Paris, London, or Milan. Whereas the other city spread out under the tents of the bazaars, a sinuous maze, interwoven with as many blind alleys as there were narrow streets, and a place whose dwellings had not changed for several centuries, reflecting the different Muslim cultures that had succeeded one another in Cairo. The first city was clean, had no smell, and was, by contrast, well-to-do; when evening came, the restrained laughter of the young English people mingled with the rowdier mirth of the French and the Italians. The second city was dusty, and smelled of leather, exotic flavors, the sweat of a heaped-up mass of humanity, whereas when night fell, the song of the muezzins brooded from the top of their minarets over a horizon of roofs as jumbled as an angry sea. One was economic and political, the other as mystical as it was historic.

Humphreys, the director of the Keoraz Foundation, greeted the two detectives in his office, on the top floor. He was a forty-year-old Englishman, powerfully built with a bushy beard, and in every respect except his personality, he resembled Professor Challenger, whose exploits the famous Arthur Conan Doyle had recounted in his novels.

Without asking them, and despite the early hour, he poured out two brandies, one for himself and one for Jeremy, while Azim received a glass of water.

"So, tell me, what can I do for you?" he asked, sitting behind his overladen desk.

"As I explained to you yesterday on the telephone, it concerns the children of your foundation."

"What you have told me is terrible. You mean to say there is a child-killer here, in Cairo? Do you have any leads?"

Jeremy shielded himself with a hand gesture, signifying that he could go no further. "The investigation is under way," he replied. "Have you found the children's files, as I asked you to do yesterday?"

The director laid a finger upon a slim pile of folders. "Everything is here, all four little ones."

"You have consulted the files, I should imagine. Have you any remarks to make? We are seeking any link among them, or any unusual detail."

Humphreys tightened his fingers, which let out a series of sharp cracks. They were deformed by arthritis. "No, nothing. Or at least . . . a few details, look."

He slid the cardboard folders toward the English detective.

Humphreys seized his glass and savored the bouquet of his brandy before trickling a mouthful down into his throat. He had swiveled around to face the window, and was now gazing at the bell tower of the church.

"Although we didn't meet at the time, I remember that you were among our volunteers, Detective."

Jeremy looked up from the files to study the director as he

continued: "I . . . I don't see how to tell you this, but . . . well, perhaps you don't remember, but those four children whose folders we are examining were all in your classes, Mr. Matheson."

Azim frowned. He examined his colleague, whose eyes widened more than was necessary.

"Excuse me?" stammered the English detective.

"Yes," Humphreys went on, "it is as I thought, you had not noticed. They all passed through your hands, when your name was put forward to conduct our reading sessions. I can see that you don't remember; look, I understand, there are so many of them, and to many of us, they all look the same."

Jeremy opened the folders rather roughly to examine the few typed pages they contained. He passed from one child to the next with growing unease.

"Is it an important detail?" asked the director.

Jeremy straightened up and fixed him with a steady gaze.

"What do you think?" he retorted coldly.

Sweat had inundated his brow in the space of a few seconds.

Azim dragged his chair forward until he could rest his elbows on the edge of the desk, and politely demanded, "Could you draw up a list for us of all the children in Detective Matheson's classes, please?"

Humphreys scrutinized the small, turbaned Egyptian before looking for his English colleague's reaction, awaiting confirmation or a veto. The director visibly had little regard for "locals," Azim noted. For a man heading a foundation designed to help street children, this was disturbing. *Yet another politician who's accepted a post for the benefit of his own future, rather than for love of the work,* he mused.

Jeremy indicated his approval of Azim's idea with a movement of his index finger.

"Good; I should be able to obtain it for you by Monday or Tuesday. I say, now that I think about it, there could be a link. We—the foundation—reported a burglary back in January. And . . . the strangest thing is that nothing was stolen. The back door was forced to gain entrance to the premises and the offices. The crook must have expected to find plenty of cash; I remember that a door had been broken down in order to get into the room where our safe is kept."

"Was much money stolen?" asked Jeremy.

"No, the safe clearly proved to be beyond his means; he didn't even open it! Two broken locks for that!"

"Is there nothing else in that room?" demanded Matheson.

"It's where our archives are kept—our files on the staff and the children."

"And now you tell me?" raged the English detective.

Azim was starting to worry about his partner's state of mind.

"It could be an important piece of information," cut in Azim, seeing the director's disconcerted expression. "What do the files on the children contain?"

This time, Humphreys did not hesitate to answer the little Egyptian: "The same thing as I've brought you: the information we need to know about the child; name, date of birth if known, place where the parents can be contacted, medical remarks, and records of schooling. One particular teacher is assigned to each child, and it is he who updates the files regularly on his pupil's progress, along with any remarks about behavior."

"Medical remarks, you say?" repeated Azim.

"Yes, of course, just in case—you never know. The majority of these children arrive here at the instigation of their parents, who want to give them a chance in life, to acquire knowledge and the skills they need to live. We select children on the basis of an application and an interview. And when they are accepted, our first task is to send them for a medical examination, which is something they have never received before."

"Where does this take place?"

"At the Lord Kitchener Hospital, which is the best of its kind along with the Anglo-American Hospital, except that the Lord Kitchener is bigger and we know the doctors."

Azim was surprised. "Lord Kitchener?"

He turned to Jeremy. "What was the name of the doctor who performed the autopsies on the victims?"

"Benjamin Cork."

"Ah! Dr. Cork!" exclaimed the director. "Of course, he's one of the doctors who examine our children."

Azim raised his eyebrows in alarm. "We are starting to have a great many coincidences!"

Jeremy, who was as morose as ever, disagreed with a shake of the head. "No, it can all be explained. The Kitchener Hospital specializes in women and children, and Dr. Cork specializes in children, that's why he carried out the autopsies. Nothing abnormal, Azim. English-speaking Cairo is as small as the Arab-speaking one can be immense."

"Very well," conceded Azim. "And what about these four child victims? Anything in particular in their files?"

"No, I've checked, nothing more," Humphreys assured him. "They . . . they were attentive, two were a little unruly, lacking in seriousness. All were very curious, and they accepted additional lessons. That's all. I shall allow you to take these files, but kindly bring them back to me when the investigation has been concluded."

"Does your patron have the keys to the building?" asked Jeremy.

"Francis Keoraz? No, it's not necessary, he's the . . . generous spirit behind the foundation, but as for the rest, I'm responsible for everything here. He drops in to see us from time to time, to say hello to the children, nothing more."

Jeremy rubbed his earlobe and smiled thinly.

The director picked up his brandy glass and emptied it with a lick of his lips. A few minutes later, the two detectives were in the street.

Azim sounded Jeremy out. "Do you really not remember having those children in your classes?"

Jeremy walked along, gazing into the distance. "No," he replied evasively.

"You gave reading lessons, didn't you?"

"Yes. More like reading sessions in English. I didn't teach them anything, I'm not qualified for that; I read them stories, which most of them didn't even understand. They didn't have the level of language needed; the best of them could barely stammer a few words of English, but it was an initiation like any other, a way of training the ear. Listen, Azim, we've already talked about this, and I told you I did it for that woman. She's the one who insisted that the foundation must take me on. I didn't derive any pleasure from it, I wasn't interested in the children, so as for remembering their faces. . . . "

Somewhat embarrassed, Azim smoothed down his mustache. "The thing is . . . it is becoming very personal," he said. "First your link with the foundation, and now your link with these four poor children. I think it would be better if you—"

Jeremy halted. "If I what?"

The Englishman's flaming gaze was trained on Azim, who realized it was pointless to insist. However personal the investigation might become, he would never succeed in making Jeremy Matheson see reason. And referring the matter to their superiors would be catastrophic. Matheson knew far too many influential people to be thrown off an investigation he wanted to conduct at any price. The sole consequence would be that he, Azim, would be sidelined from this sinister story. And he wanted to finish what he had started.

"Nothing . . . nothing." Azim raised his arms in surrender. Disappointment was written on his face, and this had the effect of calming Jeremy's anger.

When Jeremy spoke again, it was more calmly: "I am sorry,

Azim. All of this is becoming very personal, and I have no intention of running away to wait for other detectives to come and tell me what is going on. It is my task to understand, to sort out the problem."

Azim twitched. *Sort out the problem?* He had spoken as if he already knew what was afoot, the nature of his link to the murders. Azim decided not to pick up on this for the moment; circumstances were not favorable to him. He simply continued the conversation: "The boss asked me to draw up a detailed report for him today, and I cannot hide all of this from him."

"I know that. He won't drive me off the investigation, whatever happens. I have too many friends who could harm his career. Do your job."

The two companions continued their walk along the avenue with its intermittent traffic. After a time, Azim changed his approach and announced his deduction out loud: "I think we both agree that the burglary at the foundation, in January, has a direct link with our crimes? I am tempted to think that the killer broke in in order to consult the children's files and—for reasons as yet unknown—he chose children who had been present at your reading sessions. He may also have gained an idea of his future victims' personalities through the report cards written up by the teachers."

"I agree. He considers their character, their personality, through teachers' records. He knows their basic traits, some of their flaws, and consequently how to manipulate them."

"Particularly since according to Mr. Humphreys, they were all very curious. By the way, what did you think of the director?"

"I don't like him."

"I am pleased to hear you say that. I share your opinion. Tell me, I am sorry to return to the subject, but that doctor, Dr. Cork— why didn't he say anything when he did the autopsy on that child? He knew him, did he not? After all, he is one of the doctors who check out the foundation's pupils, so he must have recognized the child, don't you think?"

"I think he did recognize him," replied Jeremy with a black look. "And in his way, he gave me to understand that. But he is above all a professional."

Azim gazed at his partner for a good ten seconds, then raised his eyebrows. "What is the plan for this afternoon?" he demanded finally.

Jeremy kept on walking, watching the cars that overtook them. "You write your report; I need a little time alone, to think."

Azim opened his mouth, but immediately decided to say nothing.

They parted beneath the sun's increasingly incandescent eye.

Jeremy stopped for lunch opposite the central railway station, then walked along the railway lines and across them to get back home.

He stepped under the canopy, pleased to find a little shade, and immediately stopped in his tracks, all his senses on the alert.

The nape of his neck started to prickle. As a hunter, he knew how to recognize the confused signs given out by the body and the intuition.

He was in danger.

Imminent danger.

· 23 ·

Marion reread the last lines in the diary:

I halted in my tracks. That shiver up the back of my neck, that stretching feeling at the base of my ears: I knew how to interpret them. Through hunting African predators on their own terrain, I had

*developed the kind of intuition that belongs to people who live within
striking distance of nature. I knew how to recognize the association of
my body with the still-wild part of my mind as the herald of a possible
threat. The extreme concentration of my senses had just captured subtle
alterations in my environment, and there was a distinct possibility of
imminent danger.*

The account of this investigation was becoming more and more
intriguing, and now it had the added spice of a hint of action. Marion was captivated.

This man Humphreys, the director of the foundation, seemed
strange to her. Of course, she had to bear in mind that everything
she read passed through the subjective filter of Jeremy Matheson;
in the end, her deductions were more than slanted, if not posi-
tively determined by the detective's own opinions. Whatever
the case, all the murdered children had a direct relationship with
the foundation; that wasn't a coincidence but rather a link between the killer and his victims. And that lead had still to be
followed.

Suddenly, Marion cast a worried glance at the pages of closely
spaced handwriting.

To what extent was all of this true?

How much was invention, and how much reality? Had there
even been any child murders in Cairo in 1928?

Marion looked around the living room. If only she had an Internet connection, she could have done a bit of research. She swore.

*These monks—when it comes to technology they can't even be both-
ered to install the basics. . . .*

And she hadn't seen a computer at Béatrice's place either.

Maybe in one of the many rooms at the abbot's residence?

If not, she would have to spend some time in a library that was
well provided with old periodicals, and with a little luck she might
unearth a few articles mentioning this affair. It was sufficiently

sordid to have crossed the Mediterranean and entered French newspapers of the time. . . . At least, she hoped so.

Periodicals of the time.

She clapped her hands in victory.

There were heaps of them in the library at Avranches—she had seen whole piles of them, sorted them herself, in ecstasies over the outdated charm of the dust-scented covers. It was possible that the answers to her questions could be found among those pages.

She sat up on the sofa.

It was dinnertime, a little late to go and ask someone on the Mount to drive her to Avranches and have the doors of the town hall opened up for her.

She gave a long sigh.

Her curiosity would have to wait until tomorrow.

She had enough to keep her going, she thought, picking up the black book.

Hunger was beginning to bother her, so she decided to make the suspense last and postpone her reading until later. She opened her refrigerator in search of meal ideas and then put on a pan of water to boil. An omelette with potatoes and bacon.

If she didn't want to get fat she would have to watch her food intake more carefully, and ask Brother Damien if he was against the idea of having a jogging partner. Running along the causeway would be energizing to begin with, until she had familiarized herself with the landscape, but then it would become painfully monotonous when she'd learned every square inch of the route by heart. But there was still the splendid view of Mont-Saint-Michel itself.

She would begin the following Monday: It was settled. Another three days of loafing around and then she would start toning up and slimming down her body.

Marion enjoyed her omelette in the muted light of the living room, without music, her only company the sinister melody of the wind sliding over the rooftops.

"And just think: Right now there's probably a poor guy out

there, waiting for me to come and place the diary at the foot of the tower," she murmured between two mouthfuls. "Imbecile . . . "

She constantly wondered about the nature of the link between her mysterious correspondent and the diary she had appropriated. Was it his? Unlikely. Jeremy Matheson was around thirty in 1928, so he would have been around one hundred today. Difficult.

But possible.

Particularly since there were very few old men on the Mount.

Brother Gilles.

And that man Joe!

They both seemed very old, but whether they were a hundred years old or not. . . .

And Jeremy was English.

Except that, after seventy years of speaking French, he could have lost his accent. . . .

No, she was going much too far. The diary's author was rotting in a tomb somewhere in the world. However, someone on the Mount knew about the existence of this black book, and wanted to get it back. Someone who had misappropriated it?

Or simply stored—or hidden—it in the library, so as not to be caught unawares one day with this kind of nosing into his affairs. . . . Marion didn't know what to think.

She finished her meal with a yogurt and thought about allowing herself a glass of alcohol to round off the evening. From Monday, she would be strict with herself, so she could allow herself this luxury. . . .

She poured herself some gin and orange juice in a big glass and stretched out on the sofa with the black book under her arm.

Whomever you are, waiting in vain for me out there, I am going to continue this tale without you, and perhaps in a little while . . . perhaps I'll join you. . . .

· 24 ·

Jeremy stood stock-still, alert for the smallest movement around him. A train passed in the distance, the noise masking any other sounds.

He knew that someone had come, or was perhaps still there. Someone had visited his rail car in his absence.

Objects had moved in the progressive, meticulous collection of dust that he had fostered in his jumble of possessions.

Tiny details, yet significant in his eyes. Not a regulation search, just a curious, wandering hand that had traveled across his things.

He approached the door of the rail car and seized a tent pole that was lying there with some other bits and pieces. He slid it down the wall noisily.

The daylight filtered in through the windows, although it was partially absorbed by the velour wall-covering. He climbed the three steps and inspected the main room.

Nobody.

Nothing had moved.

He went to the bathroom and opened the door with the end of the tent pole. Empty.

He went to the bedroom.

Suddenly, the smell of perfume attacked him. Wafting up his nostrils, it slid down his body, gushed up again into his memory and fell upon his heart with the painful caress of a feather whose edge was as sharp as a razor blade.

That scent was so familiar. So sweet and so razor sharp, all at once.

Jeremy let go of his improvised weapon and sat down on the bed.

It was a fruity, almost masculine perfume.

It was the one she wore.

She always placed a drop of it between her breasts before making love.

It was then that Jeremy realized the photo was missing from the bedside table. She had taken it.

His wrist encountered a sharp corner.

A handwritten card.

Your invitation to this evening's celebration at Shepheard's, "A Senegalese Extravaganza." Fancy dress. Your one and only opportunity to question my husband for your investigation. Enjoy yourself.

Jezebel

She was playing with him. As cruelly as a cat with its mouse, refusing for hours to put it to death, prolonging its death-agonies purely for its own amusement.

Night was falling over the city. On the sharia Ibrahim Pasha, the gaslights grew brighter, casting blue and orange halos over the fronts of the buildings.

The celebrated Shepheard's Hotel was ready for what was to be dubbed "the ball of the decade." Under the vast entrance canopy, at the top of ten red-carpeted steps, two palm trees guarded the front door. Hosts of candles in lanterns had been added at the last moment to welcome the guests.

Jeremy, who had come there on foot from the railway station, walked past the Albanian porters and up to the lobby entrance. He showed his invitation card to a man in fancy dress, who in return pointed out the main restaurant. Outside the main doors to the large room, a couple were distributing turbans to the male guests and animal-shaped bracelets to the women.

Jeremy declined the head-covering, considering that his safari suit was sufficient to gain him access to this soiree.

The hotel was talked about all over Europe and even in the United States. Once again, Jeremy saw that its reputation was not undeserved.

The walls were covered with long, lush lianas; palm trees stood against the walls like living columns, while enormous fans made the leaves move almost silently. Monstrous masks of mythological creatures appeared here and there under the vegetation, lit from inside by enormous candles. On carved perches, an entire gallery of multicolored birds were hopping around to the accompaniment of the guests' laughter. Jeremy immediately spotted a tiger and further off a lion with its teeth bared. The standard of the taxidermy was admirable. Other large mammals lurked among the foliage, between the round tables. These were covered with brightly colored tablecloths, and on each one stood a massive candelabra, around which a snake coiled, glistening in the light from the flames.

On either side of the main aisle, carefully plaited native huts had been erected, forming a path to the far end of the room, where a scene depicting a temple to the goddess Kali awaited the dancers. The goddess's statue was several yards tall, with candles burning in its eye sockets as it looked down upon the stunned guests. At its feet, a group of Senegalese musicians was playing a monotonous rhythm on percussion instruments.

The drums made the air quiver, and the red lamps trembled in harmony, as though under their spell.

More than a hundred people were gently jostling one another in shimmering costumes, glasses of champagne in their hands. Among them, Jeremy quickly spotted important politicians and industrialists, such as Aboud Pacha, the seventh richest man in the world.

Everyone was celebrating a dazzling victory by the horse belonging to the hotel's director, Charles Behler, in the Allenby Cup, earlier that day. Joy, wonderment, and prestige radiated from every pore.

"I see you found my invitation." It was Jezebel.

Jeremy turned and saw her, attired in a light dress covered with beads. The fine layer of crepe beneath them was barely sufficient to conceal her breasts. Only Jezebel could allow herself such indecency without provoking a resounding scandal.

"You broke into my home," said Jeremy by way of greeting.

"There was a time when that didn't worry you."

The response was sharp. "Once upon a time, yes."

"Well, well, so the big cat is turning into a viper! If you want to meet my husband, he's over there, with the chief of police . . . "

She pointed to a table a little to one side. Jeremy's gaze traveled back to the perfect curves of her shoulders, her fragile neck, the veins palpitating with the pressure of her emotions.

Or the lack of them, he mused.

Her long black hair was now drawn together in a cleverly constructed chignon, decorated with pink and violet flower buds.

"Thank you," breathed Jeremy.

He turned his back on her and went straight across to the two men.

The police chief recognized him and stood up.

"What a pleasant surprise, Detective! I imagine you're here to mix work and pleasure; marvelous cocktail party, I tell you!"

Jeremy shook his hand and responded with a false smile.

Opposite him, Mr. Keoraz was less warm. In his late forties, with graying hair meticulously parted down the middle, his face wore the stern expression of men who have little imagination. His chin bore the marks of rushed, rough shaves; his lips were slender, hardly there at all, and his nose as sharp and pointed as a mountain ridge.

"Detective," he greeted him.

"Allow me to introduce Mr. Keoraz," said the police chief. "Gentlemen, I shall leave you to get to know each other, I must go over and say hello to the maharajahs of Kapurthala and Mysore."

Jeremy found himself alone with the powerful patron. "In fact, we have already met," he said. "At the New Year's dinner, a little more than a year ago."

"I know." His voice was as sharp as his profile.

"I have a few questions to ask you, and as you are a busy man, I am taking advantage of this fleeting opportunity."

"You are right to do so. I am an organized man myself; it is the key to all successes."

At this, Keoraz indicated a sheaf of papers, pinned together. Jeremy strained his neck to see that it was a copy of the report Azim had written that afternoon.

"You—"

Keoraz cut the detective short: "My friend, your superior, was eager to deliver this copy to me right away, it seems, fresh from the progress your investigation has made. For a man like me, it is important to know that the investigation is being conducted swiftly and efficiently. It does after all concern my foundation."

A demonstration of power, Jeremy realized. Keoraz was displaying his omnipotence, showing that it was pointless to do him harm or try and impose anything on him. He was leading the dance; nobody was going to lead him.

Behind the millionaire's back, Jeremy spotted Dr. Cork and his white beard; so, he was here too.

He looked down again and saw Keoraz signal to someone to come over. The foundation's director, Humphreys, appeared at his side.

"Good evening, Detective. How have you fared since this morning? Ah, you don't know my assistant, Pierre Berneil!"

The director stepped back to allow room for a shorter man, who walked with a stick. He greeted Jeremy with an unmistakably French accent.

Keoraz took advantage of this to get to his feet, picking up the police report. "I have to go, so much to do. . . . Detective, come and see me tomorrow evening, at our house in Heliopolis, you know it don't you? I was given to understand that you and my wife were close at one time; she must have spoken to you about it if you have seen each other since then."

Jeremy nodded silently. There was nothing else he could do; Keoraz was running the game.

"That will give me time to consult this report, and find out where you have got to," Keoraz said. "Time presses, Detective, and the last thing in the world I want is another murdered child. . . . "

He nodded nonchalantly to the assembled throng and vanished into the costumed crowd.

Azim stretched out on the camp bed next to his desk. He was exhausted. He lacked the courage needed to carry out the latest tasks he had imposed upon himself. He opened one eye in the direction of the wall clock. In any case, it was too late now.

Have a bit of a rest; that was what he must do. So that he could attack the next day with greater skill.

Four dead children.

He opened his eyelids again. How could he sleep when he knew that children might be dying out there?

He swore in Arabic.

What more could he do? There were already four dead, and . . .

Very softly, Azim got up.

Thinking hard about it, they believed there were four, but that was since the killings had been close together. Who was to say that the killer hadn't struck earlier? An isolated incident, dealt with swiftly, and with no repercussions.

Azim grabbed his turban, jammed it on his head, and went off toward the stairs. He walked up to the third floor, where the archives were stored. There was nobody there, it was already too late.

"Damn!" he hissed between clenched teeth.

Without knowing precisely what he was looking for, it was

impossible to find it in the endless filing system that occupied the fourteen bookcases.

He went back downstairs and stuck his head into several offices, until he unearthed a familiar face.

"Inspector Dodgson! I have a question."

"Go ahead, my dear fellow."

"Do you recall any incidents involving the murder of a child? Or of murders committed with great savagery? Ones where the body bore the marks of unbelievable rage?"

Dodgson let go of the pipe he was holding in the corner of his mouth. "Ah. This is about your investigation. The little ones who were broken in two."

He observed the little Egyptian over the top of his thick brown-rimmed glasses. "Gracious me, no," he replied. "Not before your own investigation. But I'm not the person you should ask, that's old Nichols—he's the memory of the entire police force. He retired about six months ago, and is waiting to be repatriated without the slightest impatience. Do you want me to call him? I have his number."

"It is perhaps a little late."

"Not at all! He goes to bed late, and he'll be pleased that someone's asked for his help. Sit down, old chap, and I'll look up the number."

In less than three minutes, Nichols was on the other end of the line.

"No? It doesn't mean anything to you either?" repeated Dodgson, a little disappointed. "Ah well, never mind. Take care of yourself, and I'll see you on Sunday for that game of cards."

He hung up and resumed sucking on his unlit pipe. "Sorry, old chap, no luck this evening. He doesn't remember any child murders as atrocious as these. All the same, how does someone get to be so utterly insane? Snapping a poor kid's spine. I hope you're intending to have him shot, if you catch him!"

Azim patted the inspector's shoulder amicably and went out into the corridor. "Sir?"

Azim saw a woman carrying a portable typewriter. One of the secretaries. This one was working late, he noted. "Can I do something for you, madam?"

"Actually, I am the one who may be able to do something for you. I heard your conversation with the inspector, and I . . . I remembered a case, less than two months ago."

Azim leaned against the wall, forgetting decorum.

"It was a murder, in that squalid Shubra district to the north of the city," she went on. "A man . . . how can I put it? Snapped in two? I was the one who typed the investigation report to make copies of it, that's how I remember. And it was . . . appalling. Really. The man had been slaughtered, his limbs shattered, and the vertebral column broken in two."

She laid a hand on her chest as she strove to get her breath back. "My God, it was incredible. And . . . even his tongue had been ripped out, the poor man."

This time Azim saw tears well up in the secretary's eyes. He approached her. "Come, come," he said clumsily.

"Oh, that's not all. There was an element of real perversion to it, because something else was found on his body, all over the place."

She stifled a retch. "S-semen. Human, if you see what I mean."

Azim shivered. This time it was very similar. The same barbarism, the same eagerness to want to shatter the human body. And finally the same act of perverse debauchery: The murderer had spread his semen over his victim.

The secretary had already produced a handkerchief, which she used to dab her moist eyelids. "You should talk to the detective who conducted the investigation, sir. It was Detective Matheson."

Now, the shiver turned into a cold sweat.

· 25 ·

Marion opened her eyes quite early on that Friday morning. She had sat up late with the diary, and yet her desire to go and investigate in Avranches had proved even more pressing than an alarm clock.

At nine o'clock she was in the streets of the village, the black book buried in a pocket of her trench coat. She passed by Béatrice's shop, which was not yet open. Marion rang at the adjacent door and her red-haired friend invited her upstairs.

"You're an early bird! Pour yourself a cup of coffee, I have to dry my hair," Béatrice called back over her shoulder.

Marion opened cupboards in search of a cup and poured the gasoline-colored liquid into it.

"All I need is a cigarette, and I've got the perfect 'fresh breath' morning cocktail," she murmured.

Béatrice reappeared, rubbing her hair. "Insomnia or a compulsive desire to chat?" she asked. "Wait, let me guess! You've exhausted all your copies of *Ici Paris* and you're desperate for gossip, so you said to yourself, 'my little Béa will sort me out.'"

"Why, has something happened in the village?"

"Stop dreaming. Your presence is already an upheaval in itself. So, is everything okay?"

Marion nodded as she gulped down the coffee.

"I have a favor to ask you," she said, getting her breath back. "I need you to lend me your car for a few hours."

"Whenever you like. Except this morning. Grégoire has gone off with it—he's running a few errands for me and the old man."

"What old man? You mean Joe?"

"Yes, I can see that you've made each other's acquaintance. Greg does his heavy shopping and Joe gives him a little cash as a thank you. So no car this morning. Is it urgent?"

"Not urgent. . . . It's mainly my impatience."

Béatrice started plaiting her hair. "Admit it, this is about your famous old book."

Marion nodded. "I'm getting hooked."

She almost mentioned the episode the previous evening, the envelope and the mysterious demand, but she refrained. She had promised herself that she would say nothing until she could see things more clearly.

"Well, tell me, what's happening in the book?" Béatrice insisted.

Marion finished her coffee and arched her eyebrows. "I'll tell you everything but I would like to find a driver before lunchtime, so I must run. Thanks for the coffee."

Marion bounded into the street and the damp coolness of the village instantly assailed her.

She was going to have to turn to the brotherhood.

Exactly what she would rather not have done. If the writer of the letters was one of its members, he would swiftly learn that she had spent part of her Friday in Avranches, in the library archives. She could, of course, wait until the afternoon, when Grégoire would be back.

But her impatience wouldn't hold out until then. She climbed the steps until she was looking down on all the roofs and left the secular path for that of the faith. She entered the abbot's residence and got lost in the labyrinth of narrow corridors and spiral staircases before happening upon the room where the brotherhood ate their meals. There was nobody there.

She heard Brother Serge's sharp voice, echoing from behind a door. ". . . matters, that's politics. What worries me is what they may have in store for us. I will not allow myself to be ousted for the benefit of these manipulators."

"Calm yourself, you dramatize everything. There is no question of . . ."

The second voice was that of Sister Anne; Marion recognized it instantly.

She decided not to interrupt what sounded like an important debate, and turned on her heel. On the ground floor, she spotted the stern profile of Sister Luce, who was hanging laundry in a large room.

"Excuse me," Marion ventured softly. "I'm not disturbing you, am I?"

Sister Luce's facial features contracted. Marion compared this effect to a spider on its back, which draws its feet up against its abdomen, an unappetizing defense reaction. Then the sister turned to face the intruder.

"What do you want?"

"I'm looking for someone to take me to Avranches."

"To Avranches? Is that all?"

Marion bit her tongue. She must not respond to provocation. *Let the old bag wear herself out.*

"Yes, as far as that," she replied with a broad smile.

"Go and see Brother Damien. He's most inclined to go traveling by car."

Brother Wrong Way; him again, thought Marion.

The old woman grabbed a pair of pajama trousers and hung them on the drying rack.

"Have you any idea where I might find him?" Marion persisted.

If certain members of the religious community welcomed Marion, others saw her as a source of trouble, someone on retreat but a little "special," imposed upon them and trampling all over their tranquil spirituality.

Sister Luce answered without stopping for breath, "Without a doubt he's at the bottom of the village, at the post office, as we had mail to send out."

Marion thanked her and wandered around for another five minutes, trying to find the way out, before going all the way back down rue Grande to the post office where she did indeed see

Brother Damien. He refused nicely, with that permanent affability that was all his own, for today it was the day of the Passion, devoted to fasting, reflection, prayer, and meditation. Marion insisted, stressing her growing boredom, and promised that he would have all the time he wanted for his spiritual activities, and that they would return before the end of the afternoon. Faced with this suffering soul, he gave in with a sigh.

Once they were inside the Simca, Brother Damien chuckled. "I'm driving you to Avranches, but I don't even know what we're going to do there!"

That was Marion's problem in a nutshell. Not telling him the truth, while gaining access to the library's attics—and then finding some way of getting him out of the way.

"It's to keep me busy," she said finally.

"So I imagine, but doing what?

Now that she knew he liked running almost every morning, his physique worried her. He had that round, friendly face typical of people who enjoy their food, while his body was that of an athlete; this discordance between his head and the rest of him surprised her. Brother Damien was one of those slightly plump men who had taken up sport intensively, to the point of trading in his flab for muscle, and yet his face had remained the same.

"Tell me, would it bother you if I joined you to go jogging?" she asked, changing the subject.

Brother Damien was surprised. He opened his hands, which were on the steering wheel, and flexed his fingers several times, like a cat enjoying being stroked.

"With me? Er . . . fine, why not? It's just that I usually run alone."

"If it bothers you, I won't insist."

"No, no," he replied unhurriedly. "All the same, I should tell you that I run a lot, so . . . "

"I think I understand. I'll accompany you over the first stretch and then leave you to continue at your own speed. It's just that if I'm going to get started I don't want to be all alone at the beginning, it's more motivating for me."

He moved back and forth on his seat, all the time keeping his eyes on the road. "That's very true, it's better when you're starting out."

"I'll start on Monday."

"Er, no, not Monday—it's a day of prayer. And this time, no exceptions. I'll come and collect you on Tuesday morning."

Marion nodded.

"So, what are we going to do?" he repeated.

"Some research."

"Excellent! And in the library, too! You know, I love puzzles; I'm an inveterate crossword puzzler—the moment I have any free time, I pit myself against a little grid. Those intellectual games do me a world of good! So, how can I be of use to you?"

Marion wanted to say, "By going and locking yourself away somewhere, far away from me, until this evening," but restrained herself. She also refrained from admitting to him that she was also a lover of crossword puzzles. She had no desire to spark off an involved conversation about different people's little tricks for completing their puzzles.

"Since I'm going to spend some time here, I thought I should know about the history of the area," she finally managed to say. "I was thinking of obtaining information about the region, its history, anecdotes about it . . . "

"In that case, it's not the library we should be going to, it's the mus—"

"No," she interrupted him. "I saw some periodicals dating from the first decades of the twentieth century in the attic, and I'd like to look through them."

Brother Damien looked as though he didn't share her opinion, but seeing her determination, he capitulated.

They returned to the poorly lit room and its freshly cataloged shelves of knowledge. Marion remembered having arranged the newspapers in the left-hand part, right at the bottom of the shelving. She got rid of Brother Damien by asking him, "If you could find me everything in the way of magazines, newspapers, almanacs, and so forth . . . up to the 1950s. Anything that's likely to teach me the typical history of the place."

Brother Damien did not hide his disagreement with this idea of coming here and proceeding this way in order to learn about the region, but all the same, he complied.

Marion easily found the newsmagazines she remembered: the *Gazette de la Manche*, the *Petit Journal*, and *L'Excelsior*. She didn't bother with the first one; it was too local.

She picked up the heavy piles and made small heaps of the publications corresponding to the era she was looking for, the first part of 1928. All the issues from January to April of that year, she put on one side. Sitting cross-legged between two high walls of books, she sorted out everything she wanted to dissect.

Then she moved on to the search proper. Page after page, she skimmed all the copies piled up between her legs. From time to time, Brother Damien came over and showed her an article, asking her if it interested her, and if he ought to put it on one side. Marion nodded politely and returned to her reading.

The part devoted to international news was essentially slanted toward politics, with the addition of a few comical snippets and major scientific news. The morning elapsed to the rhythm of words printed on pages turned brown by time.

After three hours of reading, Marion looked up and noticed that she was just next to the spot reserved for foreign languages. The place where she had discovered Jeremy Matheson's personal diary.

She checked that it really was in the pocket of her trench coat, with the same anxiety as a mother watching her child playing far away in the park. The rough touch of the cover reassured her.

At half-past twelve she abandoned Brother Damien, who repeated that he was fasting, and went to order a seafood salad in the café opposite the town hall. There, she read *Ouest-France*, which was still running her story on page one.

That crazy story that had exiled her here.

Far from home, from her family, and from her few friends.

It was nine days since her arrival on the Mount. She wasn't really missing anybody. Except her mother. Particularly the telephone calls, in fact—exchanging news, sharing opinions on the events of the day. Hearing the sound of her voice.

Her work colleagues were not vital to her equilibrium. She had known that for a long time. They had never really gelled together. Some were too pedantic, others too superficial, or too systematically intellectual. No, she had never really felt at home among them. And her childhood friends had for the most part remained in Lyon, her native city; they had lost sight of one another over the years.

Marion ran a finger over her upper lip. The scar was fading; soon it would be no more than a memory.

The memory of the bluish green neon lights in the parking lot of her apartment building.

Of that man on his motorcycle, one evening when she was returning from the movies, alone in her basement parking garage. He had braked right in front of her.

The bike had revved, several times, by way of a warning. Behind his dark visor, the man had stared at her from less than a yard away. His right hand kept on twisting the throttle, to make the engine roar.

Marion saw him raise his hand, almost in slow motion. And yet she hadn't managed to run away.

His fist landed on her mouth, cutting her lip on her teeth.

She fell backward, more shocked than really in pain.

And the motorcycle started moving in circles around her. Tight circles; the notched wheels brushed her ankles, her fingers.

Marion couldn't get up. She rolled up into a ball.

And the engine roared in her ears, yelling at her, insulting her, threatening her, promising her the most terrible torments.

Suddenly the front wheel lifted up, then came down again less than four inches from her head.

Marion wept.

She was unable to leap to her feet.

That was the worst thing of all; that weakness.

More even than the attack, it was her terrified reaction that had traumatized Marion. Pure, incapacitating terror.

The wheel that had come crashing down on her hair loomed over her, the motorcycle roaring again and again.

Then it moved slowly back, before roaring away and disappearing.

It took a quarter of an hour for Marion to manage to sit up, and another ten minutes to get to the elevator and reach her apartment. As soon as the motorcycle had stopped in front of her, she had realized that this wasn't just some random delinquent, but a messenger.

A messenger carrying a warning, when she had thought he was bringing her death.

As the DST told her, she wasn't just *disturbing* things, she was *shaking them up*. And people were going to make her understand that.

The DST could come to her assistance, as long as she agreed to disappear. Those she had harmed had cruel methods.

Either she kept silent, or *they* would take it upon themselves to silence her.

As long as she refused to put herself under the DST's protection, she would be in danger.

Marion asked the DST agent—not without a certain effrontery—why they didn't kill her if the others were as determined as all that.

The man smiled. "We're not in a film," he replied. Killing somebody was complicated. And the risks were so great that they weren't worth the bother.

But her case was different. People would perhaps attempt to frighten her.

And . . . it might go further than that. It would start with telephone calls in the middle of the night—nothing said, just the sound of breathing. Then the letter box would be regularly forced open and emptied of its mail. One day her car would be ransacked. Then her apartment. It was even possible to pay one or two dropouts to set up a rape. That had already been seen. The people she had shaken up were powerful—and determined.

And however improbable it might seem, murder could be the ultimate step in their policy of silence.

The DST knew them, but remained powerless. It would take all the power of the whole system to keep Marion safe. The law, the police, public opinion, and the media. The media was the easiest. The others took longer. A few weeks. A few months. They didn't know how to answer her. And even then, she would have to be cautious; anything was possible, after all. Even famous men *disappeared* sometimes. Divulging the matter to the press could only protect her if it was accompanied by every precaution. How many men had fallen mysteriously in recent years? Had Pierre Bérégovoy really committed suicide? Then what had become of his precious notebook, which never left him? Had François de Grossouvre really fired a bullet into his head without anybody hearing, right in the middle of the Elysée, while the autopsy had brought to light "a frontal dislocation of the left shoulder and a surface bruise" on a man who was found sitting at his desk? Had Jean-Edern Hallier really fallen off his bicycle all on his own and shattered his skull in the gutter?

Anything was possible.

Marion had always regarded herself as a strong woman. A woman with a resilient character, who knew what she wanted. And at the most crucial moment of her existence, when she should have shown her strength, struck that motorcyclist, run away to save her life, she had collapsed.

The next day she called back her DST contact to accept their protection and disappear. It was the best thing to do, he repeated. The safest.

She didn't have the means to hire her own bodyguards and the DST didn't work like that. Their method was more expeditious, and safer: to make her vanish for as long as it took to prepare for her return, and her future safety.

Marion folded up *Ouest-France* and paid her bill before returning to find Brother Damien, who was sitting contemplatively in a corner.

"I was meditating," he explained.

To curtail any explanation, Marion smiled back at him and went straight off to sit between her mini-mountains of newspapers. She resumed her research with an issue of *L'Exelsior* dated March 1928 and its rather fuzzy photographs.

She exhausted the pile devoted to this title in an hour and a half, and moved on to the *Petit Journal* and its illustrated supplement. Brother Damien had been particularly silent since she returned from her lunch break. She wondered if she had annoyed him by avoiding his presence. She had her answer shortly afterward, in the form of a gentle snore. He had fallen asleep.

Around three o'clock in the afternoon, the lines started to merge as she skimmed them, the headlines didn't mean much, and she realized that she was spending a lot less time on each page than she had done with the first issues.

Yet it was at that point that her eyes halted on an evocative headline: TERRIBLE DISCOVERY IN EGYPT—MURDERED CHILDREN!

Her hands gripped the paper and she pulled it closer to her face.

The discovery, two days ago, of the lifeless corpse of a Cairo boy brings to four the number of victims of an infamous monster who is terrorizing the beautiful Egyptian city. The local police, assisted by a British inspector, are making every attempt to apprehend the bloodthirsty maniac who prowls the narrow streets of the northeastern suburbs. According to the spokeswoman for a fashionable women's club in the city, "So far, this sick individual has only attacked children from the outlying districts, but who knows if tomorrow he may not haunt our squares and the most famous streets in Cairo!" This sad affair is beginning to worry the English and French families, of which, as we know, there are many, and the governor, Lord Lloyd, may well issue an official communiqué to reassure them in the coming days. Once again, the charms of the land of the pharaohs are associated with the blood and mysteries that seem inseparable in the shadow of the pyramids.

Besides the emphatic tone of the article, Marion was appalled by the distance and lack of compassion that emerged from it. Particularly on the part of that woman who was unmoved by the dead children but was worried in case the expatriates' offspring might be potential victims. Marion had difficulty believing that anyone could be so detached. It must surely be a quotation taken out of context, or distorted by distance. . . . Marion attempted to convince herself as best she could.

Beyond this observation, she now possessed the proof that Jeremy Matheson's diary was not the fruit of a delirious mind.

You knew that. It's too personal, too well constructed to be an invention. . . .

The article finally enabled her to base her credulity on solid foundations. Each line of this private diary was now even more redolent of the scent of life gone by.

Jeremy Matheson was real.

And perhaps he was even still alive, somewhere. . . .

· 26 ·

March 1928.

Alcohol fumes still hung in the air of the bedroom, heady and sickening. Jeremy opened one eye, and his consciousness attempted grimly to extract itself from the tenacious limbo of sleep. Little by little, light forced its way into his brain.

The smell overwhelmed the detective, and a violent spasm shook his stomach.

He lunged forward, so as to vomit on the floor and not on himself, but nothing emerged from his furred-up mouth.

The beating of his heart began to be echoed by the heavy, obsessive pounding in his forehead.

It was as if all the alcohol he had drunk the previous night had accumulated behind his eyes after drying out his body, swirling around until it sucked in his eyeballs and his brain in one uncontrollable movement.

He clawed at his hair, groaning.

A black patch appeared where he had expected only an expanse of fuzzy whiteness, facing the window. He blinked hard until he managed to focus on it.

A man was standing there, and had already been talking to him for some moments.

Jeremy propped himself up on one elbow.

The face acquired greater contrast, and features appeared against the backlighting.

"Azim?" asked the Englishman in a cavernous voice.

"Get dressed, we must talk."

Jeremy grumbled.

"Come on, on your feet," ordered Azim roughly.

"What time is it?"

"Time to talk."

Jeremy raised an eyebrow, and straightened up. He disappeared into the bathroom where Azim heard him grousing as he took a cold shower.

A few minutes later, Jeremy was combing his hair clumsily while his companion sat at his desk.

"Well?"

"Why didn't you tell me?"

Jeremy stopped, the comb still in his hair. "Tell you what?"

"Don't take me for an idiot on the pretext that I'm not English—or worse, because I'm an Arab! I know why you wanted this investigation at all costs! I know!"

"Oh, no, Azim, you don't know anything—"

"The murder in Shubra. The same violence, the inhuman rage, and the same manifestations of perverse pleasure. You were there, you conducted the investigation! I have read your report."

Jeremy tossed the comb onto a lacquered table. He turned around, slowly, then went to fetch his cigarettes and lit one.

"Tell me why you're angry," said Jeremy, suddenly calmer.

"You had evidence that could be material to our investigation. You should have shared it with me!"

"Nothing conclusive. I had nothing that could help us. I would have told you; I needed a little time."

The Englishman had recovered his serenity. He gazed at Azim through the cloud of smoke that enveloped him, trying to sound him out.

"Are we partners or competitors?" demanded the Arab. "If we are working together, I would like us to be able to share everything. I do not hesitate to keep you informed of my wildest deductions—this story of the *ghul* bears witness to that. In return, I expect the same openness, Mr. Matheson."

Jeremy breathed out two tendrils of smoke. "I am sorry. I didn't mean to hurt you."

He held out his hand, with the cigarette held between index and middle fingers, and indicated the sofa. The two men sat down facing each other. Jeremy rubbed the nape of his neck with his free hand, seeking the right words with which to begin.

"The murder in Shubra was the slaughter of a poor guy, a vagrant. When I arrived on the scene, it was . . . worse than after a bombardment. The vagrant had been broken in half, literally. The jaw had been dislocated, to make it easier to smash his teeth and tear out his tongue. He was in pieces. That day we were short-staffed, and I had to do everything on my own. Including collecting up the bits of his corpse in the middle of that filthy hovel."

Jeremy paused to draw on his cigarette.

"It was a crime that passed understanding. A kind of savagery the like of which I had never seen. A totally gratuitous murder. I questioned the locals; people knew the victim vaguely by sight—a local vagrant who had no links with anyone, and absolutely no property that anyone might have coveted. He had purely and simply been torn to shreds for pleasure. Anyway, I did my job, looked for clues, witnesses: nothing. The whole thing was done with complete anonymity. I found nothing. The investigation had reached a dead end."

He took a final drag and crushed the cigarette butt in a dirty glass that had been sitting on the table since the previous night, then went on, "When I heard those two coppers talking in the corridor about the slaughter of a child, describing pretty much the same thing I'd been confronted with a month earlier, I saw red. Because I hadn't been capable of tracking down that . . . madman, a child had endured the same unspeakable torments."

For the first time since the beginning of his confession, Jeremy looked Azim straight in the eye.

"It is up to me to find whoever did this. I have to sort this thing out quickly, I and nobody else. If I could have nicked that piece of filth just after the vagrant's murder, those four children would be alive now."

The metallic echo of a train passing close by filled the long silence that followed.

"We will have him," Azim said at last, "I assure you that we will. Now, you say you found absolutely nothing at the first crime that might help us?"

"Nothing at all."

"Very well."

Jeremy recovered his composure. He took a second cigarette, which he held between his fingers without lighting.

"We are invited this evening to the home of the foundation's patron," he said. "That swine has obtained a copy of your report. He now knows everything about our investigation to date."

Azim appeared vexed by this news. "Really? Is he as influential as that?"

"He is rich. And he has been in Cairo for a long time. Two cards that ensure he wins every game."

"I think you are going to have to go there alone; I have already planned my time. Since this story of the *ghul* seems insane to you, I have taken it upon myself to deal with it and carry out a little more research."

"Meaning?" asked the Englishman.

"I have two or three little ideas to look into. But I would prefer to keep them to myself, unless they come to something."

"Azim, don't waste your time on this wild-goose chase."

"Let us keep a clear head. We have nothing at the moment, and I am no use to you, so I shall do as I see fit."

Jeremy opened his mouth to insist, but realized how determined his colleague was, and that it was pointless going on. "Very well then, if you have nothing better to do. . . ."

"What about you? How are you going to occupy your day?"

"Delving into Keoraz's past."

While Azim was pounding the streets in the eastern districts, Jeremy was visiting his various sources, beginning with a few journalists in whom he had absolute confidence. He then headed for the British Embassy, where he gained access to the archives without having to make use of his address book.

Methodically, he assembled all the possible information about Francis Keoraz.

Born into a moneyed London family, Keoraz had studied at Oxford before taking the reins of a family import business. He had not fought in the Great War. While others were dying at the front, he had met his first wife, who became one of the last victims of the Spanish Flu epidemic in 1919, just after giving birth. Immediately, Keoraz left for Cairo with his baby son, fleeing England and his grief. He had taken over as head of his father's bank, and made it prosper as the years went by.

Keoraz was famous for his phenomenal rages, and his taste for power and domination. The few unwary people who had deliberately got in his way had been swept aside, trampled on; and in his fury at not being obeyed without question, Keoraz had unrelentingly hounded them to ruin and even dishonor.

He was the kind of individual who made vindictive enemies.

His remarriage had silenced rumors that he was homosexual—despite his son—for he was not known to have made any feminine conquests since his arrival in Egypt. All he had needed was to meet Jezebel Leenhart.

Keoraz had only to ask and he could have every influential person in the city at his dinner table, including members of the government.

He loved, or rather had loved polo, which he had played until he tired of it, as he had done with the majority of his pursuits. Keoraz was a nomad when it came to his passions; settling down—whether it applied to his moods, his hobbies, or his life in general—was not his style. Once he had acquired and mastered something, it invariably became dull in his eyes.

That was what had fascinated him about Jezebel, Jeremy realized.

Nothing and no one was more versatile than Jezebel.

Nor less capable of being tamed.

She represented a challenge of which he would never tire.

Keoraz was one of those people whom common mortals regarded with hatred. He had been born into opulence, made use of it in order to find his own way, and whatever he had attempted, the outcome had always been success. Many people called him "rich" and "born lucky" behind his back, but he justified his successes with just one word: *work*.

Through having everything, Keoraz had lost pleasure in everyday things. This could explain why he had turned to charity. Once a man of his ilk had conquered everything he had desired, and lived a life centered on himself, he turned toward others.

He was looking for new satisfactions.

New pleasures.

Jeremy read his notes, summing up what he knew. Keoraz would set himself up as a role model, despite his volcanic nature and his domineering temperament.

Jeremy reread the last few sentences.

And a sly smile appeared on his face.

A role model.

Or—why not—a man who had broken down the last barriers that resisted him on the planet. The barriers of morality.

Because of his thirst for power, his tyranny and permanent success, he had slipped, losing control of his desires and ambitions, listening to the last facet of his character that he had never satisfied: the predator. For once in his life, he had abandoned full control of his being. Allowing the beast—the hunter!—to express itself.

He had come down from his luxurious villa to roam the anonymous alleyways of the poor districts, swathed in a black cape.

And the first vagrant who came along had served as a temple.

In which to house faith in his violence, which he had held back for so long.

A temple wherein he could liberate his rage.

A transitory temple, whose beauty lay in disappearing as his inadmissible passions unwound; a temple that crumbled, carrying away what could not remain, which must not remain. This shameful offering.

And for the first time, the game had caught hold of Keoraz.

Far from being sated or relieved, he had the *need* within him.

The need to begin again.

This time, he had crossed the last frontier, attained the very purity of horror, the quintessence of destruction.

Children.

And because he was no longer in command, because the monster within him was guiding his pleasures, he could no longer stop. This would never end. Never.

Except in blood.

Jeremy closed his eyes, pondering the clarity of this argument. How could it be ignored? Was he himself in a state of grace, enabling him to see how all the elements fitted together? No, nobody could argue that jealousy was blinding him, absolutely not. The logic of this study was far too coherent.

One afternoon.

That was all it had taken him to see right through Francis Keoraz.

· 27 ·

A bird was twittering on the window ledge.

Marion opened her eyes.

Immediately she felt the warmth at the base of her belly, between her thighs. The ghost of a man left her skin, slipped under the sheets and melted away with the last vestiges of night.

Marion blinked several times.

Her breasts were tense, and she felt as light-headed as if she had just made love. Her body was needy. Her buttocks contracted and shifted gently, in search of vanished pleasure.

She had been dreaming. About him.

Jeremy had come to visit her.

To make love to her.

The memories of the last pages she had read came back to her.

The detective's deductions about Francis Keoraz's personality.

That perversion cultivated by a life of excess and never-ending success.

Marion's muscles relaxed, and her excitement ebbed away. She pushed aside the sheets to let the cool morning air play over her naked body.

She needed a good shower. To warm her up, wake her up, and wash away her nocturnal escapades and their salty taste on her skin.

As she sat down with her cup of coffee and a slice of toast with honey, Marion was still accompanying the English investigator in his quest.

He was gifted with insight into the criminal mind. "The hunter's mind," as he called it. Nevertheless, Marion thought he was rather too sudden in deducing that Keoraz was the child-killer. True, the sadistic light that Jeremy had thrown on his personality could only confirm this suspicion, yet she thought he was too hasty. Despite his denials, was there not a certain unhealthy jealousy that, knowingly or not, had led him to view Keoraz as the ideal culprit?

However, his reasoning about what the millionaire was like deep down completely held water.

Marion had often talked to investigators from the judicial police who were passing through the institute, and she remembered a conversation with a young cop who was really keen on detective stories and criminology. He had explained to her how criminal research had taken a giant leap forward in thirty years, with computers, digital fingerprint files that could be consulted from anywhere in the country, plus the contribution made by science and DNA, not to mention the olfactory techniques that were in development. Nowadays, investigations relied on concrete facts, tangible proofs, whereas before a case might be sewn up on the basis of an unstable alchemy of personal conviction and the "balance of probability." On the basis of an abstraction, men and women had been sent to prison, and sometimes sentenced to death.

In the old days, an investigation was conducted on the strength of testimonies, and above all confessions. In the absence of either, only the inspector's logical deductions could enable a suspect to be identified.

That was what Jeremy was doing. Without material clues, he had only his own reasoning to help him find a culprit, to halt the massacre of children as swiftly as possible.

In the absence of tangible proof, he had to reassemble the facts and find a credible candidate, using only his intuition and experience.

Had Jeremy rushed toward the Keoraz solution because it was the only one at the time, or did he have a great detective's instinct for getting so quickly onto the right track?

Marion couldn't wait to read the next part.

"First of all, go and get some air," she said out loud. "It'll do you good."

She wrapped herself up in her trench coat, again taking care to bring the black book with her. It was settled; she wasn't letting it out of her sight again.

The bird she had heard when she awoke was still there, two yards above her, on the little wall of the cemetery terrace. She didn't know what species it was. White and black, or maybe blue. . . . A brave bird to face winter on the Mount.

You mean a disoriented bird . . . who should have left here ages ago.

"We can judge the state of our planet from their behavior," said a man behind her.

The warm, steady voice could only belong to Joe.

Marion turned to greet him.

"Hello, Marion."

"Hello."

"When the earth is not faring well, her children start doing curious things. The birds don't migrate at the right time anymore, females stop feeding their little ones, and sometimes the world's belly itself grumbles and strikes our civilization. Notice how there is never any hatred in it, nothing but a warning shot across the bows, a flash of the teeth. Hatred belongs to humans."

"A warning shot that sometimes kills thousands of men, women, and children."

"A drama, a trauma for us. The merest flick of a finger on the scale of life. It is man in his individuality and in the present moment who creates intense emotion. The death of a human being is appalling, but when you talk about ten thousand deaths in the year 1500 and something it seems almost less serious. In appearance . . . everything is a question of scale."

"You're very philosophical this morning."

"Ah, well, you've caught me on my way to church."

Marion's face lit up.

"So you spend time with our beloved brotherhood!"

Tall and charismatic as ever, Joe clasped his hands behind his back. "Wrong, my dear."

He spun around to shoot a glance at the parish church behind him. "I was having my morning walk before going to pray to our good Lord, here. I leave the abbey Masses to the tourists and people who like religious grandeur."

Marion gave him a rueful smile, to show that he had figured her out.

"But perhaps you would do me the pleasure of coming to my table this evening for dinner?" he ventured. "I think that my advanced age permits me to issue that kind of open invitation without appearing vulgar."

Marion gave him the most charming of smiles. "What can I bring?"

"Oh, you won't find anything on this pebble, so just come with your good humor; it will intoxicate you better than any expensive wine. Eight o'clock at my door. Have a good day, Marion."

Marion saw him enter the church of Saint-Pierre by the side door, then she walked down toward the entrance to the village. For the first time since her arrival, she was surprised to find several tourists walking along the medieval roads. But of course, it was the weekend. Marion walked out onto the causeway and started a long walk to the foot of the sanctuary. Taking advantage of the low tide, she walked past the fortifications, around the Gabriel Tower, which brought back memories of the riddle, and ended up at the chapel of Saint-Aubert on the northwestern side of the Mount. The trees laid bare by the November cold creaked in the wind, huddled close together on the slope that ran under the Merveille.

From here, the bell tower displayed an intimidating power. Its carved apertures looked down over the bay with more certainty than a moral lighthouse, dictating everybody's behavior in the name of religious precepts, and, from its great height, reminding them of the punishment in store for disobedience.

Its shadow crushed Marion.

She sat down to gaze at the sea of damp sand and the distant polders, on her left. She stayed there for a moment, before walking back.

Walking past the square at the entrance to the village, Marion felt a flash of happiness as a little girl ran into her and clumsily excused herself. The little one was no older than ten, and her red spectacles were now sitting crookedly on her nose. Marion squatted down to her level to set them straight, pretending to squint, and the little girl gratified her by laughing out loud. The parents were just behind, keeping a watch on their child. Marion acknowledged them as she walked past.

Her chest suddenly lifted; all at once the air had a bitter taste. The taste of her personal situation. Her solitude. Her single state. Her age. Contact with children soothed her heart. But it also rebounded back on her, with all the appropriate cruelty.

Marion generally avoided these kinds of thoughts. They didn't get her anywhere. Well, nowhere pleasant.

Half a dozen tourists were sitting down to eat at Mère Poulard's and this demonstration of fresh life inspired Marion. She went in, to associate herself with these faces. She ordered the famous omelette and enjoyed the conversations that surrounded her—however banal they might be—even more.

She drank four cups of tea in all and treated herself to two portions of *tarte aux pommes*, stretching out this moment of relaxation into the middle of the afternoon. When she reemerged onto rue Grande, she bumped into Sister Gabriela, the young nun with the musical voice. They chatted for a few minutes before Marion offered to help her with her task, which consisted of putting up flyers reminding people that there was going to be an orchestral concert in the abbey on Monday evening. Marion received the news with surprise and pleasure; at least it would occupy one of her evenings.

She got back to her little house late in the day, and took a hot bath while listening to the music that boomed out of the stereo on the ground floor.

She then faced the dilemma of choosing what to wear for dinner. She didn't have much to choose from, as she had left most of her wardrobe back in Paris. She didn't want to be too dressy, so as not to make Joe uneasy, but she didn't want to be too casual either, in case she offended him. Eventually she decided on a pair of black, front-pleated trousers, and a thin roll-neck sweater, for which she had paid a fortune on a wild spending spree, beneath a very classic woollen waistcoat. The mirror reflected back the image of a woman who was still beautiful, with soft skin, well-tended features, and a desirable figure.

Not for much longer if you keep stuffing yourself like this. . . .

A woman who took care of herself.

The image of a woman who was nearly forty years old.

Single.

She bit her lower lip.

The white streaks within her blond hair did not look out of place. On the contrary, they conferred on it that original, almost exotic aspect that went well with her musical laughter and teasing looks.

Marion picked up a barrette and drew back her hair into a low bun on the nape of her neck. Just a hint of makeup and she would feel ready.

As if she was going on a date.

With a man who was at least eighty. . . .

She considered herself pathetic.

But any pretext is okay if it makes you feel just a little bit beautiful, from time to time. . . .

And at eight o'clock precisely she knocked at Joe's door.

The old man had put on a beige suit for the occasion, and a shirt with a starched collar, around which he had knotted a maroon scarf. He had not, however, shaved.

She handed him a bottle of red wine.

"I had this in one of my cupboards—a present from the brotherhood for my nights of desperation," she joked. "It might help if my good humor lets us down. . . ."

He took it from her and showed her inside.

"I hope you're hungry," he warned. "After all these years, I'm still incapable of getting quantities right. I've made enough for an army!"

Marion discovered that he had brought out the good china and an embroidered tablecloth in honor of the occasion.

"It's because it's Saturday evening," he explained, following her gaze. "Do please sit down."

A game of chess covered part of the coffee table in the lounge; the pieces were still arranged as though a game were in progress.

"Do you play?" asked Joe.

"I'd love to, but I'm afraid of being bad at it."

"Well you should try! I have a shortage of opponents here."

"Who was your opponent today?"

Joe rubbed his hands. "Grégoire, Béatrice's son. A very good player."

"Him? I wouldn't have imagined him playing chess. . . ."

"And yet he does. He's a good kid. He's withering away on the Mount, I'm afraid. He needs life, and a male presence; I don't think I'm wrong about that."

Marion searched the old man's face. His gaze was still fixed on the gaming board. He looked almost sad.

"You like him a lot, don't you?"

Joe nodded. "Grégoire often comes to play against me, and we talk, about everything and nothing. He's just a kid who could do with a father, that's all. It's difficult for him, living with his mother so far from everything. Béatrice made this choice for herself, because of a personal desire; but Grégoire hasn't come out of it so well, what with so much solitude."

Joe straightened up and his jovial mood resurfaced. "Right, then, let's eat—if you'd like to."

He served them coquilles Saint-Jacques, which they devoured, joking about the fact that nobody could have secrets when you lived in such a small village. Everyone knew everything about everyone else.

"That's precisely the trap," retorted Marion. "You can come here to bury a dark past in daily routine, behind a mask you can quickly create. And precisely because everyone thinks they know everything about everyone else, the secrets remain buried deep."

Joe's face lit up with a broad grin. "I can see you're beginning to figure out the spirit of the Mount," he said proudly.

"It's the spirit of small communities. And of islands. I've already discussed it with Béatrice."

He lifted a finger to emphasize that he understood where her deductions were coming from.

They got to know each other a little better over the sea bass with mashed potatoes and leeks, each going a little further into the other's private world. Joe confided to Marion that he had always been a bachelor before trying to get her to speak in turn. The bottle of wine emptied as the meal progressed, and Marion felt the alcohol getting a grip on her. A certain feeling of euphoria invaded her little by little. She felt good in the company of the old man, was enjoying the delicious dinner, and she willingly allowed herself to become intoxicated.

She ended up depicting herself as a woman who was a little too pushy, too demanding, perpetually unsatisfied. Barely had she become involved in a serious relationship and she was already identifying her partner's faults. She ended up seeing nothing but those faults and swiftly getting rid of him. At work, she wasn't sociable enough, not sufficiently fond of her colleagues. At the end of the day, she was living in a kind of autocracy, with two or three girlfriends whom she went out with occasionally, when they managed to get rid of their husbands and find babysitters for their children.

She almost mentioned Jeremy Matheson, drawing a parallel between them, but just avoided the blunder.

During dessert, Joe drew her a less-than-glowing portrait of the members of the brotherhood whom he knew. Brother Gilles was his favorite target; he regarded the man with the bird of prey's profile as a more formidable hawk than those who currently inhabited the White House. A manipulative man, he was even more pernicious since his dreams of acquiring a more prestigious title had been shattered when his superiors realized that there was more ambition in him than faith. The only pleasure he had left was in exercising his low-level power over the members of the community and glorying in it.

Brother Serge wasn't much better. Joe reckoned he was worthy of being a Mafia godfather; with more than one eye on his flock, he had the reputation of being very authoritarian and a little too strict, but Joe and he had always kept their distance from each other, as Joe had had a real affection for the brotherhood's former superior, who had left almost ten years earlier.

Next, Joe described Brother Christophe—Marion's "Brother Anemia"—as a big, rather dim owl, and he made Marion laugh when he admitted that he would not be surprised to happen upon Brother Christophe covered in cabalistic tattoos and sanctifying the name of the Devil. . . . His manner was just too nice to be sincere.

Sister Luce was the female counterpart of her acolyte, Brother Gilles, treacherous and malign. "An arid heart" was the expression he used to describe her, and Marion wondered for a moment if that hid a secret of their common past. She imagined a story of platonic love between Joe and Sister Luce, under the jealous eye of Brother Gilles, which would explain this distance between the two men today.

Joe admitted he knew nothing about Brother Damien, who had arrived too recently in the brotherhood, except that he "had the ingenuousness of a simpleton painted all over his face." He spoke about Sister Anne, who was the closest member of the brotherhood to Marion, as a kind, intelligent woman, a woman you could trust. As for the others, Brother Gaël and Sisters Gabriela and Agathe, in his eyes they were no more than "young religious people who were still full of hope and promise."

Reassured by all these confidences, Marion explained to her host her mania for attaching dreadful nicknames to everyone and Joe could barely contain himself when he heard about "Brother Wrong Way" and his consorts. He was reassured to learn that he did not have a nickname.

Marion was staggering a little when she got back home, around eleven, after promising to return soon so they could fall about laughing again.

She went to bed in a good mood, with shining eyes.

The desire to read a little before going to sleep insinuated itself through the wine fumes. She went downstairs to fetch the diary from the pocket of her trench coat and quickly returned to the warmth of her bed.

Soon, only her night-light was still lit. She had only just opened the book when a flash of lightning lit up the cemetery beneath her window.

The first drops of rain began to fall, slow and hesitant.

Marion snuggled down in her bed and picked up the story where she had left off.

· 28 ·

E very man knew what he had to do.
If everyone was well coordinated, the plan could work.

Azim went over everything one more time, to check that he had not missed a single detail.

The volunteers would be at their posts in less than an hour. The day he had spent wandering around el-Gamaliya had not been in vain. The old hashish smoker had agreed straightaway, despite his fear. The trader had yielded as soon as Azim reminded him that it was about saving children. The two men had immediately set to work to find other volunteers. Around half the men needed were found among the relatives of the victims. The other half were assembled before the end of the day, for Maghrib.* Azim's idea was basically very simple, and relied as much on their ability to cover the whole district as on luck.

The *ghul* had been spotted four times, within a small area, and always in the Gamaliya district. Azim hoped that with men stationed on the roofs in strategic positions, if the *ghul* happened to pass through the district, it could not fail to be noticed. This meant covering several acres of narrow streets and jumbled buildings. With the aid of the old man and the clothes seller, his witnesses, Azim had drummed up and motivated around thirty lookouts. One by one, they were posted on the balconies of buildings with strict orders not to move for any reason. The arrival of an imam among them silenced the practical jokers and reassured Azim that they would respect their undertaking, more through religious fear than a sense of duty. The spiritual leader had joined the men when it got back to him what was being prepared. It was whispered that a *ghul* was on the prowl, and that it was going to be spotted that

* The time of prayer, just before dusk—the Arab day begins at sunset, not at sunrise

very night. "And what if one of the faithful finds himself confronted by it, what will they do?" exclaimed the imam before demanding that he be taken to the volunteers. Only prayers to Allah could drive away the monster, he had declared before a sea of respectful faces. If such a creature was indeed roaming their streets, it was up to him to make it flee.

Despite his police badge, Azim knew he carried little weight beside the imam. He had just replied that if the *ghul* was spotted, it would be his job to go to the spot to check that it was indeed a demon and only then could the imam come and repudiate it. If it was in fact a flesh and blood criminal, the police would deal with it and arrest the individual.

Azim knew the risks he was running. If they really did get their hands on the culprit, he would have to be swift and skillful. The men would not be slow in wanting to carry out the sentence themselves, without judge or jury.

What exactly did he expect to find? A man or . . . a *ghul*? If he was unsure, it was because of the statements of the two witnesses, categorically stating that what they had encountered was not human. Azim did not know what to think. Everything was converging on the mythological hypothesis. . . . And yet the steamroller of Western education and its rational certainties had already done a good undermining job, starting with police college. He could not deny that deep inside, he believed in a basically human explanation of the drama.

The sun set while everyone obtained a few provisions and a blanket to confront the long night that awaited them, and they all dispersed toward their lookout posts.

A furniture seller at Khan el-Khalili* whose nephew was among the volunteers agreed to lend lamps for all the lookouts, which would serve as a signal. If someone spotted a hooded figure moving strangely, his instructions were to light his lamp quickly and

* A gigantic bazaar, famous in Cairo.

shake it in the direction of the highest observation point, where Azim would be posted.

Darkness took possession of the narrow streets.

The shutters closed one after another while the few streetlamps were lit.

The heat lessened slowly, and with it, the hundreds of scents floating around el-Gamaliya made their way back toward the closed shops, stables, and attics, all peaceful once again.

Conversation, banter, shouts, and arguments were silenced within the shelter of the ancient walls.

The stars started to pierce the ceiling of the world, in ever-greater numbers. Azim gazed at them in silence. It was as if the earth was just a building and the sky another, he thought; two celestial neighbors sending back their light to each other, the lights from households observing each other without seeing, millions of lives, millions of miles away.

The silhouettes of the minarets seemed to sway against the relief map of the cosmos.

In the distance, the muezzins sang out the call to prayer.

And the hours passed.

Heliopolis was a flat town, a town of columns with its horseshoe-shaped arches and its accolades, a city with broad, clean streets erected in a very fashionable Moorish style.

Jeremy got off the streetcar opposite the Helipolis police headquarters, and walked a little further to reach the Keoraz house, which stood next to the golf course.

A wall three yards high encircled and protected the millionaire's sanctuary. This was a man who prized privacy and serenity.

Or who likes living sheltered from curious eyes, protecting his dark activities. . . .

Jeremy rang the bell beside the iron gates, and a guard swiftly appeared. He let him in as soon as he saw his police identity card.

The Romanesque villa was built on top of a little artificial hill, and was reached by a pathway of crunching gravel that ran across a sea of perfectly kept lawn. When he arrived at the top Jeremy halted, stunned.

The last twenty yards consisted of black marble flagstones, flanked by silver and golden sycamores, with two very long pools filled with mercury, in which the Milky Way was reflected with perfect clarity.

Torches burned every five paces, to bring out the full effect of the terrace. In addition to the silver-and-gold leaves on the trees, little chimes of the same metals hung from the branches, so sensitive that they sounded when guests walked past.

Jeremy tiptoed through this fabulous setting, surprised by the fluidity of his movements on the ground. The guard was now walking in front of him, making the metal chimes tinkle in his wake.

Keoraz appeared right at the end, emerging from the vestibule and waiting between the columns at the entrance. "Mr. Matheson! How do you find my little Mesopotamian-style garden?"

"Clean."

Keoraz, who had probably been expecting the usual gushing compliments, fell silent.

"And shiny," added Jeremy.

"I confess I did not create it. . . . I had it built on the model of the garden that belonged to Khumarawayh, an emir of the Tulunid dynasty. Do you know of him?"

"Not at all."

"Late ninth century. One should take an interest in history, Detective, it is the foundation stone of our future."

So he knows history too, and probably Egyptian legends! noted Jeremy, concealing a contented smile with difficulty. He was corresponding more and more closely to the ideal profile. Keoraz possessed the knowledge that would enable him to mask his crimes with scene-setting that would remind people of the famous ghoul.

"Do come in, we're just about to have an aperitif in the atrium."

He dismissed the guard and led Jeremy into the house, from which they reemerged almost immediately, entering into an internal paved courtyard, with an impluvium, or Roman pool, in the center. Two purple sofas decorated with black cushions embroidered in gold thread awaited them. Hanging torches encircled them with their warm, moving light. Frescoes depicting rural views covered the walls between each door.

"Take a seat. What would you like to drink?"

Jeremy didn't have a chance to reply.

"Whiskey." Jezebel was standing in the doorway leading to the main rooms.

"You always drink whiskey, don't you?"

He nodded, but did not say a word.

She had slipped into a dress trimmed with red fur, and was holding a cigarette holder at the end of which one was burning.

Keoraz observed the pair's interaction before commenting.

"I have an excellent one. I shall fetch it myself. Please excuse me, but I can no longer bear the house staff. I've sacked almost all of them. In the end nobody serves one better than oneself."

At which he left by one of the side doors.

Jeremy, who was sitting down, stood up again as Jezebel approached.

"You can drop the gallant behavior," she said, sitting down opposite him. "So, it wasn't too difficult, coming here?"

"I already knew the address."

"I wasn't talking about the route. I meant the decision."

A mocking smile was visible on the carmine lips. "You won't even call me 'Mrs. Keoraz.' It must have cost you dear in pride, coming to our happy marital home."

"Pride has nothing to do with it."

"Oh, yes? What then? Simple *affection*?"

"A tenderness that relates to our past."

Her smile broadened. "Of course . . . I had forgotten, forgive me."

Keoraz reappeared with a tray and three glasses. He offered the detective his whiskey and took two glasses of champagne, one for his wife and one for himself, before sitting down very close beside her.

"My dear fellow, I have set aside my entire evening for you," he said.

"Before anything else, sir, I should like to ask you if you have read the investigation report."

The millionaire raised an eyebrow and stared at him in amusement.

"What do you think?"

"It ought not to have happened like this, and you should know that I regret it."

"My interests are involved. I believe I have every right to protect them, and hard luck if it conflicts with your sense of procedures. We are far from the metropolis here, and that brings an element of fluidity to our protocols, a flexibility that is the sole advantage of this corner of the world, and not to use it would be risible."

Jeremy swallowed a mouthful of whiskey and decided to attack. "You could be among the suspects. Reading the investigation report could pose a problem."

"Me, a suspect?" It was so grotesque that he could only laugh.

"Have you lost your mind, Jeremy?" scoffed Jezebel.

"I am serious. Moreover, what do you do with your nights, Mr. Keoraz?"

"Detective! Are you here to resolve this affair and help me or to seek to do me harm? Be quite clear, so that I know who my friends are, and who my enemies."

Jeremy drew out a cigarette from his pack and lit it, explaining with emphasis, "I do not seek to cause you any trouble, sir, I am just doing my job. If I do not do it, people could make use of that procedural error to exonerate the guilty party."

He assumed a sharper tone and added: " 'Detective Matheson,

how can you eliminate any other people if you have not questioned all the protagonists?' . . . coming from a barrister, that would do a great deal of harm to our prosecution."

Keoraz drank his remaining half-glass of champagne in a single gulp. "Very well, then let's go to it. What do you want to know?"

Jeremy observed him, trying to see through his businessman's hard outer shell, to get a clear idea of his real state of mind. But nothing filtered through. Nothing but his smooth surface veneer, characterized by the perfect line of his hair part. He was as cold as a lizard.

"I appreciate this," said the detective finally. "To begin, where do you spend your nights?"

Amused by the question, Keoraz laid his hand upon his wife's. "Here, at home. And sometimes at the Mena House, in Giza."

"Do you sleep alone?"

"What kind of question is that?"

"Answer it, if you please."

Jezebel did so: "You know me, Jeremy; you should know the answer."

Jeremy digested the innuendo, forbidding his imagination to gain the upper hand. "It is Mr. Keoraz whom I would like to hear," he retorted.

"No," confirmed Keoraz, "I do not sleep alone. Jezebel is with me."

"So she is your alibi for the nights when the crimes were committed?"

"Of course! If I need an alibi. . . . But I do not think we are at that stage, Detective."

Jeremy swallowed another burning mouthful. "You must admit that it is a rather flimsy alibi," he said. "If one partner is a heavy sleeper, it is difficult to confirm with complete certainty that the other partner did indeed remain in bed all night."

"But I am confirming it," insisted Jezebel.

Jeremy prevented himself from replying. He was going too far, going beyond the professional, allowing jealousy into his reasoning. He was going to discredit himself, become an object of ridicule.

He raised one hand in apology. "Very well. I had to ask those questions, I am sure you will understand."

Jezebel nonchalantly tossed her cigarette butt into the central pool. Her husband ground his teeth, sparing her a scene in front of the detective. He allowed his anger to dissipate and turned to the detective: "I think I understood that there were no tangible leads up to yesterday. Have matters developed?"

"I am sorry, but I cannot discuss that with you; please don't regard it as personal. Let us say that the investigation is proceeding."

Keoraz was about to reply when his expression changed completely. From being hermetic and distant, it became almost tender. "Whatever are you doing out of bed?"

Jeremy watched him get to his feet to join a boy aged around nine, who had just entered through one of the wooden doors. The little boy had the same sharp profile as his father; he was holding a teddy bear in one hand and his baptismal medal in the other.

"Allow me to introduce my son, Detective. George Keoraz."

Jeremy gave the child a little wave, but received no response.

"Well, then, come with me." Keoraz spoke to his child with a gentleness that did not suit him. "You should be in your bed, you have your piano lesson tomorrow with Mrs. Lentini, and if you don't sleep you won't be strong enough to take the train. It's like when you go to school, you . . ."

The businessman took his son in his arms and talked to him quietly.

A warm hand brushed Jeremy's knee. "Are you staying for dinner? The one time you come here, it would be a pity not to take advantage of it. . . ."

The roof of the building where Azim was keeping watch was in a condition that reflected its age: not so much impressive as worrying.

Beneath his feet, cracks ran right across from one side to the other, even more detailed than the lines on a palm. The roof was reached by an open trapdoor, through which poked the top of a ladder, looking for all the world like the horns of a hidden devil.

Wooden poles sat in rough-hewn holes, providing the support for a fabric roof, under which two hammocks hung. A jar of water and a pot of dates were their only accompaniments on the carpet of the shelter.

Azim was dozing in one of the hammocks, his breath whistling through his mustache. His fellow lookout, a man named Khalil, was seated against the roof's coping, his arms resting on the shaky old masonry. He was gazing watchfully into the night.

While all the rest of the district was sleeping in the darkness, the main roads gave off a gentle light as their streetlamps waned.

They had all been watching over el-Gamaliya for hours already, with not a sign of the creature.

Khalil had a panoramic view of all the different sites where the signal might come from. No movement, no light.

Sleep wove its cloak of silence over the city, smothering sounds, numbing minds, and rendering bodies unconscious.

The young man rolled backward and got up to go and fetch a handful of dates. The detective was snoring very softly, his feverish sleep preventing him from relaxing fully.

In the distance, a shutter banged loudly, making Khalil start.

Azim opened his mouth several times before sinking back into the warmth of his dreams.

Khalil started walking back and forth across the roof, rhythmically pacing. All the excitement of the previous evening had faded, and now that the veil of time had filtered all emotions, all that remained was boredom. Khalil went and sat down on the parapet.

He shivered as he ate another date.

His blanket was in the hammock, and he thought about fetching it to wrap around himself. The nights were beginning to be as cold as the days could be suffocatingly hot; this year, the desert's breath had decided to engulf spring and impose a precocious summer upon Egypt. Still, if they at least avoided an invasion by locusts that would be something, noted Khalil.

He stretched up his arms and yawned.

A lump of stone tore away from his impromptu seat, immediately disappearing into the darkness of the street, fifteen yards below.

Khalil fell backward.

In absolute silence.

He barely made a sound.

His hands fell swiftly back on the low wall that was dragging him down into emptiness.

His fingers scrabbled around in emptiness.

And his nails scratched something hard.

He tightened his palms with all his strength and pulled in his abdominal muscles, his torso leaning dangerously over death.

And Khalil gently rocked onto the right side, unable to breathe.

He let himself fall between the cracks on the roof, thanking Allah in a trembling whisper.

He had so very nearly fallen, to be crushed down below on the beaten earth, the bones of his skull pulverized like pottery, his brains spread about in the rubbish. Khalil returned his attention to the stars.

So very nearly . . .

If he had been wrapped up in his blanket, he would not have survived.

All at once the air seemed more flavorsome.

The wooden ladder made a cracking noise.

Khalil turned toward the trapdoor. Nobody.

He approached, dragging his tanned-hide moccasins in the dust, and leaned over the hole, holding one of the ladder's uprights with one hand.

It was completely dark down below. Khalil could not make out anything.

One of the rungs of the ladder creaked again.

Khalil crouched down and stuck his head down into the dark square.

Maybe it was the young girl from the first floor?

"Is there anybody there?" he whispered. "Mina, is that you?"

A shape unfolded, only three feet from his face.

Two yellow eyes.

Not human.

Khalil leaped back with a shout. He supported himself on the ladder to get further away and it began to sway.

A furious yowling sound rose up out of the hole, and the dislodged cat fled, meowing discontentedly.

Azim had swiftly extracted himself from his hammock and was already running to help his companion, one hand on the holster of the gun that hung on his belt.

"What's going on?" he stammered, not yet properly awake.

Khalil began to laugh with relief.

"What? What was it?" demanded Azim, who did not share the joke.

"Nothing, it was just a cat. It frightened me."

Azim let out a long breath, emptying all the accumulated tension out of his chest. He ran a hand across his face.

All at once, Khalil leaped to his feet. "The signal! The signal!"

All traces of joy had left the young man, who was pointing to the north, his eyes wide and staring.

Azim followed the direction he was indicating and saw, right on top of a small building, a light that was being swung from right to left.

Azim clenched his fists.

At last.

The *ghul* had just emerged from its lair.

· 29 ·

All of the part that Marion had just read was strangely written. Scarcely had he finished his observations on Francis Keoraz's culpability, than the author—Jeremy—had drawn a large arrow pointing to the very last pages. There, Marion found a long supplementary chapter solely about Azim and the account of that night, dedicated to tracking down the monster. Apparently, Jeremy had partly used what his colleague had told him, but also various witness accounts that he had briefly been able to gather, like that of Khalil, whom he had met personally.

Nevertheless, Marion suspected Jeremy of indulging in entirely imaginary digressions with regard to Azim's emotions. At times, he wrote as if he had been in the little Egyptian's skin.

She found this redirection to the back of the notebook bizarre, as if it were a passage added on at the last moment, impossible to insert except by means of this arrow, drawn at the top of the pages. So she decided to alternate reading it with the chapter she had got up to, a little more than halfway through the tale. This way, she moved successively from Azim's hunt in the narrow streets of the eastern districts to Jeremy's dinner with Mr. and Mrs. Keoraz. The suspense was even greater.

She sat up a little higher in bed and checked the time on the alarm clock.

Half-past midnight.

It was late.

So what, my dear? It's Sunday tomorrow. . . . And besides . . .

She was going to read, on and on. Enjoy herself. At least finish the passage at the end of the diary, with Azim.

Outside the rain had stopped. Marion glanced swiftly through the window.

The cemetery terrace shone silver from the moon, which was

finally emerging from behind the clouds. The wind whistled through all the streets, along the fronts of the buildings, and twisted and turned among the headstones.

The stone crosses in this morbid forest bore a figure of Christ on their trunks, divine fruit bearing witness to the passage of the seasons according to their respective states of decrepitude. Among all these tortured and dislocated bodies, Marion spotted a face.

A round head, turned white by the moonlight.

The eyes were more real than reality.

Tiredness and the half-light abated.

And Marion realized that the face was not mounted on a cross.

But on a living body.

It really was someone.

She started.

There was a man in the cemetery, and he was watching her.

Marion hurriedly turned out her light, plunging the bedroom into darkness. She got out of bed and approached the little dormer window.

She took care to hide behind the wall, revealing nothing but her right eye to distinguish the outside world.

The man was standing amid the tombs. His hands in the pockets of a windbreaker. He was hopping from one foot to the other, trying to see what had just happened in Marion's bedroom.

It was Ludwig. The night watchman.

Marion sighed. A cloud of condensation formed on the window in front of her mouth.

Ludwig bent forward, his tongue on his lips. He raised a hand, then hesitated, not certain of what he was seeing, and just on the off-chance gave Marion a friendly wave. She was careful not to respond.

She waited until he shrugged his shoulders and strolled nonchalantly out of the cemetery to head back to bed.

That was all she needed. *A night watchman who was a Peeping Tom!*

How long had he been spying on her? Didn't he have anything better to do?

At this hour of night, on the Mount. . . . No, probably not. . . .

The idea of a fifteen-year-old kid trying to see her getting undressed made her smile, but Ludwig. . . . He was a responsible adult. . . . *Stupid bastard!* she raged.

She promised herself that she'd make him feel uncomfortable the next time they met; she'd have to find exactly the right words to put him in his place and remove any desire in him to do it again.

After all that, the desire to continue reading had evaporated. She no longer had the heart to immerse herself in 1920s Cairo. And even less to switch on her bedside lamp again!

Marion rolled over in the sheets, ready for sleep, but she moved around a lot before she closed her eyes, thinking again of Ludwig. Stupor was turning increasingly to anger.

The wind grew in intensity, wailing like a flock of nocturnal birds. It hovered over the village while the sea battered at the gates of the seawall.

· 30 ·

Marion hung on to the guardrail to climb the steps that ran along the ramparts.

The storm had made its presence felt in the small hours.

The shutters slammed against the walls with suicidal violence.

The sea clashed its undulating cymbals, bringing forth a tremolo of foam that spurted onto the towers, soiling the stone with this choleric ejaculation.

Marion bent low so as not to give too much purchase to the powerful winds. She held her coat tightly to her with her free hand, her bag swaying against her painful hips. As soon as she awoke, she had decided not to read in her living room anymore but in a more favorable context, in one of the rooms of the Merveille.

It was while climbing the staircase of the inner Grand Degré that she realized the extent of the danger. Her desire to read was changing into a stupid idea, a regrettable whim. Here the wind was even stronger than in the village; it hurtled down from the top of the steps to the bottom, poured into the canyon formed between the high walls of the abbot's residence on one side and the church on the other. Its vehemence was even more terrifying than its intermittent howling; it tangled itself around Marion's legs, flattened her clothes as if to smell them before trying to knock her down. Each time she lifted a foot, she ran the risk of losing her balance and falling backward.

There was something baleful about this wind.

Normally so rational, she couldn't prevent herself from thinking about the film *The Exorcist*. She had the impression that a supernatural force was throwing itself from the top of the steps to sweep everything away, that the wind itself was the Devil's breath. In the midst of this chaos, the brotherhood's hearty singing of the Sunday morning liturgy took on a redemptive air.

Marion managed to push open a door that she immediately closed by throwing all her weight against it.

She shook her head.

I've never seen a storm like it!

In better spirits, she thought back to her fantasy of the Devil trying to hurl her into the sky. It was a load of nonsense, but it didn't surprise her; she'd always had a dazzling imagination.

She crossed a passageway, and went down a staircase into a more modestly sized room.

The wind was chanting its invocation even inside the walls of the abbey, whistling and echoing in the bowels of the church before hammering on both sides of the high windows.

Marion checked that the diary was still in her pocket.

She had chosen a good day to come and read here.

She wandered according to her instinct until she happened upon a locked door. Searching among the keys on her bunch, she eventually found the right one and entered a long room on the intermediate level of the Merveille, the Salle des Hôtes. The absence of tourists in the winter had enabled the brotherhood to convert it back into a workroom. Several wooden desks stood facing one another, in the middle of tables covered with old books. Marion checked that there was nobody about before approaching.

The brothers had collected large quantities of very old paper, aged to differing degrees, and inks of various types in order to carry out restoration. Fragments of virgin parchment were piled up between bowls of colored pigments and all the instruments worthy of the Inquisition that were used in the repair of manuscripts. Some of the writings dated back to the thirteenth century.

Marion wavered among the chairs.

The place was ideal for reading. Alas, the brothers and sisters might come and work here during the day; apart from the fact that she was doubtless unwelcome in this room, she would lose the tranquillity she sought.

Marion closed the door again behind her and strolled a little further, then pushed open another door, onto a passageway from which she overlooked the Salle des Chevaliers, the former scriptorium. Here, she would be left in peace.

She settled herself beneath one of the windows so that her eyes would not have to strain in the half-light, checked once again that she was alone, and returned to that night in March 1928, when Azim was tracking that enigmatic ghoul while Jeremy was spending the evening at the Keoraz house.

Then the wind came and flattened itself against the glass behind her, as sharply as a presence, pressing its face close so that it too could read the fabulous tale.

· 31 ·

O nce dinner was over, they went into the small drawing room. Jeremy had tried to decline the invitation, with a thousand credible pretexts he'd prepared to save himself, but none of them had got any further than his thoughts. He had remained silent until he could no longer get out of it.

Francis Keoraz led the conversation, which centered on himself and his success, describing his triumphs with surprising lassitude. After an hour, Jeremy had come to regard this ordeal as an unhoped-for opportunity to gain a better understanding of who Keoraz really was. Search his attitudes to discern breaches, gain possession of his mind in order to map out its twists and turns. It was presumptuous, but Jeremy found the idea quite attractive.

He took care not to divulge personal information when Keoraz questioned him, nevertheless Jezebel enjoyed making a few barbed comments intended for him.

Curiously, as the meal progressed she became less caustic and more attentive, sometimes even conniving. Twice, addressing Jeremy, she asked if he recalled such and such a day and a detail that she conjured up from their past life. Each time, the detective caught the bright flash of jealousy's blade in Keoraz's eyes.

At least they shared that, he noted with bitter irony.

The master of the house served them a liqueur that he had brought over directly from Scotland, and opened a fine metal box of Nestor cigarettes, from which Jeremy helped himself.

"Do you play billiards, Detective?"

"On occasion."

Keoraz directed an amused smirk at him and signaled him to follow him into the adjoining room. A superb wooden billiard table stood there, illuminated by its fringed lamp.

Jeremy drew on his cigarette and let out a grunt of satisfaction.

"They're good, aren't they?" chuckled Keoraz with a knowing air. "I buy them by the box at Groppi's, they cost me a fortune! But this tobacco is worth every piaster spent on it . . ."

"For those who can afford it," Jeremy couldn't stop himself adding.

They each selected a cue and Jeremy began the game. Jezebel sat down on a velour-covered bench, her glass in her hand.

"Do you frequent a club?" Keoraz asked after several minutes' play.

"Every one in the street. Every place where there's a billiard table, a partner, and an invitation."

Keoraz leaned over the green baize. "Join us sometime at the Gezira Sporting Club, you'll have an opportunity to carry off plenty of presumptuous scalps."

"I shall think about it."

Keoraz took aim, sliding his cue back and forth across his hand, his face stern. He struck the ball and observed it as it moved across the table.

"Why did you create this foundation?"

Keoraz, who clearly had not been expecting this question, abandoned the rest of his turn and turned questioning eyes on Jeremy.

"Why?" he repeated with unexpected seriousness. "What kind of man do you think I am? A miserly, inflexible blackguard? Or a philanthropist, hiding under the appearance of a sour-tempered businessman? Oh, don't take the trouble to answer, I can see from your face what your opinion would be. And you want to know, Mr. Matheson? You would have only half the truth. I am both, Detective. Like everyone on this planet. I am neither white nor black, merely colorless and striving not to lose my way by being blinded by one color or another. As I move along, I take on the hue beside me and falter before I recover my balance. And so on . . ."

Jeremy walked around the table to gauge the best angle before playing. "Not everyone in the world is necessarily gray, if I may say so," he commented.

"That is not what I said. We have no color, we take on the color of our thoughts, our actions. And those are as changeable and diversified as a painter's palette."

Keoraz offered Jeremy the billiard rest, but he refused with a brief shake of the head.

"My foundation is all I can do to say to this country that I like it, Detective, in my own way. I have so much money that I can no longer count it; what could I do to say thank you to this city? Take care of its offspring, the men of tomorrow. In the Cairo tradition, I set up a teaching foundation, a little like the *waqf* * that made it possible to build those immense fountains one sees in the streets, with a room upstairs in which to teach the Koran. The difference is that my foundation is slanted toward general learning, and is open to those few families that agree to send their daughters at the same time as their sons."

"So the formidable Mr. Keoraz offers culture to the children of Egypt!" Jeremy declared with emphasis. "Admirable!"

"You don't believe it, do you? You are one of those skeptics who want to know what I am concealing behind this act of compassion and generosity, which is somewhat improbable coming from a hardheaded millionaire businessman. I say it again, here and now: there is nothing. Nothing more egotistical than a feeling of lightness when I get up in the morning. You would say that I created this foundation to buy back my conscience, but I say that it has given me a form of serenity—it is a matter of one's point of view, I would imagine. I am not the demon some wish to see in me. As I told you: I am similar to all men, neither completely bad nor really good."

"And yet bad men exist. Monsters capable of the worst atrocities."

Keoraz held his cue in front of him, vertically, and leaned his hands on the top of the heel, about level with his breastbone. "That is the question, my dear fellow. The rift of evil."

* A pious foundation also known in Northern Africa under the name of *habous*

Jeremy took up a playing position. "The rift of evil?" he asked. "I've never heard of it."

"The rift between those who think that monsters exist, and those for whom Man is born good, or at least neutral, and becomes what he is by dint of his experiences. Is evil an entity or a corruption of our society?"

"Rousseau?"

Keoraz winked at the detective. "Very good. But not just Rousseau. The rift of evil is a question that has been haunting our race since the dawn of civilization. Are we the fruit of our experiences or are we born predisposed to those experiences? Are the worst criminals all that way because they have experienced the worst torments in their development to manhood, or is it because they were born with this inclination toward violence?"

Jeremy delayed his shot long enough to ask a question. "Don't recent thinkers on the subject of the mind say that it is the child, through its development, who constitutes the foundation of our character? A child who is persecuted at school by the other children could perhaps develop a sort of . . . defense mechanism, hating the other children without any distinction among them and—"

"Tut-tut-tut, Detective, I must stop you there. The question is not about what that situation might engender in the head of a child, but 'why did we arrive at this situation?' Why did this child arouse the anger and hatred of his comrades? Through his misdeeds, his wicked words, or his calumny, I suppose. Why did he have this basic attitude?"

Keoraz had entered into the state of earthly detachment experienced by great orators, who are captivating as much because of their charisma as the emotion they put into their words. He continued: "Is evil an affectation that we contract through having lived, like a sickness of the soul, in a way similar to melancholia, or is it that mysterious force that inhabits our cells from the first sparks of our creation? Two distinct visions of the essence of evil. That is the rift of evil. An eternal debate on the existence of good and evil, or on the colorless and chameleonlike nature of Man."

Jeremy jabbed his cue forward and missed his shot.

"Well, well, Jeremy, is this debate about our nature awakening some kind of contradiction in your mind?" teased Jezebel, momentarily casting off her haughtiness.

The detective swapped places with the millionaire, ignoring Jezebel. "I confess I do not know on which side of this rift of evil I should stand, I . . . I have from time to time observed the terrible nature of certain individuals among us. I do not say whether we are born evil or become that way; I am very afraid that the two are not so far apart. But I know that existence carries this evil within it. And that even the best people can sometimes topple over onto the other side, contaminated without hope of remission. Man is capable of anything."

The tone he used and the expression on his face commanded Jezebel's respect. "You talk as if you were a victim of this transformation yourself."

There was no hint of a question in what she said, nothing but a troubled observation.

"In a way."

"Are all detectives burdened with this wound?" she asked, almost tenderly.

"This has nothing to do with my job."

Keoraz understood all at once. He laid his cue on the edge of the table. "The war . . . ," he said.

Jeremy raised his eyes to look at him. Keoraz went into more detail, "You are of the age, and in the physical and intellectual condition to have served during the Great War."

Jeremy ran his tongue over his lips. He looked around for his glass. Jezebel got up and brought it to him without a word.

"It is in extreme conditions that a man reveals his true nature, is that not a well-known fact?" he said, taking a drink. "From experience, I say that evil is as much an essence in the cosmos as a fever in our society."

Keoraz approached, carrying a crystal decanter, and topped Jeremy's glass.

"However atrocious they may be, the barbarous actions in time of war are, alas, completely in context," suggested the millionaire.

Jeremy drank again, taking two long swallows. "The context is a pretext. What I am talking about doesn't concern the killings against the Germans. But what happened within a unit. Among British *gentlemen*."

Jezebel folded her arms across her chest.

"During that fearsome era of organized slaughter, I was present at the most infamous persecution. A group of perverted NCOs, deranged by spending too much time in the blood and the mud. And a young soldier who was too naïve. Young and handsome like a beach after the tide has gone out, leaving it with not a scar upon it."

His moist eyes trembled under the light from the billiard table. "I saw them persecute him. Turn him into their whipping boy, by turns a means of physical, moral, and sexual release. He was spared nothing. Nothing. It lasted eight months. And between each torture: the battles, the pulp of flesh pulverized in the air by the din of the guns, the agonized cries of men who'd been playing cards three hours earlier, and the only point of reference that arid land, a field plowed by weapons and gorged with blood, where nothing grew but the roots of despair."

"Didn't anyone intervene to save this young man?" demanded Jezebel indignantly, her voice a whisper filled with emotion.

"We were cut off from the rest of the troops, in an isolated post, commanded by an officer too blinded by dignity to allow himself to believe that his men could do such a thing. During the war, the chain of command was the only constant that could be respected. You could die of hunger, cold, or bullets, but you could never call your hierarchy into question. The punishment would have been the firing squad. And the torturers were all noncommissioned officers. Picking a fight with them would have been tantamount to suicide."

Without a word, Jeremy picked up the decanter and poured himself another glass. "One day, a man—his name was Dickey—intervened. He couldn't bear the young soldier's tears anymore. Seeing three of the four NCOs approaching to lay into their 'object,' Dickey got up to bar their way. He was away three days in the hospital, and when he came back, the NCOs gave him a hard life. He died a week later, in a trench. From then on, the unit chose to close its eyes and ears when necessary. The majority of the men had at least a fiancée, if not a wife and children, and they wanted to go home. Death was already too constant a visitor to the trenches and the barbed wire for them to go out of their way to provoke it. And in time of war, it is easier to close your eyes."

"And what about you?" inquired Keoraz.

"I waited until it passed."

"How did it end?" asked Jezebel, troubled.

"In blood." Jeremy finished his drink, gazing into emptiness. "One day," he went on, "the young soldier refused to submit. It was one time too many, I imagine. The NCOs fixed their bayonets and amused themselves with him. One by one, the other soldiers emerged from the tent. The torture lasted several hours. The sheets were covered with blood afterward. This time, the torturers couldn't hide all the horror, and the unfortunate was sent to the hospital. It appears he said nothing for several days, not one word, not one cry of pain. He just shat blood. With a swollen face and an enormous gash on his chest."

In the silence that followed, Keoraz lit a cigar without taking his eyes off the detective. Jezebel wept.

Her incandescent green eyes were covered by a veil of tears; she pursed her lips tightly to hold in the sobs as best she could.

"What happened to the NCOs?" asked Keoraz.

"They were sentenced to death by court-martial. But in the time it took to convict them, they had decimated half the unit in suicidal attacks."

"And the young soldier?"

"I don't know. He died or as good as died, I would imagine. Unless the evil entered him by dint of his having been confronted by it every day. Whatever happened, his life was shattered."

Jeremy swung around toward Jezebel, who gazed at him unblinkingly, the tears rolling down as far as the lines of her lips, where they gathered into a glistening pearl.

What did she see in him now? What image was drawn up by the mention of his name, of their shared memories? He who had always lied when she asked him questions about his past at that time, about his service in the war, who had disguised this truth behind tirelessly repeated lies until he had convinced himself they were true.

"You see, Mr. Keoraz," Jeremy said in a voice that was abnormally low and trembling, "evil men do exist, men who are capable of the worst things. There may be those who become that way, victims of evil who carry around their pain like ghosts unable to find absolution. In any event, there are people who do evil without fighting against it, without apologies, without any inner struggle; on the contrary, they rejoice in it. Those people are monsters."

He leaned forward to hand Jezebel a handkerchief from his jacket pocket. Without even looking at his audience, he continued in the same tone, laden with anger and suffering: "And those men do not deserve any trial; all they deserve is death. Only death."

His thighs bulging from the effort, Azim climbed the last of the building's stairs and finally reached the roof by means of the ladder.

Khalil was waiting for him and stretched out a hand. "Well? What did you see? Was it really the . . . the demon?"

Azim collapsed onto the carpet, reaching out for the water jar. Khalil poured some out for him to drink.

"False alarm," grunted Azim between two gulps.

"But . . . but the signal . . ."

"A man who was too jumpy, who grabbed the lamp as soon as he spotted a shape moving strangely. It was a lame man, not a beast from Hell."

Disappointment appeared on the young man's face. "Do you think we'll really see it?" he asked.

"I don't know, Khalil, my plan rests on a crazy probability. The *ghul* has been seen in this area several times in the past few weeks; if we are lucky, then maybe. . . . Come on, rest now, I shall keep watch and you can relieve me for the last few hours."

Khalil lay down in one of the hammocks and swiftly sank into an agitated sleep.

Azim wrapped himself up in a blanket and sat himself at the corner of the building, overlooking the torpor of the district. The curtain of stars lit up Cairo's anarchic silhouette.

Azim was not at all tired. His run through the narrow streets had rather reinvigorated him, as the fear had mingled with excitement in a volcanic cocktail. All the same, what emotion! Approaching the suspect had sent terrible shivers through him, one hand on the stock of his revolver, ready to draw and fire.

If it had really been the *ghul*, shooting at it would not have been any great help to him. According to the legends, only the power of prayers had the ability to ward off the demon.

"Come on, admit it," he whispered to himself. "You don't believe that. If you did, you wouldn't have charged right up to it, knowing your weapon would be no use. You think that behind all this are the machinations of a man."

Then who was he? Why had he taken an interest in children at night? In sniffing their clothing, and trying to enter their bedrooms as the trader had testified?

A little disoriented, Azim's gaze strayed over the cracks in the roof.

He no longer knew what to think. The tiredness . . . the emotion . . .

He must concentrate, not doze off, wait for the signal. Nothing else . . .

Azim waited, with the greatest vigilance.

The hours went by, little by little. The streets were still as silent as ever. The cold became thicker, pressing blankets to clothing and skin even more as the night wore on.

Azim ate a lot of dates as he waited.

To his great surprise, the imam came to pay him a visit a little after one in the morning. He found it pointless to wait at the mosque for someone to fetch him and had decided to go around to all the lookouts to bring them support. Azim and he spoke a little, essentially about the *ghul*, which the imam barely dared name. The little detective was disturbed to discover that the religious man seemed to fear the monster. Sweat beaded his brow when they discussed the imam's decisive role if the human factor was eliminated.

The imam left an hour later, declaring that he would keep an eye on the roofs and the lanterns. If the signal was given, he would wait five minutes, allowing Azim the necessary time to judge the situation in situ, and then come to help, remaining within hearing distance just in case.

Azim returned to quietness and solitude.

His thoughts wandered. And halted at his colleague.

Matheson did not believe in the supernatural. He refused to keep an open mind about this lead, even though it had been verified by two distinct witnesses. The Englishman had an unappealing reputation in the Cairo police force. He worked alone, and when he was forced to do otherwise, he did not share, leading his investigation in his way, keeping silent. He was a bad partner. But an excellent detective.

His reputation as a "trustworthy man" ensured that he found all doors open, or almost. People said he was mysterious about his private life. Azim, who was beginning to get to know him, preferred the adjective *reserved*. Matheson did not share easily—neither his work, nor his private life. And he had the same attitude of savage defense as wounded animals, preferring to be left alone, to bind his wounds, in this case a wounded heart.

Yes, the more he thought about it, Matheson was—

Azim leaped forward, suddenly getting to his feet.

A lantern was frantically waving to and fro in the distance.

With such intensity that the flame had difficulty remaining steady. The person giving the signal was terrified.

He wasn't just giving the signal, no . . .

He was appealing for help.

· 32 ·

Marion looked up from her reading.

The storm was blotting out the sun, darkening the Salle des Chevaliers. The pillars added to these areas of shadow by masking the far corners; the only things missing were burning torches on the walls, and you would think you had stepped back into the Middle Ages.

During her first hour's reading, Marion had heard religious chants filtering down from the church above, reinforcing the impression that she was outside the world. Now there was nothing to accompany her but the anger of the elements outside; they hurled themselves ceaselessly against the window behind her, tapping and raging on the glass, and making her jump.

Intermittently, a long, high wail sounded along the stone corridors, wandering along, dying from door to door, and then losing itself in the Mount's foundations.

Marion rummaged in her bag in search of the one or two biscuits she'd brought with her. She ate them slowly, savoring each mouthful.

Jeremy's confidences regarding his wartime experiences had particularly upset her, and she found herself dwelling on his reflections on evil and its roots. In parallel, Azim's watch on the streets of Cairo with his men was heart-stoppingly suspenseful. At the end of the day, the irony of the situation was almost comical. While one was tracking down evil, the other was attempting to understand its essential nature.

Marion shook the numbness from her legs by walking around the nearest fireplace, beneath the shadowy eaves, as far as the raised passage on the south side of the chamber. She imagined this place with its walls decked in rich tapestries, as much to keep in the heat as to partition the hall into smaller rooms; with roaring fires in each hearth, and monks bent over their desks, illuminating manuscripts with stiff pages. The smell of the candles must have imbued every inch of the place, down to the carpets covering the floor. And the light could only have been a vast, moving creature, flowing among the draperies, its spectral leopard skin spotted with black and amber, undulating across the soaring ceilings.

She was there. She could almost hear the quill pens scratching over the parchments, the clink of the jars containing the inks, the isolated creak of a chair, and the soft rustling of sleeves on the wooden tables.

Marion threaded her way among the monks as they worked, between the cold pillars, to reach the window and her possessions.

Little by little they evaporated, leaving only damp grayness behind them. Marion drank a little water from her bottle, put it back in her bag, and turned around to look at the landscape through the window.

The trees down below were shaking dangerously, their branches clashing against one another and threatening to snap, and all the bushes were under attack from the incessant winds' wantonly destructive breath.

The rain was falling almost horizontally, slicing through the air. At this altitude, the sea became confused with the sky; whirlpools of little droplets rose and fell all over the place, except when they merged and imploded.

Marion breathed in noisily under the effect of such a sight, then she returned to her book, leaving the Mount to its battle with nature and time.

She had reached a passage about Azim, the famous chapter exiled to the very end of the diary.

I find it easy to imagine Azim running along the district's still-warm paving stones, in the middle of that starry night, then pounding the beaten earth of the narrow streets, forced to bend double at the sharp twists and turns, so as to get by more easily, and only just avoiding all the detritus that littered his path. As he approached the area where the alarm signal had originated, Azim suddenly forced himself to calm down, slowing to a walk to get his breath back and to ensure greater discretion. He must be careful. He was on the trail of a ghul. . . . His mind was torn between his ancestral beliefs and the more Cartesian training that the colonial world had instilled in him. That was the source of the dilemma in his mind. What was he really expecting to find? A real demon or a sick person in disguise? The weight of his revolver did not give him any real comfort. Azim was on the . . .

Marion stopped reading.

The door of the raised passage had just opened.

A hooded silhouette appeared up above.

Its gaze began to roam the hall; then it halted. It swung round to face Marion, and the hood slid back.

Brother Gilles laid his withered hands on the metal balustrade and stared at her. Eventually he spoke. "Ah, it's you," he said cheerlessly.

"Hello."

"You shouldn't be here, there's a storm. You'd be better off in your room."

Marion gave her coat the most discreet tug possible, just enough to cover up the black book. She didn't know if he had spotted it.

"I wanted to take advantage of the atmosphere," she replied.

"You chose a bad time, and in future it would be better if you had someone with you when you came up to the abbey."

Marion displayed the impressive bunch of keys with which Brother Serge had entrusted her.

"I have the best possible guides," she replied with a hint of jaunty insolence. "A little patience, keys to open every door, and all the time I need."

Marion was jubilant. This man who liked nothing better than to control everything on the Mount was visibly furious.

Brother Gilles's glittering eyes pierced right through her. "Well, don't come to me complaining if you get lost or catch your death . . ."

He added something else between his teeth that Marion couldn't catch, and continued on his way out, leaving the door open behind him.

She picked up the diary again, hoping that the monk had not noticed anything.

Marion had forgotten where she was up to.

Azim.

The signal.

The ghoul.

Yes, that was it. The ghoul . . .

· 33 ·

Azim hurtled down the narrow streets at full speed, his leather soles echoing on the paving stones or thudding against the beaten earth.

He changed tack and lowered his center of gravity at each

hairpin bend, compensating for his mistakes at the last moment by steadying himself with a hand or an arm against the wall of a house, and headed swiftly down the next street. The darkness did not make his task any easier; he could not make out the holes, detritus, and other objects littered across his path as he ran, and several times he almost fell.

As he neared the building where the signal had originated, Azim slowed down. He must not allow himself to make a sound. The advantages of his plan also resulted in weaknesses. From down below, the signal was not visible.

There was no quick way for Azim to find out if the lookout was still in position, waving his lantern, or if he had stopped.

There was just the crossroads left and then he would be there.

The little Egyptian slid along the wall, trying to get his breath back. The street he needed to go down was ten yards farther on, gaping wide and sinister. Azim mopped the sweat from his face with his sleeve and ran the tips of his fingers over his revolver. There was no longer anything magical or reassuring about the touch.

It was a *ghul* he was tracking.

He entered the dark street. Rectangles of fabric were stretched out at intervals between the fronts of the houses, to protect them from the sun. But at this time of night, they made the place even darker than a moonless night.

Azim briefly considered the top of the building where the lookout must be standing. How had he managed to see the monster passing below with all these draperies? True, they didn't cover the whole street, but all the same they did limit the field of vision. . . .

Perhaps he didn't really see it! thought Azim. *Perhaps it's another false alarm.*

Immediately he remembered the panicky way the lantern had moved. No, the man who had given the signal had been really terrified, to the point that he no longer realized he was shaking the lantern too hard, reducing the strength of its flame and rendering his actions almost pointless.

He had seen something.

Azim continued on his way, all his senses on the alert. He moved one step at a time, searching the shadows, his concentration mingled with the beginnings of panic.

He could hardly make out anything.

Caution told him to stop right there and then, and retrace his steps. But he did nothing. What if he was right? What if the child-killer was within his reach? Azim had no right not to continue. If another boy was slaughtered, how would he feel?

He was moving forward slowly when he caught the sound of breathing.

Slow and deep.

The beast must be lurking in some kind of recess a little farther on, on the right-hand side.

Azim unfastened the buckle of his holster and withdrew his revolver. He knew it was useless, but the feel of it in his hand gave him the strength he needed to approach.

It is not a ghul. . . . It is a man. . . .

Azim was no longer sure of anything.

Three more feet.

His heart was pounding beneath his shirt, urging him to run away, each muffled blow hammering home the fact that it had no desire to stop beating. Azim carried on, and gained another foot.

His revolver was weightless now.

Azim noticed that he was letting his weapon slip out of his fingers. He swiftly tightened his grip, trying to refocus his attention. Fear hampered him.

He was almost there.

The breathing grew harsher; a rasping sound.

Azim raised his weapon.

The recess was close enough to see now.

The shadowy corner became more clearly defined.

Azim began to make out a rectangular shape.

A shutter.

Then he saw.

A man was asleep there, snoring in the shade of his shutter.

All the tension that had overtaken him left the Egyptian's body. It flowed all the way down to his heels and then trickled away, to be replaced by a single fear that left his legs too light, in danger of giving way beneath his weight.

He must go on.

A cat began to yowl furiously from an alleyway a little farther on. Then there was the clatter of wooden boxes being knocked over, and hurried footsteps.

Silence immediately regained possession of el-Gamaliya.

Azim holstered his gun and covered the rest of the distance separating him from the thoroughfare.

He flattened himself against the corner, with just the very edge of his face showing.

All was calm and deserted.

Then the cat appeared.

It halted in the middle of a crossroads, its ears flattened back. From where he stood, Azim noticed that the animal was probably feral. But the cat shouldn't be afraid of humans, just wary of them.

Azim crept out of his hiding place and approached the animal, all senses on the alert.

The cat let out a meow as shrill as if it had caught its paw in a painful trap and rushed off into the night.

Azim did not move.

He was totally visible, in the middle of the street.

A long shape unfolded from a dark corner of the crossroads.

Its torso rose, followed by the rest of its body, and then finally its head.

It was enveloped in a shapeless robe of coarse fabric, concealing its body, and its face was masked by a voluminous hood.

Azim could not breathe.

The shape climbed onto a dilapidated chest, and crouched down.

It seemed to the detective then that it tilted its head back slightly to . . . sniff the air.

Suddenly, it leaped forward, soundlessly but with surprising speed.

It was running after the cat.

Azim was petrified; he dared not follow.

He had seen it.

The *ghul*.

It existed.

The wild cat began to yowl again, and spit ferociously. In a second, the hoarse cry turned into a shriek of pain.

And then nothing. Not a sound.

Azim must act. If he remained there, the *ghul* could run away, or it might see him if it reemerged and retraced its steps.

He gulped in oxygen and returned to the crossroads as silently as possible, before slipping into the corner where the creature had disappeared.

Scarcely was his back against the wall when he detected movement out of the corner of his left eye.

It was reemerging.

Azim flattened himself as much as he could in the darkness.

The monster was less than nine feet from him. Motionless.

It was holding the cat in one hand. The poor beast was hanging completely limp, a dark liquid trickling onto the ground. Soon, there was enough blood on the ground to produce the damp, liquid sound of a continual flow.

The *ghul* lifted its prey up to its mouth and Azim heard it sniffing. Successive, short, whistling breaths. *As if it was attempting to recognize the smell*, thought the detective, as fascinated as he was terrified.

The demon's face was still invisible beneath its immense hood.

Still carrying its trophy, it set off again.

And entered a blind alley.

Azim closed his eyes very briefly, trying to recall the place.

It was the same dead end the old hashish smoker had pointed out to him.

Azim scoured the darkness, determined not to lose sight of the tall silhouette.

A good six two, at least, he noted. It was good to know that his police instinct for morphology hadn't left him yet.

The *ghul* paused in front of a door at the far end before pushing it open and disappearing inside.

Thirty seconds later, Azim was outside the door.

From inside the abandoned house, he could hear the heavy scraping of someone pushing a massive object against the wall.

Azim waited another minute. Still no sign of life.

Then he too pushed open the door and entered the wolf's lair.

Throwing caution to the wind, he flicked on his cigarette lighter.

Timidly, the flame rose and cast an orange halo over a small downstairs room littered with rubble. A partially collapsed staircase led upstairs.

In the corner opposite the entrance, a large rotting chest had been used to collect stagnant water.

The water was rippling as if someone had just thrown in a sizable object.

Or as if someone had moved the chest!

Azim knelt down beside it and tried to get a handhold on the sides. The *ghul* couldn't have gone upstairs; that way was impracticable.

He must be losing his mind. If there was one thing he must do it was run far away from here. Alert the imam, so that he could come and put an end to this abomination.

But Azim was incapable of turning tail. He wanted to know the truth. To stick to the monster until there could be no further doubt. To discover its lair; to know.

There were no handholds on the chest.

Azim seized it in both hands and pulled it with all his strength.

It made a shrill grating sound as it slid aside.

And a staircase leading down to the cellar opened up beneath it.

Azim spotted a sticky stain on one of the stone steps. The cat's blood.

The detective held his lighter in front of him, cutting an amber-colored swath through the darkness. He descended the staircase, almost trembling, and emerged in a cramped, musty-smelling room. The only furniture consisted of two barrels, eaten away by the damp.

Azim raised his flame a little higher above him.

An immense eye was trained on him.

As dark as Joseph's Well at night.

The black eye was weeping in the detective's flickering light.

It was a hole knocked through the wall, about three feet high.

A way through, wide enough to enable a person to enter on his knees. A few roots protruded from it. The earth was clammy, opening itself to the cellar in an almost obscene manner, with its brown, sweaty flesh, its pendulous white veins, and its sickening odor of decay. Azim turned around to check that there was no other way out.

If he wanted to follow the *ghul,* he must plunge into these sinister entrails.

Azim crouched down and stuck the hand holding the lighter into the opening.

The monster had hollowed out his lair like a snake burrowing into the ground to enjoy its prey.

The detective bowed his shoulders and entered the house's interior.

Instantly the air became thicker, the light more confined.

Azim began to move forward on all fours, using his right elbow to pull himself along so as not to let go of his only source of light.

Within three movements he was covered in soil.

The roots rumpled his hair with their hooked tendrils, while the points of stones scraped his knees.

He could no longer see any more than twenty inches in front of him.

All that awaited him farther on was a circle of darkness. Movement after movement, he crawled farther into this nothingness, leaving the world of the living for that of the demons.

He had difficulty breathing; the narrowness of the passageway was oppressive.

The flame started to falter.

Then the passage in front of him opened up its maw, liberating dark shadows that crawled convulsively toward Azim.

The flame guttered, and then died.

Azim just had time to see the black hole before him forming its round mouth into a greedy smile.

And the eternal night of the lair put out its tongue and engulfed his entire being.

· 34 ·

While she was reading in the timid daylight, inside a building buffeted by extreme weather conditions, Marion saw the reflection of a massive shadow moving behind her, a shadow that spread itself right across the room before disappearing almost as swiftly.

This made Marion forget the Egyptian tale. She was fifteen yards above the pathway and there was no balcony.

She kneeled on the bench and leaned toward the window.

Outside, the storm was shaking the trees and bushes.

Suddenly, the wind gusted violently beneath a branch, tearing it off and hurling it toward the heavens. The enormous section of tree cracked and spun around in the air, then suddenly rose up toward Marion.

She threw herself backward, letting out a cry of surprise.

She saw the branch graze the wall of the Merveille as it flew up, casting a broad shadow on the ground as it passed the window.

The elements were being unleashed; maybe it was time to get a little more worried, to join the brotherhood at the abbot's residence, or go back home.

You're safer here, in the heart of this stone fortress, than in your ridiculous little house! And in any case, you can't go outside in this weather, you'd end up getting hit on the head by a roof tile.

It was just a bit of wind, that was all.

The storm produced strange sounds in the Merveille, whistling, banging, grating, sometimes down below, sometimes up above.

Marion sat down again to eat the sandwich she'd made that morning before she came. She unwrapped it from its tinfoil and started eating, munching on it rather halfheartedly.

The Salle des Chevaliers now resembled an ancient crypt in Marion's imagination. There, she saw a procession of people in red robes and gowns, walking along with candles in their hands, preparing for an odious sacrifice to the glory of the Devil.

Marion began laughing softly.

All she had to do was let her thoughts wander, and she could see anything and everything here; she had the imagination of a child.

She lifted her sandwich to her mouth.

Her eyes wandered up again to the raised passageway.

A shape was hidden in the darkness of the door left open by Brother Gilles.

It was impossible to make out properly from where Marion was.

All she could see was dark fabric, and a voluminous hood pulled down over the face. An allegory of death.

Marion stood up.

Whoever was standing in the doorway took a sudden step back.

"Hey!" Marion called.

The silhouette disappeared into the darkness.

"Hey!" she shouted again, much more loudly.

And she ran across the hall, up the steps and through the doorway. She had a choice of several exits from the adjoining room.

The corridor bore right, then bent at a sharper angle.

Marion rushed around this corner and just had time to grab hold of the wall so as not to crash into the tall, robed presence in front of her.

Marion sidestepped and made a grab for another jutting edge on the wall beside her.

"Well, well! Whatever's the matter with you?" asked the presence unhurriedly, with that dismantling of sentences into distinct words that was a trademark of Brother Christophe.

Marion looked him up and down as she got her breath back. He didn't seem at all tired, barely even surprised.

"I . . . I was looking for someone," explained Marion.

"By running? It's dangerous here, you could split your head open on a sharp corner, or by falling down one of our many staircases."

"You didn't come across someone just now, did you?"

Brother Christophe—Brother Anemia—shook his head without bothering to think. "No, nobody at all. Who are you looking for in such a hurry?"

"Er"—Marion took the time to breathe in before going any further—"someone who played a . . . prank on me."

"Who would that be?"

Marion opened her hand wide, signaling her confusion. "I don't know. Someone wearing a robe like yours, but with their head covered. I was reading in my corner and whoever it was was watching me—there you are, you know everything. And I really think he—or she—went that way."

"Well, no. This place is vast, you know; you can soon get the passageways mixed up when you don't know it, and the sounds all echo in every direction, particularly today with the wind. Anyway, I hope you haven't hurt yourself?"

Marion reassured him with a shake of her head.

She realized then that she had left the diary in the Salle des Chevaliers. Within reach of the first person who might come upon it.

"Thank you," she said. "I'll see you soon."

The brother had no time to reply; she was already retracing her steps at top speed.

She got back to the immense room with the round pillars.

She saw her things, lying at the foot of the bench, at the back of the room.

Her coat spread out.

She ran faster.

The black book was indeed there.

The sandwich was right beside it.

She sighed, hands on hips.

This time she couldn't put it down to paranoia; she had *really* seen somebody spying on her.

This had gone too far. She'd have to talk to Sister Anne about it.

But what if Sister Anne was in on it? It was rather a catch-22 situation. . . . But what was the nun going to say anyway? "Calm yourself, nobody here is watching you." Probably something along those lines. So who could she talk to about it? Joe? Béatrice?

Béatrice was the most likely to be objective. Marion knew she wouldn't look down on her with a mocking smile.

There was nothing for it but to catch and unmask this person, and demand an explanation. Nevertheless, the idea of sharing this with someone made her feel better.

Yes, she was going to go back down to the village and ask her new friend for advice.

Marion stood by the window and noted that the storm had not abated.

In an hour or two, if the elements permitted, she would go back home.

She picked up Jeremy Matheson's diary.

· 35 ·

Crushed by the shadows' suffocating caress, Azim seized his lighter in both hands and hurriedly put his thumb to the striker wheel.

It sparked, but it could not drive back the darkness.

Azim panicked. He knew he could not retrace his steps—moving backward here would be very difficult and take a long time.

Then he imagined what might happen if the *ghul* retraced its steps and loomed up in front of him, right before his eyes.

That might already be happening.

It was approaching, crawling silently in his direction, its nightmarish claws tearing up the earth less than three feet from him. It was very, very close. . . .

Why had his lighter gone out?

It had run out of fluid.

Azim shook the object gently. No, it was almost full.

A draft.

No! A movement *of the air!*

Something—or someone—was moving in the passage, and this had caused a sudden indraft that had put out his flame just like someone blowing out a candle.

That meant that he was not alone in the lair.

Azim tried to light his lighter one more time.

The flame rose up with reassuring elegance.

Azim hardly dared turn his head to look in front of him; the terror of what he was going to find there made his whole body shake.

The disfigured face of the *ghul,* its pointed teeth emerging from its slobbering maw.

His eyes pivoted around slowly.

There was nothing.

Nothing but this hand-excavated underground tunnel.

He started moving again.

Eventually he detected a widening of the tunnel.

It opened out into a corridor.

Azim emerged from the hole at top speed, half-suffocated. He straightened out his legs in the dusty corridor. Fallen rocks blocked one of the ways out, leaving only one possible way to go.

Where was he? The walls were made of stone; holding his flame close, Azim thought he could make out the vestiges of age-old decorations. Paintings several centuries old, obliterated by time's eraser.

He walked about ten steps forward and discovered some pieces of broken pottery, which he stepped over. The ceiling was high, around twelve feet. There was no doubt about it, he was walking through a secret underground passageway that was associated with several mysterious structures in ancient Qahira.* The corridor eventually opened out into a larger chamber.

Reaching the threshold, Azim knew he was vulnerable, revealing his presence with his light, but he could not do otherwise. He could only hope that the *ghul* had been in a hurry and hadn't noticed its pursuer, and that it wasn't lurking in a corner waiting to ambush him.

The detective's foot encountered something very small. He looked down.

What looked like an old papyrus lay rotting on the ground.

Azim went down on one knee and lowered his lighter.

The document was written in Arabic. It resembled an administrative note from some ancient time. Since the eighth century, official papyri had no longer been written in Greek but in Arabic, which seemed to prove that the place Azim was walking through came later—or at least the period of its use, before it was forgotten. Azim picked up the papyrus, which he rolled up very gently before slipping it into his jacket pocket.

* An old city that, with Fustat, formed the modern-day city of Cairo

Trusting his sense of direction, Azim estimated that he could not be very far from Khan el-Khalili's bazaar. His knowledge of the history of Cairo led him to make logical deductions, and he nodded to himself in agreement, alone in the darkness. He had an idea of the place in which he found himself. He was in old Qahira, where Gawhar had begun building gigantic palaces at the end of the tenth century, the largest of which extended over more than twenty-two acres. Historians of the Arab world had testified to the place's many marvels. From the depths of his memory, Azim trawled up the name of Nasir-i Khusraw, an eleventh-century traveler, who had revealed the existence of a sumptuous underground passageway, enabling the sovereign to go from the great palace to the more westerly small one. A gallery so vast that one could ride through it astride one's horse. This legendary underground thoroughfare had just taken shape beneath his feet, Azim realized.

The detective breathed out the dusty air that clogged up his lungs. His mind had wandered through history for ten seconds, the time it took to rid himself sufficiently of fear and remain in control of himself.

Other, more macabre historical facts jostled in his brain.

If he was indeed near the foundations of Khan el-Khalili, that implied that he was no longer very far from a cursed place. Indeed, the great bazaar had been built on an ancient tomb that had been emptied of its sacred bones. The *ghul* could not have dreamed of a better setting for its malevolent nature.

Azim entered the chamber, his feeble light illuminating only a tiny portion of it. Trying to keep tight hold of the lighter, he burned his index finger on the metal. He stifled the pain by biting his upper lip.

He swiftly noticed another bloodstain on the ground. The *ghul* had been through here with its cat, preceding him by barely five minutes. Azim could not suppress a shiver, which shook him violently.

What madness had taken hold of him? There was still time to

retrace his steps, to run and alert the imam. . . . Azim did not listen to his own reason; his legs were already making their way through the terra-cotta debris, almost a thousand years old.

Whatever there might be farther on, he prayed that he would come upon a staircase, so that he wouldn't have to go back into the vile tunnel, to crawl through that hell.

Three-quarters of the room were invisible to him, as his flame was not sufficiently powerful. Azim walked forward, following the nearest wall, in the direction seemingly indicated by the monster with the increasingly rare drops of blood it left in its wake.

An opening on the left.

Another chamber.

The blood trail led into it.

Azim stepped through the stone door frame, crossed six feet of corridor, and entered what seemed to him—from the muffled sound of his footsteps—to be a more modestly sized place.

It gave off a terrible stench of acidic urine. Another, more rancid one swiftly mingled with it: a smell of cold meat, the one that always haunted butchers' cellars.

Azim first lit up an iron coat peg that had been fixed to the wall very recently. Part of it disappeared under the large, hooded cape that was suspended from it.

Gooseflesh prickled the little detective's arms.

It was the *ghul*'s robe.

He was very close.

This time he drew his revolver; it mattered little to him that it might not be effective, he needed its powerful feel.

The orange halo lit an upright barrel, filled with a dark liquid. Azim advanced slowly, searching all around him, on the lookout for any sign of life, any movement, fearing that someone might approach without his noticing.

He bent low enough to see into the barrel.

The liquid was in fact water.

Reassured, Azim straightened up.

It was at that moment that the horror appeared.

It was revealed in the quivering brightness from the lighter.

Just beside the water barrel. The corpse of a man.

It was hanging on the wall, part of the face skinned alive, the flesh still sweating a variety of organic matter. The end of the nose had been torn off, along with most of the cheeks and lips, opening the whole of the mouth and teeth to the air. The yellow enamel of damaged teeth gleamed in the light.

It was the body of a black man, probably a Sudanese, guessed Azim, and it was completely hairless.

He could not have died more than an hour or two earlier. His eyeballs were still moist, and the left one was abnormally swollen.

Something disturbed Azim, beyond the mutilations that had been inflicted upon the poor man; a detail he could not identify was causing him concern.

Azim drew back and turned around.

He lowered his arm to cast light on an old table.

He stiffened.

The corpse of the cat had been placed upon it.

Suddenly he raised his weapon in front of him, like a shield, searching the darkness that extended beneath the thin veil of flame.

The *ghul* wasn't very far away, he was sure of it.

In fact, it was probably right here, with him.

It was watching him.

Azim did not notice the subtle displacement of air behind him.

The shadows that wove a wall behind him barely revealed the silhouette of the tall Sudanese. And in this compact darkness, the corpse moved.

Furtively, the head lifted up. Its eyes shone in the remnants of the light, immense and round. They fixed on Azim.

The jaw with the broken teeth opened a little way, and a translucent, opaque thread flowed out of the mouth onto the chin, then onto the floor.

And the entire corpse slipped into the gloom, without a sound.

Azim, who had heard nothing, explored the room a little more.

The remains of fresh food shared a plate on the table. Bits of chewed-up bread, reduced to a viscous paste, and a strip of meat, one side of which had been sucked for so long that it was falling apart in places.

Azim's foot caught in something soft.

He lowered the lighter, to discover a heap of stinking fur and viscera. The whole thing was seething with plump maggots.

Dogs, cats, and even a few jackals, all disemboweled.

Azim walked around the charnel house, and halted in front of a filthy straw mattress, part of which was covered by an equally dirty blanket.

What he saw next to it turned his stomach.

Chains had been riveted to the wall. It was modern work, in no way linked to the archaeology of the site. The chains ended in leather bracelets, small in size.

For the wrists and ankles of a child.

An empty bowl accompanied a tiny chest. Azim came closer to look inside.

The contrast between the object and its environment was painful.

A toy. The chest contained a wooden train, a locomotive, its tender and two wagons, the whole thing mounted on wheels so it could be pushed around with a finger.

Azim thought he felt something brush past behind him, and he spun around.

The flame flickered and the shadows grew more opaque; it bent, contracted, and the detective was blinded.

Then the flame stabilized and regained its slender vigor.

Azim could not detect anything abnormal.

Get out. That was what he must do. He had seen enough. He knew where the monster had its lair. To remain was becoming suicidal.

One detail that doesn't fit.

Azim couldn't forget the corpse's atrocious features.

There was an anomaly in that face, beyond the tortures.

No, not an anomaly. Not that . . .

Azim attempted to drive this obsession from his mind but it clung on, like a necessity.

Like a survival instinct.

He had seen something, but couldn't work out what.

Death was very recent. Not just that.

It was something to do with . . . movement.

The black man hadn't moved, of course not. So why think of that?

No, not movement, more . . . the gaze. The eyes.

Suddenly, the truth leaped upon Azim as powerfully as an animal charging at its prey. Once again every ounce of substance left his legs, and his strength betrayed him, taking refuge in nothingness.

The eyes were not perfectly motionless.

That's impossible! roared Azim inside his head. *Impossible! I would have seen it!*

Not if it was very slight. Not immediately.

And despite the lack of light, Azim remembered then that the pupils had had a reflex. The image appeared in his head as if in slow motion, broadcasting extracts of his memory like a film in the cinema. Silent and yet so precise.

He identified the detail that hadn't quite fitted in at the time.

That subtle change in the pupil.

Too closely synchronized with the flame's approach to be a postmortem reflex.

The Sudanese was not dead.

Azim brandished his weapon and his light in the direction of the corpse, and took the three steps necessary to discover the empty wall.

The tall black man was no longer there.

Azim realized at last what he had gazed upon.

The *ghul*.

He had stood four inches away from what he thought was a corpse hanging on a hook, when it was in fact a demon standing with its back to the wall.

The *ghul* had allowed him to come.

And now it was lurking somewhere, not far away from him.

· 36 ·

Azim dropped his weapon on the ground.

Bullets could not harm a demonic creature.

Why deny the truth? Now he knew. He could no longer deny the evidence. Demons existed.

And he was going to die here.

Eaten alive. He saw himself howling as the monster tore out his guts and devoured them on the floor.

A tear trickled onto Azim's cheek, bringing him back to reality.

He was panicking. His feet held back when he wanted to go forward.

His trousers were sticking to his thighs.

He had urinated on them.

Run away. He must run. Back to the tunnel dug out of the earth, back to the surface, the night air.

Azim wanted to leap forward, but his muscles would not obey his command. He took several strides, as disjointed as if he were a badly operated puppet. His hand found the wall's support to get a grip on himself again. He used it like a rail, as fast as he could, seeking to get back to the small corridor.

Then the large chamber.

The air there was more breathable, the smell bearable.

Azim could barely see anything now. Tears were blinding him and the flame of his lighter was dying because of the jolts and his jerky movements. Nevertheless he found the tall corridor leading to the one way out he knew of.

He was being followed. He was certain of that.

The presence of evil was palpable in the air.

The Egyptian detective knew that he must summon up every ounce of strength. With each second that passed, he expected to feel the keen pain of teeth sinking into the nape of his neck.

It was going to happen, that was for sure.

Faster.

The entrance to the earth tunnel appeared.

Azim felt a surge of pleasure, but it was immediately swept away by terror.

A shard of pottery had cracked behind him.

The *ghul* was on his tail.

Azim rushed forward into the narrow, sticky passageway.

All at once his lighter went out.

The detective didn't bother to relight it. He abandoned it in his panic.

Frantically, he crawled.

Another nine or ten feet and he would be in the cellar.

Another nine feet, no more.

Another nine feet, barely.

He was almost there.

The darkness seemed less dense to him up ahead.

The cellar approached.

Life was still possible.

Another nine feet or less.

Maybe six.

And he would survive. And he would sur—

Azim closed his eyes.

And he wept, as a cry tore from his throat; a cry more harsh and hoarse than any animal could make.

His ankle had just been gripped by a hand with long, twisted fingers.

* * *

Jeremy Matheson was stretched out on the sofa in the main drawing room. The remnants of a log were disintegrating in the fireplace, the wood opening its sooty belly in a sonorous grating noise, spreading its reddened entrails amid the ashes, which flew up like little flakes of dead snow.

He was bare-chested beneath a thin blanket.

His forehead felt heavy, his throat dehydrated by too much alcohol.

The mansion was quiet; Keoraz had gone off to bed some time ago. They had talked, at length. And drank.

Keoraz, the perfect suspect.

Jeremy had observed Jezebel a great deal: her cold beauty, her piercing gaze.

Suddenly there was a rustling sound behind him.

That of a light fabric flowing across the stone floor and the carpet that lay on top of it.

Jeremy sat up and turned around.

A hand brushed his cheek, long fingernails lightly touching his mouth.

And someone gently covered his lips, preventing him from uttering a word.

Jezebel appeared in a long silk robe, hanging open to reveal her naked body.

Her nipples, of the palest pink, merged with her white skin. She was breathing hard, creating a vertical line on her belly, above her navel, her delicate breasts rising above her visible ribs. Her almost hairless pubis opened in a triangle like the Nile delta, a promise of fertility and fulfillment.

She pushed Jeremy back until he stretched out, and pulled off his trousers before climbing astride and sitting on him.

Her womanhood was wet, her nether lips parted by desire.

She must have been thinking about this moment for a long time already, to the point where her mind felt as though it had opened up more fully than even her most intimate parts.

All at once desire rushed through Jeremy, like an orgasmic discharge, lifting his penis, swelling his entire manhood; he contracted the muscles of his arms, his pectorals, taking Jezebel by the shoulders and drawing her firmly toward him. Her small breasts caressed his chest, cooled by the air. Their two skins pleased each other, spoke to each other, developed gooseflesh at the same time.

Jeremy held his mistress an inch above him, and ran his suddenly moist tongue along her neck.

She tilted her pelvis and her sex met his.

Like two friends rediscovering each other after a very long wait, they barely touched each other, tasting each other, mutually savoring the moment, barely daring to let go of each other, almost trembling at the thought of embracing as powerfully as they could wish. Then Jeremy seized Jezebel by the neck and forced her to lower her guard.

Slowly his member penetrated her sex.

The sodden heat sent a tingling sensation right through him. And took possession of his reason.

She felt the tenderly rigid warmth of her lover slide into her, open up a path to ecstasy with exquisite friction. And the sweet inflammation of her senses began.

Jeremy moved back and forth inside her flesh, cradled by her fluids, the sap building up behind the gates of resistance, ready to explode in a fecund star-burst.

Jezebel forgot what she was, where she was. Her muffled moans rose into her throat, but did not cross the threshold of her mouth. Her fingers tightened about Jeremy, her nails tearing a furrow through his flesh.

She moaned again.

Eyes closed.

Again.

A kind of tremolo replaced her moans of happiness.

Strident . . . electric sounds.

The telephone was ringing in the distance. Behind Jezebel's back.

She vaporized on him, and the blanket fell to the ground.

Jeremy opened his eyelids, groggy and suddenly bitter.

It was dark in the drawing room.

The telephone was ringing.

Jeremy managed to sit up on the sofa, one hand between his eyebrows. His head was thumping.

He remembered drinking. Exchanging words with Keoraz. And Jezebel insisting he lie down here.

The telephone bell trilled on relentlessly.

Someone took it off the hook. Jezebel's voice answered.

Despair bored a hole through Jeremy's breastbone, wrenching aside his chest muscles, driving its fist deep inside and crushing his heart.

He had not possessed her. She had not taken that step toward him. It was all nothing but an illusion.

His trachea suddenly tightened; a ball of anguish swelled inside him before rising painfully along his too-narrow throat. He wanted her. This couldn't be real, impossible, no, no, she wasn't married to that fellow, she had never left him, she loved him, she was offering him her company and her body as fervently as he was offering her his soul.

A second later she was standing in front of him. Her immense green eyes fixed on him. She was wrapped up in a satin dressing gown, as cold and beautiful as an easeful death.

"It's for you," she announced.

He grimaced. Not serene yet.

"It seems urgent," she added, her voice softened by the vestiges of sleep.

Jeremy stood up and staggered to the telephone.

"Yes," he said weakly, his mouth furred-up.

"It's me, Azim! I've been looking for you for ten minutes, I've called everywhere! I have—"

"Calm down, I told you I was coming here last evening, what's the—"

"No, no, listen to me!" cried the Arab detective. His voice was jerky with emotion; he was practically shouting into the receiver. "I found the child-killer! I followed his trail, I know where his lair is; it's a *ghul!* Do you understand? It's a *ghul!* Appalling! That's why the child had white hair! That's why! I thought I was going to die! I thought it had caught me but it was a root, just a root! And I know where it's hiding!"

Jeremy's head had cleared in the space of three sentences. "Go over that again, Azim. What exactly happened? Tell me."

The Egyptian retraced his nocturnal steps from the idea of tracking down the monster to the root that had clutched at his foot. His words came at an incredible rate; he took less than three minutes to tell Jeremy everything. However, he was quite incapable of explaining the location of the entrance to the secret passage, and the absence of street names did not help. All he could do was go back there and hope he didn't get lost.

"Very well, Azim. I will join you there. Where are you?"

"In the little square next to the Huisein mosque in the Gamaliya district. I am on the police telephone, in the corner of the square."

"Huisein Square," repeated Jeremy. "Very well, I can't miss you. Don't do anything else, above all don't do anything else, and wait for me, I'll find you. I'm coming right now."

He hung up. Keoraz had entered the drawing room soundlessly. "Is it an emergency?" he asked.

"I have to go. My colleague may have identified the murderer."

"I can drive you. I've bought a new Bentley. I can do over a hundred in it, you know, you'll be at the Huisein mosque in a third of the time. Did I hear correctly? That's where you're to meet?"

Jeremy returned to the sofa to get his shirt and put his shoes on. "It's very kind of you, but I'd prefer to go there alone."

Keoraz was about to insist when Jeremy added, "I'm going to borrow a vehicle from my colleagues at the Heliopolis police station. Thank you for your cooperation and your hospitality; you will soon have news from me, sir."

Without looking at Jezebel, he got dressed and went out into the cold night, heading for the police station less than five minutes away on foot. He didn't give the duty officer a chance to protest and helped himself to one of the cars, which he managed to start at the first attempt. He drove down to Cairo and wound through the complex tracery of streets before parking near to the mosque where Azim was waiting for him.

Jeremy searched high and low in every direction.

He found no trace of his partner.

The telephone post was there all right, but Azim was no longer there.

Jeremy waited an hour longer, hoping to see him emerge from one of the narrow streets.

Then he went back to sound the alarm.

· 37 ·

Béatrice cleared away the plates and placed two liqueur glasses on the waxed tablecloth.

"Will you take a drop of Calvados?" she asked Marion.

Before she had a chance to reply, Marion found herself with a large glass of eau-de-vie in front of her.

"So who do you think it is?" Béatrice persisted.

"That's just the problem, I can't work it out. They're all equally likely to be the mysterious figure who's spying on me."

Marion had told her everything during dinner. From the Gabriel Tower riddle to the regular espionage she felt she was being subjected to.

"Well . . . there's that Brother Gilles, I can't stand him," added Marion.

"That wizened old prune? Sorry, but I can't imagine him running along dark corridors in the abbey."

"It only lasted a few seconds and then I lost him. Even he could have done it."

A howl of terror shook the panes of glass in the interior door separating the sitting room from the kitchen.

Grégoire was watching a horror film on TV while working out with a small dumbbell to develop his biceps.

"Greg!" shouted his mother. "Turn the sound down a bit." Then, turning back to Marion: "I swear to you, he's crazy about these fantasy films. . . ."

"I don't know what to do, Béa. I don't trust the brotherhood; they're weird."

"Kind of like an occult sect? Is that how you see them? Sorry, darling, but that's not possible. They're completely straight. Cranks if you like, but they're the height of propriety. They've been on the Mount for quite a while and everyone knows them. You've nothing to fear."

"And yet someone broke into my place, and not just once! I'm being spied on and . . . look, the other evening it was Ludwig! He was in the cemetery, ogling me."

Béatrice turned her glass around in her hand, warming the Calvados inside it.

"Ah, Lulu," she said unconcernedly. "Okay, I have to tell you, big fat Ludwig has a thing for you. It's not a secret anymore. He's hoping you'll phone him—apparently he slipped you his number the other day."

Marion held her head in her hands, elbows resting on the table.

"For pity's sake, not that . . ."

"Afraid so! And just wait until he corners you, he'll give you the big spiel: 'I was a top-class rugby player, you know.' He does it to every remotely pretty woman who comes to the Mount—ask the waitresses at Mère Poulard's! They can't take any more of it. He's forever telling them how he played for a good club, Lille I think, how he could've turned professional if he'd kept playing . . . and all the bloody nonsense he can come up with to make himself look good."

She paused to savor the bouquet of her Calvados.

"Please, please, keep him away from me," begged Marion.

"I don't have the power. Just avoid going out in the evening!" Béatrice joked.

"In any event that doesn't solve my problem. Who's harassing me? No matter how often I go through all the possibilities, I can't see it. I even suspected Joe!"

"Nothing to fear there. Gentle and pacifist as a Greenpeace activist stoned on marijuana."

Marion smiled at this mental image. "You're very lyrical this evening," she commented.

"There are days like that. . . . As for old Joe, if I may say so, he never leaves his house except to go on his walk to Tombelaine; apart from that he stays in practically the whole time."

"Who then?"

"Me."

Marion stared at her. Béatrice had just gulped down a mouthful of Calvados; no trace of relaxation was visible now on her features, she was pensive, a dark look in her eye.

"What?" exclaimed Marion.

Béatrice's pupils slid in her direction. "Me. I'm the one who's watching you. And do you know why?"

Her lips were moist.

"Because I'm a lesbian and I'm madly in love with you!" she declared, howling with unrestrained laughter.

Marion relaxed. "You idiot . . . just for a moment . . ."

Béatrice was delighted. "You believed me, eh? Okay, come on, stop stressing. I'm going to tell you what's going on. One: The members of the brotherhood are maybe a little too conscientious, and they let themselves into your place to check that you didn't have any drugs or stuff like that. Two: You spend too much time up there, all alone, and this old rock starts to play tricks on you. You see monks wearing habits, well, that's hardly surprising as they live here. Your imagination just livens the whole thing up a bit. . . . And, er . . . three: The letters are just a game, one of the monks who's bored to death and doesn't have enough God to keep him busy. Stop being paranoid; I assure you you're getting worked up over nothing at all."

"I've not even been here two weeks yet, and I don't know if I can put up with it any longer."

Béatrice gave her an encouraging look. "Of course you can! If not, what are you going to do? Go back to your little house in Choisy-le-Roi, and rediscover Parisian drizzle?"

Marion gazed at the warm hue of her liqueur.

"You chose to take some time out here, so take advantage of it!" Béatrice insisted.

Marion pushed her glass away. "Béa, I have to tell you . . ."

Instantly, Béatrice sensed that her friend was deadly serious.

"I'm not on retreat here." A red light went on in Marion's mind. She was going too far. She was destroying her own cover story. "I'm here because I have to disappear from the face of the earth for a few weeks or months, I don't know how long myself. People have to forget about me, for as long as it takes for something to happen in Paris. At the moment I'm being bounced about among all the different departments, all the different possibilities, the legal procedures—it's now that I'm vulnerable."

The alarm sounded inside her head. She could no longer go back. In five seconds she had just exploded all of her previous lies. And all the efforts of the DST. What was happening to her? Why was she cracking now?

Béatrice swallowed noisily. She no longer looked remotely like someone about to laugh. She glanced toward the connecting door with the sitting room, checking that it was firmly closed.

"It was the DST who brought me to the Mount one night."

"The DST?"

"The French secret service. They're in charge of protecting the homeland. That sometimes involves matters that threaten state security. Its equilibrium."

"Shit," murmured Béatrice. "What did you do?"

Nervously, Marion smoothed an eyebrow. She'd started now, and she'd have to go on. "Nothing. I was there at the wrong time, that's all."

"Did you threaten to kill the president, or what?"

Marion waved away the idea and threw her head back. "I don't work in an ad agency. I'm actually a secretary. At the Paris morgue."

Béatrice's eyes widened in amazement.

"When I came back from vacation, very early one morning, I happened to walk through a dissection room. There was a copy of an autopsy report lying on the floor. I thought there had been an autopsy during the night, it happens sometimes, when there's a real emergency, and that the doctor had just finished his report and brought it down to give to the officer from the judicial police. And that he'd forgotten one copy, which had fallen on the ground. So I picked it up. And skimmed through it."

She paused. The emotions of the memory and its consequences hit her all at once. "At the end of September, a famous politician died at home of a heart attack."

"Yes, oh well, that's something everybody knows! Especially with what's been said since."

"He was autopsied discreetly one night at the Médico-légal Institute in Paris. And it was that report that I found."

Béatrice frowned as Marion's account poured out in a disjointed flood: "The medical examiner who carried out the analysis of the body stipulated that there had been no heart attack, but poisoning, which was shown by the specialist's toxicology reports. The man had died from ingesting too much Arpamyl, a drug belonging to the group of calcium-inhibitors, prescribed for problems with heart rhythm. When I read that I was surprised, but no more than that; I hadn't fully understood. It was just a political matter to me. I took the report back up, and placed it among my documents while I waited until a bit later to go and hand it back to the doctor concerned when he arrived. But the day went by and he didn't come. On the radio, they were still mentioning a heart attack as the cause of death; they even stated that this had been confirmed by the previous day's autopsy. I sensed that something didn't ring true. So I kept the copy. That evening, they were still saying the same thing. The following morning, the doctor who had carried out the autopsy in question came back. I went to find him to discuss it with him. Immediately he shut his office door and asked me to give him back the report. He confided to me that this was an affair of state, that he and I weren't in a position to judge such things, and that we must forget everything. I could clearly see that he was afraid—he was sweating with anxiety—yet I refused. At that moment, medical secrecy and all the rest seemed completely futile to me. If people talked about serious lies, about a suspicious death, that changed everything. The doctor almost threatened me when I left the room. I immediately faxed the report to the editors of all the major Paris dailies."

"You did what?"

"I was afraid. And I thought it was the best thing to do. And I called an officer from the judicial police, a cop I knew, to explain it all to him. Later that evening, two guys came to take me to one side and chat with me. Men from the DST. And all the shit started."

"Did they threaten you?" Béatrice wanted to know.

"No, on the contrary. They told me that things were going to be difficult for me. That I should keep my mouth shut for the time being, and above all not talk about what I had done. It was during the following week that the real scandal erupted, when it emerged that the last person who had visited the politician was unknown, but had been traveling in one of the cars attached to the Elysée Palace. The press lost no time divulging information that smacked of heresy. That the president's wife's hypertension was treated with regular doses of Arpamyl, exactly the substance that had killed the poor man. The media emphasized that there were sizable differences of opinion between the two major politicians, that they were making things difficult for each other for the coming election.

"This story is completely nuts, I know. Everyone says it's impossible that the president could be mixed up in the murder in any way, and at the same time the others say that on the contrary, it's the final act of a man engorged with power, overshadowed by his own ego, who no longer has any idea what he's doing because now he only lives for this illusion of permanent success. They say it's the vice of power, its hidden face, I've read all that. But the idea of me being the originator of the whole sordid mess. . . . Good grief!"

Marion couldn't stop herself now. "Public opinion started really rumbling, massively, when a new autopsy of the corpse was ordered by way of a second opinion and it was discovered that it had disappeared. The body had been taken from its drawer in the morgue without anybody noticing, vanishing forever. It's then that I fully realized the real implications of what was happening."

"I remember. Even here people threatened to march on the capital if they weren't told the truth. And they're still talking about it in the cafés!"

Marion continued her explanation as a kind of catharsis: "The medical examiner who had conducted the initial autopsy denied the new version in its entirety; he confirmed that death had been caused by a heart attack. He had been well-briefed—him and the man who carried out the toxicological analyses. I don't know what they were told, but it worked. They stated that it was a hoax. The autopsy report received by the editors was a forgery. And yet the sender's fax number corresponded to that of the Médico-légal Institute. The press set out to find the person who sent it. Me."

"Did they find you?"

"No. The cops I'd contacted managed to keep the secret. During this time, they registered an official interest in the affair and opened an investigation. I was told that I would be called as a witness if there was a trial. It was at that moment that the DST came back to see me. They explained that things were going too far, and I must be put somewhere safe."

"Since they're the secret service themselves, what were they afraid of?"

"The president's personal bodyguard. The shadowy men in his party. Who knows? They didn't tell me anything."

"I don't understand. If the DST deals with the balance of the nation, why are they protecting you? Usually, in films, they don't get bogged down in details. Bang bang, one shot with a silencer, and the embarrassing witness is feeding the fish in the Seine."

"In films . . . in reality, the DST aren't mercenaries in the pay of the president. They really do act for the good of the country. That's what I was told. And they've proved it with me. A scandal implicating the president in a case of political murder causes a stir; if in addition to this you discover that he's had someone assassinate the girl who made it all public, it's civil war! It seems to me that there are interminable power struggles among all the country's official organs. The DST distrusts the bodyguards at the Elysée, and certain police officers and gendarmes, and so on. So they stick me a long way from everybody, long enough to clear away the undergrowth and see things more clearly. And then bring me back to life. And if there were to be legal proceedings, well, I'll have my bit to say, as a witness. . . . All this because of an autopsy report that went astray, the sort of thing that's so stupid that you can't believe it could happen. Put that in a film, and everyone will think it's ridiculous. And then reality shows you that it's even more simple and ridiculous. In the meantime, I have to hide."

"So you came here. Could it last a long time?"

Marion rubbed her temples; she was tired. "I don't know. Long enough for things to calm down, I was told. That's the worst thing. Not knowing when I'll be going home."

Béatrice finished her drink. "My God . . ." She comforted her friend, placing a hand on her back.

"I'm going to go," announced Marion.

"Do you want to sleep here? I can make you up a camp bed on the settee. . . ."

"No, that's really kind. But I'm going to go back and read a little, that'll give me a change of thought. I'm sure to see you to-morrow."

Marion left her confidante on the doorstep. She could feel Béatrice's eyes on her until she disappeared around the corner of the street.

· 38 ·

At nine o'clock in the morning, the heat was already so intense that all the Westerners went out with parasols in their hands.

Jeremy Matheson paid a dragoman to accompany him into the districts of Abbasiya and Gamaliya in order to find out what Azim had done the previous day. Through his guide and translator, he asked a thousand questions, little by little building up a picture of his colleague's actions.

Early in the afternoon, he emerged from a long conversation with the imam who had accompanied the lookouts the previous evening. His name had swiftly come to Jeremy's ears; news of the nightlong watch and search organized by the Arab detective had reached everyone in Gamaliya. On the other hand, Azim's disappearance had made tongues harder to loosen, but it had not taken Jeremy long to find the appropriate keys, using gentleness, bribery, or a degree of violence where necessary.

Khalil, the man who had waited on the roof with Azim, joined them at Jeremy's request.

He and the imam gave a complete account of the night, Azim's plan, and how he had responded to the terrified signal of one of the lookouts posted in a southern sector of el-Gamaliya. The man on duty had spotted Azim approaching without managing to follow him for very long, as the detective had melted into the labyrinth of narrow streets and not reemerged. At dawn, all the lookouts had dispersed, sensing that the *ghul* had struck again, this time choosing an adult victim.

Leaving the mosque, Jeremy knew two things about the *ghul*: its physical description, which Azim had given him swiftly over the telephone, and the fact that its lair was in a basement in the southern part of Gamaliya. Jeremy hurried back to his rail car, where he took a shower. The cool water was insufficient to wash the stickiness from his skin and clothing. Unease was still weighing hard upon his heart, as heavily as a migraine on his forehead.

Jeremy picked up the telephone and called Keoraz's secretary. He wanted to hear the sound of his voice. To know what he was doing. He couldn't let go of him.

The secretary explained that it was impossible to reach Mr. Keoraz. Jeremy insisted, introducing himself as a detective, and the secretary confided that her employer was in town, shopping for a surprise for his wife. He would be back in two hours.

Jeremy hung up without another word. He opened his mouth and gulped in great lungfuls of air.

He was taunting the serpent, and in return he must accept being bitten.

Imagining Keoraz's repulsive physique offering Jezebel a new dress drove the breath from his body. How had they got to this point? Jeremy stood up, went to pour himself a drink, and stopped on the way. This wasn't the time. He had better things to do.

He arrived at the police station on the banks of the Nile in the late afternoon. The pain in his chest had faded.

The terrible news had been awaiting him for less than an hour.

Azim had been found.

In a tomb at the caliphs' necropolis.

Jeremy had someone drive him there, his head leaning back and his eyes closed throughout the journey. To all outward appearances, serene.

He said not a word, walked across the sand to the ancient building, which had partially collapsed, and entered what must have been a lobby.

The setting sun illuminated the center through broad, open apertures, radiating in brilliant red pools, making the grains of sand sparkle pink, orange, and carmine.

Azim was on his knees, his face totally buried in the ground, with only his black hair visible above it. His hands were tied behind his back with a rope that was worn, but stronger than a man's wrists. He was no longer wearing his trousers.

A wooden stake, the same dimensions as the shaft of a spade, was sticking out of his anus, a frothy white substance still covering part of the stake. A large quantity of blood, which had not yet entirely dried, stained the area between the detective's legs, and his thighs were covered with it.

The end of the shaft was flattened, split by powerful blows.

The scenario was crystal-clear.

The wooden bar had been forced into Azim's anatomy by smearing it with soap before making it penetrate further than was anatomically possible by hitting the end with a mallet.

A slow, unbearable death.

Inspectors, mainly Arabs, were milling around the edges of the scene, running up from all over the city to take stock of the horror.

They spoke in low voices, sickened, drawing their own conclusions. To judge from the evidence, Azim had been killed here, as the necropolis was deserted in the small hours and nobody could hear his screams; it was convenient. So the killer must have had a car in order to get here with his victim, which excluded 90 percent of the population.

Jeremy heard someone whisper that he recognized the torture; it was an ancient punishment dating from Egypt's Ottoman period.

Whoever had committed this monstrosity was playing with history.

Francis Keoraz had proved that he knew history, that he loved it, thought Jeremy, *once again.*

The detective signaled to a group of men he trusted and ordered them to ensure that the autopsy was carried out that same night, by Dr. Cork; by him and nobody else.

Jeremy returned to the vehicle that had brought him there and, without waiting for his driver, took the wheel and drove at top speed toward the ancient wall that was supposed to protect Cairo.

Once back at Cairo's central police station, he rushed to the office where Azim had worked and sat down on his creaking chair. He opened each file that lay within arm's reach and inside the drawers; he analyzed each of his colleague's recent notes, but found nothing.

Their direct superior, Calvin Winscott, crossed the central aisle that cut the large room in two. He changed trajectory immediately when he spotted Jeremy sitting at one of the desks and came straight toward him.

"Matheson, we've been looking for you everywhere for an hour, there's a panic on here, damn it! They're waiting for you downstairs, move yourself!"

Jeremy, who was finishing flicking through Azim's diary, did not answer.

"The two of us must have a little private talk," continued Winscott. "This case is far-reaching now, there's no question of you being on your own anymore. I'm going to put an entire battalion of men on the case. I want to know where we are. Are you listening to me?"

Matheson nodded vaguely.

"For the love of God, are you going to pay a little attention to what I'm trying to say to you?" raged Winscott. He seized him by the shoulders, forcing him to look at him. "Jeremy, we have just found out that the whole of Heliopolis is in a state of siege. Every officer is being rounded up."

Winscott grimaced nervously, revealing his teeth, before adding, "Keoraz's son was abducted this afternoon. Mr. Humphreys, from the Keoraz Foundation, is waiting for you downstairs. He wishes to speak to you personally."

· 39 ·

Humphreys was waiting in a room next to the reception area, his voluminous chest stretching his shirt under a tailored waistcoat. He was running his fingers through his long beard, like a comb. When Jeremy entered, he jumped up faster than if he'd sat on a spring.

"Detective—"

Jeremy signaled for him to follow without a word. They left the building and went to a café kept by a Greek, a little farther on. The place was frequented only by Westerners. There, Jeremy asked for two whiskeys and, with a nod, ordered Humphreys to sit opposite him.

"I have come on behalf of Mr. Keoraz," began the director. "You know that his son was abducted this very afternoon. Mr. Keoraz wishes to assure himself that you are going to put everything in motion to find his son in the shortest possible time. The child is frail and—"

"Why is your boss addressing his questions to me?" There was not a hint of compassion in the detective's voice; he was as cold as a stone.

"Mr. Keoraz fears that the abduction may be linked to these murders you are investigating. First they involved pupils from his foundation, now it is his own chi—"

Jeremy stopped him with a gesture of the hand. "The killer attacked those children because they were right under his nose. They represented enviable and easy prey."

"How can you say that? It's imposs—"

"Not at all!" cut in Jeremy. "I can say it because we know that the killer is someone close to the foundation. It is someone who knows those children, who can approach them without frightening them. He broke into the foundation one night to secretly consult the pupils' files, to find out as much as possible about them, and he knew the premises. He didn't break down any doors other than the ones that led to those files—I have that on your own admission, Mr. Humphreys."

"You suspect one of our own people?" demanded the director indignantly, clapping a hand to his beard.

"Someone who knows me."

"That makes no sense!"

Jeremy put down his glass just as he was about to raise it to his lips. "Whoever did it took care to select children who had attended my reading classes."

"You think that I, or even . . . Mrs. Keoraz could do such a thing! You are completely wrong!"

"No, it is a man, which excludes Jezebel, and it is not you, either; you have the keys to the foundation, you wouldn't have taken the trouble to break down the doors to come and consult the children's files. It's someone well-organized, who has sufficient power to have access to information relating to my work. It's someone who would know that a violent crime committed in Shubra on a day when I was on duty would be entrusted to me, and that sooner or later I would make the link with the slaughter of the children, the same barbarous scenario. Someone who has orchestrated everything since the start, in minute detail, in order to drag me into this chain of events. Someone who wants to implicate me as much as possible in these murders; who wants me to know that he's addressing me, that it's done partly for me, against me. He has spun a web of blood, in which Jezebel is also ensnared. I can only see one person who fits."

Humphreys shook his head vigorously, refusing to believe in this absurd theory.

"You are losing your reason! Mr. Keoraz's *son* has just been abducted! In broad daylight, while he was returning alone by train from Cairo, at a busy time that was supposed to guarantee his safety. His piano teacher saw him into the streetcar, and his governess was to collect him on arrival. It is a Machiavellian network that is behind this, and you—you are accusing his own father! What kind of investigator are you?"

"On the contrary, there is no network behind this abduction, just one individual. One individual who knows the child. So that the child agrees to follow him without attracting attention. The trip is a long one between Cairo and Heliopolis, there are many stops, they could have got off anywhere. The fact is that I called your boss this afternoon. Do you know where he was? In town. Looking for a surprise for Jezebel. For two hours, at least. What better alibi than that? All he needed to do was visit a store quickly, buy his gift, and go off to fetch his son and leave him somewhere, probably a house he had bought or rented under an assumed name. He will claim to have strolled from shop to shop, knowing that the salesgirls will have had so many customers that they will be incapable of saying whether they saw him or not. When people of the stature of Keoraz are concerned, the balance of doubt is always in their favor."

"You are talking nonsense!"

Jeremy charged at Humphreys and seized him by the beard, flattening his own face against the director's perspiring features. "You will go back and see your adored patron and tell him that I am going to make him pay for what he has done," Jeremy warned him in a whisper. "Sooner or later he will make a mistake."

He leaped to his feet and left the café without a backward glance.

* * *

It was nearly midnight.

In the hospital basement, Dr. Cork moistened his cracked lips with a thick tongue.

"Why is it always me?" he asked, in a voice imbued with a tiredness that was not physical.

Jeremy came straight back with, "Because I trust you. There aren't many doctors in Cairo who carry out good autopsies."

"There aren't many detectives in Cairo who order an autopsy for every one of their investigations."

Jeremy nodded and lit a cigarette. "We make the ideal couple," he commented in the cloud of smoke that enveloped him. "So, what about Azim?"

The doctor folded his arms across his chest before moistening his lips once more.

"Slow death, probably took a few hours. Phenomenal agony. This stake was inserted into his anus."

He indicated the piece of wood, about four and a half feet long and at least two inches in diameter, which was lying on a table. Half of the shaft was covered with half-dried blood.

"Penetration was forced by striking the end of the stake that remained outside the body, until—little by little—it perforated the intestines, the stomach. . . . In short, until the pain immobilized him completely. The torments were such that Azim was incapable of moving once he was impaled, that is for sure. Which signifies that the torturer did not have to stay around to wait for his death."

Seeing Jeremy's impassive expression, the doctor went into more detail: "The guilty party did that to this unfortunate man in the middle of the tombs, and once he had carried out his crime, he was able to go away, leaving Azim to suffer, as hemorrhaging emptied his body of every drop of blood. The murderer did not need to be at the scene for more than five minutes, I would say. Afterward, every shudder must have traveled right down to Azim's guts, forcing cries of pain or tears from him; I don't really know what a man might do at that stage. It is unthinkable that he got up, or even tried to remove the stake. His hands were tied behind his back and, again, I must stress: The stake went all the way up to a point beneath his sternum. The slightest movement would have made him mad with pain."

"So he waited to die . . ."

Jeremy spat out the smoke from his cigarette.

"Just a moment!" he exclaimed in astonishment. "If the killer didn't stay there, then why did Azim have his head buried in the sand?"

Cork brandished an index finger in his face.

"Because Azim did not wait for his last breath. I think that after an hour, his suffering was so extreme that he attempted to speed up the process. Unable to move his body, he must have started by striking his head against a stone. I've been told that there were two large stones beside him, with a little blood on them. And he opened up his forehead and right temple. A little more and he would have broken through the cranium. He gave up just before that happened. He probably waited another while, and tried something else out of despair."

Cork's somber gaze was fixed on Jeremy. "Azim pushed his face into the sand, by crawling I imagine, in order to suffocate himself."

The doctor stressed the point with a nod.

"That is what finally killed him. Oxygen deprivation. He has all the symptoms."

Jeremy sighed, and brought his attention back to the sticky-looking length of wood.

"Another thing," added the doctor. "The poor devil was brought to us as he was found, without his trousers. On the other hand he still had his jacket on, and from it I removed his wallet and . . . a sort of rolled-up papyrus. It is written in Arabic."

This time Jeremy did not hide his surprise. "A papyrus?"

"Yes, small and in very poor condition. It must be really old."

"Can I pick it up?"

Cork shrugged.

"Of course, except that at the moment it is in the hands of a colleague. Oh, don't worry, he is a trustworthy man! He works with the American University; they call him whenever they find skeletons in the digs. He's an anthropologist, and he has assured me he will swiftly obtain a translation of the text for me. I shall give it all to you the minute it comes back to me."

Jeremy nodded and seemed on the point of leaving when he laid a hand upon the doctor's shoulder.

"Doctor, when you did the autopsy on the body of that young boy, you recognized him, didn't you?"

Cork opened his mouth and a gurgling sound rose up from his stomach and escaped. But no words emerged, just a long, weary breath.

"He was one of the children you medically examined on behalf of the Keoraz Foundation, wasn't he?" persisted Jeremy.

"He was indeed a child I knew. And . . . I gave you to understand that, Detective."

Jeremy gave him a sad smile.

"And my words should not be taken lightly," added Dr. Cork. "When you find whoever did it, put a bullet in him from me. Personally, if I have the opportunity, I won't hesitate for a second."

· 40 ·

Marion's morale matched the color of the coffee she was stirring.

Why did she have to go and lower her guard the previous evening? A nice evening with a friend, a touch of melancholy, the feeling that she was all alone, too alone, and she had revealed it all.

Béatrice knew everything.

Marion hardly knew her; her trust was based on only the most random of instincts. As she had confessed everything, she had imagined that she would feel better afterward; she'd hoped that sharing her secrets would lighten her load. But it wasn't anything of the kind. It was worse, even.

Not only was she no stronger, and felt no better supported; what was more, her paranoia was resurfacing. And what if Béatrice had already told the Mount's other inhabitants everything? Worse, what if she had alerted the newspaper editors in order to sell the identity of their mysterious informant to the highest bidder?

And, since misfortunes never came singly, she couldn't get the chorus of Johnny Hallyday's song "Black Is Black" out of her head: *"Noir c'est noir, il n'a plus d'espoir . . ."*, which she had heard on the radio while having her shower.

She no longer knew what to do. Her cover was blown, as they said in spy novels. Should she call the DST and ask them to come and fetch her? What was she going to tell them by way of explanation? That one evening when she was tired, she had divulged everything? Beyond humiliation, that testified to massive negligence. Wouldn't they be within their rights to reply that they were going to abandon her, that she would be impossible to protect if at the end of ten days she fell into a depression and revealed everything to the first person who came along?

Marion was tired.

Since October, her life had been nothing but unremitting anxiety, watchfulness; those who wanted her to shut up had tracked her down—they were sufficiently powerful and organized to do that—to the point of sending a motorcyclist to her underground parking lot to terrorize her. They hadn't suspected she was in contact with the DST at that point, a state of affairs that had certainly changed since. Her enemies had to track her down, sound out each possibility, to find her. If that was the case, in future they would be less lenient, thought Marion; they wouldn't take any more risks, and would stake their all, by killing her.

The DST had taken it upon themselves to find a little forgotten corner so that she could be forgotten, while waiting for the judicial police to need her testimony. If they ever got to that stage . . .

Her situation was nothing but a vast blur, with no line to mark the horizon.

What have I done?

She put her head in her hands.

Did she have a choice? She had to wait. Until the DST contacted her. It was better that way.

And to kill time, she still had her book.

Thinking about it, that story was at least as crazy. By proxy, she was living through an investigation that had taken place more than seventy years previously.

With a little luck and a morning on the Internet, she could find information complementary to this investigation and might even find out how it had all ended.

And deprive yourself of discovering it all through the private diary?

No, she wanted to finish it, go right to the end. Take things in order.

Suddenly, a knot of anxiety returned and her stomach contracted.

What if the diary came to a dead end, without divulging the story's last word?

Then she would somehow obtain an Internet connection, and unearth the truth by herself. If there had been an article in the *Petit Journal*, there would surely be more details elsewhere, in the English-speaking press at the time, in Internet archives.

And what if the child-killer was still alive?

Marion asked herself what she would do if she happened to meet him. An old man.

She would denounce him to the police, of that she had no doubt.

After such a long time, was it just ancient history?

Not in her eyes, not when children had been slaughtered.

Reading would distract her, carry her far from here and from her problems.

Marion went upstairs to put some warm clothes on, and as she had done the previous day, she made herself a sandwich before adding a blanket to her bag. She left late in the morning and headed back to the lofty heights of the abbey.

She returned to the Salle des Chevaliers and its shadows, as elegant as they were threatening. It was the perfect setting to accompany her on her journey.

Marion was nearing the end; the number of pages left to read was dwindling, and the pace quickening.

She unfolded her blanket beneath the window she had chosen, and prepared to leave the twenty-first century.

When she opened the flyleaf of the black book, she had the feeling that she was opening a door.

The words were a magic spell.

She spoke them delicately to begin with, then sped up.

Mont-Saint-Michel disappeared.

The sun began to shine.

Exotic smells wafted under her nose.

And the sounds of a bygone age rose up all around Marion.

· 41 ·

At six o'clock in the morning, Jeremy Matheson was walking aimlessly beneath the ramparts of Saladin's citadel. The tall towers of the Mehemet Ali mosque rose up like two candles, ensuring that a little light continued to be cast over the shadows of the city.

His feet were bruised; he had been wandering like this for quite a while already. His mind was in turmoil. He had walked through several districts with twisted alleyways so narrow that three men could not walk abreast, and reached a less compact, less mysterious city, crossing main roads as straight and spectacular as the Champs-Elysées in Paris. It was already too early to see hordes of cars invading the streets; in two or three hours' time, the noise of their engines would swallow the sound of the wind and of the craftsmen who were already at work.

Jeremy went over and over the entire investigation, searching for the weak spot.

Keoraz must fall.

To begin with, Jezebel wouldn't understand. Worse, she would certainly feel hatred toward him, for having revealed her husband's terrible personality. However, with time all would become clear to her and she would open her eyes and see what he, Jeremy, had accomplished. She was going to have to become strong. And he would be there to support her. To prevent her from stumbling.

He was going to hold her hand, and would walk discreetly in her wake for as long as was necessary. For her. Without asking for anything in return.

She would be hard with him, as she generally was; intransigent and cruel. Odious, sometimes. It was a protective mechanism, her way of defending herself against the emotion he inspired in her. He could not believe that their love had turned upside-down, to the point where it had become this vicious hatred. Deep inside, she still felt an enormous affection for him, and it was this very affection that was making her crazy. She was making him pay for this feeling that overpowered her whenever they met.

He was going to have to be patient. Loving, too.

Support her.

Jeremy realized that he had just crossed Saladin Square, and was now under the walls of the prison.

The sky was whitening behind the citadel.

Gunshots crackled, loud and furious in the dry morning air, echoing against the high, encircling walls of the inner courtyard.

Jeremy halted and closed his eyes.

He rummaged in his trouser pocket, found a pack of cigarettes, and lit one.

How many of them were there? Jeremy wondered as he inhaled the tobacco smoke. What had they been thinking about in those last minutes? While he had been striding across the square, they had been emerging from their cells, knowing that they were taking their last steps, that this was their last dawn, and that they were leaving their lives, and existence altogether, because they had been unable to conform to a society that was banishing them forever.

He was smoking peacefully here, and they already no longer existed.

Inert bodies, riddled with bullets.

The condemned men executed in the solemn silence of early morning, almost anonymously, as if there was a certain shame in applying the sentence.

Behind the streetcar rails, just after a block of dwellings partially hidden by the prison, a gigantic cemetery stretched out, as big as five of Cairo's districts. Here generation after generation fell into obscurity and were forgotten, the men and women who had filled this city. All those men who had paused one day to think about the others' deaths, all those women who had wept over the loss of one of their own.

Jeremy dispatched his cigarette end with a flick of the finger and walked back across the entire square, in the direction of the Hasan mosque, in order to reach the main boulevard.

He felt exhausted, detached from his body; a sort of far-distant drunkenness.

He waited for the first streetcar and headed back into northern Cairo, to the headquarters of the Egyptian police, where he had his office. In order to overcome his fatigue, he obtained a map of the city and drew up a list of all the hospitals near to the Shubra district. He had his strategy. His battle plan.

If the murder of the vagabond in Shubra really was the child-killer's first crime—it displayed the same symptoms of inhuman frenzy—then its perpetrator might perhaps have frequented the surrounding hospitals. During their last telephone conversation, Azim had briefly recounted his adventure, and his discovery of the monster: a bald black giant, with cheeks laid open over damaged jaws. He had shouted that it was a ghoul.

The folktale explanation of this individual's monstrous nature was not the only one.

If such a man had killed in Shubra, then it was possible that the local hospitals knew him through having dressed his strange affliction.

There were not very many medical establishments in the vicinity, and the Jewish hospital was quite a long way away for a man who probably had no means of travel apart from his own legs. And he probably moved around at night, so as not to be seen.

Jeremy borrowed a car and spent two hours at the Lord Kitchener Hospital, which he knew well since it was the workplace of Dr. Cork, to whom he systematically entrusted his autopsies. Nobody seemed to remember a black giant whose face was half-eaten away.

So he headed for the second and last establishment, the Bulaq Hospital. First a nurse recognized the description given by Jeremy, then a doctor. He was not the sort of patient one would forget.

The man had come for treatment once, more than a month and a half previously, at the end of January. They had even attempted to have him admitted to an institution, at least for a few weeks, long enough for his health to improve, but he had fled before the vehicle arrived. The man lived on the street, and was more like a stray dog. He did not speak, had flesh missing all over his body, and was undernourished. He had been brought here forcibly, by police officers from the Shubra station, who had found him crouching in a local ruin. His terrifying appearance had at first led them to think he was a corpse, his cheeks eaten away by animals, until he moved.

Frightened and then curious, the two local policemen had brought the giant, who had not shown any hostility.

He had not been seen since. Either he was dead or he was very discreet, holed up in some sordid den in the area.

As for his affliction, the doctor was uncertain. It had the look of leprosy, but was not. The man's cheeks were eaten away, fleshless, and part of his nose had also gone, while one eye was abnormally open, almost hanging out. The giant's jaw was impossible to open, as though it were stuck in a closed position, which explained his malnourished state, as the patient was reduced to swallowing only semiliquid foods, which he had to introduce into his mouth through the slender openings between his rotten teeth.

Shortly after lunchtime, Jeremy was on his way back.

Francis Keoraz had an armada of contacts at his disposal. It was entirely feasible that this sinister story of a man-beast had reached his ears and he had undertaken to find this creature, which—with good organization—had not been difficult. The individual Azim had called the ghoul was now locked away or simply housed somewhere. Keoraz was keeping him by providing him with a roof and food.

Jeremy went to sit on the terrace of a café in the gardens of the Royal Yacht Administration, which was very close to his office and faced the Nile, in which a platinum sun was reflected.

Mentally, he prepared his report.

The black giant was assuredly an immigrant from the Sudan, rejected by his family because of the ugliness of his affliction, whatever it was. He had grown up in one of the hovels in Shubra, an area as wild as the savannah of the African predators. A district where neither the police nor the civilian authorities had yet penetrated, in a universe that escaped both rules and prying eyes. Alone and disfigured, he had developed according to his own mental image, inventing his own rules. Perhaps he quite simply hadn't grown up in his mind. He was still the child who had suffered from his illness, whom his parents had rejected in the face of his contemporaries' jeers and blows.

Yes, the theory worked.

And it was this hatred that was rising back to the surface.

His barbarous nature was merely the mirror of his sufferings, and the children were in his eyes the cause of his woes, the source of his loneliness.

He was externalizing his own inner hell.

That held water.

And Keoraz . . . the personality of Francis Keoraz was already known. Jeremy had drawn himself quite a precise picture of it, the picture of a man of power, accustomed to having everything, possessing ever more, doing ever better, without limits, until he lost himself.

The appetite for power had engendered a spiral into dementia.

But Keoraz was a civilized man, too imbued with this upbringing, and even if he felt beyond morality today, he was not capable of all the atrocities committed on the dead children.

He used the ghoul.

He manipulated the black giant, like a real puppet-master. He pulled the strings, guiding the wounded man onto the path of hatred, initiating him into this form of outlet that killing could release. An absolute liberation, and in the end, a source of pleasure for him.

And Keoraz enjoyed this authority; from a distance, he observed the ignoble deeds of *his* monster. Like a Frankenstein, he was the shadowy figure behind the creature on which everyone focused.

No, Jeremy thought. He must specify in his final report that Keoraz did not only experience an orgasmic pleasure in this omnipotence over others and over life and death, but he was even more sordid: he literally achieved orgasm! The semen found on the roof above the crime scene where the second child had been slaughtered bore witness to that.

While the ghoul struck, Keoraz kept his distance and watched, feeding his depraved fantasies.

Jeremy shook his head somberly.

Keoraz was going to get away with it.

The millionaire was treacherous and wily. To the point of abducting his own child so as to ensure the support of public opinion and in order to establish his apparent innocence while he felt threatened by the investigation. Jeremy had no doubt that Keoraz was one of those beings apart, beyond egotism, with a permanent instinct for survival, implying that he had no real attachments, few emotions, and above all: a total feeling of detachment in relation to the world. Keoraz was, in his own eyes, simply a consciousness in the middle of a game; everything, all forms of life, were merely instruments for his own amusement, his personal development.

There was one question that remained unanswered: To what extent was he cold and distant? Would he be capable of putting to death the fruit of his own flesh?

Jeremy clenched his fist. Keoraz must fall.

Only one element was lacking in order for this to happen: proof. A concrete sign linking him to the crimes, to this . . . ghoul.

But that was now just a question of time.

Jeremy paid for his coffee and called in at the police station to make sure that there were no messages for him. The agitation was at its height; separatists were going around the city, performing various acts of vandalism, and all fit men had been summoned as reinforcements to contain the rioters.

For years, demonstrations had been degenerating into violence and there had been a succession of political deaths, but no agreement could be found that would satisfy all the factions.

Jeremy dodged the call-up and headed for Cairo's eastern districts, taking care to make a broad diversion via the north, in order to avoid confrontations in the streets of the city center.

He searched for an hour, the time it took to find the dragoman who had helped him the previous day to converse with the natives. He paid the guide in exchange for a service: to list and locate all those who had helped Azim to track the monster on the night of his disappearance, in order to tighten the net around the ghoul's lair. He must begin with the imam he had met the previous day, as he must know most of the local inhabitants. He would be a perfect point of departure. Among the witness statements, there might be clues to glean, and with luck, something enabling him to unearth the creature's lair. The dragoman must ask all the questions, and if he obtained interesting results, he would receive a commensurate reward.

Jeremy had dinner in the area by the railway station, where the riots seemed to have had no impact.

Then he went home, his eyesight affected by the heady vapors of the wine he had drunk.

Night was falling over Cairo.

He was not drunk, far from it; just a little tipsy, enough to warm his heart and give himself courage.

All the same, when he stepped under the awning that adjoined his carriage, it took the detective five steps to halt after realizing that there was an unusual object in his field of vision.

A cardboard tube had been laid on a chest, just beside the entrance. It was about sixteen inches long, similar to those used to store maps in libraries.

Jeremy opened it and took out a piece of papyrus. A note from Dr. Cork accompanied it.

It was not yet completely dark, and by bringing it right up to his nose, Jeremy managed to decipher it.

This is an administrative document dating at first sight from the thirteenth century. It deals with the upkeep of the basements of a palace and expenditure on the construction of Sultan Qalawun's hospital. Mention is made of stopping up the underground passageways linking the small palace to the grand palace. My friend also sent me an explanatory note;

these underground passageways are situated approximately between the
present-day Huisein mosque and al-Azhar University. They have never
been discovered, but several archaeologists are working on it. And do
you know what? In the list of these archaeologists that my friend gave
me is the name of one of our clients: Frederick Winslow, the poor fellow
murdered by a bullet a month and a half ago, your "shitty investiga-
tion" as you called it. He claimed to have found a way in to these un-
derground passages, it seems, just before he was killed. Call me
tomorrow morning or drop in to see me.

Best wishes, Dr. Cork

Jeremy was about to crumple up the note but prevented his fingers from giving free rein to his anger. The wine made his head
spin for a brief moment.

Winslow was not only an archaeologist murdered in haste, he
was a personal acquaintance. Jeremy and he had often chatted at
the city's high-class soirees. Winslow did not have a good reputation; he was known as a "handyman," willing to arrange discoveries to give them even more value. He did not respect protocols, and
went off on his own. He didn't dig on behalf of any museum, and
liked to offer his services to the highest-paying collectors. It was a
"shitty investigation" all right. Jeremy had not failed to emphasize
the number of suspects it was possible to find. Between Winslow's
corrupt colleagues in the world of archaeological mercenaries, who
were ready for anything, and some crazy fanatic obsessed with the
preservation of ancient sites, the leads could go off in all directions,
and Jeremy had still found nothing when he set aside the case to
take on that of the slaughtered children.

Jeremy swiftly took his bearings.

Now, even the most obtuse magistrate could not deny his conclusions. There was more than one link between him and his murders. Everything the killer did was carried out with the intention to
do him harm. To focus on him.

Once again reality went further than fiction. No sham, nothing but a perpetrator who had been obvious since the start and whom time had eventually confounded. No final revelations, like in an Agatha Christie novel. Nothing but the simplicity of the clues, the sad evidence of reality. Keoraz was his first suspect, and at the end of the day he was the guilty party.

In a novel, the medical examiner would have committed the crime, Jeremy decided. He lived among blood, and he was an old soldier, traumatized by the war. . . . He knew the children through the foundation, and might have encountered the ghoul one day when treating him at the hospital. And it was he who had autopsied the archaeologist, Winslow. He could then have broken into his home to consult his notes.

And in a novel written by a woman, Jezebel would have been the perfect culprit. An unbalanced woman, without real roots; an orphan in search of points of reference. . . .

All sorts of mad theories.

Jeremy carefully rolled up the papyrus and put it in his jacket pocket.

He was about to enter the carriage when his foot slipped and he came to a sudden stop.

The door was open. He hadn't noticed that when he arrived.

The alcohol flowed back down from his consciousness to his guts, freeing up an extra part of his attention.

Just in time to hear the soft padding sound of footsteps, carefully withdrawing across the carpet.

· 42 ·

Francis Keoraz.

Marion was almost disappointed. The culprit seemed too obvious. And yet, as Jeremy emphasized, reality was often as simple as that. No last-minute revelations, no diabolical machinations, nothing but one individual's banal trajectory that progressively veers toward drama. Through her experience as a secretary at the Institute in Paris, she knew that criminal investigations all centered essentially on the same thing: a story of jealousy, greed, and desire. JGD. The majority of violent deaths came down to the same culprit: JGD. Jealousy, greed, desire.

One or the other guided the hand, if not the mind, of all murderers in our world.

Except serial killers.

They were different. They could not be compared with the other offenders. Notions of a quest or of personal development, balance, survival, came into play in their macabre mechanics.

But almost all the crimes committed outside these atypical monsters reflected in one way or another the presence of JGD.

JGD speaks.

Man acts.

Keoraz was of a quite different kind. Marion amused herself characterizing him according to her own jargon. From a compulsive sadist, he had become an obsessive plenipotentiary in the pay of an ambition devastated by his own successes. One and the other had become confused, to the point where they had given birth to the destructive pervert.

The terms were perhaps a little strong, but Marion was proud of her analysis. She put herself in mind of novelist Patricia Cornwell, who had worked in a morgue before using what she had learned and heard to create her own stories.

I'm less talented, and a lot less wealthy!

Finally, Jeremy Matheson had *sensed* from the start who was responsible for these crimes. For a second, Marion was tempted to conduct her own investigation, to go on the Internet and find out how it had all ended. She rejected this idea immediately. She still had a few pages to read. Who better to tell the epilogue to this turbulent drama than the man who had had a ringside seat?

Another twenty or so pages and she would know.

And what could you say about that . . . ghoul?

Marion had allowed herself to be carried away by the tale, not really asking herself questions except through Jeremy, not looking herself for the answers to the various riddles when she was in a position to solve some of them. Then she took the time to focus on the problem.

The ghoul.

It was a man, of course, not a demonic creature. A man suffering from an affliction that had eaten away his skin. At the start, Marion had thought of leprosy, as suggested in Jeremy's tale, but that didn't last the course. Then she had remembered the name of that sickness that continued to ravage bodies today, notably in Africa.

Noma.

Suffering in its purest state.

A gangrenous affliction that eats away the tissues of the mouth and face. Marion remembered it in particular after she had seen a television program about this plague. She had typed a long report on noma in the form of a memo to all hospitals and medical-legal departments in the country, after an infant was found to have died from the illness in a vile squatter's house on the outskirts of Paris.

The scientific name came back to her.

Cancrum oris.

Still little known by the general public, and yet so nightmarish. The illness was not contagious, and only affected very poor communities with appalling levels of nutrition and care of the mouth and teeth; beyond a very few immigrants, the affliction was never encountered in France. Nevertheless the experts had grasped the full horror of its physical mutilations and deformities, and of all the psychological and social consequences.

In the 1920s, suffering from this illness meant social exclusion, rejection, and hatred. This man, already sapped by infection, had been jeered at, persecuted, and bullied—to the point where he had gone into exile, forced to hide himself away. This was an individual who had been totally taken apart psychologically.

Marion imagined the life he had led.

His acts of barbarity against children were intolerable. And yet the most dramatic aspect as far as Marion was concerned was to understand where this capacity to destroy innocence had come from. He certainly felt nothing but hatred for other men, all the more so for the children who must have mocked him as much as they feared him in the street. Jeremy had figured him out very well. The hunter had briefly but precisely exposed the process of creating the monster within the monster.

The investigation was on the point of being wrapped up.

Marion resumed her reading, pulling the blanket over her legs to warm herself up.

The storm had ebbed away, but outside the wind continued to express itself with a degree of rage, reaching deep inside the abbey the moment an opening presented itself.

A high-pitched moan rose up from the building's entrails, swelled in the spiral staircases as though they were celestial flutes, and the whole of the Merveille began to whistle.

Suddenly the wind dropped.

The stone pipe-work emptied, the spaces underneath doors that served as mouths became silent, and the wind ceased to grind away at the beveled edge of the steps.

And during this interval, Marion heard the click of the lock, which someone was attempting to muffle.

She stiffened.

Was she being locked in? It was the door opposite, on the raised passageway, the very same she had entered through, an hour and a half earlier. Marion remembered then that she had locked it behind her.

Someone was opening it.

Very slowly, so as not to be noticed. Taking advantage of the wind to conceal their presence.

There was someone on the other side; someone who wanted to approach without Marion noticing.

The mysterious hooded presence. Without a doubt.

The resemblance between it and the ghoul who had prowled the streets of Cairo in 1928 would have had an ironic flavor if the circumstances had been completely different.

Marion put down her book on the blanket and stood up without making a sound.

She was not in a police investigation; it wouldn't be sufficient for her to glean clues gradually in order to unmask the person who was spying on her.

She must take the initiative. Make things happen.

Walking on tiptoe, Marion made her way between the columns, then climbed the stair to the passageway and halted in front of the door.

She held her breath and knelt down.

Her mouth was producing too much saliva.

She swallowed.

Marion laid her hands on the door, and brought her eye up to the lock.

The hole was black.

She scanned the darkness.

Without noticing the shape that was softly appearing behind her.

A robed shadow moving along with the hood pulled down over its face. Cleaving the space in the Salle des Chevaliers.

Marion could not make out anything; all she had was the certainty that there was no key in the hole, and yet she could not make out what lay beyond it. She prepared to open the door, as rapidly as possible.

To play on the effect of surprise.

If Brother Gilles really was behind this, he would be caught red-handed.

Behind her, the shadow was walking quickly.

Marion placed her hand on the iron door handle.

She heard the rustle of fabric.

Her eyelids lowered as she worked it out.

Behind . . .

She swung around.

The strange apparition was less than three feet from Marion's things. She realized that it definitely was her stalker when it stretched out a gloved hand toward the diary.

"Hey!" shouted Marion.

The hand closed on the black book and drew it into the folds of the robe.

"Drop that right now!"

Marion hurtled down the steps.

The silhouette that so closely resembled the Grim Reaper spun around and lunged forward.

Marion saw it running just ahead of her, reaching a postern gate at the northwestern corner.

Marion was on its heels.

The individual ran down a spiral staircase, heading for the storeroom. Its pursuer slowed down so as not to miss a step and risk falling. She came out in the vast chamber on the lower level. No trace of the fugitive.

One half of a double door was just closing, letting in the daylight and the cool November wind.

Marion pushed it open and saw the silhouette, sprinting through the gardens down below. It was establishing a considerable lead.

Furious, Marion strode over the first steps and jumped the remainder, landing on the winter-shriveled grass. She rushed off in pursuit of the thief, who zigzagged between the trees in the garden, plowing through bushes and trampling on clumps of flowers. This person knew perfectly well where they were going.

Marion forced herself to run faster, with every ounce of her strength.

Despite everything, the fugitive was getting farther away, and changed direction with great agility.

Then came a long straight line, at the foot of the Merveille. Marion closed her eyes for a second to give herself energy.

She concentrated on her breathing. On the way her arms pumped back and forth, whipping the air with her hands. On the rhythm of her thighs.

Lift your knees, bring your heels up to your backside.

Her target did not enjoy the same freedom of movement, since its legs were hampered by the long robe.

And little by little, Marion caught up.

Instead of bringing her to life, the oxygen was burning her lungs.

Then the fugitive halted in front of a door at the end of the esplanade, took a bunch of keys identical to Marion's from the folds of the robe, and started looking for the right key.

Her keys. In the confusion, Marion hadn't brought them. If the other person succeeded in locking the door behind them, it was finished; she would lose her quarry for good. And the black book along with it.

She forced herself to breathe out as far as she could, and greedily took her fill of fresh air.

She sped up a little more. She was on the point of collapse, she could feel it.

And the silhouette raised a key to its eyes before sliding it into the lock.

· 43 ·

Marion was nearing the end of the chase at top speed.

She was going much too fast. She must slow down.

The door opened.

The thief was about to disappear.

Marion did not slow down; on the contrary, she put everything she had left into one desperate gallop.

The wall rose up suddenly.

The silhouette withdrew the key from the lock, preparing to cross the passageway.

Marion saw the stonework fill her field of vision, far too rapidly.

She just had time to fold her arms in front of her to protect herself.

And she crashed straight into the individual who was attempting to flee.

The impact was so hard and so sudden that the two bodies were thrown together, violently crushing the fugitive against the stone.

Marion fought for breath, all the air suddenly expelled from her chest. Her thief acted as a buffer, absorbing most of the impact and crashing into the wall.

The bunch of keys fell to the ground. And so did the book.

All the same, Marion was groggy, and she staggered, instinctively drawing back. The hooded figure grabbed the door handle so as not to fall over. With a clumsy grab, it retrieved its keys. Marion was recovering slowly. She realized that the other person was in no better state than she. It was groping around with its gloved hands, in search of the book.

Her head still spinning, Marion approached.

"No, you don't," she managed to gasp. "Oh, no . . . if you want . . . the book . . . you . . . you'll have to ask me for it, face-to-face."

She came closer.

Immediately, she sensed panic in the figure, which leaped forward and slammed the door shut behind it.

Marion recognized the sound that followed as the sound of the key relocking the door.

The thief was escaping.

And the irregular pounding of footsteps sounded on the other side of the wall. The figure was having difficulty in getting away, still suffering from the recent collision.

The thief had escaped.

All the same, he or she had had to abandon the book in order to do so.

Marion collapsed to one side, and hugged it to her.

· 44 ·

Jeremy climbed the steps up to the rail car, all his senses on alert, already concentrating on the evasive move he would make if he detected a hostile presence, preparing to strike.

The darkness was too intense to make out his surroundings clearly. The blackness of the night was amplified inside by the narrowness of the windows.

First he heard it coming.

Then he saw it.

A silhouette, rushing to meet him.

He did not move.

It raised an arm to strike him.

Jeremy made not the slightest attempt to escape.

And he took the violent slap full in the face.

"How can you think that?" cried Jezebel, the sound of sobbing still in her voice.

He had recognized her shape, the way she moved, and her perfume the moment she appeared in the half-light.

"Humphreys came to the house to report what you said about Francis. His *son* has been abducted! What more do you need? Well? Tell me, Jeremy, what more? Does he have to die himself? Or will you go on relentlessly pursuing his corpse? In the end, what has he done?"

She turned away and, clearly on edge, strode back and forth across the sitting room.

Jeremy breathed out through his nose. Suddenly, the alcohol

and the tiredness weighed a little more heavily upon him. He picked up a packet of matches and struck one to light an oil lamp, whose light licked at the velvet drapes and the wood in the room.

Jezebel was now standing very straight, facing him.

The short flame sparkled against the jade, ebony, and ivory of her eyes, emphasizing the sleek lines of her beauty, her pale pink lips, her porcelain skin, and her intoxicating curls. She shone like a precious stone.

Jeremy gazed upon her like a work of art; his eyes lingered on the beauty spot placed in the middle of her cheek like the signature of a great master.

"Don't tell me this is because of me," she said, her challenge barely louder than a whisper.

A fringe of tears appeared along the bottom of her eyelids.

She whispered again, painful effort distorting her intonation: "Why can't you forget me, Jeremy?"

Jeremy, whose shoulders were drooping, drew himself up. Raising his head, he swallowed, then poured himself a glass of whiskey, and gulped down a mouthful straightaway.

"Don't pursue him, please," she murmured. "He is my only family, you know that."

Jeremy rubbed the palm of his hand on his jaw, the skin scratchy with a fresh growth of beard, then massaged his temples. "Look on the desk," he said eventually.

Jezebel hesitated, then went over to the desk.

"Do you see that notebook in the middle?" he asked. "That's the diary I began at the start of this investigation. This evening I shall add my final thoughts to it, my recent conclusions, and it will be almost finished. The truth is inside it. If something were to happen to me, everything is in there. I want you to know that."

He turned to look at her. "Do you still like Puccini?" At which he wound up a gramophone, which launched into the opening notes of *Turandot*.

Jezebel remained silent for a few bars, then she sat down at the desk and started playing with a lock of her hair. Her other hand stroked the wooden surface of the desk, lightly brushing the objects placed upon it; her eyes lighting on a pile of dog-eared books.

"*One Thousand and One Nights*," she said as she read the spine. "Francis is crazy about it," she admitted weakly.

Jeremy snapped back instantly: "I know, I remember now that it was with those stories that he seduced you at the New Year's party. . . . My murdered colleague believed that was a lead for our investigation. Myself, I think that the killer uses them to play on myths, to re-create a legend. Because that immortalizes him, at the same time keeping the superstitious natives away."

Jezebel's fingertips moved to the area between her eyebrows, and she shook her head. "Why do you persist?" she wanted to know. "You know that Francis is not a monster. He hasn't killed anyone, you know that."

Her voice was saddening and sweet. Jeremy thought he could make out a tear, trickling along the bridge of her nose.

"You know me," she went on. "I can sense what people are like, I'm not wrong about what they are. It's in me. I am an orphan from Alexandria, a little girl with foreign parents who abandoned me in this land where I am nothing, and I have become a respectable woman. Thanks to that gift, I can *feel* people. I have created myself all by myself, you know that very well; I have climbed the steps of the world without any help. Today I have found Francis, and I know what he is, I know his good qualities and his flaws. He is hard, it is true, but he is absolutely not the man you think he is. You can't pursue us like this, you can't."

Jeremy drank a mouthful of whiskey, listening to the words of this woman he loved. Puccini was growing more passionate.

He was willing to give anything to feel her snuggle into his arms. To make love to her, one more time. He missed the warmth of her body, the folds of her skin, the taste of her sex, and of her tongue with its sweet flavors. She was standing there, only a few feet away, within reach. And yet so far away.

"You have to accept that I no longer belong to you," she continued. "I am going to be blunt with you, Jeremy. I can feel people, and when it came to you, I never managed to work out what you were. At first, that's what attracted me to you, that savage charm that great explorers have. Then that was what irritated me, before . . . before it began to scare me."

She gazed at him in the amber-colored chiaroscuro that divided the desk. "You have never really understood why I have been so hard with you since we parted, have you? To help you to draw a line under us. And because your fidelity and your naïve hope got the better of my patience in the end. By constantly harassing me with your indiscreet questions about my relationship with Francis, you pushed me to the limit. If you and I didn't stay together, it is because you disturbed me, Jeremy."

The green of her eyes hypnotized the detective.

"In your soul, you possess the indifference of those who have gone too far, too far into nature, too far into solitude, and who have never returned. You are never entirely here, Jeremy. There is always a part of you that remains there, in those strange lands that you alone know, in those memories of war, in those wanderings through the savannah, and here"—she raised both palms to the ceiling—"in the muffled distance of this rail car. What is inside you escapes me, and makes me afraid. I think that you are a delectable lover, but you will never be an attentive husband, still less a good father. That goodness and that ability to give to others are no longer possible for you; you have lost them over the course of the last ten years, in all of this tormented life. The other evening, when you were telling that sordid story of what you experienced in the trenches during the war, I understood; that is why I wept. I understood, you know. And yet you are still this . . . ghost; you are never really here. You are not like us. I am sorry. . . ."

She wiped her eyes swiftly, before delivering the coup de grâce: "But you cannot hate Francis for bringing me everything that you could not give me."

Not another word sullied the intensity of their gaze as they looked into each other's eyes. Puccini and his dramatic melodies carried them into this soul-to-soul exchange. At last, Jeremy put down his empty glass and broke the bond by turning around to go and fetch an object wrapped in a piece of cloth.

"Soon you will really understand who I am," he said at last. "I am your guardian angel, Jezebel. And like all angels, I am half invisible. One day perhaps, you will see me as I really am."

From the cloth, he took a Colt M1911 semiautomatic and the magazine that accompanied it, loaded it, and slid it into a holster that he retrieved from a shelf.

"And Francis is the devil in disguise. You have been manipulated, that's all."

Jezebel darted her flaming eyes at him and, with a furious sweep of her arm, knocked over everything on the desk.

"*Enough!*" she shrieked.

Then she jumped up and ran outside.

Jeremy clenched his fists.

He put on his holster under his jacket, picked up his diary, which he slid into one of his pockets, and left in the furious wake of this ethereal siren.

He ran behind her to sharia Abbas, where she jumped onto the first streetcar that came, just as the doors were about to close.

Jeremy sped up, the alcohol making his blood heavy. His poorly oxygenated brain weighed three times as much as usual, and his legs would not obey him as quickly as he wished. He forced the pace even more, struggling for breath, and leaped onto the rear footplate of the streetcar while it was picking up speed.

The lights of the city hummed in the darkness; they processed into the distance behind the windows of the tram, drowning in between the passersby and the cars that were driving in the opposite direction.

Jeremy opened the door and entered the compartment. He pushed his way through the other passengers and seized Jezebel by the wrist. "You are going to hate me," he carried on. "I know that. I shall be your scapegoat, but one day, one day, you will understand. You will accept the truth. You must know that I will be there, I will wait."

Roughly, she tore her arm from the detective's grasp. "You are making a monumental mistake, Jeremy. Monumental. Jealousy has made you lose your reason. And by accusing Francis you are going to destroy your career."

She was about to run away from him when he grabbed the central pole and used it like a turnstile, swinging around and reappearing in front of Jezebel. "Your husband is guilty. He has enough influence to have found the so-called ghoul, and to use it to carry out his dirty work. He knows Arab myths well enough to play on them; it is his smokescreen to direct us onto the wrong track. The victims are children he knows, since he has them right in front of him—children from his foundation. After all, why search further afield? All he has to do is discreetly gain access one night to the children's files. The nights of the murders, you say he was sleeping with you, but how can you be so sure? You sleep heavily if I remember well. . . . And the night Azim was killed, he heard me repeat the address I was to go to. With his powerful car, he could have got there before me."

"Francis did not go out that night!" shouted Jezebel. "After you took off like a whirlwind, we went back to bed. It doesn't hold water . . ."

"All right, and how long did you stay awake before you fell asleep? Hmm? How long? Two minutes? Five? It doesn't matter, he'd have waited, and his famous superfast Bentley would enable him to make up for lost time and reach Azim before me."

Jezebel pushed away the detective, watched in alarm by the other travelers who had witnessed the scene. "Francis is not a criminal!"

Jeremy reached into his jacket and took out the old papyrus that had been found in Azim's clothing. "And your husband adores the history of Cairo. He is at the head of a bank that finances a number of archaeological searches; he must have learned of the existence of old underground tunnels, where he hides his 'ghoul.' Soon I shall have all the proof I need against him."

Jezebel was no longer listening to him.

The streetcar slowed down. A more and more compact crowd filled the pavements and the middle of the road for a hundred yards. Eventually the car stopped and the doors opened.

Outside, in the gathering darkness, the demonstrators were mingling with a tide of curious onlookers, young sensation-seekers, and anti-English slogans sounded alongside those extolling a strong Egypt, governed by the people's representatives. The current regime was being castigated for its indulgence toward the British occupiers.

Everyone was walking quickly, shouting as they moved back up the boulevard.

Jezebel slipped between two groups and melted into the masses. "Jezebel!" shouted Jeremy. "Jezebel!"

He pushed away the bodies that stood in his way, zigzagging through this forest of flesh, shouts, and growing hostility.

Arms were raised to protest, and mouths directed aggressive reprimands at him.

Jeremy struggled not to lose sight of his target. Jezebel's black hair rippled to the rhythm of her random movements. Jeremy had the impression that her long hair escaped all the laws of earthly attraction; it was as if it floated in water. Jezebel had slipped in among the procession.

Suddenly, a furious face occupied his entire field of vision.

An old Arab, who started insulting him in the language of the prophet Mohammad.

Jeremy pushed him out of the way without gentleness, to regain sight of the enchanting apparition. He sought her in vain.

Dozens of heads, even more turbans, fezes, tarbooshes, but no more Jezebel with her accentuated movements.

Jeremy was finding it increasingly difficult to breathe. Perspiration was running down the length of his spine. All the protests, the braying, the yelling whirled around his ears, forming a great merry-go-round of confusion and suffocation.

Windows shattered, shopfronts were smashed in by bricks before collapsing with a clatter. The din of the malcontents rumbled like a wave, spreading toward the back of the human snake.

There was a bend in the street. A fabulous halo of lapis-lazuli blue rippled across the fronts of the buildings. Their stone was covered with a luminous, electric blue skin, moving like water on fire, striped with red veins, and in the panes of the bow windows volcanoes were reflected, spitting out bubbling sapphire lava.

Negotiating the bend, Jeremy was stunned to discover what was suffusing the whole street with this extraordinary brightness.

All the lampposts had been decapitated, and the gas was shooting several yards into the air, burning skywards in a flaming column, a real artery of buzzing fire, of a magnetic blue that changed to orange at the summit and whistled furiously.

Then he spotted Jezebel, twenty yards ahead, pushing away two men who were ranting and raving at her. One of them stepped behind her and caught her by the hair.

Enraged, Jeremy shoved aside the onlookers in front of him, cleaving the crowd.

Jezebel started to scream as she was being manhandled.

A youth, excited by the general revolt, recognized Jeremy as one of the British occupiers and stepped into his path, determined to prevent him going any farther.

Over his shoulder, the Englishman saw that Jezebel had been dragged to one side, and slapped twice.

His fist clenched and dealt the youth a stinging blow to the liver. He bent double, then fell on all fours, expelling all the air from his lungs. Jeremy wasted no more time, and stepped over him.

The first individual did not see him loom up and was immediately felled by a powerful blow between the shoulder blades. He fell forward and broke his nose and several teeth on the pavement. The other let go of Jezebel and ran forward to grab the detective by the throat. Jeremy sidestepped him and raised his knee, striking the man hard between the thighs.

The blow hit home but also unbalanced Jeremy. He saw the street spin around and only had time to put his hands forward and cushion his fall. He blinked. The alcohol was no longer having any effect on his senses. Out of the corner of his eye, he noticed that his adversary, who was lying just under his own legs, was attempting to get to his feet.

Jeremy raised his thigh and with all his strength brought down his heel on the troublemaker's chin. Something broke under the violence of the impact.

Jeremy grabbed hold of the metal grille in front of the building and used it to haul himself to his feet. Jezebel shrank back, afraid.

The detective spun around and saw a band of angry men bearing down on him, led by the youth who was still holding his belly.

Hatred was written all over their faces.

Six were approaching him, and there would soon be ten of them.

They were going to break him into pieces. Him, and then Jezebel.

Jeremy unfastened his holster and brandished his gun.

"*Halt!*" he roared.

The group paused in its march, while the hundreds of others passed by, speeding up their pace, heading for the front of the assembly, barely paying any attention to what was being played out between this couple of Westerners and a faction of their own people. The outcome of the confrontation was in no doubt.

Emboldened by the weight of numbers, the youth rushed at Jeremy.

Jeremy lowered his arms.

The lampposts poured out their sparkling torrent above their heads.

The crowd chanted its nationalistic litany.

There were hundreds of passersby, and they were almost running.

The shot from a .45-caliber weapon barely made a sound in the general chaos, stifled as it was by the chest of the youth who was at its business end when Jeremy pulled the trigger.

The boy's eyes changed all at once. The vengeful fever turned into incomprehension. Jeremy saw no pain there, only disorientation, and then fear.

The youth died in the grip of terror. He collapsed, his eyes searching for some possible escape, some comfort, but already he saw nothing more than his own abyss, which was progressively engulfing him.

He closed his eyes, refusing to drown in nothingness like this, and was shaken by one final convulsion. His hands flopped limply to the ground and began to turn cold.

The other men who accompanied the boy watched him die, then turned their eyes on Jeremy. The detective realized that they were going to charge. His weapon mattered little; they were going to rush him, in a single movement, to submerge him and make him pay for what he had done.

A din grew louder from the front of the tumultuous procession. A roar that was transformed into terror.

Shots rang out between the façades of the buildings. Sharp and metallic. Rifle shots, Jeremy guessed.

The army was charging.

Already the demonstrators were running in the opposite direction, terrified.

Jeremy turned his attentions back to the danger that directly affected him. Several individuals were approaching him, looking menacing.

He checked that Jezebel was definitely behind him, and put his finger back on the trigger. Panic was flowing back from the front of the human mass, all the way back to where they stood.

More than half of the shadows around them were now running in the opposite direction.

The rifle shots rang out again.

Jeremy saw two silhouettes sidestep the fugitives to go around him and attempt to take him from behind.

A third charged at him, full-out, just avoiding the angry mob of fugitives.

Jeremy could not fire; there was movement everywhere. Any bullet would go through several bodies before reaching his attacker.

Suddenly, the human tide became so dense and so violent that everyone was carried away by the tidal wave.

Unable to resist without falling and being trampled underfoot, Jeremy allowed himself to be carried along, pushed, and propelled by the power of this wave of flesh.

His attackers were swept along just like him, dispersed, moving their legs as much as they could to remain at the surface.

The tide burst as it reached a square, plunging its offshoots into the narrow streets that opened off it in all directions.

Jeremy threw himself into the recessed doorway of a house and waited for the main body of the herd to pass. He looked for Jezebel among the faces.

And he found her, on the other side, terrified but safe and sound. He lost her as she swiftly left a busy thoroughfare to escape the mobs along an adjacent street.

Jeremy threw his head back against the wall, and let out a long breath.

The worst was yet to come.

Tonight was going to be the longest and the most sinister of Cairo nights.

· 45 ·

Children's laughter awakened Marion.

Her tongue was coated, and her head filled with a throbbing pain.

She no longer knew where she was. The room was going around.

In the rail car . . . I'm with Jeremy, in the rail—

No, she was in Cairo. She'd been attacked during the riot.

She remembered a shape that looked like death, pursuing her. No! She was the one chasing it.

The diary.

Mont-Saint-Michel.

Marion remembered. She was in her place. In her little house.

For a moment she no longer knew who she was. Her life had become transposed with the earlier life of Jezebel.

She was Marion.

She had got back the black book. Jeremy Matheson's private diary. And she had gone back up to the Salle des Chevaliers, more angry than worried. Someone had been playing games with her. Had she misheard that click in the lock? Was it in fact that of the postern door, or had the thief caused a diversion at the main door before running round to enter behind her back, so as to sneak the book away from her?

She had not found the answer. In the end it mattered little.

Then Marion had gone back down.

To see Béatrice; she'd needed to talk.

The shop was shut. Closed on Mondays. And nobody was in the apartment upstairs.

Marion had noticed Ludwig coming out of an adjacent street, and had flattened herself in the dusk to avoid him before going back to her place to take refuge. This was not the moment for him to come and whisper sweet nothings in her ear.

She stood there in the living room for five minutes, and then started crying. She was lost. Incapable of making the right decision. She'd found the telephone in her hand, while she punched in the number written on a card in her purse. The man from the DST.

She'd hung up before the first ring.

And paced up and down instead.

When her feet started hurting, she sat down and poured herself a gin and orange. Then another. And so on.

Her mind had grown calmer, and she had picked up the book to flick through it; and even before she meant to, she was reading what came next.

She fell asleep at the end of the riot, when Jezebel ran away.

Knocked out by the alcohol.

She had slept for two hours.

Now the children were making a din underneath her window.

Night had fallen. And there were no children on the Mount.

Marion blinked, very slowly, but did not get up.

She opened her mouth, and her lips came unstuck like chewing gum being peeled off linoleum.

She reached out to grab the top of the sofa and pulled to haul herself up. Her nose made contact with the cold glass of the bay window.

Down below, in the street, dozens of people were walking up towards the abbey, each at their own pace, the children in the lead.

The orchestral concert.

Marion had helped Sister Gabriela put up the flyers in the village square last Saturday afternoon.

She looked at her bare wrist and realized that she hadn't worn a watch since she arrived here. She found the time in the kitchen. Twenty past seven.

The concert was in less than an hour.

Marion had no desire to attend.

She wanted to be home. In her *real* home, in Paris. She wanted to go to bed in the evening and set her alarm clock for the following morning, the very same one that made her grumble at quarter to seven when she had to get up and go to work. She dreamed of being able to forget all this.

Why did somebody persecute her? Who?

Matheson's private diary lay upside down on the sofa, open at the point she had reached when she fell asleep.

It was impossible that there was any relationship between this diary and what had happened to her in Paris, the case of the suspicious political death. So whoever was pursuing her here simply wanted to get the book back. What was there in it to arouse such determination?

Marion picked it up.

There were only a few pages left to read.

And perhaps then, she would know.

She sighed with all her soul and sat down in front of the gin bottle.

The diary fell open on her thighs and the pages turned one after the other until they stopped, suspended in midair.

Marion pushed away the bottle of alcohol.

And returned to her place.

That night in Egypt, when the worst was yet to come.

· 46 ·

Jeremy returned to the eastern districts, to see the dragoman he had engaged to find all those who had participated in the nocturnal vigil along with Azim.

Azim had discovered an old underground complex, in which the ghoul was hiding, somewhere under el-Gamaliya. He had brought back an old papyrus that identified the underground chambers in question as being in a part of the city between the Huisein mosque and the al-Azhar University. But Jeremy had still to find the entrance.

The dragoman was at home, with his wife and children. Nobody was sleeping, despite the lateness of the hour. Rumors of a riot in the center of the city had reached them, and they were all waiting for news. The dragoman greeted Jeremy with an immense smile, counting the piasters the detective had just handed him by way of invitation.

The dragoman had identified several men, and had questioned them; and he presented the information to the detective, not leaving out any detail. Jeremy drank tea with him, and he was brought a handful of dates which he nibbled in silence.

After an account that was careful—the dragoman had an exceptional memory, retaining all the names of the protagonists—but useless to Jeremy, he concluded with what seemed to him to be the least important information: "That is not everything, effendi. I was also directed to two old men this afternoon. They cannot stop talking about this beast, this *ghul*, to everybody, they are becoming obsessed with it. They are annoying the people in the *qawha*. The first one says he knows who is behind it all. I met him just now, I don't think he has all his marbles anymore. For him, the *ghul* is his neighbor in disguise. He says his neighbor is mad, that he's a child-killer and—"

"Where does this old man live?" asked Jeremy, who was in a hurry to get to the end.

"In the northwest of Gamaliya, in Bab el-Nasr, very close to—"

"Too far," cut in the detective. "What about the other?"

"He's a fanatical hashish smoker. He's been frequenting the *ghoraz* for too long. He says he knows where the demon lives. In a blind alley, in the southeast of the district."

Jeremy spat out his date. "Not far from the Huisein mosque?"

"Yes, that's right."

The Englishman leaped to his feet.

He remembered Azim, and his two witnesses, the two men who said they had seen the ghoul. One was an old hashish smoker. And it was close to the place where the underground tunnels ought to be.

"Take me to him," he said. "Come along, time is short."

They unearthed the old man at the back of a smoking club well known in the district, with his eyes red and shining. He did not balk at taking the two men as far as the entrance to the blind alley in question when Jeremy promised him a little money in exchange.

The narrow streets were deserted and dark.

They walked along carrying a lantern containing a small candle, which quivered in time with its bearer's footsteps.

The three men moved soundlessly under the *moucharabiehs* that made the narrow alleyways even darker, stepping around the empty stalls, until they walked down a confused maze of passageways, some covered, some dilapidated, which served as shortcuts.

From a distance, they resembled a little firefly, looking for the way out of a giant stone labyrinth.

At last they ended their nocturnal walk at the entrance to a blind alley made up of ruined houses.

"It is here," murmured the old man in Arabic. "I'm not staying much longer, it's dangerous."

The dragoman translated for the detective.

At which the old man seized Jeremy by the sleeve and waited.

The Englishman sighed, took a banknote from his pocket, and handed it to him. The man was about to leave when Jeremy held him back by the shoulder.

"Which house is it in?"

The dragoman acted as an intermediary between the two men.

"He says he doesn't know," he reported.

"In that case, ask him if he knows where the Huisein mosque and al-Azhar University are."

The old man hesitated, before pointing both arms to the right, in vaguely the same direction. This gesture seemed to direct their searches more to the houses on the right side of the blind alley.

"It's better than nothing," grumbled the Englishman, handing the lantern back to its owner.

The dragoman instantly translated the old man's few words. "He says you can keep it. You'll need it more than he does if you intend to go in there."

The old man was already walking away.

"Tell me, are you really going to enter these ruins to look for the *ghul*?" asked the dragoman anxiously.

Jeremy gave him the promised money. "There's no need to follow me. Your journey ends here, my friend."

The detective turned his back on him without further ado, and plunged in among the crumbling façades, full of gaping holes like greedy mouths.

Jeremy heard the guide's footsteps hurriedly moving away.

The first building on the right side was impossible to get into, as the ceiling had collapsed. Jeremy swiftly checked out the second one. There was nothing inside but rubble. The third required more effort, as it included a cellar that he inspected carefully.

Inside the next one, he was astonished not to have access to a basement. He searched every corner, his dim lantern in his hand, until he halted before a sizable wooden chest filled with stagnant water.

He placed the lamp on the ground and leaned on the wood with all his strength to make the water bucket slide across the floor.

The hole was underneath.

Jeremy picked up his lantern again and descended the steps before swiftly coming back up to move the water-filled container back into position as best he could, in order to keep the entrance hidden and not reveal his presence.

Once he was down below, he could not miss the hole that had been made at ground level. A recent hole.

Had Frederick Winslow made it himself, in order to enter the archaeological underground chambers he so coveted? It was possible. Winslow was the type to search on his own, keeping to his own corner, not telling anyone about his discoveries except those close to him and his employer if any. Or had he not had time to finish, and Keoraz had completed the job himself, to ensure he possessed a lair nobody knew about, once the archaeologist had been eliminated?

Jeremy bent down and had to put his arm with the lantern through the hole to ascertain the endless depth of the passageway. The earth was damp, sweating in places, and many twisted roots hung down, like desiccated hands. Now Jeremy understood what Azim had said, "I thought I was going to die! I thought it had caught hold of me but it was a root, just a root!"

The little Egyptian's voice echoed deep in the tunnel, distant and ghostlike. "Just a root . . ."

Jeremy kneeled down and entered the passage headfirst.

He crawled as fast as he could, on the alert for the smallest sound. He soon began to breathe rapidly, paddling around in a swirl of mud and decomposing vegetation.

It became difficult to move forward with the lantern, forcing him to move it in stages. The candle flame almost drowned in its own wax when the jolts were too severe. He found a lighter, sticking out of the soil. Azim's. He recognized it immediately; his former colleague very rarely smoked, but was never parted from his lighter, always very proud to be able to light other people's cigarettes.

He must not feel claustrophobic, thought Jeremy. He wriggled about like a worm in the belly of the earth, twisting the different parts of his body to move forward in this humus-filled intestine.

Finally Jeremy emerged in the underground tunnel.

The dust filled his nose.

Once he was standing upright, the detective took his weapon in his right hand, and raised his lantern. The darkness swallowed up the edges, gnawed away at corners that were too sharp and totally engulfed all perspective beyond six feet.

He entered a large chamber. The feeling of insecurity suddenly took a firmer hold of him.

Don't make a sound, he repeated to himself. *Be careful where you walk. . . . Be on the lookout. Don't hurry . . . there you are . . . don't leave anything to chance, make sure there is nothing behind you.*

He turned around to carry out this command.

In his wake, the darkness had closed in again, depriving him of any points of reference. Was he going to be able to find his way back? Azim had managed it. All he had to do was follow the line of the wall . . .

Jeremy took a step forward and, in panic, hurriedly opened his lantern and blew on the flame.

The smell from the dying wick rose to his nostrils.

He had just caught sight of a glimmer of light.

Weak and moving, but a light all the same.

It was coming from a corridor on his left.

Jeremy approached, holding his breath so as not to betray his presence.

The corridor, which was very short, led to a modestly sized room whose details he could not make out from where he was standing. He put down his lantern and took his Colt in both hands. He moved toward the doorway.

The place was as sinister as it was pestilential.

Two candles danced on a worn-out table.

Beyond the table rose a pile of dead animals. Some of them were seething with plump maggots.

Someone was making a snuffling noise.

A long, sticky breathing sound.

Jeremy aimed his pistol in the direction in question.

And his entire being froze with the shock.

· 47 ·

The ghoul was indeed there.

It was tall and misshapen. Its bald pate gleamed in the candlelight, one eye abnormally open, almost dangling, the nose eaten away by disease, the cheeks and lips missing, opening the whole jaw to the air. The creature was enveloped in a long robe of coarse cloth, as dark as its skin, with a voluminous hood pushed back onto its shoulders.

And it was playing.

The creature was holding George Keoraz, aged nine, in his arms. The child was motionless, inert and partially undressed. The ghoul was holding one of his arms, and using it to push along a little wooden train.

It snuffled again, tilting its head back. Sucking in through its teeth the spittle that the absence of skin could not hold in. When it did that, it resembled a wild beast sniffing the air.

Jeremy could no longer move.

It was then that it noticed him.

Its good eye locked onto him, then onto the weapon pointed at it. The eye turned toward something, lying on a stool.

Jeremy followed the look.

It was an assortment of elongated rings, each made to cover the whole of the last joint and extend beyond the end of the finger. The rings were made of metal, and ended in a claw, carved from bone and set into the end.

So that was the secret of those hands with their endless fingers and inhuman nails. A craftsman who worked metal in a souk had made them. It was just a case of paying the price—there was no shortage of bones or metal in Cairo.

Jeremy realized that the black giant was about to make a dash for his weapons.

Fear unlocked his body and he took a step forward, keeping a firm grip on the gun.

"Shhhhhh," he hissed, hoping to dissuade the ghoul from attacking.

Did it realize the danger represented by a firearm?

It let go of George Keoraz, who collapsed completely.

"Don't do that!" yelled Jeremy, trying to get a little closer.

And it leaped for the stool.

Jeremy was forced to hold fire, as the child was in the possible trajectory of the bullet. He threw himself backward, trying to flatten his back against the wall so as to gain distance between himself and the ghoul, and to make sure that he was in a good position to take aim.

His shoulders made contact with the wall.

He refocused his eyes, just in time to see the monster's terrible face bear down upon the candles.

And blow them out.

· 48 ·

A childish fear.

A feeling of powerlessness and insecurity that went back to a child's first, faltering attempts at speech. Written in the genes, a warning system from the reptilian brain, dating from the epoch when the whole of humanity knew what terrors could be lurking in the darkness.

That was what took hold of Jeremy.

The fear flowed out from the ancestral parts of his mind like the blood of a hunted animal that knows it is mortally wounded.

Jeremy began to pant.

The ghoul knew where he was when it extinguished the flames. He had to move. Immediately.

Jeremy moved his pelvis sideways; he had enormous difficulty commanding his body to move.

The claws whipped through the air, just in front of him.

Then once again.

The third salvo gouged the detective's forearm, and he let out a howl of pain.

He fell to his knees and dropped his Colt, which landed on the ground.

The ghoul plowed into the wall just above him.

Jeremy rolled forward; he detected a presence that just brushed past his shoulder. He rolled again, to move away from it.

The monster snuffled behind him.

Jeremy held his breath; it made him too vulnerable, giving away his position. He probed the earth beneath his palms, in search of his weapon. Advancing very slowly and carefully, in silence.

The ghoul collided with a large object to Jeremy's right.

The next moment, there was an enormous crack as the wood of the barrel split open as it hit the ground, several gallons of water pouring out.

The liquid reached Jeremy immediately, drenching his legs and his sleeves.

Feverishly, he felt all around him.

His weapon; he must find his weapon.

His fingers came into contact with warm skin.

The child's ankle.

He moved away and continued his desperate quest.

He was beginning to suffer from lack of oxygen; he must breathe more of it in. Soon, it would be impossible for him to go on without breathing more deeply.

The ghoul was moving somewhere behind him, ready to sink its lethal nails into his soft throat.

A metallic surface met his fingers.

It was his Colt.

He seized it firmly and raised it in front of his face.

His head was spinning. But he must not breathe in as hard as he needed to, must not allow himself to be pinpointed by the sound.

Now there were two hunters.

The first mistake would be fatal.

He rotated around, very slowly, so as to face the direction in which he had seemed to hear the ghoul a moment earlier.

Nothing.

Water was trickling between his calves.

The ghoul sucked in saliva through its teeth.

Just in front of him.

Less than three feet away.

Jeremy pulled the trigger with all of his strength.

Again.

Again.

His ears rang.

An immense body collapsed into the flood of water and Jeremy opened his mouth to swallow as much air as he could.

Then a sound of rasping rose up out of the damp darkness, mingled with muffled gurgles.

The man deformed by sickness, destroyed by society, was dying in this cold tomb. Then he began to gasp convulsively.

And silence returned.

The detective remained motionless for several minutes. Unable to stand up. He waited for a sign from the creature.

When numbness threatened to cut off his circulation, he got to his feet and set about relighting the candles with the aid of his lighter.

The black giant was stretched out on the floor, with three bullets in his chest.

He carried his sufferings away with him, and those of his victims.

· 49 ·

Jeremy placed his Colt on the table and rushed toward the child.

George Keoraz was sprawled on a vermin-covered straw mattress, the lower part of his body overlapping onto the soaked ground. The detective took the boy's head in his hands, and bent over him to listen to his breathing.

He could detect no sign of life.

Jeremy was about to unbutton the little one's shirt when he noticed that it was already open. He pushed back a shirttail, repressing the obscene images suggested by this detail.

And he pressed his ear to the child's chest.

His skin was warm.

No mechanism was beating inside the thoracic cage.

His baptismal medal slid down his neck, on the end of its little chain.

Jeremy parted the slender lips and probed the mouth with his index and middle fingers. At first sight there was nothing blocking the throat.

It was then that the detective saw the marks on the child's neck.

What he had taken for an effect of the shadows that were so much in evidence here, was in fact deep bruising.

George Keoraz had been strangled.

The ghoul had played with him, taking him on his knees, to the point of squeezing his frail neck with its enormous hands, and tightening the pressure little by little, until the child's legs stopped kicking.

Until he became a docile doll that could be played with.

Jeremy let go of the corpse, and covered the upper part of his face with his still wet hands.

His rage echoed off the underground stonework, the sound growing as it ricocheted and reverberated.

Then he stood up, and laid waste to the room.

He overturned the few shaky bits of furniture, wading in the lake of water that covered the ground.

And he sat down, exhausted, on the last stool still standing, facing the table.

Flasks filled with brown liquids had fallen and shattered. The entrails of the dismembered cats and dogs were clumped together amid the debris of broken glass. Jeremy realized that all the corpses had been skinned at the hindquarters. The hunter in him understood immediately.

The animals' anal glands had been removed.

There could be only one reason for that.

To frighten animals.

It was probably one of the giant's old rituals, from the time when he lived alone on the street, to protect himself from famished stray dogs, a childhood memory of his village's hunts, a local belief that required that children should be daubed with this substance to repel predators. It was a practice that Jeremy had seen before in southern Sudan. The smell of these mixed glands on human skin disgusted certain animals.

Protected in this way, the ghoul had prowled the streets, frightening potentially aggressive dogs.

A whitish skin was floating like a jellyfish in the half-light.

It was drifting toward the detective.

Jeremy's vision was blurred; he focused through his anger, which was ebbing little by little.

It was a pair of trousers.

He leaped up to seize them.

There was no doubt that these were the ones Azim had been wearing on the night of his death. Keoraz had brought them here, into his lair, as a morbid trophy.

When he noticed the metallic reflections caught by the candle flames, he began to tremble. Jeremy fell to his knees and picked up the metal tin.

Nestor cigarettes.

He opened the lid. There were about twenty left.

Keoraz's voice, honeyed and obliging, came back to him: "I buy them by the box at Groppi's, they cost me a fortune! But this tobacco is worth every piaster . . ."

He closed his eyes.

Francis Keoraz had sacrificed his own son for his survival.

Jeremy looked up at the menacing curves of his Colt on the table.

He knew now what he had to do.

But before that, he must testify. Explain everything. Secure his future. And Jezebel's.

Jeremy took his diary from his jacket pocket and sat down at the table for an entire hour. He wrote down everything he had just done. Made sure that nothing was missing.

He went back and inserted an arrow into the account he had given of his night with Mr. and Mrs. Keoraz. This arrow led to Azim's story. Jeremy wrote this according to what his colleague had told him briefly that night, on the telephone. He completed it with what the imam and Khalil had said, then his own deductions in light of what he had just discovered, allowing himself a few purely imagined details.

Everything was there. His private thoughts. And his investigation.

In order to understand who Francis Keoraz really was.

What kind of monster he truly was, beyond that poor unfortunate he had manipulated in order to commit the crimes.

Once he had made the last full entry in the candlelight, Jeremy left the diary open and picked up his weapon.

He was going to alert his police colleagues by telephone to the existence of this vile cellar, so that they could collect the child and to ensure that they had all the evidence in their possession. He would say nothing more on the telephone.

Meanwhile, he personally was going to sort out the problem once and for all.

Before society and its flaws got hold of the case. Before the millionaire could exercise his influence to save himself, before he could play with the permeable joints of the system.

The rift of evil of which he was so fond was not going to stretch out its tentacles and engulf civilization; malign corruption would attain no hold on Jeremy Matheson: Of that he was very sure.

Francis Keoraz was going to confess everything.

Or die.

The flame of one of the candles faltered, and a track formed, down the edges of which transparent wax trickled.

Behind the burning halo, the detective's silhouette faded away.

The wax ran down about four inches, with increasing effort; its blood solidifying more as it traveled farther from its heart.

Jeremy Matheson's diary lay beside it, the hot rivulet bearing down on it.

Then the trail of wax halted, broadening and swelling at the very end.

It began to harden.

And became white.

And cold.

The two candles went out.

· 50 ·

Francis Keoraz will talk. Or die. I am leaving this diary here, and preparing to go, leaving in my wake the lifeless body of the child. And perhaps after I have left, death will summon up that sense of propriety that is invisible to the living, and cover this tomb with its cape,

wrapping the room in a cold shroud, while the candles extinguish them-
selves, as if by magic.

The diary ended on these mysterious words.

Marion turned the pages that followed. There was nothing new, just the chapter added on at the very end concerning Azim's wanderings, which she had already read previously. She examined the spine of the notebook, checking that no pages were missing. Everything was intact. Old, but completely undamaged.

So ended the strange film that Marion had played to herself throughout her reading. These visions of a bygone age came to an end on a question mark.

What next?

She closed the book with the leather cover and gazed at it for a moment.

What next?

It couldn't end like that. There was no conclusion, no epilogue, nothing.

A little voice inside her played devil's advocate: *You weren't reading an ordinary type of story, you were reading a* true *story. What were you expecting from reality? It isn't perfectly ordered or structured; reality is a tale filled with weak points and blanks, and dotted with question marks, the answers to which are not always given at the end. Truth is like that, not otherwise. Imperfect and incomplete.*

Jeremy Matheson had not been able to save the child. He had confronted the ghoul before leaving for the Keoraz house, armed with his personal belief, and with too many pieces of evidence for it to be a coincidence.

What had happened afterward?

Did Keoraz confess? Threatened by Jeremy's Colt, probably. . . . Under the Medusa gaze of his wife. Was Francis Keoraz charged? Or had he committed suicide in a moment of sudden lucidity?

Having read the diary, there was another hypothesis, very probable despite its dramatic side.

Jeremy had aimed his pistol at the child-killer to make him confess.

Rage and disgust had pulled the trigger.

Marion swore out loud. If only she had the Internet, in a short time she could have found out what happened via the press archives.

There was still one problem.

Now that she had read everything, Marion still could not see what would lead an individual to want to get the diary back at any price. What did it contain that was so precious? Nothing . . . nothing but the truth about an old story of child murders.

The truth . . . and the confidences of a wounded man.

Jeremy had given himself up to it wholeheartedly.

Jeremy . . .

Marion did a quick calculation. If he was still alive today he would be a little over a hundred years old. Difficult.

But possible.

Joe and Brother Gilles were the only old men on the Mount.

Neither of them seemed that old. And yet, was she capable of assessing their precise ages? No . . .

Then there was Sister Luce.

Jezebel?

No, nothing about the nun suggested the elegance and grace of which Jeremy spoke. Even with time, Jezebel couldn't have lost it all, and Sister Luce had a fearsome profile, as sharp as her nature.

Jeremy.

Marion kept coming back to him. A lover. That was what he was. He attracted her to the point where she saw him everywhere.

What if you proceed in the other direction?

What data did she have to help her identify the mysterious figure who was harassing her?

Whoever it was knew both the Mount and the abbey well.

Everyone here was capable of that.

Whoever it is has the keys—not just to the abbey, but to my house. Exactly the same bunch as the brotherhood has.

So, someone from among the brothers and sisters.

A copy could have been made.

What else did she know?

It's a very athletic shadow . . .

That had been proven by their high-speed chase.

Brother Damien. He often ran in the mornings.

Ludwig. Used to play rugby.

Don't forget the kid. Grégoire. He works out.

Three possibilities.

What else?

The riddle . . . it's someone who likes to play. The moment I arrived, I was presented with that intellectual challenge. And according to the second letter, there might well have been others, if I hadn't found the notebook, which caused offense.

Brother Damien was a game-player; he liked crosswords.

And yet he didn't have the right profile. Was he hiding behind a mask? That seemed unlikely . . .

Marion couldn't seem to get Brother Gilles out of her mind.

Too fragile to run through the abbey. No . . .

How about a double act?

Brother Gilles giving the orders, and Brother Damien subject to his authority, using his physical condition in the service of the older man.

The portrait didn't fit.

The old monk was too much of a killjoy and too dull-witted to appreciate mental games, and still less riddles. Marion couldn't see him in his cell, enjoying himself as he created a puzzle for her arrival, just to welcome her and test her ability to respond. That wasn't his style at all.

There's a direct relationship with one of the protagonists in Matheson's diary. If not, they wouldn't try to take it back from me at any price.

The idea of a two-man team worked.

The evidence was right under her nose.

Marion couldn't refute any longer what, by default, had to be the sole answer to her questions.

For several days already, she had been thinking about it, but refusing to accept it as a probability. She liked the old man too much.

See what's staring you in the face! Even his name is a clue!

It was as simple as that.

Joe was Jeremy.

And now everything took on a new meaning.

· 51 ·

Marion switched on the light in her living room.

The brightness emphasized the warmth of the materials there. Fabric, velour, wood. For the first time, she noticed a similarity with Jeremy Matheson's rail car.

Joe was a diminutive of Jeremy.

He played chess, stimulated his mind with intellectual games, and had the mentality of a man who enjoyed playing with riddles.

He wasn't acting alone, of course.

Grégoire.

The young man was much closer to Joe than she had supposed.

"He needs life, and a male presence; I don't think I'm wrong about that," Joe had said during their dinner.

Grégoire executed his commands.

As the ghoul had executed those of Francis Keoraz.

It was the youth she had pursued that same afternoon, who had panicked at the thought of being caught before abandoning the book to run away. Grégoire was clearly fascinated by this man who would have been a good model for his father, who undoubtedly told him stories as crazy as in those fantasy films he was so mad about. And he had at last found in Joe a means to escape the Mount's monotony.

Jeremy had taken refuge in France before the war, to flee his own country. For what reason? Was he wanted for the murder of Francis Keoraz? Or did he wish to be forgotten by his fellow countrymen after the notorious affair, which had probably earned him a sad kind of fame that he would gladly have done without?

He had ended up far from everything here, in the shadow of the church. Preserving his private diary as the last witness of his former life.

Marion slipped on her trench coat and picked up Matheson's diary before stepping out into the cool of the night.

She headed straight for Joe's house.

After she had hammered on the door several times, it finally opened.

Marion tensed as she guessed that it wasn't the old man standing behind it. She relaxed as soon as she recognized Grégoire.

He gazed at her with a resigned look.

They didn't say a word.

Marion held the diary under her arm. The youth noticed it, and his gaze traveled to Marion's face.

Eventually she asked, "Is he in?"

Grégoire remained impassive. Finally he withdrew, making way for her.

When she was in the main room of the house, Grégoire replied, "Joe isn't here. He's up there, at the abbey."

His voice was measured. Marion detected no signs of anxiety or fear in it.

"I've finished it," she said softly, showing him the diary.

"That's what we thought, that you'd finish it today."

Marion gazed around the living room as if she was there for the first time. Looking for some detail, some clue that would tell her more about the old man's personality. About what Jeremy Matheson had become after all these years.

"He has hardly any accent," she commented.

"He's been living in France for so long. . . ."

"And he doesn't look his age."

Grégoire's eyebrows arched, and he gave a sort of twisted grin. "Look . . . ," he began. "About this afternoon, I wanted to apologize . . . I didn't want anyone to get hurt. It wasn't planned, I was just supposed to get hold of the old book, that's all. I didn't want us to come into contact and—"

"Drop it, Grégoire. You'll learn with the years that we're responsible for our own actions, their consequences don't matter much. There are times when it's good, no . . . vital, to ask ourselves questions *first*."

The youth, who hadn't been expecting a sermon while he apologized, went into a huff and folded his arms across his chest.

Marion refrained from adding that, in the final analysis, it was he who had suffered more from their physical confrontation.

"If it's okay with you, I'm going to stay and wait for him to come back from the concert," she went on.

"In fact, he suspected you'd come to talk to him, this evening or tomorrow. He's not in the hall, he's on the roof. I'll explain to you how to get up there."

Grégoire described the route to take and accompanied her back to the door.

"One last thing," said Marion. "Why did Jeremy abandon his private diary among the books in the Avranches library?"

Grégoire scowled. "Jeremy?" he repeated. "Jeremy Matheson? But he never abandoned his diary in Avranches. . . ."

"But it was he who—"

"Matheson disappeared in 1928."

Marion shook her head. "No, Matheson is . . . wait a minute. Joe is Jeremy, hasn't he ever told you?"

Grégoire looked at her as if she had just proffered the worst kind of insult. "What are you talking about? Haven't you got your information straight? Jeremy Matheson disappeared in March 1928, and his body has never been found. Joe is not Jeremy!"

He gave his head a slap. "You don't know, huh?"

"Know what?"

"Who he is *really*."

· 52 ·

Grégoire leaned against the front door.

"You haven't done your research, have you? Don't you know what happened that night?" he went on.

Marion's heart began to beat faster, making her chest rise and fall.

She was experiencing this with a sense of involvement that went way beyond her. She hadn't just read a private diary, she had shared a *real* life.

Grégoire began: "The night Jeremy Matheson disappeared, the police received a telephone call from the detective, explaining where to find the body of Keoraz's son and that of the ghoul. When the cops got there, they found everything as described in the notebook you've read. Except that the son wasn't dead. He was sitting in a corner. Not in a good state, but alive. In the confusion, Matheson had made a mistake. He was so convinced that the ghoul had already killed the child that he barely checked. In fact, the little boy was unconscious when he arrived, but absolutely not dead. He came to shortly before the cops arrived."

Marion held the diary tightly to her.

"George Keoraz was treated," the young man continued, "he grew up, and went off to study in England, before coming to France, which he liked so much that he stayed here to live. That is where he entered holy orders. He settled on Mont-Saint-Michel with other members of the religious brotherhood to which he belonged. After a few decades, internal tensions led his superiors to want him transferred elsewhere. He refused. He was more attached to the Mount than to the rest. After a year, he left the brotherhood to move into this house. He stopped attending the abbey and went to the little parish church instead. And he got old."

"Joe is George," murmured Marion. "George Keoraz."

"Yes. A former member of the brotherhood."

"That's why he had the keys. He'd kept his bunch from back then."

"Copies." Grégoire nodded. "So he could get into any part of the abbey, even into your house."

"Which also explains the tension between him and Brother Gilles. . . ."

Grégoire hesitated before answering. "I think it's because of Sister Luce. . . . They were both very close to her and that created problems," he admitted with an absence of embarrassment that testified to his lack of maturity.

Suddenly, all the various elements came together inside Marion's mind. She opened her mouth without saying a word.

Jeremy Matheson had disappeared that night. He was certainly dead.

She realized why Joe had been so motivated to get the diary back.

It contained all the truth about his father.

The truth that had not emerged. Which had cost Jeremy Matheson his life.

Joe had striven to take back the book so as not to sully the memory of his father if the truth came out.

Francis Keoraz had killed Jeremy that same night. While the detective was at his house, attempting to make him confess, the millionaire had got the upper hand, and he had made the body disappear.

The investigation into the child-killer had eventually been closed.

The ghoul was an ideal culprit. A monstrous madman.

Perfect for the public opinion of the time.

And Francis Keoraz managed not to be tainted by the scandal. He remained undisturbed.

In one way or another, Matheson's private diary had remained in the Keoraz family's hands.

"I must see him," declared Marion.

Grégoire stepped out into the street and raised his eyes to the fantastical bell tower of the abbey church.

· 53 ·

From the western terrace, Marion had a splendid view over the area bordered by night's starry sheet. Behind her, the lyrical melodies of Vivaldi and his *Four Seasons* filtered out through the tall doors of the abbey church. The winter allegro non molto was just beginning.

She took a deep breath, pushed open the door as quietly as possible and entered the nave. About a hundred people were in the concert audience, seated on benches, concentrating on the music. Marion passed by via the aisle and headed for the south transept, trying not to attract attention. There, she found the door Grégoire had told her about. It was wide open.

Marion stepped through it and set off up a particularly narrow spiral staircase.

Her thighs soon showed their displeasure by growing heavy. The intoxicating echo of the music resounded in the dark stairwell.

Marion reached the first landing, where she rested for a moment before continuing. Grégoire had told her to go right to the top.

The last step ended outside a door, which Marion half-opened so she could go through.

The wind instantly grabbed hold of her. It charged at her, sniffing at her more suddenly than any wild beast. It seized her clothing, tousled her hair, and threw her roughly backward so it could whirl around between the gables, beneath the bell tower, like an invisible guard dog in the pay of God.

Marion accustomed herself to this turbulent presence.

She took in her surroundings, concluding that she was lost in a forest of pinnacles, flying buttresses, and spires growing out of the roof, sometimes merging, sometimes exploding next to one another in a petulant clump.

Powerful floodlights were trained on the most ornate walls, projecting golden curtains between the tall, dark stained glass windows and the mutilated faces of the gargoyles.

A bridge of carved granite soared above the void, joining up with the turret from which Marion had emerged onto the roof of the choir. A series of steep, concertina-like steps led upward, running along its back.

Marion ventured onto it, gripping the guardrail with all her strength. The bridge was so intricately carved as to make the entire structure almost fragile. Whipped by nature's powerful breath, she pitched dangerously for a moment before concentrating on her feet to escape the dizziness.

She gained a little more height and stopped, two steps from the top.

An imposing silhouette awaited her.

"The lace staircase, that's what we call it," said George Keoraz by way of a greeting.

He reached out his hand to her. "Will you allow me?"

She didn't know what to do and ended up reaching out her own hand. He took it and helped her to haul herself up.

"I like coming up so high, it's an exquisite experience for the senses, and it's conducive to thought. I didn't know if you would finish the diary this evening or tomorrow; uncertain as it was, I came here to meditate."

He was obliged to shout to make himself heard above the surrounding wind. Without letting go of her hand, he led Marion along a parapet, which was so low that it scarcely reassured her, to the northern side where the wind was more forgiving.

From here, the bay looked endless.

The stars were reflected in the sea's calm waters, creating a landscape with no visible horizon.

The Mount floated at the heart of the universe.

"Between ourselves, I must tell you that you are a very mediocre liar," he said. "On Thursday, when we met, you asked me if there had been an Englishman on the Mount, on the pretext that someone in town had led you to believe that there had been. It was rather laughable, but entertaining. Particularly since at the time I thought you had confounded me."

Marion attacked back. "Dragging Grégoire into your personal quest wasn't such a great idea."

George responded first of all with a grin. "On the contrary. On the contrary . . ."

Then he went into detail: "It enabled him to feel important. To share secrets, converse with an adult; and he has taught me a lot of things. He's a smart lad. And he would have held it against me if I hadn't involved him. I simply regret the physical confrontation you had today. It ought not to have happened. He was not supposed to take the diary back from you unless he considered it was possible to do so without your noticing. Then he panicked."

He folded his hands behind his back. "Nobody was hurt, that's what matters," he concluded.

"He told me who you were. I confess I thought you were Jeremy himself to start with."

"Matheson?" he exclaimed indignantly. "Do I look that old? Don't be deceived!"

"You used to be a member of the brotherhood. Why did you hide that from me?"

George gave her an amused look. "You didn't ask. In any case, sooner or later you would have found out. It's of no great importance."

The floodlights were attracting a whole cloud of insects, which themselves were encouraging greedy bats to fly over.

"Why the riddle on my first evening?" asked Marion.

"Oh, that . . . because I have a taste for games. To combat boredom. Like everyone else, I knew that the brotherhood was going to take in a woman on retreat for the winter. I wanted to mark the occasion, welcome you in a more . . . original way. I have a mischievous spirit—let's face it, it's all I have left. And believe me, when it comes to that game, I confess that I can prove formidable. I take a sadistic pleasure in it. I would have played with you until I went too far, until I'd worn you down; that's my personal sin. The taste for intrigue, always going just a little further. I had it in my mind to communicate in this way with you for a while."

"Until I found the diary . . ."

"Yes, that on the other hand . . . I confess it disturbed me a little. It was Grégoire who mentioned it to me. The evening of your discovery, you went to see your friend Béatrice; you showed it to her and talked about it. Her son was there too. That's how it all began. It ought not to have happened. If it was in my power, I would wipe this whole story from your mind."

"You shouldn't have left it within reach of the first person who came along."

"The attics containing old stock in Avranches are not open to the public, and there was little chance of anyone coming to look for a book in the English language around here. . . . That diary is a private story. It is the intimate history of my family, mine. You shouldn't have read it. In return, I bestowed on myself the right to enter your lodgings in your absence, to search and take it back. Unfortunately, you always had it on your person."

Taking advantage of the old man's eloquence, Marion gave her curiosity free rein. "Why was the diary in Avranches?"

George frowned. "Through cowardice, I suppose. When I arrived here, around sixty years ago, I chose not to have this diary in my cell, in case someone happened upon it. I hid it among the other works in the library we had here at the abbey, with the English-language books. The fact is, the collection was swiftly transferred to Avranches. I made sure that mine was lost among the rest, in the attics. And I left it there. Unable to destroy it, and not brave enough to carry it with me."

A little nervously, Marion ran her tongue over her lips. "I don't understand why you kept it. It's a piece of evidence with dangerous implications for your father's memory."

George gazed admiringly at the placid stretch of water radiating from the foot of the Mount.

"You came here to me after making skillful deductions," he said. "However, there is an error of interpretation in your logic. And it is a monumental error; I am even surprised that you committed it."

He turned to face her. "My father was not guilty of any crime. It was not him."

· 54 ·

A bat skimmed past Marion's hair. "How can that be?" she demanded, taking no interest in the small mammal.

"Marion . . . you astonished me that first night when you played the game and swiftly deciphered my Polybus square. I would have thought that the truth would not escape you when you read the diary. Think. There are important clues in what you have read. Who is the real guilty party?"

Marion had absolutely no idea. Everything was so crystal-clear in the diary; why try to cast doubt on it? Was George trying to divert attention so as to save the memory of his father? Marion couldn't believe that; it would have been puerile on the part of George, and she thought too much of him for that.

"I don't know," she admitted. "Don't be offended, but Francis Keoraz is the obvious culprit."

"That is what it said. I am asking you what is more sustained, as well as more coherent. My father? No, that has no meaning. Except for Jeremy Matheson's pathological jealousy. Come along, make an effort."

Marion couldn't work out what he wanted. Nobody else could be guilty, the investigation had been skillfully conducted, and everything could be explained. There was only Francis Keoraz.

"Set aside what is written about my father, can you do that? And now, if you had to accuse one of the protagonists described in this diary, which one would your suspicions most likely fall upon?"

Marion sighed.

Although the wind was weaker on the north side, it was forcing its angry moans between the open arches of the bell tower. Suddenly it fell silent. In this short period of time when the elements spared the Mount, Marion heard the melancholy strings floating up from inside the church.

"Jezebel."

She had said it without thinking, just because he was insisting on a name.

George looked annoyed. "No, of course not. She could never have done such a thing. . . . Try harder."

Tired of playing the game, Marion chose another name from the diary at random. "The doctor . . . Dr. Cork?"

George made a little sound with his mouth to demonstrate his disappointment, and folded his arms across his chest. "No. And yet you had him right under your nose the whole time you were reading," he said sharply.

"Azim? No, he died during the investigation. . . ." She looked for an answer among the stars. Then she stared at her own hands. She hesitated.

George leaned toward her. "Do you have an idea?" he whispered, very close to her face.

"I . . . I don't think it could be possible. . . ."

The insects were crowding against the overheated floodlights and burning up in such great numbers, that they gave off an almost caramelized smell.

"But," he urged her to continue.

". . . Jeremy?"

"Why do you say that?"

"I don't know."

He stood up straight. "I am going to tell you: because sometimes he frightened you a little. He intrigued you, that great *white hunter.*" He laid strong emphasis on the last two words.

"And I am going to tell you," he went on. "You are completely right."

Marion raised a hand, palm upwards, in a sign of incomprehension. "You're talking nonsense! Jeremy wrote the diary. He conducted the whole investigation, he has nothing to do with these murders, it's—"

"Jeremy Matheson," he said, hammering home each syllable. There was a faraway look in his eyes. "He fooled us all."

Marion seized the diary she had brought in her coat pocket. The cover creaked at her touch.

"He deceived us all," lamented George. "And that diary is his greatest success."

"No," objected Marion. "He investigated the murders, he—"

"He insisted on conducting the investigation. To ensure that nobody would pick up the trail leading to him. At the risk of shocking you, I shall state that almost everything in the diary is true, the facts and the emotions. Jeremy only doctored certain events, and omitted others. As one may be surprised to read, he took that case very much to heart. And with good reason . . ."

"What are you saying?"

"After going through his notes, one becomes more intimate with him, and could almost say that one knows him a little. Did he give you the impression that he was somebody extremely compassionate, in particular with the natives? And generous? Is he that by nature? What do you think?"

Marion remained silent, staring at George, trying to work out what he wanted to prove.

"Myself, I would say no," he continued. "It doesn't feel as though it was in his nature. And yet, in a rather intriguing first passage, he gives money to all the families of the murdered children, the ones he goes to see with Azim. It's an interesting act of kindness and compassion. All the same, it doesn't feel in character for the hunter he is. Could it be that this act constitutes a means of paying his debt, trying to gain forgiveness for murdering the children?"

"George . . . you . . ."

He raised a finger to silence her. "Wait until I have finished, please. Remember the day when he and Azim are standing around the body of the murdered child. Jeremy has difficulty containing himself; he doesn't seem to be in his normal state. It isn't the barbarity in itself that disturbs him, he is in fact under the influence of his unhealthy excitement, at the memory of what he has done. In the same way, a few minutes later, he is obliged to drive 'crazy images' from his mind—images that have nothing to do with an imaginative compassion or a curious gift of insight, but which are quite simply memories of the atrocities he has caused."

George could hardly get his breath back for what followed. "And when Azim comes to tell him that all the murdered children belong to the same foundation, remember how he admits feeling ill, livid. We are supposed to believe that it is because he feels personally attacked by the killer, since he too frequented the foundation, whereas in fact he realizes that the investigation has just taken a giant step in his direction."

"That doesn't make sense! So why would he confess to feeling ill at ease?"

"That is precisely Matheson's strength. He hides the absolute minimum. He takes no risks. If Azim for his part had written a private diary or spoken with someone about this conversation between them, testifying to Jeremy's uneasiness, he would have been embarrassed."

Marion counterattacked. "No, that doesn't stand up. From the start, Jeremy shows his skill in the investigation, he makes discoveries at the scene of the crime, and deductions that are correct. If he was guilty, he would keep quiet!"

"Not Matheson. On the contrary, he establishes his authority over Azim. Whereas the Egyptian detective hasn't advanced in several weeks, he gets things moving in a tenth of the time. This enables him to take command of their partnership easily. And nothing he says compromises him in any way. For already, he knows that he is going to lay the blame on his great rival, my father. He will accumulate evidence accusing Francis Keoraz, redirect leads in his direction, even create them."

The old man gazed at the bell tower. "There is something even more disturbing," he declared. "Remember when he's discussing the very first murder with Azim, the one where the vagrant was killed in Shubra? He explains that he questioned everyone, looked for any witnesses, and he also says that it was a day when they were short-staffed, so he had to do everything on his own. Now, he admits several times in his diary that he doesn't speak Arabic. So how did he manage? Must I remind you, as he says himself elsewhere, that it is an extremely poor district? So nobody speaks English."

"Obviously he didn't bother mentioning that he had a dragoman with him," stammered Marion, suddenly less gung ho.

George shrugged his shoulders and continued: "Jeremy Matheson was not the victim of a perverse child-killer who hated him sufficiently to orchestrate everything in such a way that the crimes would be loosely or closely connected with him. That is a risible argument. Matheson had a connection with each detail of the investigation because he himself was the killer! Listen: He followed Jezebel into the foundation to please her, and it is there that he saw all those children, potential targets. It was he who investigated the first murder at Shubra, and he swiftly found the guilty party, a black giant suffering from noma—that is the probable name of the disease that had transformed him into a . . . ghoul. Matheson did not track him down in order to arrest him, but to bend him to his will. He knew an archaeologist with whom he often chatted, as he confesses; he must surely have told Matheson about his latest discovery, perhaps even taken him there before Jeremy killed him. Matheson then had a hiding place for his 'hired monster,' whom he asked to do to the children he would supply what he had done to the vagrant, in exchange for a roof and liquid food. Next, he went off to find children studying at the foundation, children about whom he knew a very great deal after breaking into the establishment's premises and consulting their files. Armed with this precious information, he manipulated the children when they finished class at the foundation, far from witnesses. He promised them money, incredible knowledge—about the legends—or anything that would be attractive to a young kid from those districts. Let us not forget that the children knew him; he had been a reader at the foundation! He would set up a secret meeting, if possible at night, if they were able to leave their homes without being noticed. And we know what happened after that."

The wind, which had proved timid on the northern side, suddenly gusted, slamming into George Keoraz and battering his cheeks.

"In reality," he shouted to make himself heard, "I am quite convinced that he spoke Arabic. He had been living in Cairo for nine years, and it was difficult to be a detective in a city like that for almost a decade and not have learned at least a smattering of the language. It's a question of logic. And he had read *One Thousand and One Nights* as the end indicates, when Jezebel comes to his home and sees the book. He tells her that it was his colleague Azim who thought that the killer had used it, without having the nerve to say that he had just bought it and read the whole thing in just a few days. In my opinion he had had it for a very long time. Between his books and his 'friend' the archaeologist, he had enough sources of information to delve into history for the method of torture inflicted on Azim, not to mention the fact that he was a constant visitor to *qawhas*, where Arabic was spoken and a succession of storytellers recounted ancient legends. Jeremy had come to know Egypt through this mythological culture, and when he saw the deformed black giant, he remembered those tales about ghouls. Was it then that the whole scenario unfolded in his mind? Remembering how Francis Keoraz had charmed Jezebel by telling her the story of *One Thousand and One Nights*, deciding to give free rein to his insane impulses, and falsifying them so that he could one day accuse his great rival? Or was it later, while listening to frightened gossip, that he stage-managed everything? And then attributed this madness to my father, on the pretext that he was a history enthusiast."

Marion caught him by the wrist. "Tell me, George, have you been dissecting the whole diary like this for the last seventy years?"

He observed her with a sad look on his face. "I didn't even need to read it twice. I knew what I was looking for."

"But why are you so sure you are right?"

There was a touch of incredulity in his voice as he answered her: "Have you forgotten? I am George Keoraz. I was that abducted child. . . . And who do you think it was that got onto the train that day, to take me away?"

· 55 ·

George rubbed his chin and lips with his broad hand. "It was he, Marion. That is why I am categorical. I am not suggesting anything to you. I am stating it as a fact. Jeremy Matheson got on that train. My father had introduced him to me the previous evening, and he was a police officer; that was enough for me to agree to get off with him when he told me my father had sent him to fetch me and take me to meet him somewhere other than had been planned."

Marion's throat tightened again as she saw tears in the old man's eyes.

"He delivered me into the hands of that creature, so that it would be less alone, so that it could . . . *play*. And he didn't return until the evening, staying just long enough to torment me himself. What is more, in his diary he is not precise about what he did that day. If you read attentively, you will note that he mentions having investigated Azim's disappearance that morning, and going back home for a shower in the early afternoon. Then he tells us about the end of his day in his office and the discovery of his companion's body. There is not a trace of what he did between his shower and his arrival at the office, a few hours later. And with good reason. He was busy following me when I got on the train, and taking me away to his sordid hiding place. The previous evening he had heard my father talking to me about my piano lessons, about the streetcar . . ."

He stood there without adding anything for a moment, beneath the stars. Marion could not tell if he was hiding his emotion as best he could, or if he was searching for something else to add.

"That night, he wrote that he saw Humphreys early in the evening—the conversation lasted a quarter of an hour—then Dr. Cork at almost midnight. Between the two, we know nothing."

The old man's head rotated on his shoulders like an owl's, to take in Marion's reaction. "He was with me during that missing time."

Marion's hands tightened around the diary until the leather was digging into her skin.

"The hours passed, and the shock treatment to which I was subjected disconnected me more and more from reality. I lost consciousness the next day. Only to wake up when the barrel was knocked over and the water flooded over me. It was completely dark; I was suffering from cold sweats, fever, and unbearable pains. I remained motionless for a long time. My throat had tightened up, and I was having difficulty breathing. Then I groped around and found some matches, and a candle. The monster's corpse was there. I don't know what really happened between the two. I think Jeremy came to check that I was dead, which is what he expected from the ghoul. And that he killed his slave so that he could not betray him in one way or another. The notebook was on the table. I opened it, and saw that it contained his words. I don't know what came over me, but I stole it. I hid it among my rags and the police arrived shortly afterward."

A salvo of applause rang out beneath their feet. The concert was at an end.

"I didn't open my mouth again for five weeks after that. I didn't say anything about the notebook either; I kept it like a trophy, secretly. And I read it. One page from time to time, when I was alone. It was after I'd finished it that I got my voice back. I went to see my father, and asked him if he was really a murderer. Then we had a long conversation, whose epilogue I was not to learn until ten years later, when he left us. Jezebel admitted to me then what had happened that night, between them and Jeremy. For he did indeed come to the house. He got past the gates and entered the house; and he aimed a weapon at my father. He manhandled him to get him to confess that he was the child-killer. He yelled at him, holding a tin of cigarettes in his free hand, saying that it was proof that he had found in the monster's lair. Proof that he had been able to buy from Groppi's, since my father had given him the name of his supplier on the night they had dinner together. He became mad, struck my father, again and again. He wanted at all costs to make him confess in front of Jezebel. So that she would realize. Jezebel ended up seizing the revolver we kept there for our own defense, and she fired at the detective."

Marion's eyes were fixed on him. George Keoraz was telling his story with great difficulty; his voice was less assured than usual, and his hands were shaking.

"Jeremy Matheson died instantly, with a bullet lodged right in the middle of his brain. Jezebel and my father did not know what to do. They panicked. They had just killed a police officer. A police officer who had accused my father, what's more—which could constitute a motive in the eyes of a particularly obtuse judge. So they weighted him down and put him in one of the mercury pools in the garden, while they waited to find a better place. A whole army of police officers turned up shortly afterward, not to arrest them but to bring me back. And my father eventually buried Matheson in the desert, a few days later. An investigation was opened into his disappearance, but it came to nothing. According to the people who knew him best, he had become more and more impulsive in recent months, sometimes irascible. His character changed, and the beast in him rose to the surface. Instinct was beginning to take hold of the hunter. For my part, I claimed to remember nothing; I lied because I didn't know what to say anymore. They concluded that the child-killer was the black giant, and everybody was happy. I found out later that Jezebel had searched in vain for Matheson's diary. He had confided its existence to her, and she was anxious to know what it contained in reality. I never managed to admit to her that I was the one who had it."

George swallowed several times in succession, and turned to Marion. "Do you still doubt the identity of the real child-killer?"

She wanted to say something, but the strength needed to push out the words instantly evaporated.

"You are wondering why, aren't you?" guessed George. "Why did he do all this? He was a tortured soul. A man who had lost all notion of emotion. As Jezebel told him on the evening when she came to find him in his rail car. She could not work him out. Because he was not a man in other men's image. He was not really human. In a certain way he was unbalanced, but although sick he was conscious of his perversity, and it caused him pain. I think that if Jezebel meant so much to him it was because her strong, original personality had made him experience feelings again that he was normally incapable of feeling. And these odious crimes, through their extreme nature, made him feel emotion. He was nothing but an empty shell, weeping over the nothingness that he could not fill except with uncontrolled, immoderate sensations."

A group of bats in formation skimmed the two human shadows on the top of the abbey church, more than a hundred yards above sea level.

"To define him, I must tell you that the major part of his delirious fantasies about my father's perverse personality were merely a transposition of his own. His pages of psychological analysis are nothing more than a transfer of what he was himself, to the scapegoat he had devised. He could eliminate his rival in love and exonerate himself in one fell swoop. Having said this, the criminal processes he attributes to my father's mind seem most grotesque when one reads his diary; on the other hand, they become more plausible once they are replaced by Jeremy himself. All one has to do is replace the intoxication with power that he claimed was the breaking point—as a point of departure—for my father with the terrible consequences of the war that turned Jeremy Matheson into a disembodied creature, and we can grasp his nature."

George clapped his hands in front of him. "In the final analysis he was a damned soul. The war had succeeded in dehumanizing the child he had been."

Marion shuddered.

The war. The tortures Jeremy had seen inflicted on that poor soldier.

George pointed to the diary. "Take hold of the first page, and tear the cover. Go on, don't be afraid, I covered the book myself, back then, so as to camouflage it."

Marion followed his instructions and pulled on the leather. It grumbled as it tore.

"That's enough," ordered George.

He leaned over and slid his fingers under the tear in the leather, searching for something.

"There . . ."

The old man drew out an old sepia photograph.

"There you are, look. That's Jeremy Matheson."

Marion took it and looked at the author's face with a degree of apprehension. In appearance he was as he had described himself, a handsome man, but with an expression that darkened his face. In fact, it was even disturbing. There was an enigmatic glimmer in his eyes, as imprecise and changeable as those holographic photographs in which the facial expression changes when the viewing angle is altered. A look of cold, permanent anger, Marion decided, without much confidence. *Or a persistent suffering, which consumes him.*

And then another flash of intuition came to her. A more disturbing one.

That glimmer of light belonged to a lifeless body, floating in the very depths of him. The glimmer of his soul.

In his eyes there was a terrifying fogging, which belonged to a consciousness that had been dead for a long time, having abandoned its body to drift aimlessly.

He was harboring his own corpse.

Beside Jeremy stood a magnificent woman. Marion had no difficulty in identifying her. Her class and her impetuous nature were imprinted on her features. Jezebel.

The photo had been taken on a beach. Jeremy was in short bathing trunks, in accordance with the fashion of the time, revealing a chest disfigured by a long, swollen-edged furrow.

Marion turned over the photograph.

Alexandria, September 1926.

"The photo was acting as a bookmark in the notebook when I found it," commented George. "An error on Jeremy's part, committed because of his affection for Jezebel."

George revealed the final cog in the insane mechanism that constituted Jeremy Matheson. "When he was a little drunk, on the evening they dined together, he told my father and Jezebel an anecdote in confidence. You have probably guessed that he lied about that, too. He did not see that young solder being mutilated and raped for so long by vile noncommissioned officers. He didn't see it, he lived it. He *was* that soldier."

Marion ran her index finger over the slender curve of the scar on the detective's chest. The photo quivered in the wind.

"That was why Jezebel wept that evening," emphasized George. "She understood. When he talked about the mutilations by bayonet, and a gash across the chest, she remembered that enormous scar on his torso. She grasped the sufferings he had endured during the war. After each slaughter, when he had to go and attack the Germans, he returned, astonished that he was still alive, covered with the meat of his comrades, and confronted another hell, while waiting for the next attack that would in turn burst open his flesh."

Marion scrutinized the photograph and the man who had made her share his existence, what she had thought was his investigation, his pain. She imagined him wandering along the sordid alleyways of Shubra, to flush out the black giant, approach him, say a few words to him in Arabic. Then she imagined him bringing his "hired hand" down into the underground chambers, to shelter him there. Promising him food. And inciting him to liberate his anger with the children he would procure for him. Jeremy had savored the spectacle. He had also killed his own friend, the archaeologist who had told him about his discovery, this ideal hiding place. He had slaughtered Azim because he was on the point of uncovering the whole thing.

It was he who had burgled the Keoraz Foundation to consult the children's files, find out how to approach them and how best to bribe them. Marion closed her eyelids when she realized that he had perhaps knowingly chosen the hemophiliac boy, so he could feast his eyes on the interminable tides of blood that were going to flow.

The whole diary came together within her: the characters, the days, the heat, the architecture of Cairo. As she read, she had made a film play in her head, and now she experienced the whole thing again, this time on fast-forward.

Suddenly, the image silently froze.

And a new scene added itself to the others. This one didn't come out of the diary, but from the memories of a wounded old man.

It was an afternoon in March 1928.

Sharia Maspero was packed with passersby. French ladies simpered and laughed in the shade of their parasols, Cairo governesses pushed baby carriages in the shade of the palm trees that traced a strip of greenery between the street and the majestic Nile. Men in suits jostled each other and apologized politely on the sidewalk, outside large, five-storied modern buildings, all in stone and steel, and with open windows at the top, protected from the unbearably hot sun by drapes.

Recently made cars purred on the roadway, inviting the cameldrivers and carts pulled by mules to get a move on with blasts from their fake horns. And in the middle of this street, everyone cleared the way for the approaching train, which gave out metallic clicks and sparks amid its crowning glory of cables.

A woman with an Italian accent leaned toward a young boy dressed in leather sandals over white socks, shorts and a shirt stained from eating aniseed balls. An itinerant seller of oranges stopped beside them and offered fruit. The woman dismissed him with a firm refusal, showing that she was well used to such things.

"Don't forget to do your scales," she reminded the child. "Every day."

The streetcar squealed to a halt in front of them.

The doors opened and the boy climbed aboard, waving good-bye to the Italian woman.

"I'll see you next week," she shouted, over the din of the closing doors.

The streetcar shook itself and picked up speed. The lively colors of the shop windows slid by as the train passed through the high-class districts.

The streetcar was very full. All the seats were occupied and the boy was hesitant to go back into the compartment reserved for women, where there were still some empty seats. He did nothing: "It's not done," he had often been told.

He grabbed hold of a strap and was about to occupy himself by looking at the fine cars when he recognized a face among the passengers.

It was a rather tall man who was gazing at him, a smile on his lips. His expression broadened, giving way to real pleasure.

"Hello, George!" he said.

George recognized him. He was the guest who had been at their house the previous evening. A police officer, his father had told him.

"Do you recognize me?"

The boy nodded. "Hello, sir."

The man didn't talk very loudly, just enough to be heard by the child.

"It's good luck for me that I've found you here," he replied. "I was afraid I'd miss you. I had to run to catch the streetcar, you know."

George nodded out of politeness. His gaze was immediately captivated by the roar of a car overtaking them.

"Do you like cars?" asked the police officer.

"Yes, I adore them. My father has a Bentley. Do you know what a Bentley is, sir? It's a very fast car, the fastest!"

Around them, two stern-looking men were reading their newspapers, and a little farther off another was picking his nose as he watched the landscape glide past.

"Oh, yes, I know what a Bentley is. And do you want to know something? My own car is even faster than a Bentley!"

George frowned, as if that seemed inconceivable to him.

"It is, I assure you. Tell you what, if you want I will take you for a drive in it."

George wore the expression of a child who is incredulous but fascinated.

"Right, but before that," the police officer went on, "I have to tell you that it's your father who sent me. That's how I knew you'd be on this train. He told me to come and fetch you and take you to him at the polo ground. Have you seen a polo match before?"

"No," the child replied immediately, with enthusiasm in his voice.

"Well, I think that's why your father wanted to give you a surprise. You'll have to come with me, so I can take you to him."

George ventured a timid nod. He wasn't entirely trusting, but wouldn't dare rebel against an adult. "Are we going to go there in your car?" he asked.

The policeman began to laugh softly.

"Yes, you'll see it. And even get inside."

The child seemed reassured.

The police officer straightened up. "Here we are, this is where we get off. Come along."

He held out his hand and wrapped it around the boy's. Together, they stepped out into the stifling sun.

"Is your car here?" asked the boy.

"We're going to my place first, to pick it up."

From inside the streetcar, they could be seen walking into the distance as the doors closed.

The police officer's voice was now muffled by distance and obstacles. He said, "Once we're at my house, I'll introduce you to a friend of mine. You'll see, you're going to be able to play together."

And they were lost in the immensity of Cairo and its seething masses.

Marion clenched her jaw to silence the pain that threatened to rise up from her belly.

She stroked her lips with her fingertips, as if to claim possession of her face, to put herself back in context, lost as she was amid all these lives.

She spotted the fleeting pencil of light from a lighthouse far away on her right.

And all these stars, the sole and silent witnesses of human tragedies since the dawn of time.

Very slowly, she slipped the photo back inside the diary and held it in front of her before handing it to the old man. "This belongs to you, I believe."

He took it and made it vanish into a pocket. "You know everything now," he concluded.

"Except the reason why you kept this diary after all this time," she said, with great respect in her voice.

He gave her a weary smile. "It has helped me to understand. As for the rest . . . I was a child. One does not always know what drives a child to act. Today I am an old man. It's not dissimilar."

"And between those two ages?" she asked gently.

"I tried to understand Jeremy Matheson."

Marion swallowed. She dared not ask the question that hung upon her lips. George encouraged her to speak with a nod of his chin.

"And . . . did you succeed? I mean, beyond the hatred?"

He tapped the pocket containing the diary. "Sometimes I weep over the nature of his existence."

Marion pulled her coat closer to protect herself from the wind.

"Now, my dear, I would like you to succeed in telling yourself that all of that was just a story. A long and strange story, a very long time ago. And I hope that with time, it will become no more than a vague memory—and out of respect for me, that you will eventually forget it. If I was a magician, I would remove it from your head."

He laid a hand on her shoulder and showed her the way back to the lace staircase.

As she started walking, she thought she detected a movement out of the corner of her eye.

George was wiping his cheeks.

·ᘐᕬᘑ·

· EPILOGUE ·

·ᘑᕬᘐ·

Marion embraced Béatrice and walked down rue Grande.
They had said their farewells.

Only two days had passed since George Keoraz's confidences,
and a limousine was waiting for her at the foot of Mont-Saint-
Michel.

She had only spent two weeks there.

Sister Anne had come to inform her the previous evening; they
were coming to fetch her. She was going back to Paris. Marion had
received a telephone call that same evening. There were develop-
ments; a judge had taken the affair very much to heart, and she
was summoned without delay. And after that . . . they hadn't been
able to answer. She would be accommodated at a hotel for a few
days, and then after that they would have to decide. Nothing was
settled. Her vagabond existence still had a long time to run.

She was leaving this place earlier than expected, in a peculiar, almost piquant context.

Marion had gone to George's front door early in the morning, to leave him a letter.

A letter that she had spent all evening composing, only to end up with just:

> *Thank you for having shared your truth with me.*
>
> *Marion*

It didn't reflect what she bore in her heart, but it was better than nothing, she had decided.

Today, she was still questioning herself with guilty doubt.

She couldn't repress a deep distress when she thought of George Keoraz and his story. And yet, there was still a part of herself that was attached to Jeremy. To what he had made her experience. Could he be the monster George described?

Sometimes, Marion wondered if the old man hadn't exploited every weak point in the detective's account in order to find another explanation, which would exonerate his father. A process he had begun very early, when he was only a child. Obliterating the presence of his father in the streetcar to replace it with that of Jeremy. For his part, the English detective had not necessarily made mistakes in his diary, only omissions, clumsiness or errors due to fatigue.

Scarcely had Marion thought up this theory when she drove it away, blaming herself for calling the old man's words and sufferings into question.

Marion reached the square at the bottom of the village. Sister Anne and Brother Serge were waiting for her there.

They greeted her and the sister handed her a bag of regional specialities.

Marion got into the back of the car, her suitcases already jammed into the trunk. They were about to set off when she spotted

Grégoire emerging through the gates beneath the wall and running toward her.

"Wait!" Marion called out to the driver.

Grégoire halted beside the open window.

"My mother wants to give you this," he said, getting his breath back.

Marion took the wrapped gift, improvised with old paper that had been reused, and opened it. It was a dog-eared, crumpled book.

"*How to Win Friends and Influence People,*" she read out loud.

Couldn't find anything better, it's a little souvenir of me. For your next life, wherever you settle. Good luck, big girl. I'll be thinking of you and I'll keep an eye on the newspapers and wait for you to head back to my shop one day.

Béa

Marion's smile was filled with emotion.

"Thank her for me."

"That's not all," Grégoire stopped her." I . . . I have to tell you something. It's . . . in a way, it's important."

Marion waved at him to continue.

"The diary you read."

Marion glanced at the men in the front of the car. "Well?"

"I think you'd rather know. It's a forgery."

"What?"

"Yes, it's a forgery. I had to tell you, so you knew before you left."

"What are you saying?"

"They made it all up. To help you pass the time. People say that here, for people who aren't used to it, the worst thing is boredom. So the monks made this false private diary. They have a workshop for restoring old manuscripts up there. They got the right kind of paper, and then they wrote this story in the hope of entertaining you, occupying you. So you wouldn't be just marking time."

"Grégoire, are you kidding me?"

"I swear I'm not."

He looked more than serious, almost desperate that he must confess to her.

"They found a news item in newspapers of the day and embroidered what they wanted around that. Then they put everything together, in Avranches, and sent you there with the idea of slipping you the book to read on the pretext that it didn't correspond with the cover, but that none of them read English. Stroke of luck—you found it all on your own."

Marion's legs were trembling, her hands moist.

"Even the photo's a fake. It's an old thing they had and they used it to make up their story. Joe was in on it, because he was a member of the brotherhood, that is true, and as he was an outsider in your eyes, he could inspire more trust in you."

Marion was lost. She no longer knew what to think.

"I'm sorry to tell it to you like this. But it was better that you should know."

She wanted to reply that she didn't believe a word of it, that none of it had had any effect on her, but she just nodded silently.

What was she to believe? This unexpected revelation or George's more dramatic one? Then there was a third . . . Jeremy's, the one he had written in his diary.

Ill at ease, Grégoire drew away with a "bye" and a small wave.

The limousine pulled away and the electric window slid back up.

Marion's hair whipped against her face and then fell back down. She was leaving the Mount with her eyes filled with questions, searching its complex architecture in the hope of finding answers there.

She was leaving for another world, taking with her this story, no longer knowing where it began and where it ended. A story that was taking control of her.

Her story.

The Mount remained visible in the rearview mirror for a long time, powerful and massive; watching over the bay.

It was watching over its secrets. Just as it watched over its inhabitants.

Béatrice's words came back to her: "They stick together, take the blows, and if they have to, they can keep a secret, a secret that shouldn't leave the Mount."

The sun tentatively appeared from behind the clouds.

And Mont-Saint-Michel disappeared behind a bend in the road.

The black book lay on a bench; a hint of sunshine had just settled on its leather cover. Care had been taken to sew up the torn part that had housed the photograph.

The gilded letters of the title shone feebly in this rare glimmer of light.

The Narrative of A. Gordon Pym.

The title of an unfinished novel to hide a private diary.

Grégoire approached and sat on the bench.

A hand with worn-out skin, prominent veins, and age spots settled on the book.

"Did you tell her?" asked the soft voice, with just a hint of an accent.

Grégoire turned toward the old man. "Yes."

Joe nodded. He waited several minutes, until the sun came back to warm him a little.

"Do you think there was any point?" Grégoire asked eventually. "Telling her that."

"Yes. I do."

"Why? I'm not sure about it. . . . The truth . . ."

"The truth? What is truth at the end of the day? Can you tell me?"

In a learned, steady voice, the old man recited what he had so often thought: "If you believe in a fiction, it becomes truth. A person's truth. But a truth in that person's eyes, assuredly. As truly as the witness to a miracle, an appearance of the Blessed Virgin, believes what he has seen, other people's opinions do not matter; everything is in the focusing. Beyond the great principles of our world, there is not only one universal truth, there are our personal truths as well. And there is a personal truth for every person on this planet. . . ."

Joe savored the sun for another moment.

"Let her choose her own truth," he added. "Sometimes it is enough to know how to read between the lines. To be attentive; and she will know what she must believe."

His hand stroked the cover of the diary once again. "After all, ours concerns only us."

.꙳.

· ACKNOWLEDGMENTS ·

.꙳.

A nd so this story ends.
      Don't be surprised; there is nothing frustrating about this
slightly . . . odd ending when you think hard about it. All the keys
to reading it are given.

I should like to thank here all the bookshops that have always
been behind me, since the start of my adventure.

This novel about truth is dedicated to them.

My publisher and the whole formidable publishing team deserve thanks beyond my ability to give them.

I thank François Saint-James for his knowledge of Mont-Saint-
Michel, and for our nocturnal wanderings along its alleyways and
corridors. If there are any mistakes concerning the Mount, they are
my fault. Also, please forgive me for depicting a rather "austere"
religious fraternity; this was for the needs of the novel, and is absolutely not a real portrait.

A short note concerning Cairo in 1928. The majority of the places or events described existed. For example, the Allenby Cup soiree at Shepheard's Hotel is real; I have not exaggerated anything. The decorations, the ambience, and the personalities mentioned were there that evening. The old-fashioned charm of the streetcars, the story of the underground passageways beneath the palaces, gardens with mercury pools: All of this contributes in a certain way to the feeling of melancholy, which haunts all of this part of the novel. I should like to specify it, so that—in your mind—these memories may go beyond the framework of a simple romantic image.

Finally, if you, my reading companion, would like to go further and think more deeply around this novel, I invite you to recall the Polybus square . . . 25 35 24 34 33 15 11 45 45 23 15 32 11 12 35 34 33 54 44 24 45 15.

www.maximechattam.com

Until we meet again.

—MAXIM CHATTAM
Edgecombe, February 4, 2005